The Sound
of the
TREES

THE SOUND
OF THE
TREES

A Novel

ROBERT
GATEWOOD

Picador
Henry Holt and Company
New York

www.picadorusa.com

Picador® is a U.S. registered trademark and is used by Henry Holt and Company under license from Pan Books Limited.

For information on Picador Reading Group Guides, as well as ordering, please contact the Trade Marketing department at St. Martin's Press.
Phone: 1-800-221-7945 extension 763
Fax: 212-677-7456
E-mail: trademarketing@stmartins.com

Library of Congress Cataloging-in-Publication Data

Gatewood, Robert.
    The sound of the trees: a novel / Robert Gatewood.
        p. cm.
    ISBN 0-312-42188-5
    1. Mothers and sons—Fiction. 2. Runaway children—Fiction.
3. Family violence—Fiction. 4. Runaway wives—Fiction.
5. New Mexico—Fiction. 6. Boys—Fiction. I. Title.

PS3607.A79 S68 2002
813'.6—dc21   2001051703

First published in the United States by Henry Holt and Company

First Picador Edition: June 2003

10 9 8 7 6 5 4 3 2 1

For Ma and Dad

All the bushels in the world

I shall set forth for somewhere,
I shall make the reckless choice
Some day when they are in voice
And tossing so as to scare
The white clouds over them on.
I shall have less to say,
But I shall be gone.

—ROBERT FROST,
from *"The Sound of the Trees"*

I

ONE

THEY RODE OUT from the house in the predawn quiet. Against the cold brown sky its appearance was wind-broken and funereal, and neither looked back once they passed.

Lord, the boy whispered to no one.

They rode the horses at a trot to the north. They passed the town still shrouded in darkness and they did not speak. They rode away from the main road, through sedge and willow, past the lake where fog pooled so thick it looked like grounded cloud. They rode under the low sagging telephone wires and into the arroyo where they disappeared around a small bluff gouged out of the rock by waters that no longer ran there.

Once the boy looked back at his mother and she was crying, her hair spilling out from the clothespin bun and her shadowed face averted. He held her a moment with his gaze, then turned ahead and kicked his horse onward.

Trude, his mother called out as they came onto level ground. Trude.

The boy stopped and waited, his hat held low to his head with his free hand and his shirt collar drawn up high on his neck. He quartered the horse and faced her. As she came on he noticed her delicate hands wringing the bridle reins. In light of everything that had gone to packing the night before, she looked small and unaccounted for.

Trude, she called breathlessly when she finally shouldered her roan to his side. Darlin, are we sure about this?

Jesus, Mama. He did not lift his eyes from his saddle nor did he take his hand from his hat. Just look at your face.

She put a hand across her cheek and turned away. They were quiet for a long time, sitting there in the cold country morning.

Colorado ain't that far, the boy said, placing his own hands on his knees to give brace to the idea. And the way they talk about it. Most beautiful country in the world. And the biggest ranches.

His mother let the reins fall and brought both hands to her face.

We barely got any money, she said. And we don't even got the truck.

Shit, the boy said, neither of us can drive anyway. Besides, the bank can take the ranch from him all they want. But they ain't takin Triften. She ain't dollars, she's my horse.

So we're ridin all the way up to Colorado with scarcely any money at all?

Name a better way, he said.

He paused briefly and studied her with her eyes near frantic and lost on the vast landscape before them. Away from the town all detail washed away. Even the trees, which clambered out toward the hills, appeared formless and bleak. The boy heeled his mare and squared up to her. He reached out for her shoulder and said more gently, We got to, Mama.

His eyes were the clear blue of his mother's, but without the sick sparkle now alight in hers.

Don't you see that? Mama. I know you see that. We got to.

When they reached the edge of town the boy's mother whoaed her horse and gathered her hair back up in the clothespin. The boy sat and waited while she looked with a furrowed brow down at the town where trucks were warming the air and the sound of storefront shutters being pitched open came dull and insignificant across the gulch.

I can't up and leave without havin said my piece to the girls, she said. It won't take but thirty minutes.

The boy squinted hard, looking out at the lightening sky to check the sun's progress. His mother shook her head and stared at her hands that worked the bridle reins methodically.

I've seen it take six men to clear him out of a bar. And prohibition ain't even seemed to graze him. His daddy bought that land in '01, but once he was gone. Well. She looked out at the hills. Hatley, she said. She looked at the boy. Your father. He didn't take no shame in drinkin it away one acre at a time.

The boy's mother turned and surveyed the dark plains, her knees bent up high against the horse's barrel, her back all bone and wrenched muscle in the paling light.

I guess some things can't be fixed, she said finally. I guess no matter how much straightenin you may do in your mind, some things always come out crosswise.

The boy watched his mother keenly now. Though grayed and neck-bruised, he could see her old beauty yet, and he saw by the tightness of her mouth that she had at last resigned herself to their leaving.

Alright, Mama, he said. I'll meet you here come the half hour.

His mother smiled at him with a brightness that he could not remember seeing for a very long time. Something in it that reminded the boy of how she had been when he was still a child. He could not help but smile himself and he lowered his head and put his hand atop the crown of his hat to hide it from her.

I'll drop in and see Doc, he said.

His mother gave him a firm nod and told him again thirty minutes and she told him not to worry. But the boy was no longer worried. It was as if the idea alone of leaving his father behind were enough for him to become a man. A new man in a new world where things were as he remembered them once to have been, and he presided over his horse with great dignity, turning her in a sidestep down the path as the moon collapsed under the earth and the sun rose red upon the shivering grass.

HE REACHED THE doctor's yard with a long shadow coming off him and the fog clearing and the night all but over. On the front porch a brass lantern struggled on its twisted chain. The bulb hung dead and black in the gloaming. The boy's mare stepped backward nervously by the side of the porch and he eased her down with a low whistle. He dismounted and struck a hand across his pant leg and pulled off his gloves.

From the hill where the doctor's house stood the boy could see far off in the distance to where the mountains loomed like polished bowls of stone turned asunder. They appeared to him the same way in which they did in his dreams, and he recalled how often as a child he had dreamed of the roaming bears that ruled them. He remembered how he had dreamed a sky the color of the blue flowers that grew on the tree outside his bedroom window and how he dreamed of the blunt brown heads working beneath it like stones pushed along the bottom of a clear running stream. He dreamed he walked in the deep green grass among them, following the tracks of their lead-black paws out upon the snow to where the waters froze and the world itself seemed to pause to let them pass. He recalled also how he had dreamed himself into the warm folds of their skin and the tremorless pools of their black eyes. And in the dream he began to call to them in their language, which was absent of words, and his throat became clean with the sound, but when they reached the forest they would no longer let him follow.

He went up the porch steps and knocked on the frame of the screen door that was pitched open and creaking in the wind. When the doctor finally rose and came to let him in the boy stepped back and pushed his gloves into his back pocket.

Trude. The doctor pressed his hair back with the palms of his hand. What time is it in your world?

The boy raised a hand in apology. I know it Doc. Sorry. I just wanted to say you a good-bye.

Where you goin at this hour, son?

Up north.

North you say? Well boy, there's a lot of country to the north you know. It ain't New Mexico all the way up on into heaven.

I know it, the boy said. We're goin to Colorado.

The doctor's face was broad and stubbled and high in the cheekbone yet all sense of meanness in his sharp features dissolved when his heavy white eyebrows slackened. After a moment he took the boy by the arm. Well what are we standin here with the door open for, he said. Get on in.

He led him down the hallway past the standing clock and the book-shelves filled with the hand-worn medicine journals and past the parlor table where the phone sat mute in its cradle and into the study. The doctor stepped aside to let the boy pass. The room smelled thickly of leather and cigar. Trude sat in one of the heavy green armchairs. The doctor turned the hot ash of the fire and slowly gave it kindling and lit a cigar and sat facing him in the other armchair. The boy shifted his feet upon the dark rug.

Well, you got me up and smokin now. You want some coffee?

Thank you. No sir. I'm in a bit of a hurry.

That's right, the doctor said. He wiped the loose ash from his knee and folded his hands in his lap. Now who is we, and where are you goin?

Me and Mama. We're goin to Colorado. And you know about the ranch.

The doctor worked the waist belt of his bulky robe tighter but did not take his eyes from the boy. The boy shifted his feet again and just then realized he was still wearing his hat. He took it down and set it in his lap.

I know about the ranch but you all got a few more days yet. And what about your father? I thought he said you'd go to Utah to stay with his sister for a while.

He ain't comin.

The doctor stopped pulling on his belt. He fixed his gaze on the boy. What? he said. Now what does that mean? Why?

Well.

The boy looked down at his hat. He closed his eyes and took a deep breath to stay himself. After a moment he breathed out and looked up squarely at the doctor. The doctor saw how it was in the boy's eyes and lowered his chin.

Yes, he said after a long while. I see.

The sun rose in the window behind the boy and a long pallid ray ran along the arm of his chair. He held it in his hands and watched it, weak and quavering on his skin.

I guess I always knew it was the right thing to do.

Yes, the doctor said. Yes. But Trude, you ain't but seventeen.

Eighteen, sir. And I don't see how that's got anything to do with Pa losing the ranch nor balling fists at her.

They sat. The doctor ran his fingers along his eyebrows. The boy stared down at the rug.

Why's it got to be Colorado? Why not just down the road? What's wrong with Jimenez? Or Bayard?

Because, Doc. Down the road ain't leavin. It's just a ride.

But why Colorado? Your ma and you. You ain't Lewis and Clark.

The boy fiddled with his hat. I know it, he said. But we want a fresh start. God knows she needs it. Colorado, it just feels right.

The doctor studied him. I want you to take my car, he said at last.

No sir. No. The boy's eyes quickened and he shook his head. Not a chance, he said. You need it to get to the sick. Besides. Me and Mama been over this already. I can't drive a lick and she's no good at it neither. I doubt there's even roads to get us up there. Not ones I'd know. Not through the mountains.

Maybe not through the mountains. But you can go ahead and take a train that skirts around east a bit and can get you straight to Santa Fe. Or Albuquerque. Hell, if you take the car it's not but sixty miles before you hit paved road.

The boy shook his head again, almost a lament in the slow sway of it. Too much money for the train, he said. And I don't want yours and neither of us can drive, like I said. Besides, I can't leave Triften. You know that. She just wouldn't have it, and I guess neither would I. Most times in the last few years she's the only company I've had. I'd just as soon make a clean cut. We'll make it. We will.

The boy roused his head from his lap and looked into the doctor's eyes.

Don't you believe it?

Yes. Of course I believe it, son.

The doctor took the belt ends in his hands again and wound them deliberately over his fingers. As if to demonstrate some procedure of thought. At last he looked up at the boy and sighed.

You best take care then, he said. You hear me? You best stay as close as you can to the towns. Now I know you ain't never been one for signs and borders or the like. But remember, you ain't never been out of Grant County before. It's rough country up there if you're plannin to shoot the mountains. It's country most folks ain't never heard of, let alone seen. And I don't care how many trucks or trains you got to get you there.

Yes sir. We'll be careful. I'll make sure of it.

The boy paused, staring blankly at his hat and the shadow it cast upon his hands. The doctor watched him through the dusty slats of light that were now unfurling from the window. Then the boy raised his head.

Now I know you all are friends and I don't expect you to like it, but I came to say you a good-bye and I do expect that he won't get wind of my plans from you.

At this the doctor straightened up in his chair. His face fell grave and he puffed his cigar, looking at it momentarily then setting it in an ivory ashtray and turning the ashtray with his strong fine hands and finally turning his eyes to the fire. I reckon you're right, he said. It had to come to this.

The boy peered into the fire and they both did so for a long time. Upstairs the boy could hear the doctor's wife splashing quietly over a washbasin. He looked at the mantle clock and it ticked the seconds in the stillness, and finally he rose.

The doctor pulled long on his cigar.

Have you considered that he may follow you?

The smoke crossed the room. It rose up at the boy's waist while he turned his head and gazed out the window behind him.

I done considered it, yeah. Depends on how he feels when he sobers up. Depends on whether or not he's stashed enough money for himself. Depends if he even wants to find us. But just the same, if we go on up through the mountain passes, can you imagine him givin chase? I mean, if you want another reason for not takin the train or your car. There it is. You think he could stay set on a horse anymore? I don't know. The boy lowered his hat, then placed it atop his head again. He raised his hands as if he couldn't think what more there might be to say. Depends on a lot of things, I reckon.

The doctor set the cigar in the ashtray again. He swept a hand across the rubble of white hair on his chin. Then he took in a deep breath and rested his fists on the chair arms.

Sometimes your father used to come here at night when he was very drunk. I'd let him sleep it off on the cot in the back and in the mornin I'd feed him eggs and coffee. We were always good friends, your pa and me. He'd tell me he didn't want to go home because he was afraid of himself. I always thought that was a curious thing, but your father is a curious man. But you know, the doctor said, raising a hand toward the boy then placing it on his chest, he does have somethin that at least resembles a heart in there.

The boy stared at the hand on the doctor's chest. How long we known each other Doc?

The old man shrugged. He strained his eyes in remembrance, and it was clear from his frown that such memories were of little use to him. Long as you've been around, he said cautiously.

And you've always taken care of me with my ridin injuries and the like. Right?

Oh well yes, the doctor said, straightening up in his chair again, but look at all the ribbons you took in on account of your roping. Best young rider in the tricounty district last year.

Well sir, with all due respect, I ain't but once been injured by horse or cow.

The old doctor slouched down in his chair. He turned his head back toward the fire.

I got one more question for you, Doc. The boy now stood full in the wake of light, and it flooded over him from his back and shoulders. Is the story they tell about when I was born true? I mean, I'm leavin now and I won't see him again I reckon and you're the only friend around here I got. It'd mean a lot to me if you could just go on and say it.

The doctor rested his chin in his hand. He looked at the smoke drifting up his fingers. At long last he thumbed out his cigar in the ashtray and rose into the light of the coming day. He crossed the room and put his hands on the boy's shoulders. For a while he studied his face. Smooth and sunken as if drawn out by some indelible sorrow, yet with the boy's wheat-colored hair spraying from his hat brim and fluttering over his long eyelashes, the doctor once again saw the child he knew, and he moved his hands from the boy's shoulders to cup him under the jaw as though he meant to bear the boy's soul where he himself could not.

It's true, he said, now correcting the boy's hat on his head and trying for a tender smile. He damned you when you were born.

At the door the doctor waved him off sadly and the boy turned and regarded him and put a finger to the fork of his hat. He saw the doctor's wife descending the stairs with her long gray hair coming down over her shoulder and he wished the doctor well and began to walk his horse back toward the north and into the ashen country that awaited him.

Two

THERE WAS AN untraceable updraft that struck the boy and his mother as they crested the sand hills north of town. The winds kneeled and shot up again in great whorls. The roads and buildings had swiftly receded, and the country spread vacant and bitter before them. The boy shepherded his mother along the gray ridges of the hills, neither of them able to see but a few feet in front of the horses.

It's always hardest in the beginning, he called to her.

His mother tried to nod but it was difficult to move at all. Her gesture came out stilted and unnoticed. The mule carrying their provisions bayed and staggered on the lead rope.

Come on old timer, he called out, keep it steady.

With quick clutchings of his off hand the boy towed his mother's roan and kept his mother close enough to his shoulder that he could see her hair blustering beside him. He held his hand aloft and squinted out from under his hat brim. The wind groaned and groaned. It seemed to harbor a prejudice against them. And though it strapped the boy into virtual paralysis he turned his burning neck from time to time, surveying the land they had passed. He searched the land for a sign of his father with his eyes so absent of color it seemed he feared the stalking of a ghost.

Hours passing into the afternoon, they came out of the bottomland and perched over a bluff and there took to a low alcove of volcanic rock.

Here, the boy called above the din.

He came down and helped his mother calm her roan and hobbled the horses and mule on a lone acacia tree that was rooted precariously on the slope of the outcropping rocks. A swatch of burned crabgrass garlanded the tree which itself writhed in the gusts of wind. When the horses trod over the crabgrass it did not bend but crackled, and they lowered their long heads as if to sniff out some treachery beneath them.

The boy took his mother down from her saddle. The last of the thick fall heat blew in her hair. He held her face in his hands but she was looking away, her eyes wet glass. Set here, he yelled at her.

His mother did not move for a moment, then her eyelids stammered and her eyes settled on the boy's face. She nodded absently and bent and braced herself on one of the boulders and lowered herself into the belly of the cave.

The boy held his hat down with his hands and lurched back toward the mule. He uncinched one of the saddlebags they had secretly packed in the dark of the previous night, running his fingers blindly along the leather strap and pulling it loose from the animal's barrel and then went stumbling and ducking into the cave.

Tarnation.

He slapped his pant legs and shook off his hat. In the muted cup of the cave his voice resounded flatly. His mother looked up from her folded hands.

Damnation, darlin. I believe what you say here at this point is Damnation.

The last word she uttered slyly, smiling at the boy with a smile it seemed she had retrieved from pure sadness.

The boy went to wrestling open the sack, shucking his gloves and making fists of his hands to bring the numbness out of them. He drew out a small pouch of cornbread biscuits and wiped away the sweat beading up on his forehead. From his bib overalls he took out his dirk knife and unthreaded the cord and laid the cotton open on a flat slab of volcanic glass.

He removed a parcel of deer meat folded in wax paper and unfolded it with his raw trembling hands and laid it next to the biscuits and finally from the side pouch he fingered loose a beef bladder corked by bee's wax which was filled with the last milk from their lost cattle.

Should be the best dinner we've wanted in a long time, he said.

They ate slowly, looking out at the desolation and the driving winds. The boy swallowed and pointed a finger at the scene before them. You see Mama, he said, that old truck would've buried us alive.

His mother shimmied closer to the boy and put her arm around him, and for a while they sat knotted so.

Darlin, she said. If we had that truck we wouldn't be here.

After some time the sun moved behind the bluff. They watched in silence as wide shadows swept dark and weary across the desert floor. A solitary crow spun down and called out. The boy's mother withdrew her arm and laid her head back against the rock.

For as long as he could remember they were never given a choice or a chance of their own in any matter, and all they had been offered in their lives was very much like the soft greasy bills of money that passed through generations of hands. Farmer's hands and forger's hands and cobbler's and merchant's and the hands of old woodworkers long exhausted in their trade. Many hands laid upon those bills but none who could stake a claim upon them, as if they themselves had been swallowed into the commerce of a void. He wondered if the world would recover. If it could recover. And beyond that, if they could.

After a while the wind abated. The boy's mother rose up gingerly and pushed back the straw that had become her hair. The boy flicked away the cigarette he had been smoking and pulled on his gloves. I don't believe we'll make it to Silver City tonight, he said.

His mother pulled on her own gloves. How far is it? she asked.

It's a piece yet, he said. When we get there we'll bunk a night and map out our path. And if it takes till tomorrow, it don't matter. The boy stopped and gazed out at the clearing stretch of country before them. Beyond the boulders the desert appeared even more desolate, without wind or water, rise or tremor, as though it had fallen into a dream and dreamed of the only thing a desert could imagine, which was itself stretching out forever.

What we got plenty of is time, he said.

The boy's mother leaned against one of the boulders and closed her eyes while the boy collected the animals. When he had them ready he called out to her.

His mother jerked up awkwardly from her elbows. She squinted across the mouth of the cave at her son. The boy held up his hands in question until she finally got her legs under her and stumbled to the horses.

What were you doin over there?

What? Oh, nothin. Thinkin.

About what?

Trude. Honey. What do you think?

In the early evening they downstepped the horses into a ravine. The storm passed, only thin blue clouds like old rags slung along the skyline. With the wind gone the boy watched his mother more intensely. She appeared weaker than when they had first set out and the boy wished the sandstorm had not caught hold of them but he pressed on, concerning himself with his mother's condition and watching for the ghost. Or worse, for the man himself.

He could not summon what possible deeds would follow if indeed his father was tracking them. He could not imagine his hand or breath anymore. He remembered only that glass stare he and his mother had dreaded each night of the last year during which all reason seemed to have abandoned his father, sitting together on the davenport in the evening and trying not to hear the truck rumble into the yard or anticipate the creak of the door.

At the dusking hour they came to the confluence of two creeks which joined into a slow-moving river lined with box elder. A small congregation of Russian olive trees and in the near distance a grove of salt cedar. The boy ran a finger across his brow and spat and pushed back his hat. He looked up at the rising moon and then toward the lights of Silver City. He estimated they were still at least three hours away. Then he looked at his mother bow-shouldered on the roan and whoaed the mare.

Ma, he called. This looks like a place just as good as any to lay for the night. I can catch us some fish.

His mother said nothing nor did she make any motion of agreement, but came down from her horse and hobbled her in the grove of salt cedars and walked down to the river and sat at its edge.

The boy watched her thin silhouette against the water while he put his mare and mule up. Her flickering shadow commingled with the shadows of the olive trees and for a moment he could not discern limb from limb, tree from mother, as though the coming night meant to show him that in this world all becomes darkness, equal and without end.

He took a roll of cotton twine from his rucksack and cut a piece with his knife. He pried loose a tack nail from one of Triften's shoes and bent it and tied it upon the string. From another parcel of wax paper he took a slice of roasted chili pepper and slid it upon the nail and finally went down to the river and sat next to his mother.

He looked at her from the corner of his eye. She dipped her hands in the water and rubbed the base of her neck with one hand, supporting her body upright with the other. The boy turned back to the river and dropped the line into the black water.

I never meant for him to hurt you like he did.

The boy did not move at her voice but kept looking straight at his line dipping in and out of sight. Wasn't any easier for you than it was for me, he said.

His mother turned away, looking long into the dark rustling grove. But you were his only son, she said.

Hell Ma, I know it. And it ain't fair and it ain't right and God knows it ruined us in that country but we're loose of him now. Shit, he said.

She turned to face him now. She wiped her eyes down with the back of her hand. Don't you cuss like that, Trude.

Shit Ma, the boy said, meeting her eyes. It ain't the cussin that's bad for us.

The boy came upon luck in the river. He pulled up two killfish and a fat trout all brightly colored and he shucked them from their skin and cleaned them and tossed the severed heads into the fire he had made by the riverbank.

The boy's mother moved closer to the fire. By the time the fish were prepared her eyes had lightened and she had stopped shivering. The ash from the piñon branches flavored the fish well and they said how well it tasted and ate everything before them with a hunger neither had noticed before. After a while the boy rose with his tin cup and walked to the river, calling back to his mother as he went.

Big old place, Silver City. Ain't it?

Yes it is.

The boy returned with a cupful of river water. He sipped at it, then set it down and rolled a cigarette and gazed off at the city lights in the north.

Your father and me used to go up there in the summer when he was courting me. The boy's mother spoke into her hands that were gripped together and resting on her crossed ankles. They have this wonderful plaza with open carts and the like, she said. And they feed you and let you drink free on this particular week and the folks are fancy-dressed but nice. Charming, your father used to say. He used to walk around and nod and bow, all the while saying Charming, and that made some people laugh but not everyone.

Her eyes darkened upon the fire.

He could never settle on happy. He had somethin in him that said, It ain't enough, Hatley. It ain't enough to be happy. I don't know, she said, her hands going up to her hair.

Well, Mama. I don't know either.

The boy got up and washed out their tinware in the river. When he came back he helped his mother lay out their bedrolls, and soon after they laid themselves down on either side of the fire. No other riders chanced upon them all evening long. Way off in the distance when the breeze was gone the boy thought he could hear trucks motoring in the gravel washes on the outskirts of the city. Every once and again a piñon branch would pop in the fire and the boy would start up with his hand on the Colt revolver he had placed beside him.

When he was near asleep his mother leaned up on her elbows and whispered across the flames. You think he'll hunt us?

The boy rolled onto his shoulder and faced his mother with his eyes still closed. I don't know. Then he opened his eyes upon her. She was craning her neck out to better see him through the fire. No, he said. He's gone.

He paused at her eyes and would have turned back to lie down again but for something moving in the quiet of them. He straightened slightly on his forearms. She held his gaze there for a moment, then lay flat on her back, her eyes wide to the thickening stars.

Yes, she whispered almost inaudibly, I believe he's gone.

THE FOLLOWING DAY they breached the high country. Climbing upon the sand hills that outlined the city they passed a group of cowpunchers the boy had seen at dawn. All touched their hats as they rode up. They spat tobacco juice over the knobs of their shoulders and spoke nothing of the day or of their business but only nodded solemnly as if further transaction could only cause confusion, and rode on.

On the other side of the hills the landscape began to bloom like wildfire. Long tufts of buffalo grass rolled into orchards of apple. In a field to the east a woman bent over among the trees, tipping a water bucket at their roots. They came across a diversion dam at the river's head and they passed over fields of corn and chili and acres of cherry trees. When the boy upstepped the mare to his mother's side he saw that she was smiling.

They rode to the head of town on the main avenue where trucks were cranking and moving in and out of the side streets. As they walked the horses toward the general store a truck slipped from an alley and came barreling toward them. The horses reared up and the boy's mother's roan stammered back. She rose up on her hind legs and whinnied high and wild. A few women on the street turned, watching with clear amazement this thin bescraggled woman lofted high into the air, her hands on the reins drawn up over her head and her bone-peaked face as chiseled as a knot of walnut.

The truck squelched its brakes and swerved around them. As it passed the driver shook his head and peered at the boy who was turning Triften down and hepping her to his mother's side. The driver flung a cigarette butt out the open window, then drove on.

Whoa, the boy called. Whoa now.

He came down from Triften and eased his mother's horse. The horse was sweating and his mother too. She put a hand on the boy's shoulder to steady herself.

I sure don't remember this place movin so fast, she said. I'll be damned if he didn't drive like your father.

Come on down, the boy said.

They hobbled the horses and mule at the side of the general store and walked out into the road. The city was bustling. Men swayed through the streets in black vests and starched white linen cuffs and women sat in the shade of the storefronts nursing bottles of soda. The boy studied their appearances, the brown briefcases the men carried and the small round hats they wore and the way they tipped them tersely when they passed one another. It seemed to him an altogether other world. The boy's mother jogged up to his side and took his arm with one hand and with the other leaned into him, clinging tightly to the shirt at his stomach.

The barroom they sat in was dark, and what little light passed through the shutters shone like slatted beams of steel. The waitress who tended them was tall and lean in the manner of the coastal Mexicans with black eyes and a face like a hawk.

You all just get to town? she asked in a stilted voice.

Yes, his mother said flatly. She was watching the girl watch the boy.

From whereabouts, if you don't mind bein asked?

The boy's mother looked at her son. He smiled at her a little, then went to looking out the window at the city street.

Down by Hurley, she said.

That's a tough little stretch from how I understand it, the waitress went on, speaking more like a Texan than a Mexican girl.

A telephone rang from behind the bar and the waitress put up a finger.

I'll be right with you all, she said.

She brought them huevos rancheros and a pitcher of buttermilk. The boy picked at his eggs and went on squinting and watching the trucks out on the street.

When his father had saved enough money to buy the truck, the boy remembered how proud he had been to get the first one in town, how he washed it by hand every Wednesday night after the town council meetings when he was still a councilman, his big-knuckled hands plunging into the bucket of hot water and soap and the delight he took in squeezing the sponge over the yellow hood. He remembered also and more vividly the days when the truck had become overworked by the rutted roads and overwhelmed by rust, and how instead of attending the town meetings and washing the truck under the porch lamp, he took to sitting alone on the front stoop, a bottle between his knees and his knees held close to his chest. How he sat there without expression, without response to his wife calling from the kitchen to come in and eat something, but hauling into his lap a handful of gravel, which he would pick from and launch toward the road anytime a new and fine-looking truck raised up dust in front of the house and passed him by.

His mother regarded the boy's averted face, then reached across the table for his hands. He's gone, right? she said.

The boy turned to her, his face blank but for the light in his pale blue eyes. Yeah, he said. Yeah, Mama. He is.

When they'd finished their meal the boy ordered two cups of coffee from the waitress. For a long time the boy's mother moved a spoon through her coffee, nor did she look up from it. Where do we cross? she finally asked.

Cross what?

Cross over to Colorado.

The boy folded his hands and rested his elbows on the table and thought about it.

I think by Quemado Lake. Up near Apache Mountain. Thing of it is, I don't know for sure where the lake is when you come over the mountains. It's the one thing I can't yet figure out. But I know for a fact it's a good place to cross. Easiest country. It's still a good way from there to Colorado, but once we get there it's the best track to follow north.

He sipped from the mug of coffee and set it down and took a cigarette from his breast pocket and lit it and flushed out the match by his side. You know where it is?

His mother shook her head.

Shit, he said.

They drank their coffee. The waitress returned to check on them. The boy asked her if she knew where the lake was but she said she did not. He asked if the proprietor was around. She nodded and went to the back of the room where she yelled out for a man she called Big Heff, jutting a thumb back toward the boy and his mother.

The man raised his chin and gave a final swipe of his dishrag across the tabletop he was standing over and started across the room.

You wouldn't know where Quemado Lake was, would you? the boy asked.

I sure do. The proprietor took the dishrag from his shoulder and it disappeared in the mitt of his hand after he ran it over his sweating forehead. Pretty country up there once you get through the mountains. Them mountains is downright treacherous. You takin the train?

No sir, the boy said. We're riding.

The proprietor fingered a great slab of scar tissue above his temple where it appeared a knife had gone through. Horses? he said.

Yes sir.

The proprietor looked at the boy then out the window, turning his head to reveal the pink hairless gash. The boy's mother quickly turned away. Well. Horses? he said again.

The boy nodded.

Truly treacherous then, Big Heff said. Truly.

He rubbed at the scar more furiously, turning once to the waitress and snapping his fingers at her and pointing to a table where three men in gray button-up suits had just sat down.

Well, the boy said. Where is it, did you say?

Oh. The proprietor unballed the rag from his hand and slung it back up on his shoulder. It's up by San Juan County, he said. That's a long way off.

The proprietor studied the boy's mother again. He stopped working the scar and leaned down and put both fists upon the table. You all sure you want to ride it? You got enough provisions? He kept his eyes upon the boy's mother. I mean to say, it's already hittin on winter up there, and it gets cold. It'll be getting cold up there right soon.

I know it, the boy said. She does too. We'll be fine sir. I thank you.

The proprietor looked back and forth at the boy and his mother once more and said Anytime. Then he walked off with his hand upon the scar and his head slightly shaking.

San Juan County, the boy said.

He turned back to his mother with his hands atop his gloves.

Do you know how far that is? she asked him.

I know McKinely County is just south of it and that's a good two-week ride. Maybe longer.

When his mother did not reply the boy looked up at her. With that light so stark on her face and its wide lines and rivulets glistening in the sun, he thought how old she looked sitting there. Sitting there with her son about the same age as her husband when they married and him left behind and her without man or country, and he hoped that she did not worry about him for he felt he was burdened with enough worry for both of them. Maybe we should put you on a train, he said.

His mother raised up and shook her head. From her back pocket she took the red scarf she used to wear when she hung out the linens and wiped a ball of dirt impatiently from the corner of her eye.

We don't got the money, Trude. Besides, I ain't leavin you alone. She placed her fingers around her coffee mug and stared at them. You're all I got left, she said. She took her hands away and leaned back. Anyways, we surely can't afford to pay both our ways unless we up and sold the horses and probably a good part of our gear.

The boy's grip flexed and slackened around the gloves. Triften, he whispered. Shit. You know I can't.

She took his hands and leaned across the table.

Yes, she said. And you know what else I know? I wouldn't let you if you tried.

The boy worked a smile onto his face.

I just wish I would've went and tried to get the truck from Pa. It could have at least got us up a ways.

It'll be alright, his mother said, rubbing his thick hard hands in the small softness of her own.

I know it, he said.

In the late afternoon heat they walked the length of the street back to the general store where the horses stood hobbled. The boy took out a small fold of dollar bills from the tin talcum box they'd packed in the saddlebag. He rolled himself a cigarette inside one of the bills and motioned to his mother who stood waiting in the road, and walked up the porch and into the store.

They bought cornmeal and soap and tins of shredded ham hock and beans. The butcher cut them strips of elk meat and they bought coffee beans and milk and sugar. They bought a sack of oats and a bag of biscuits and a loaf of unleavened bread.

The boy leaned against the counter and smoked with the clerk while his mother looked idly over the bunches of flowers in the store window.

Where you headed?

The clerk's thumb was tucked into his belt beneath a huge potbelly which stuck out shameless and hairy at the navel where shirt buttons had once been but were no longer.

Colorado, the boy said.

The clerk's teeth clenched around his pipe and his tongue warbled the words from his yellow-stained beard. Long ways, he said.

It is at that, the boy said.

You takin them horses all the way up there?

Yes sir we are.

The boy let his cigarette fall on the floor by his feet and stubbed it out with his boot heel.

Shit, the clerk said. With a great heave he righted himself off the countertop and hitched impatiently at his belt.

The boy looked up from the floor. Sorry, he said. He picked up the cigarette butt and put it in his bib.

Ah, I don't care about that, the clerk said.

Shit for what then?

The clerk moved the pipe to the other side of his mouth, a thin string of spittle descending from his chin. He squinted at the boy.

Why'd you say Shit?

Oh, the clerk said, his eyes opening wide again. He wiped the yellow string from his neck. Shit for the horses.

They crossed the street to an outfitter. There the boy and his mother counted out their remaining bills and bought extra-duty leather riding chaps for the mountains and leather vests. The boy dressed them over his overalls, looking like some time-traveled farmer preparing for a war on the gentry. The saleswoman told him not to worry. She said he looked handsome. He thanked her. He bought an overcoat for his mother after much insistence, though she would not allow him to buy her new gloves despite his pleading.

I don't need new gloves, she said. I like mine fine, and they're warm and comfortable. What we should buy is some new jean pants for you. And a nice shirt.

I got all that packed on the mule.

Well why don't you wear them?

They ain't comfortable.

I suppose they're more comfortable than that vest over your bib. And I'm sure they look better.

The boy turned from his mother and paid the saleswoman. She made his change from the till and told him again he looked right fine. He smiled at her and led his mother out by the arm.

My lord, she said. Some girls got no apprehensions.

Shit, the boy said. And you wonder why I cuss.

In the evening the boy unshod the horses in preparation for the mountain shale, and afterward they ate modestly at an open-air market in the center of town.

The night was cool and the clouds luminous over the moon. The townspeople swarmed and the children chased one another around the parked trucks and squat brick water wells. Old women sat under verandas and the high archways of the government building and called their merchandise to the passersby. They sold bolts of linen and silk and calico cloth and in the darker corners young men with old faces dealt Black Horse tobacco to the businessmen.

The boy and his mother walked arm in arm and spoke at length about the goods being sold and the chandeliers in the hotel foyer they passed and the fine dress of the townspeople, and though the boy deeply considered the coming days through the mountains they spoke nothing of their journey.

The old adobe house they boarded in was owned by a prosperous logger, and when he had shown the boy's mother off to bed the boy sat with the man at his kitchen table and spoke of the north country. The boy leaned on his elbows while the man told him stories about the Colorado streams and the deep and rich forests and the air that smelled like jasmine. Through the feathered light of the lantern that hung low above the table the boy was held captivated, and he spoke unregarded to the man about how he had dreamed of such places. How he had dreamed an entire night of just a single shade of green. He told him how that night while he slept his heart soared and when he woke in the morning he had told his mother that he had dreamed all night of the country they call Colorado. He told the man how he hoped to start a ranch of his own there, where he and his mother would work and make a good life for themselves.

When the clock that hung above the oven range struck eleven the man rose and set the glass of milk he had been drinking in the sink basin and wished the boy well and told him to take care getting up there, saying at last that if he could get his mother up there unscathed, putting up a ranch would be like baking a pie.

When he rose in the morning the boy already felt it. The cold snap broke into the house and through the seams of windows and doors. He looked at his mother shivering on the cot below him. He pushed back his hair and jumped down from the bunk.

A norther's blowin in, he called to her. Time to rise and shine. He pulled on his boots. Then he leaned down and shook his mother's shoulder. Mama. Please. We can't waste any time.

His mother stirred and let down the patchwork quilt from her neck and rubbed her arms. Should we wait another day? she said.

If we wait another day it's likely to get worse. And after that it might just stay bad. Might as well get up there and get used to it before we chance upon snow. I'll saddle the horses.

Outside the light was dark and gray. The boy took his time feeling along the jawline of his horse to be sure the hackamore fit snugly. When he finished with Triften he stepped away from her and looked out. In the morning darkness the town did not appear all that odd to him, save a lone figure that presently came walking down the middle of the road.

He was hunched at the back but walked very swiftly and did not raise his head from where it was pressed into his chest. His hands were pushed deep into the pockets of his trousers and the wind blew the remains of his hair furiously about his head. The boy stopped with his hand on the back of his mother's roan and watched the man coming.

When the man finally raised his chin the boy staggered back against the crossposts of the fence where the horses were tied. He dug out the knife from his bib and held it slightly aloft from his hip. The man in the road kept coming. The wind bore down upon the road and struck up a band of dust across the boy's face. When the water cleared from his eyes he thrust the knife forward.

Hatley Mason's hands were still stuffed down in his pockets when the knife came up in front of him. He smiled stiffly at the boy and jutted his chin out, as if he were merely calling on some old friend. His shirt was torn under the left armpit and in the web of his left hand there was a crust of dried blood. He was thinner than the boy remembered him to be, but his eyes still held their same squinting fire.

Make that your last step, the boy said.

His father halted a few yards away. He raised his eyebrows at the boy. You always had that shaky grip, he said.

The boy eyed his hand on the knife. He clenched it tighter. He shot a glance over his father's shoulder. His mother had not yet come down and all the town was still sleeping. The only sound was that of the wind.

Hatley Mason made a step forward. What you aim to do, boy? he said.

The boy met his father's advance with a thrash of the knife through the air. Get clear of you, he whispered through his teeth. He extended his arm and pointed the knife at his father's chest. Now step yourself back.

Hatley Mason toed the ground but did not move away. For a moment he seemed to be contemplating something in the swirling dust. He frowned at his boot. Then he looked up and stared the boy in the eye for a long time.

Where is she? he said finally.

Blood pounded in the boy's ears. He made an uncertain step forward. She's gone, he said.

His father jutted out his chin again, this time in the direction of the horses. That's her horse there, ain't it?

The boy half turned to the horses. Then he said, She's on the train.

Hatley Mason studied his son. The boy froze under his father's inspection in the old way he had back home and had not yet forgotten, nor would he ever.

Alright. Where'd she go on the train then boy? Hatley Mason's voice was shaky with drink.

I told her to take it to the end of the line, the boy said.

His father chuckled heartily and threw back his head. You told her, he said. You did. Well how about that. He made a false smile at the boy. And what about you?

The boy reset his grip on the knife and tilted the blade forward. I'm on my way, he said. Then the boy came toward his father until the knife was a foot from his chest.

Hatley Mason looked at the knife and chuckled again, this time without heart. His face fell slack. He looked off into the distance like he meant to take inventory of all things surrounding him at that very moment. Then in one quick motion he spat and stepped back and pulled his hand from his pocket and flung something at the boy's feet. The boy kept the knife poised and did not look down, nor did he swipe away the dark red spittle that clung to his cheek.

You give that to her, his father said. He took a few steps backward. You give that to her and let her know I ain't done with her yet. Not by a sight.

Yeah you are.

Don't think I don't know how to find the end of the line, boy.

I don't.

And don't think you'll get clear of me neither. You'll never get clear of me. He squinted at the boy a moment longer, then turned on his heels and started back down the road. When he was halfway gone he turned back once more. Never, he called out. I'm your goddamn daddy, boy. You'll never get clear of me, no matter what. You've got my blood in you.

The boy did not respond but only stood firm with his knife upraised and his knees slightly canted. He watched his father until he was out of sight. Then for a while he watched the empty road. At last he lowered his knife and ran a glove across his cheek and looked to his feet. He bent down and picked the shiny little thing out of the dirt. He pulled his hat tighter against the wind, then he licked the rawhide thumb of his glove and rubbed the dust from the silver amulet that hung from a tiny silver chain. He looked down the road again, the last time. Then he held the amulet up to his face, where beneath the scores and black-ened tarnish he made out the crude inscription of his mother's name.

THREE

AFTER MANY DAYS of black clouds, descending from the mountains and bearing low upon the rutted and narrowing paths they rode, the sun broke clear and bright. With that sudden light the mountains came into high relief, gnarled and colorless as bones.

Well, the boy called. Just a few more hours and we'll be up there.

Standing her horse beneath the looming shadows of the mountains, the boy's mother made no response.

You ready Mama?

His mother tried to smile but her lips were carved flat. Yes, she said. I'm ready.

The boy kicked his horse on and his mother followed as if by mechanics, and they began their pass with the rust-colored railroad tracks in the southwest and the smoking mountains blowing down from the north.

Late in the morning they came to the head of a moss-banked creek. It was his mother who drew up her reins first, sliding down and hobbling her roan by a willow tree. She stretched out along the bank and called for the boy to come sit with her, her hair flung back in the high grass and her bone-thin forearms tucked under her ribs. The boy slipped down from his horse and watered them all from the creek. He watched all three animals lapping up the water for a while, then sidled up to his mother. Silva Creek, he said.

His mother turned a languorous head to him. How do you know?

The boy gazed around at the closing mountains and back to the southern plainlands. Such silent empty grandeur he could not help but smile. Then he looked hard at the churning water and took out a cigarette and his matchbook and lit it and put the matchbook back in his overall bib.

I been plannin this for a long time, Mama. A long time.

After a few moments he flung the cigarette into the brush and pressed his fingers to his forehead. Listen, Mama. The world was silent. Only the trickle and splash of water could be heard. Now this is country, he said.

The mother and son sat and ate by the bank. The boy said how warm it was and how from here on in it will only get colder and his mother agreed. The day was so blue and sun-filled, and it became a long hour they sat there tearing the remains of the hard bread they had bought in Silver City.

When they were finished eating the boy fiddled with the end crust, easing down onto his back and throwing it up in the air and catching it and throwing it up again.

You havin fun over there?

The boy caught the bread and raised his head above his chest.

Yeah. Something wrong?

No, no. You go on.

Thank you, he said. He threw the bread up again. I believe I will.

When he pitched the bread too far from his grasp his mother laughed out loud and the boy sat up and mock laughed at her, and soon they were speaking softly to each other, as if suddenly younger.

His mother told him of the days when he was still a child and she told him of happier days and county fairs, the boy holding his arms up for his father to swing him on, of making faces at the prize hogs and cheering as his father shot balloons with a pellet gun to win them stuffed rabbits from the scowling hawkers. She spoke of the riding lessons they took together from their neighbor Larry Bowles when the boy was just beginning to walk. She addressed him very quietly and she peered into the water all the while.

You was always so quiet around your daddy.

Yeah. I guess I was.

His mother knitted her fingers together and looked down at them.

I guess I should have learned something by that. I always felt you was smarter than both of us, even without regular schoolin.

If I'm smart in any way, it's on account of you.

His mother unlinked her fingers, then closed them again.

Out in the pastures, though, she said. She looked up at him. Out there you all seemed right together. Before the drinkin, of course. I don't know if you all talked out there or not, but your face was different out there. Both of your all faces. I remember watchin you two from the kitchen window. Could make me forget about the dishwater my hands was sunk in.

She told him in great detail one such story of his father taking him to work cattle in the morning and how the boy jumped on his back and fell back in the saddle, and she told him that that picture of the boy out there laughing with his father was once enough for her to live on. Then she paused and looked vanquished of emotion and said sadly now it was not.

The boy watched his mother pass through those stories and he watched the changes on her face that were seasons as complicated and heartbreaking as the world's own. He listened quietly and he smiled when she smiled and he looked down at the mist-risen creek when she paused to hold her quavering lip. But mostly she laughed and the boy smiled wide and the smile felt strange and warm upon his face, but it was late and they still had miles to go until they reached the mountain forests.

We ought get movin, he said.

Yet his mother went on with an intense fluidity now, as if the world's fragility and transience had suddenly struck her, and she told him finally of the time when he was a young boy and studying the Bible and his father came home violent from the fields after she found one of his bottles and smashed it on a fence post. She told him how she knew he was special and would grow to be strong and fine when his father raised a fist to her and the boy shot up and waved the good book in the air and exclaimed defiantly, *Muzzle not the ox that treads the corn*. And she told him how his father froze where he was standing and began to weep and went back out the door and into town and did not return for a week. She said it was the only time she'd ever seen him cry.

For the smallest of moments the story of his father's appearance in Silver City almost escaped his lips. After a long silence, both gazing glassily at the water, the boy looked up at his mother. Then with a siege of grief and love he told her that she was the finest woman he had ever known and he suspected there were not many ever made in her likeness, and if God played a part in anyone's life it was hers.

The day was long and patient. The boy's mother spoke no more. Upon leaving the creek she seemed to fall again into the deep grueling reflection that had claimed her and which she could not shake. Her hands worked the reins just enough to guide the horse, and her head fell into a loose slow rocking between her sculpted shoulders.

They rode for hours without stop or speech. A bobcat loped from the trees and mulled about in the horses' path as if in deep consideration of their shapes. The air began to thin in the early evening and their passage was made even slower by the darkening terrain and the forthcoming mountain chill, the boy's mother swaddled sheepishly in her son's blanket looking to be not merely in travel but in exodus.

At dusk they regained the creekbed. Its water was blacker and colder than where they had fetched from it before, and that night the boy made a tremendous fire. He made mesquite charcoals and cooked the elk meat high above it. He left his Colt bagged on the mule and now kept his grandfather's Winchester rifle under his free arm to ward off any unwelcome in their camp.

The creek ran on without repose and in the light of the fire the boy watched it move black and thick down the mountain. Both the boy and his mother stopped eating to watch silently as a white-tailed deer stepped furtively into the ring of fire.

Its coat was pure white and looked so soft to the boy he imagined if he touched it it would melt. It held itself with such grace though its ribs were exposed in the firelight and its eyes were awash with hunger. It turned its head and did not move away. For a moment it peered directly at the boy, its back arched like a cat's. The boy's rifle was pressed under his leg and he would have snatched it up but for that deep lost look in the deer's eyes. A look he could neither name nor betray. A moment later the deer sprung, a white flame among them, bouncing down the mountain slope and into the red moon which clung to the mountain ledge like a leaf on fire.

The boy looked across the flames at his mother. He shook his head. Lord have mercy, he said.

In the morning the boy awoke to his mother sitting beside the fire she had already rekindled. When he sat up she handed him a cup of coffee she had boiled. She watched him sip at the rim of the cup a moment, then held her arms tight to her chest. She looked up at the sky.

Trude, she said after some time. Now listen here. I believe it now. I believe you. When we get up there we can find us a new ranch.

He turned from the fire and she leaned forward and touched him under the chin.

Yes we can Mama, he said. Yes we can.

That morning they rode into the first mountain. They camped at noon and again before the moon came up. On those initial nights they camped in widemouthed caves and they camped in a gully one night and one night they passed a high desolate crag and they camped upon a band of quartzite with no shelter whatsoever. Around them plume agate stood ancient and treelike. They were rocks the boy had never seen before, and at times it seemed to him that they had left the world altogether. Higher and higher they rose, where the watermelon snow on the red rock gave way to a purer white, which in places covered the forest floor though it was only the first days of winter.

In the forenoon of their first Sunday out, they came trotting into a high mountain meadow. There before them appeared dozens of elk and the sun broke free and the boy and his mother sat the horses. They watched the elk gallop and mull about like a new texture being laid, and their presence against the mountains in that high sweet grass was a trellis alive and for a moment it seemed as if the world was reinventing itself and the boy was filled with an inexplicable hope.

See Mama, he said, tipping his hat back. He shook his head. Will you look at this, he said. We ain't got nothin to worry about. I'll take care of you just fine.

I know you will, his mother said, but her face was turned away and her eyes closed against the cold burning sun.

31

ON THE FIFTH day of mountain riding the boy and his mother footed their way through the snow to follow up the side of a silt stream. The icy water crashed upon the black shale walls with abandon, and there a western diamondback slid with imperceptible quiet into the boy's mother's boot and gathered her flesh in its fangs.

She had only just climbed abreast her horse again when she felt the strike of the snake's teeth. The reins fell from her hands. The bitten leg kicked out from the stirrup. Her mouth shuddered then went slack without word, until the boy turned and looked at her.

He dismounted in unison with his mother's moan. Snake, she finally cried, pointing weakly and without precision.

The boy stomped the ground and shook her leg, jumping back when snake shot out of her boot and slithered into the dark trees.

He struggled the dirk knife from his bib and took his mother over his shoulder. He set her on the ground and cut back the boot leg, finding the two blood eyes just above her anklebone. He pressed his lips against her ankle and sucked the flesh of it. He spat out a long rope of the yellow poison juice while his mother braced herself, leaning up and knocking the boy's hat off and clenching her fingers on the crown of his head.

When he had spat out the last of the wormy milk he took her under the arms roughly, in the manner of someone grown impatient, and propped her up against a rock. She moaned while he dressed the wound with a strip of his shirt he ripped off from his waist.

Shit, Mama. Hold still. Why'd you have to. Shit. Look at this. It's alright. Shit, it's alright Mama.

But it was not. His hands trembled and he could barely keep his eyes upon the flesh that was already gone black where the snake's teeth had been. After a while his mother went mute. She leaned back on the rock. She pitched her head back and watched the sky. Still gripping the boy's hair she told him it was alright, though her voice was altered and distant. As though she spoke to him from the bottom of a well.

That night by the fire she told the boy she felt better, but he had stopped listening to her for many of her words had become garbled and trailed off to nothing. He made her sit very close to the fire and draped his extra clothes around her. He listened in vain for life in the woodlands, some other presence to soothe him, but nothing came.

All night he sat and smoked and watched his mother's eyes flicker and wane. From time to time he felt her head. When he touched her she mumbled incoherently, though several times he thought he heard his father's name among her blind pleadings. Once he got up and rummaged around in his saddlebag, and when he opened his eyes at dawn the amulet was still pressed in his lap.

In the late morning the boy hefted his mother onto her roan and he handed up the reins to her and asked her several times if she wanted to rest more but she said that she did not. She said that she was feeling much better. The fever's gone down, she said.

But Mama.

We've made it this far, haven't we? Ain't no little snake goin to stop us now.

She rode before him in the morning's gray domain with the wilderness heights almost attached to the clouds as if a great hem had stitched earth to sky. The boy rode abreast of his mother and watched her with slatted eyes and would not look full upon her for fear that closer inspection would reveal too much. She was slouched horribly in the shoulders. Her feet repeatedly slipped from the stirrups, and after a while she just let them flop against the horse's flanks. She patted down her hair with a pale hand as though in fear that someone would see her looking so unattended to.

The boy could not help but think of Eve expelled from the garden, and he thought his mother worse off for she gained nothing from the serpent but went riding as though there was never any knowledge of past or future, only that riding on and on.

Let's get a rest, he said when he could watch her no more.

No, no. We've got to get on. Before the cold comes, remember?

It's goin to be fine Mama, he said with his face still averted. In a few days we'll hit another town. We'll get you fixed up proper there and well rested. I didn't tell you before. I got some money of my own saved up, he lied, so when we get north it won't take long to start our own ranch. I can sign on with another outfit for a year and then we should have enough with my wages to start up on our own. Mama?

The boy's mother had ridden well ahead of him, her eyes all over the trees and sky.

Yes?

It won't be long now.

She turned to him at last. A green pallor had crept into the skin around her eyes and mouth. She smiled weakly. I know it, she said.

They rode very slowly that day. The landscape was unvaried in shape or color and they rode the horses through a deep snow. The boy's mother made no sound. Under the horse's feet the snow ran dark and almost black in the afternoon shadows, shaped like heaps of shawls cast over a land unreal.

In the early evening the wind ceased almost entirely. Silence fell in the forest except for the distant songbirds and a remote river and the trill of its water pass. In this quarter of the forest the boy's mother drew up on the reins and whoaed her horse with a whisper. The boy pulled up behind her. She was listening to the songbirds rising there, rising among them in that mysterious forest. She listened to the river and asked the boy if he heard it and he said he did and then she looked back at the boy and her face looked serene and the boy moved closer to her horse and spoke to her but she was already dead.

He sat with the horses' breathing. By and by he dismounted, taking a long time to hobble Triften and the mule. He slid his mother's body down from her saddle, holding her by the waist with one hand and stroking her hair with the other. Her hands were the cold white of the snow and her breasts sagged and pooled beneath her armpits. He walked her body to a grove of snow-laden aspen and came back and sat at his horse's feet.

Late in the night he made camp by the aspens. From the fire he looked into the dark grove but could not see his mother there. Once he walked over to be sure she hadn't fallen into a fever fit and risen again, but there was her body limp and ragged among the pine duff. Her eyes were wide and chalky under the black lids. He bent down and pulled off his glove and closed her eyes with his fingers and went back to the fire.

He rose before dawn. He fed the animals.

All morning the boy thought about what he should do, what there was left to do for his dead mother. He knew he couldn't bury her in that rocky terrain. He didn't have a spade or even a place where he could use his hands.

At last he went into the grove where her body had slouched over during the night, as if to inspect more closely that raised gnarl of tree roots. He stood over her and worked his chafed hands together. He closed his eyes. Then he hefted her in his arms and put her horseback, stroking the roan and quieting her until she was still.

The saddle creaked under the weight of her body. He used cotton twine to tie her arms and legs to the fenders of the saddle. He tied another lead rope to the roan and fitted the headstall on Triften and took up the reins and called to the mule and rode out. He rode out this way into the deeper mountains with his mother in tow, all of his belongings in a ramshackle congregation of horse and leather.

The following afternoon he came down from his horse for the first time and ate with his chin on his chest. Afterward he took his mother down from her horse. He could no longer carry her. She was so heavy in her skin, though there was not much else left of her, and in his arms there was no trace of her warmth or her spirit, nor was there that jeweled glimmer to her eyes which he had searched into all his life.

For an endless moment he stared at her. Then, with rudiments of linen that had been packed for their journey, he began to wrap her body. He wrapped her first and slowly at the face and then at the waist where the flesh was green with poison, and then with some of his extra clothes he wrapped her entire body.

When he had finished he staggered up and looked around aimlessly. He could not understand how it had happened. It had come so fast. He thought of the doctor, how he could have helped her. He remembered invoking God's name just days before at the stream but could not find anywhere the mercy for which he had called.

At last he laid his mother upon a long slab of stone.

With the final seam of cloudlight settling at his feet he bent down and gathered up a handful of pebbles into his hands. He looked back once, the thin frame of his mother wrapped in dirty cloth on that gray and nameless rock. Then he turned the pebbles over in his hardened fingers, remembering the only words in the way of wisdom his father had ever given him. *The land is your bones and your bones is the land.* He thought about that, looking long and long into the coming night, a light snow falling hushed and calm in the dark open.

Before putting his foot in the stirrup he leaned down and scattered the pebbles back onto the earth but for one nugget that he pushed into his pocket and squeezed until it was as his heart felt. Dust.

II

FOUR

IN THE WILDERNESS of Catron County the boy made a wandering of himself. He followed no path or particular direction and he knew he would never return home nor ever lay eyes upon family again and he roamed thus for weeks. The first day out after his mother's death he crested onto another mountain meadow where he unsaddled his mother's roan and secured her tack in the saddlebag. He placed the saddle on his mule, then let the horse free with a swipe of glove across her muddy backside. She stood confused in the hazy light. He had to tell her to git, kicking his boots at her until finally the mare bolted off into the milky field. The boy stroked Triften as she watched her sister running loose, her long brown mane blowing along the white run of trees like a flag carried off in the wind. She watched her with great apprehension and the boy leaned into the mare and pressed his nose against hers, speaking to her beseechingly and telling her that was just the way the world worked.

They cleaved the mountains and rode the higher ridges with the tree line running thin and the snow snapping beneath the horse's feet, climbing into the saw-toothed rocks beneath the pendulous light as if the danger of his vigilance would foster some absolution at the mountain's end.

The days rose and fell. He ate little and sat staring at the fire every night, wherever he had stopped, and he did not consider where he had been or where he was going. But as those days alone in the mountains grew and passed, the boy could no longer fight them. He stepped into their rhythm and their rhythm was the rhythm of the wild, and the rhythm of the wild was blood-driven and raw and ruled by the bone-made body. It was the rhythm of water. It was the rhythm of the world laid bare.

He came down from his horse in a field of tall yellow broomgrass. Five weeks of rigid cold had passed across his body like a blade. His vest was torn. The chaps he had bought in Silver City were split at the seams. The horse stamped and flung back her head, watching him gravely as if she knew what all of it meant. He sat with the frozen grass blades to his shoulders. He rolled onto his side with the wind setting his hat to tittering where it lay on the ground beside his head, and in the half-light of a cloud-filled noon the boy fell into a deep sleep where once again the massive bears worked their forepaws through the deep swales of snow.

In the dream he was still the child he had been when they had first come to him, and he chased after them with the same heedless wonder as he had before, down the streams and across the snow, weaving through the aspens and the checkerboard light that spilled through the forks of their brittle limbs. He tromped through prairie grass and sage and into the lush green carpet at the edge of the forest, but once more he was turned away where the trees grew dense and the light flattened and the horizon disappeared into the broad-backed leaves and gray drifts of snow. He called out to them as he had before, a dark longing in his voice that went deep into the heaving wilderness. Yet in this dream, to his amazement, the last bear stopped where a final shadow stretched into the forest, and turned back to him. Before the boy could move closer the bear gathered itself on its hind paws and rose huge against the trees, the great hinged muscle of its jaw opening to reveal the white blades of its teeth glinting in the sway of light. As the bear came down again its hind legs squatted deep to the ground, then in one tremendous thrust from the earth it sprang for the boy, its teeth still bared and its eyes red and wild.

When the boy flung his arms in front of his face he awoke to the sound of his mare whinnying and the mule lowing like a cow. He was up on his knees as he had been in the dream, and in the fragmented moon glow he saw the bear lope off into the trees, the heat from its body rising like smoke, its breath thick in the cool night air.

He staggered up and stumbled across the field, then fell to his knees again. For a long time after he sat staring into the unlit trees.

Days passed and though he did not cross the bear again, he saw it everywhere. He saw it in tree shadow and he saw it in water. He saw it standing poised with all its nameless brothers when he woke among the salt cedars that surrounded the permanent camp he had made by the clearing where the bear first appeared to him. He saw it in the wind and he heard it in the night fires by which he slept.

His life had taken a shape, and it was the hunt. He slipped onward without thoughts beyond the bear, going days without food or water and forgetting to feed his horse and mule. His figure grew hard. In the night he could stand still among the pines and listen for hours. Through the diffused lens of moonlight his eyes moved pale to pale across the frozen fields. They seemed eyes that no longer resided in the world but rather in some alternate and forsaken place that the world had gone from. He was no longer the man he saw himself as on the first night of their leaving, nor was he the boy he had been.

From time to time he came upon land that was rich with thaw and these times were the only ones that gave him pause, if only for a moment, his knees straightening from their hunting crouch and his hand slackening on the knife. Here he remembered his mother as if she were a brief flash that once appeared before him. And though he did not think of their journey nor her death nor the ranch they once called home, he thought about how in such fertile land, where the earth was sodden and pliable and lush with grass, what a good gravesite she could have had.

DARK WERE THE trees and darker the night. In the makeshift border of rock with which he had encircled the camp, the boy stood over a fire of mesquite and cedarwood and worked the blade of his knife with a stone. He no longer belted his guns but only that knife which he whittled to an even point every night, and he no longer sought any future past the moment when he would at last sink the knife into the bear's silent and ponderous heart.

The weather had begun to turn and the columbines opened their silken arms but the boy did not take notice. And though he and his horse and mule had all three grown thin from neglect, he would not yield.

When the moon rose high enough to see by, he flung the stone into the fire and set out in the last direction he had not yet gone. He went out on foot, hunched at the back like a harridan, the eyes peering out above the collar flaps of his vest stark and caved in the flaxen light. He moved swiftly through the swales of spring grass, jumping soundlessly from rock to rock. The hand in which he held the knife poised by his waist was raw and flaking from gripping Triften's reins. His hair floated up as one yellowed wave and of the rest of his body only his jaw remained substantial.

He wore a skullcap of gray squirrel skin under his hat. On his hands he wore nothing at all. One toe stuck out of his boot where the leather carriage had become unstitched. His overalls, pressed against the bones of his chest, were brown with mud, wet and dried so many times on his body they were almost like another husk of skin.

He pulled up at the downslope of a creekbed that trickled along the mountainside, walking gingerly to where the creek disappeared down the rocks. At the bottom of a bare slide beneath the creek a valley appeared and in that valley a lake, clear and blue and without ripple. At its edge the snow blossomed like wildflower. Ice hung from limp ragbush and nested in the craws of a stand of spruce trees. The trees loomed like silver beasts unto themselves but it was the red glaze from a distant fire that caused him to descend.

As he neared the flatland of the valley he could make out the fire two hundred yards off, where a canvas tent stood warping inside the rope-and-stake structure. Its aperture wings blustered up and whistled in the licks of wind. He went hedging down the last slope closer to the warmth of the fire, the lighting of his great heaping shadow making him appear to be the bearer of some terrible woodland secret.

In the valley everything was white snow and blue moon glow and like many places in those mountains it was ruled by silence. He stopped a hundred yards away and crouched on his haunches. The spruce branches sagged toward the fire. Around the camp and upon the tent slush fell from the trees. Stepping closer the boy could see horses of great coloring and beauty, and beside the tent he saw the shape of a man.

It was the first man he had seen since he and his mother left Silver City two months earlier. He could hear him talking. His voice came loud across the field, like a snap of twigs in the quiet, yet he could see no one else at the fire. When he was ten yards away he saw the man in full, though the man himself still did not seem to notice the boy who was out in the open now, standing erect with his arms folded across his vest.

The man was dressed in a long jacket of a fine and silky fur and his hands in front of the fire were soft and unblemished. For a moment his words sharpened and his chin bobbed up and down harshly in the direction of the tent but the words were lost to the boy in the fire's noise. Then the words ceased and the man turned back sullenly with his hands clasped together. The boy called out as he stepped into the fire's light.

Evenin.

The man who until that moment seemed insubstantial now spun and fell flat in the clearing around the fire and rolled to his stomach. In his hands he held a rifle dead set on the boy's chest. The boy did not jump or turn away but simply gazed into the fire, unfolding his arms and letting them down by his sides. I ain't huntin you, he said.

It was strange to hear his own voice after so long, yet the words came, calm and slow and without inflection.

Who are you? the man called out.

Just a hunter.

The brass hammer flickered in the firelight.

Just a hunter?

Yeah.

They were both silent. The man studied the boy, his eyes slit and his head upraised from the sighting. Then he rose to his knees. He put one hand on the ground and hefted himself to his feet. The gun stayed hoisted across his forearm with his finger curled around the trigger.

I saw your fire. The boy did not take his gaze from the flames. He made a gesture with his head toward the bluff he had descended from. I was up yonder, he said.

What was it you were doing up yonder?

The last two words he spoke more deliberately, and the manner in which he spoke seemed stately and precise.

I wasn't doin nothin. Can I sit?

Look at my jacket, the man said. He snapped the back of his hand across the muddy sleeve. Ruined.

He inspected the boy a moment longer, on his face a look perhaps reserved for things he could not name. He puckered his small mouth and raised his eyebrows, but for fear or amusement it was unclear.

Sit, he said. Please.

The boy slid his knife into his vest pocket and lowered himself onto the mud, sitting crosswise from the man, who himself leaned down again to sit high upon folded Mexican blanket. He set the gun by his side and crossed his black leather boots at his ankles. Off behind them the horses mulled about, huffing and sniffing beneath the trees. The boy peered over the man's shoulder to the tent where he could see no shadow nor hear any sound. The man pressed him with a stare and asked him if he liked the horses.

Yes sir. They're some beauties.

Is that why you came down here, to see my horses? To steal my horses from me?

No.

No to see the horses, or No to steal them?

No to both. I just came down is all.

Yes, the man said. Yes, he repeated, with the same deliberateness he had used before. Do you know these horses, then?

Not by personal name, but they're all Tennessee walkers, I can tell you that.

Yes, they are indeed.

I never seen stallions run like that in the mountains.

They weren't supposed to be.

Why are they up here then?

The man breathed deeply. He adjusted his jacket and folded his arms.

You want to know why I am here? Is that it? He looked at his mud-caked sleeve again and shook his head. Very well, he said, looking up at the boy. I will tell you. Our train derailed and slid into a ravine on one of the new mountain passes. At least that's what they call it. New. The locomotive driver said it would take a few days for the trucks to get up the mountains to bring us down, so I bought these from a man on the train who was moving them for sale to Texas.

The man lit a pipe with his delicate hands, his pinky finger extended as though he was holding a cup of tea.

Must have taken some amount of money to buy them.

It did, the man said between draws on the pipe, but his voice allowed no emotion, neither pride nor arrogance nor sorrow.

You alone?

The man looked up from behind the smoke of his pipe. He nodded his head very slowly.

Yes, he said. I am alone.

His hand went down to his side and rested itself upon the rifle again. The boy's eyes went away from the fire and back to the man.

His coat had buttons of ivory the size of half dollars and he wore gold chains at the collar of his shirt. His hat was of some strange rounded felt the boy did not recognize and his pants were wide and straight without a flare at the bottom. To the boy he looked more alien than any beast he had seen in all his days in that land, and he knew no such man would travel alone.

I ain't never seen an English saddle like that around here, he said.

The man did not reply. His face darkened and he puffed on the pipe with his thin blue lips.

You from England?

Again the man made no response nor did he look at the boy. He pressed back his short oiled hair above his ears with his fingertips and leaned back and pitched his head back as if to listen behind him, at the tent.

Where you headed? the boy said at length.

There was now suspicion in the boy's voice, though he could not have said exactly why. The Englishman stared at him a moment longer, then outstretched one of his fleshy fingers and waved it about the general north. Over there, he said.

Over that mountain peak?

Yes. Over that mountain peak.

There a town over there?

But of course. What else? More mountains? I don't think so. The Englishman leaned over the fire, puffing steadily on the pipe and lifting the rifle into his lap. And you? he said.

The boy looked in the direction the man had pointed, forking his hat between his fingers and lifting it slightly off his head. He gazed out at the moon, the wide north starless sky appearing to him as if for the first time.

Same, he said.

The constant hum of the valley crosswinds was uprooted by a voice that came low and mournful from the tent. It was the voice of a girl. Her words were distorted by the ripple and snap of the tent flaps. The Englishman, whose face had fallen blank on the fire, jerked upright and uncrossed his legs. He set the pipe on the ground and squared the rifle on his shoulder again and aimed it at the boy. His eyes across the fire and on the boy were like dull green pebbles even the leaping flames could not give sparkle to.

The sound came louder now. Then the voice seemed to give up altogether on words and became a deep and breathy sob. The Englishman tilted the rifle up in the air to signal the boy to rise. I'm alone, he repeated. He let up the hammer. He looked above the sighting in question of what the boy was waiting for.

Yeah, the boy said, rising stiffly and walking backward from the fire with his eyes on the ground. You're alone.

The girl cried out again, a resounding guttural moan, and the Englishman wheeled around to the tent then turned back as quickly, clicking the hammer down again and setting his finger to the trigger, but all that remained of the boy were a few muddy boot prints and the low pound of his breath which drifted off and faded into the blue valley winds.

The tune he hummed to himself between bouts of coughing had played on the dusty old Victrola that had once occupied the parlor where his mother entertained the wives of the neighboring ranchers. It was a steady ascension of notes not unlike the grandstand music that rumbled from the aluminum horns at the rodeo grounds, and it reminded the boy not of any particular day or place but rather it gave him some distant sense of continuity in which all seemed good and warm and unbidden by time.

The illness had come with swift resolve after sleeping restlessly the night he met with the Englishman. He had kicked off his bedroll in the early morning hours, wet and sweating before the fire. He woke with a clot of blood in his throat and could only rise to kindle the fire before he was overcome by weakness.

Two days passed and all he could do was watch the fire and the trees that leaned in the soft earth around the stone border of his camp, and he watched them constantly, separate and in tandem, as if they shared some news of his demise.

The clots of blood became bigger and ran down from his lips with each cough, and lying as he was now on the cold mud floor of his roof-less home, he recalled snaking beneath the blue flannel covers of his bed and reading tales of the Indian wars. He recalled the stack of them he kept beneath his bed to hide from his mother, all written on slick yellow paper bound by raw leather spines and illustrated with explosions of gunpowder and thick-necked men whose faces were drawn with heroic intensity, always crouched behind stone walls and always lighted by a dusky red serenity as if each battle were the last. He remembered pulling the quilt up under his arms and piling the pillows behind his head, placing the book on his stomach and tilting it up with his fingers and half listening to the rusty sound of the needle pulling along the record. He remembered the murmurs of the women down-stairs and his mother's light laughter coming now and again, up the stairs and muted through the walls like a balm swept across his fore-head to assure him that the world as it was now was as it would be forever.

In the evening of the third day he rekindled the fire and climbed into his bedroll and shimmied closer to the flames until the heat of them wore on his face. Still and quiet as he was, the sounds that came to him from the woodland were haunting and unfamiliar. Even his horse and mule would not shift or stammer to relieve him of the night's anonymity. He rolled again with his arms still pinned inside the bedroll and let his nose turn under the slop of mud he lay upon.

For a while he thought about the girl's voice that had come from the tent. It was a voice he would not have recognized if he had not remembered the cry from his mother when the snake found the artery that lay beside her ankle. It was as if they shared a common voice, as if their bodies had resigned themselves to another time and place where their calls were calls come forth from the throat of their spirits.

Later in the night the sound of the Victrola came back to him from beyond the fire and the voice of the girl beyond that. He wrestled from the blanket and placed his hands on his head. The music and cries commingled until they were together and steady, a melody so unlikely as not to have been music at all but instead some old telling wrought from the bones of his painted heroes whose bodies lay scattered on the empty hillsides, their tongues black and the cores of their eyes spilled out of their heads.

At last it was his mother's voice that rose above all, without music or cries but simply calling his name as she had that dawn when they left their ranch behind. It was a sound so pure and lost, like the warble of a bird from a far-off tree, and even when he pushed down the bedroll and sat upright with his elbows on his knees it remained with him. It came and went, pausing in attendance for another wind to carry its sound, then came again. The fire was spent to embers and only a low shadow of his own body wavered beside him in the mud.

Dawn began red from the bosom of the mountains and his tears were the first since his mother's passing, and once they began they would not cease. He gripped his face full in his hands and rocked up and over his ribcage to lay his head between his knees. The voice of his mother went away and the woods were quiet but for a brisk morning wind that moaned in the treetops. Yet he went on that way, and before him passed the vision of his mother not yet of her thirty-sixth year, driven away by the violence of her man and the brazenness of her son and now calling out to the dim and vacant woodlands which were no more to the boy than his own dark image.

He woke again to a heavy sun. He sat up slowly and wiped away the salt and dried blood from his face with the back of his hand. He looked up at his horse. She had moved closer to him during the night and now stood stamping her foot in the ash at the edge of the fire's waste. He studied her chest, rippled lean with muscle and covered with a hard shell of mud. He leaned over himself and put a hand on her leg and coughed violently but the blood did not come.

Later in the morning he got up and kicked out the surviving embers of the fire. He sharpened his knife with the tune of the Victrola still upon his lips, humming to himself like he imagined the warriors of the old Americas had done when their tribe had been slaughtered and they prepared for the last battle they would ever fight beneath the wide spirit of the sky.

His knife glowed pale among the white trees. In a patch of weed and scrub he bent with his hands on his knees to study some fresh markings on a fir tree.

He had stripped down to his boots and overalls, the bib folded at his waist and cinched by a belt he had fashioned out of one of his mother's old lead ropes. About his neck was the silver chain, the lusterless silver amulet that kept his mother's name. He was thinner now than he had ever been and his whitened chest looked nothing more than a sheet of paper bound around a pole.

When he lowered himself down beneath the overhang of tree branches he heard the sound of a riverbed washing against the rocks. He followed the bark peelings closer to the river. Among the scrub a blackberry bush stood crippled in the dripping weeds. He picked one of the berries and tasted it, pinching it with his teeth like a barterer testing a coin. When he had eaten all he could he leaned back against a pine and closed his eyes.

Sometime later the boy awoke to the sun still hovering lazily above the mountains and he woke to the rushing river, but what he sensed first were the human sounds that came from the precipice shouldered above the river water. As he leaned up on his elbows there came a scream. It came again. He rose to his haunches. He listened. Again it came, and he knew it was the same voice he had heard coming from the Englishman's tent days before. It seemed to the boy a pleading, and from her crushed voice came some wild testimonies he could not piece together.

He rose against the aspen trunk. Through the low branches and creosote bush he made out the figure of the Englishman. He wore a brown frock coat and from the broadcloth at his neck hung a knot of silk. He was belted with an ivory-handled bowie knife and he stood unmoving. The boy crept closer. Against the light that dished off the water he saw in the arms of the Englishman a small package. It was wrapped in white linen and the Englishman held it closely to his chest. The boy squinted hard at the purple stain on its underside. The wailing from the girl would not cease, but the boy could not see her. He waited to see what the Englishman would do.

At length, the girl's cries subsided. Then the Englishman hoisted the package above his head very slowly, as if in offering, and held it out over the water. The cloth fluttered gently in the warm breeze. He let it go. It tumbled end over end and hit the frothing water where it bobbed and flowed for a moment, then sunk into the rapids and was gone.

The girl was suddenly crumpled against the Englishman's legs. Behind the Englishman all the boy could see of the girl were her raised fists. The man watched her for a few moments, almost with a look of playfulness, then shook her grip loose from his legs and walked out of sight.

When he saw the Englishman had gone the boy sprang up and went running back for his knife which he'd left beside the tree. The suspender branches of his overalls swung up and snapped against his stomach. He caught the knife up from behind the brush and turned and squinted against the sun and ran until he glimpsed her standing by the river's edge and stopped all at once.

In the fading light he saw her. She was dark. Her skin was like ebony afire. Her hair too was dark and it fell past her shoulders like nests of stone. Beneath the paper-thin cotton shift and the blue shawl gathered around her throat she was very thin. For that moment in which he first saw her she did not move at all. She was kneeling up with her hands pressed against her thighs. Then the girl brought her hands to her face and her eyes were terribly dark, like fire-scorched crystal, and she held her thick tangle of hair over them and began quietly to weep.

The boy's first thought was one of sadness, yet he thought other things about her in that single moment. He fumbled around the trees. He ran up to the edge of the gorge and looked around for the Englishman. Then he called out for her.

She did not seem surprised by his voice. She slowly raised her head as though she had only been patiently in waiting. He called out again. Stay there, he called. Stay right there.

The girl did not move. Even from that distance her beauty seemed a thing inexplicable to him. She was so very dark, and yet all he could see in her aspect was a clean and wheeling light. It was the kind of light he'd seen only once before, when his mother had smiled at him that morning long ago when they'd left the ranch to begin their lives again.

I'm comin, he called once more. But before he took three steps, as if summoned from the netherworld, a great paw came crashing across his shoulder.

It came so fast there was no time for thought. The boy fell to the ground and lifted his knife in the air. It crossed in front of the bear pitifully small. He rolled over. His shoulder swept up the earth's floor with its wet blood. When it rose before him on its hind legs the wake of its shadow brought out its face clearly and the boy saw that it was not the bear at all but the Englishman. The man held his ivory-handled bowie knife in front of his belt. He stood in a crouch, sawing the air with the knife. He said nothing to the boy. The boy climbed to his knees. He took his knife into the hand of his working arm and rose to his feet. The Englishman sneered at the boy just as he had at the girl. The boy lunged for him but the man stepped to the side and took the boy's arm with his free hand and struck the boy again in the shoulder. The boy fell back to the ground. His knife shook weakly before him. This time the Englishman did not wait for the boy to rise. He came down with the blade aimed at the boy's stomach, but at the last moment the boy slid from beneath him and sunk the knife in the Englishman's back.

The Englishman paused only for a moment. He looked down to where his hat had been dashed. Then he turned his small oiled head toward the path from which he had emerged. As if he was being called to from the receding trees. Then he faced the boy again and smiled. It was a curious look, as though he was uncertain as to what amused him. Finally the man climbed to his feet again, his left side badly slouched and bleeding, and loped off into the trees.

The boy tried to give chase but his knees would not hold him. He fell back to the ground and lay there on his side. Blood ran off his arm and shoulder. He slumped over to the earth. Sticks and seeds clung to the pulp of his shirt. His vision faltered. For a moment it seemed a great hood had been brought down upon his sight, then all went empty.

The last thing he saw was the butchered light of the sun spilling into the granite sleeves of the mountain peaks. And the last thing he thought he saw was the girl's eyes, raised from the lace of her hands, looking at him.

FIVE

THE FIREWEED SWEPT across his horse's chest as the boy descended from the mountains, and with each step he seemed to shed a purple skin then reemerge with the mare snorting and sweating as they went.

He had lingered in the mountains through the month of March. The Englishman had cut him twice in the same place, high on his right shoulder, but somehow had not severed any muscle and the boy suffered only a dark blue throb which he dabbed and wrapped with his mother's old scarf. Neither the bear nor the girl appeared to him again, and when the forest had been scoured to where he no longer knew where to look, he redressed himself and packed up his tinware and his bedroll.

On the first morning of April the boy awoke and tied up his rifle to the fenders of his saddle and climbed abreast the mare and took up the mule's lead rope, saying, Best get on. He pulled his hat low and rode out with the high mountain winds in his ears. He recalled the Englishman had said he was headed north, to a town beyond the mountains, and he could only believe him and believe that the girl would be with him too.

From a small lake he passed through cataracts of mist with the sun shining through them as though through bedsheets. He came through a thunder shower and later on the lower ridges the rain cleared. He rode long into the evening, and the boy was forced to stop on several occasions, for his mare had grown terribly weak.

I'm sorry babe, he kept saying to her. I'm sorry.

In the full night the boy rode out of the sand hills and into a broad sweep of buffalo plains. In the open land some lights flickered in the distance. The boy stopped the horse and struck up a match against a half-used cigarette, and through the glow he could make out a small village below.

He rode toward the light. The houses looked like skeletons of houses with their earthen walls bowing under their own weight. He upstepped the mare out of a gulch and into a narrow dirt road. Very little sound came from the houses and the feet of the horse and mule clacking in the silence came out like a clock counting a different time altogether.

As he came abreast of the houses the lights from inside extinguished into the black. At the end of the row he came to a house that remained lit. It was a tiny adobe structure in terrible disrepair, with its vigas crooked on the roof gaps and the leather cordings that bound them together looking like sutures that had been stitched through a wound that would not heal.

He stayed the horse. Through the window he could see a kerosene lantern burning deeply on a low crooked table. A man sat over a large bowl and addressed someone out of his view. He whistled to the mule and walked the horse into the yard and dismounted by the side of the house. Nearby a wheelless truck stood on blocks of cinder with its hood open. A scattering of tin cans and chicken bones was strewn errantly in the yard. He walked along the side of the house where a lone cottonwood stood with bed linens draped over its branches, and there he hobbled his horse.

He walked up the stone path to the door and took off his hat and held it at his chest and knocked on the door. After a moment a woman appeared. She tilted her head behind the crack in the door. She put a hand to the muslin wrap that secured the long ropes of her dark hair, then stepped back.

Buenas noches, the boy said.

The woman's eyes came to the seam in the door again. She looked him up and down. Finally she opened the door. Yes, she said with a heavy accent. You need something?

The boy shifted his hat in his hands and looked over his shoulder at the road.

Well. I just came through the mountains. I was hoping to rest somewhere for the night.

The woman studied him. His hair was matted against his head and swung out over his eyes. He crossed his free hand in front of his face and tucked it back behind his ears.

I know I'm dirty but it don't mean I'm bad.

He tried to smile at her but it was sorrow on his face and sorrow the woman saw.

There came some movement behind the woman and she and the boy turned. The man he had seen in the window glass came into the hall and stepped in front of the woman.

Buenas noches, the boy said again.

The man was tall and muscled and he wore his white shirt open. His face was hard as well, but in his eyes there was a sallow quality which made him appear almost penitent.

The man and his wife spoke to each other in Spanish. The man nodded to the boy and told him to come in. The boy lowered his head and stepped into the room behind them. He looked about cautiously in the manner of someone entering a church. He held his battered hat close to his stomach. The man pointed to an empty chair at the table and they all sat down.

Hungry? the man asked.

I could eat.

The woman dished him out a plate of beans and a plate of tortillas. She looked back and forth from the boy to her husband. The man watched the boy and poured him a glass of wine from a thin wooden pitcher set in the middle of the bare wood table. Next to the boy sat two young children who stared at him unflinchingly.

Where are you coming from?

The boy started to explain the part of the country where his ranch was but stopped and looked at his plate and then out the window. I come in from over there, he said. He pointed out the window toward the mountains. From the mountains.

Which mountains? the man asked.

I don't know that I could name one different from the rest. All of them, I reckon. I come in from all of them.

They ate in a silence broken only by the gnashing of the children's teeth. The woman looked glancingly at the boy. After a while she reached forward with a knife and slid more beans onto his plate. She filled his glass with the warm wine. The boy glanced at her and tilted his head apologetically and leaned back again. Gracias, he said.

He looked momentarily around the house. The light was feeble. The room in which they sat extended into both kitchen and bedroom. The beds appeared like covered bodies with the white damask sheets slung carelessly upon them. Steam rose from the kitchen basin to cloud the small window above it. There was a strong smell of cowhides in the room, and when they had finished eating the boy inquired after the man's business. The man turned a spoon in his hand. He told the boy how the hide business was no longer a true business for it was passing under new advances in that country and what his job amounted to was very little in terms of finance, and that like old Mexico itself his work was fading into obscurity.

Things have changed, you see? he said. Pero, they must. It is not for me to say.

When they had finished eating, the children rose by their mother's hand. She led them to the back of the room where the beds were and they slid under the bedclothes. Their mother bent and kissed them on their foreheads and spoke quietly to them and after a moment they rolled onto their sides. She extinguished the candle that was flickering in a pool of wax on the sideboard and came back to the table.

The man pulled back his wife's chair and she sat again and the man poured the boy more wine. The woman asked him what it was he was doing in the mountains. The boy remained silent for a long time, looking at his hands which he held folded in the cup of his stomach.

Livin, he said finally. I was livin there.

The man glanced over at his wife. She looked as if she might speak but the man stayed her with his eyes. He leaned forward over the table edge.

Why? he asked. You no go back anymore, will you?

No. I don't know.

The man leaned in again and spoke with his hands pressed together and his forefingers directed at the boy.

You should not go in the mountains anymore. You get cold and die or go crazy. Pero, one day a man could go in the mountains but that day is no longer. Man no go in the mountains anymore because he has a new place and that is here. Here is the world. The world is no more in the mountains. It is here.

I know it, the boy said.

You are a rancher.

Yes. Well. No, not anymore.

Why not?

No ranch.

Where is your family?

The boy only shook his head. He asked the man for a cigarette and the man reached into his pocket and handed him one. He lit it with a match from a wooden box the man pushed across the table.

Where you go now?

The boy pulled long on the cigarette and turned the burning end inward and watched it. He looked out the window. It was glazed with raindrops that were now coming down and casting a blue warp on the outside world.

To Colorado, he said. Good country up there I heard, and I reckon it to be true.

Colorado, the man repeated. You have work there, then?

No.

The man and his wife watched him.

Also, the boy said into his lap, I'm lookin for a girl.

Yes. You have no work and no family in Colorado?

No.

The man leaned back in his chair and undid his hands and set them in his lap.

Have you seen a man ride through town lately? Sort of a dandy. Had about five horses with him.

And this girl was with him? the man asked.

Yeah. That's him.

The man shook his head. I have not seen them, he said.

Would you have seen them if they did come through?

Yes, I don't know.

The man folded his arms across his breast and his wife watched him while she smoothed down the cloth napkin in her lap. His eyes followed the boy's back and forth from the window to his hands on his thighs. Every once in a while the boy would cough into his hand and say, Excuse me, but he did not raise his head to them. After some time the man looked at his wife and she put her hand upon his and raised her eyebrows. Finally the man straightened up in his chair and made a gentle tap on his wife's hand, and she took it away and began to clear off the table.

Is this girl your family? the man asked.

No sir.

Is the man she is with?

Not in the slightest.

No, of course not.

He paused briefly and offered the boy another cigarette. He took it. He pinched it in his teeth and lit it and drew on it and set it against the lip of the bowl.

Pero, I will tell you something, the man said, if I may.

Sure.

The man leaned up against the table and resumed the posture of his pressed hands and tilted them at the boy. You know how it is said about the dignity of man? It is said a man's dignity is his free will. Pero, you are very young, no?

I reckon.

Yes. In the very young the will is strong. Very strong. Perhaps too much. Perhaps it is no my place to say. Pero, I see in you it is strong past reason.

It's what?

The man's eyes flickered from the boy, then came back quickly to him. He asked the boy to please let him speak.

It is strong past the reason of things, he went on. It is a tricky thing, free will.

With this he wagged his hands at the boy as if to make him believe it.

It can be very good, but it is no good without reason. With reason it stays some in the mind and not too much in the heart, where it likes most to be. Pero, without reason it is too much in the heart. It makes a flood in the heart, like blood, but it is not blood. It is free will. And it tells the heart that whatever it believes is all there is to believe.

The boy took up his cigarette and rolled the ash from it into the bowl. He looked down at his lap again. Excuse me sir, he said. But I don't really care for a sermon right now.

The man laughed out loud. Though it seemed contrary to his appearance, the laughter came clear and easy.

I am no preacher, he said. Yes, one day long ago I think about it, but there is a problem with such men. They become too close to God and they forget about men. After a time they no more can speak to men because men are not perfect, like God. They talk only to a perfect being, so they forget how men are. Men are just men. Mira, what I am telling you. It is just a story.

The boy stayed looking down at his lap.

A man's will can no change everything, you see? There would be no dignity to it. It would be very bad like this, only wills fighting against each other and no seeing things outside that will in their hearts. Pero, I do not know if this is you. All I am saying is that I am looking at you and this is what I see.

He paused for a moment. Then he raised his hands palms up at the boy.

Where is this man? This man with the horses. Where is this girl? I am sorry, but you are looking very bad. Very bad and tired. And wrong. Mira, is this girl here? No, she is not here. Is she on the other side of the mountains? Is she on the other side of the mountains waiting for you? Who can say. She is gone, that is all. She is not here. Because she was with you once maybe you think she cannot be gone, but she is. Pero, this is not me. This is you and this girl I do not know. All I know is she is gone.

The man lowered his head and tilted it to try and catch the boy's eyes but the boy cast them low by his feet and would not turn them up to the man. Then the man leaned back and looked at the remains of his cigarette in the lantern's weak light.

It is no easy business, he went on with a deep inward breath, but you must be graceful about these things. You must keep grace in your heart. For it is the thing that lets you lose.

The boy raised his hands from his lap and wiped his face dry. He turned his head toward the window and away from the woman. The woman looked pleadingly at the man but the man kept his eyes on the boy while he ground out his cigarette in the bowl.

You can work, no?

The boy looked up at him with his hands still upon his face. The woman passed the cloth napkin across the table to him, but the boy would not touch it. The man now spoke with a certain patience to the boy, as though he might to a worried child. Of course you can work, he said. You can drive truck?

No.

Pero, you can work in the fields?

The boy set his hands palms down on the table. Thank you sir, he said. But I can't stay here. I got to get on.

Yes, the man said.

I reckon it's my will.

Yes.

The woman looked a long time at her husband who sat staring at the table. The boy studied the man's averted face then nodded at the woman and tried to smile at her but could not.

Explain, she said to her husband in Spanish. Digale la realidad.

She put her hand on the man's coarse hair and stroked it for a moment. Then she rose and nodded solemnly to the boy, saying, There are beans some more if you like, and resigned herself to the dark recesses of the room.

The man raised his head and looked back at her. He smiled a little. Then he rose from the table, going first to the bedside and then to the children's sideboard, and returning with the crushed stub of candle. He lit it and extinguished the lantern. The man's clean white shirt glowed brightly in the candle-light. The boy studied his face for some betrayal of emotion but none came. Finally the man sat again by the single candle flame.

He told the boy his own story about when he was young and left Mexico. He told him how he had no people anymore and that the people he met were not at all like him and didn't even speak the same words. He told him how he rode into America in the back of a dairy truck beneath empty milk jars and how he slipped past the border patrol. He told him how the men who drove him dropped him off in the middle of the desert and how he wandered through the land as if it were no land at all but only some foul dream long extended. He told the boy how he too had lost his grace and how he had tired of the world, as he suspected the boy himself had.

The man stopped to pull on his cigarette. He scratched his stubbled jaw. The smoke rose invisibly from his fingers and drifted between them where it took form in the light of the candle.

Then he told the boy that the world was tired also. He told him how the world had aged long past their knowledge and that it was tired of carrying them around on its sore back. And he leaned closer to the boy and the boy could see the man's own age and how his face was detailed by life and he knew he spoke from the heart. Then the man said that the most important thing he must remember is that the world would never quit them, that the world was like God because no matter what you do, it never leaves and it never gives up.

With this the man leaned back and stared at the table again. The boy peered out the window. Dogs were barking in the distance. A thin remnant of a locomotive's hollow whistle sounded in the night.

I ain't sayin I'm tired of anything. The boy's voice came cracked and muffled against the window glass. And I don't have any notions about quittin.

The man raised his eyes and looked across the candle's flame at the boy. Rarely do men think that, he said. But if you know how to watch a man, you can see it in the way his eyes work.

The boy put his elbows on the table and looked down. My eyes work fine, he said.

The man made a fleeting gesture with his hand. His own eyes fell to the table and his face softened. The boy worked his hands together and when the man looked up again the boy saw that his face had grown very serious.

I will tell you only one more thing, he said. My mother always warn me against this and now I warn you too. No dejes la oscuridad convertise visible.

They sat in silence. The man smoked. The boy ran his fingers along the edges of the table. The man tapped his cigarette against the rim of the bowl. He watched the boy as he looked out the window where the sun had just summoned the first film of red heat along the horizon. The man turned and looked out at the light bending around the contours of the hills.

The rain is past and gone, he said. You should sleep well.

He sat at the table in a small flume of light. The woman fed him eggs and bread and milk and coffee. The children had gone off to play in the fields and the man was straightening up things by the beds. He wore woolen slippers that shushed against the wood-grain floor.

You are leaving? the woman asked.

Yes ma'am. There's a town nearby, right?

Yes.

I reckon I should go there. I need a job. I'm near out of money.

The man shuffled into the kitchen and stood over the sink basin where the dishes from the previous night were piled up. He had shaved and his slick face shone in the morning light. There were tomatoes on the windowsill and he took one down and bit into it and set it back down. You are go to find the girl? he said.

The boy looked into his coffee. The man began to scrub the plates. Four hours in the truck, he said. But the truck is broken. I can no take you.

That's alright. I'm ridin anyways.

Yes. Your horses. I saw them this morning.

The man stopped scrubbing the plates and turned to the boy.

They are very thin.

Yes sir. I'm going to see to that.

At the door the woman embraced the boy. He did not expect her to do so and her arms around him were warm. He smiled at her and thanked her again and she stepped back and put her arm around her husband's waist. The man fixed the collar of his shirt and held his hand forth and the boy took it.

He told the boy that he hoped he found what he was looking for, whether it was the girl or not. He told him also that he hoped he would find a place to stay very soon because the language of the lone man quickly becomes a language only he can understand.

They stopped shaking. The man held fast to the boy's hand. Then he said, Go and find her. Is okay. He patted the boy's chest with an open palm. I know how it is in there. He made a shy smile. I have boys too, he said. Younger, but boys. Like you.

THE FLEDGLING TOWN he came upon stood in a valley between Apache Mountain in the north and the Tularosas in the southeast.

When the boy took the switchback on the last hill and stepped into the gravel road, he began to see the shape of it. It was built in the manner of the old Spanish piazzas. The brown adobe buildings stood in a circle and all were at least two stories high. Dirt alleyways ran back between them like wheel spokes. Inside the circle was a hard black road, glistening and bending in the sun. In the middle of the road stood an enormous willow tree. Its long arms were beginning to blossom white and at that hour they shaded the plaza almost entirely.

The horse stammered momentarily when her feet hit the pavement. The boy eased her down with his hand on her barrel and steered her to the side of the road and clicked his tongue for the mule to follow. They went slowly past the storefronts. A few people walked the porch floors and some came out to watch the boy as he passed. He looked over at the tree as he came abreast of it. A group of old Navajo women sat crosslegged around the trunk. By their sides stood cracklegged oak shelves on rusty wheels that were overflowing with buttons and mosaics and blankets and sashes of dog hair and feather.

From the corners of the new buildings children flashed in and out of sight and their calls hung in the still air and could be heard in all quarters of the town. He passed a storefront with a half-constructed facade. He turned his head and watched as two men drove latillas into the nail beds. The boy was entranced by his return to such a world of people and movement and did not notice the truck idling in the alleyway he blocked until the sound of a horn made both horse and rider jerk back.

Hey cowboy.

The man leaned his nose into the dash. The boy settled the mare and peered in through the windshield. Yes sir?

The man leaned closer to the glass.

Get the fuck out of the way, he mouthed.

The boy watched him a moment longer, then reared the mare back. The truck burned out onto the road. He watched it go and could see the driver shaking his head through the cloud of dust. Across the plaza three men were leaning on a green car, watching the boy. The boy glanced over at them as he passed. Their look was neither welcoming nor hostile. The boy balled up the reins and gave his mare a little kick.

He came at last to a cantina. In front hung a heavy canvas awning and on it an inscription that read Garrets. It batted intermittently against the wind, against the barking of workers and the rattle of truck beds in the streets.

The boy hobbled his horse and mule on the portales of the cantina. He dusted off his pant legs with his gloved hand then removed his gloves and pushed them in his rear pocket. He knocked his boots at the threshold and stepped inside.

It was a long room with a low ceiling. Pale blue electric lights hung from above in cheap plaster casings. On the counter by the door an old till stood with its drawer open and beside it was a bowl of peppermint candies and a tube of toothpicks. A glass display offered three different sliced pies which sat motionless inside of it on a metal wheel plate. Along the windows was a line of booths with benches like high-backed church pews and on the left a bar top where two old men sat drinking coffee and smoking cigars.

The two men were looking at the boy, their cigars still upraised to their mouths. They quickly studied him up and down and hunched over their coffee mugs again.

He sat in a booth by the back. A middle-aged woman sitting at the end of the counter stood and held her apron from her waist and bunched it in her hands, then dropped it and went into the kitchen. After a while she came back through the folding kitchen doors and stood by the boy. He was rolling a cigarette and gazing out at the plaza. The waitress tapped her pencil against the table. You movin cattle, young man? she said.

The boy looked up at her. A long flare of yellow hair fanned over one of her eyes. She guided it back with the pencil.

No ma'am.

The waitress pulled a crushed notebook from her apron pocket and pressed the top sheet flat. She rested the edge of her hand against it to keep it from curling up again. I figured maybe you come on before the rest of those Texans supposed to be movin through this month, she said. The fellas from Wyoming left out of here two days ago, so I figured you for an early Texan.

No ma'am. I'm just passin through.

That right? Well, I suppose you'd have to in these parts.

Ma'am?

The waitress took her hand from the notepad and placed it on her waist. This here's the only town for many a mile, she said. She paused and looked up at the ceiling as if the county map lay suspended above her. I'm goin to guess you haven't been here before.

No.

Now see, she said with some urgency, this here town is goin to be something. I came all the way from California. I heard about it all the way out there. Must mean something. Bigger than Santa Fe, they say. This side of the state, if you're goin north, you're bound to pass through here. And once the railroad gets laid. Shew.

She shook her head and smiled suggestively, looking at the boy like she had revealed some secret of which she was deeply proud. She put her hands on her hips when she saw the boy was not smiling.

Well hell, she said. So what's your plan, anyways?

The boy twisted the cigarette between his fingers. I can't say I could name it, he said.

Well, you ought to think about right here if you ain't settled on anything. She moved her hair away from her eyes with the pencil again. This place is growin every day.

The waitress returned a while later with a platter of potatoes and a fried steak and a bowl of chili peppers and an ashtray which she placed on the corner of the table. Coffee?

Yes ma'am.

She turned and the boy caught her gently by the arm. He asked her if there was a livery stable in town and she said No.

Somewhere to lay up then?

Surely.

She pointed out the window and across the plaza to a four-story inn with porches the full width of the building on every floor. Abner's, she said. It's still sort of dirty, if you catch my meaning, but that's all we got right now.

He ate in the same slow methodical manner as he had during the heavy days of the mountains. When he finished eating he sat back and drank his coffee. After a while he took out his billfold where he had placed most of his remaining dollars. He took out two bills and set them on the table. They were as soft and flimsy as cotton. He set the salt shaker upon them and put on his hat and wiped the ash from the table and started out.

Ford's stable is down the road a piece if you ain't mindin to ride a stretch.

The boy turned to the old men at the counter who in turn regarded him through their cigar smoke.

It's just west a ways and the ride is easy, one of them said. No rain or nothin here for a while and it's mostly plain and pastureland. That horse of yours shod?

No sir.

Well if you're plannin to stay here, you ought take care of that.

I don't know that I am.

Well, there's some good shows here for a kid like you.

The men smiled conspiratorially at each other. One of them had a great bulbous nose that wobbled like rubber when he grinned. The other pointed out the window to the east.

Back yonder there's a grand old place for shows.

What kind of shows?

The man with the nose scoffed.

Come on, son. Ballet shows of course. Western style.

I don't reckon I've seen such shows.

Both men laughed and pounded the counter with their fists.

Well, you ought to, kid. You ought to.

The men went on laughing. The boy walked past them and pulled open the door.

Hey kid.

He turned with his hand propping the door open and the last light from outside falling red upon his boots.

Charlie Ford. That's the man's name. He'll take care of you. May even have some work for you. He still moves em about like the olden days. You'll know you're there when you see a big old truck stickin out of the ground like a tree with wheels. No shit, kid. Like a goddamn tree machine.

The inn's foyer was dark and low. He walked past tan leather chairs that stood worn and vacant and illuminated by yellow-glassed lamps under which whorls of dust spun dully. He rang the bell at the counter. A clock ticked loudly in the empty room and finally a tall heavyset man appeared from a doorway behind the counter with a filthy napkin tucked under his shirt collar. He put a finger up while he finished chewing and pulled a pencil from his shirt pocket.

Evenin, the boy said.

Yeah. You need a room?

Yes sir.

You seen which girl you want yet?

Girl? The boy looked around the room from which no such girls appeared. No sir, he said. Just me.

The proprietor brought the napkin to his face and wiped it across his mouth. Just you, he said. He fumbled around the undershelving. I got a room on the plaza side.

How much does it go for?

Four dollars.

The boy brought out his billfold and flipped through the bills. Anything cheaper?

The proprietor put the pencil back in his shirt pocket. Son, he said, I had General Sandoz in that room last week. Said this town was goin to be the model for the new West. That's what he called it. Said every one of us would be Paul Bunyans and John Henrys before all's said and done. For that I think four dollars is cheap.

The boy moved his fingers over the bills again. He shook his head.

Where you from, boy? Mexico?

Grant County.

The proprietor looked him up and down.

You sure as hell look like you could be from Mexico exceptin for your eyes, and I'm not afraid to tell you that.

Well I ain't. And I don't rightly see where that could matter.

The man glanced over his shoulder out the door. That yours out there?

The boy turned to follow the man's gaze. Triften stood nosing the ground, the slow roll and sway of her head somehow elegant in the new dark.

Yeah.

You got any alfalfa? Or oats for that matter?

Yeah.

Then I'll tell you what. You feed my Katie Mae out there in the back and I'll give you the room for two dollars. I done forgot about goin to the store for her today. Bein so busy and all. The man shot his small eyes to the staircase. A man can tend to forget these things, he said. You can sure write me down for that.

The boy shifted his hat in his hands. Well, he said. I reckon I'm more concerned myself about bein wrote down for a room.

He held out the money and the proprietor snatched it from him and snapped down the napkin from beneath his chin. He raised a brown leather-bound book from the undershelving and took the pencil from his shirt again and followed the entries down with his finger and scratched down the boy's name.

It ain't all pillows and perfume here yet boy, he said. Watch yourself.

He handed the boy a key and went back through the door.

Yes sir, the boy said to the closed door. I'll try.

Down the gravel path that wound behind the inn the boy walked his horse and mule to the half-shut barn door. He pushed the door full open with a long creak. A fine hay dust floated in a single layer at the height of the loft. He unsaddled the horse and uncinched the saddlebag from the mule.

He brought the proprietor's horse out from her stall and in the weak light examined the ribcage, stark and black on its underbelly. He fed them all greatly and watered them in a cheap tin trough against a wall of shredded tack.

He walked to a window on the north wall and looked out through the cracked glass. The sun was like a sunken moon, its copper crown barely outlining the distant mountains and coming into the barn to cast his own shadow long and pallid on the dirt floor. The air was cool and fresh coming down from the foothills and the boy thought it was indeed pretty country and he did not stop himself from thinking that it was a sign of the Colorado country to come, and though he tried to, he could not stop from thinking how fine his mother would have found it to be.

He walked back to Triften and put his face against her neck.

We could use us a rest, Trift, couldn't we? he whispered to her. Just for a while.

A bird called out from the recesses of the night. He listened for more but none came, only the distortions of guitar and fiddle from a dance hall down the lane. Out in the plaza came the flare of gooseneck lanterns that encircled the town to burnish the sky. He touched the mare's nose when she raised her head at the distant flash of light. Then he led them all back to the stalls and drew the lock across the gate. For a long time he stood and watched the horses in the dark.

Six

THE ROAD WEST was all gravel. For the first time in many months the boy rode his mare without the mule trailing and she bore down on the wind, her hot breath burning in the morning's dark. They rode for two steady hours, past a dry creekbed where a flurry of deer were foraging the sedge and underbrush and past a procession of farm trucks in which young Mexican boys sat in the flatbeds and held to the tying rails and tilted their hats down over their sleepy eyes.

When he reached the ranch of Charlie Ford the boy whoaed his horse and looked down upon the great slab of metal and wheel before him. The pickup truck the old men had spoken of was nearly buried beneath the ground. It stood up on its end and high in the air the hood was flung open and flower and wildflower alike spilled from the chassis where the engine had once been.

The rancher was out in the pastures herding cattle into an empty paddock. Looking out at the rancher moving the cattle like a slow drift of cloud, the boy recalled the times his mother watched him riding the plains from the kitchen window when his father had not come home for days and he was forced to work the horses and cattle long into the evening. Looking out now, he noticed how well the man sat his horse. He cut the cattle with an ease more beautiful than any song or book. The mountains behind the horse and rider seemed as though they had bore those figures up from the bosom of their own dark and soundless souls, bore them up to once again make pretty the world.

An hour later the rancher rode down from the sun and into the blue shadows that the barn cast upon the boy. He was still squatting by the fence pole and smoking and watching the cattle. When the boy saw the rancher's horse start into a high trot he raised up and flung the cigarette into the grass. He put up a hand.

Charlie Ford rode the fence line with the gelding beneath him snapping the sweat from his head. The rancher was long and thick in the shoulders and tall besides and he wore no beard nor mustache but only a red stubble which he wiped with the back of his hand. His blue shirt was stained purple with sweat and as he came upon the boy he declared, What a day, stepping down from the stirrups and into the fresh cold mud.

He fixed the belt buckle at his waist and struck off a pair of yellow cowhide gloves. Well now, he said. Can I help you with something, son?

The boy took down his hat and fingered back his hair and held the hat at his hip. I come about my horse, he said. He walked over to the mare and took her by the lead rope and stroked her nose. Her name's Triften.

Charlie Ford looked the horse over, slapping the gloves he held bunched in his hand against his pant leg. Good lookin, he said. You aimin to sell her?

No sir. Hell no.

Charlie Ford watched the boy's face tighten and he put up a hand. No offense meant, he said. Just that it's gotten so that anyone who comes by here seems to want to get rid of somethin they can't use no more. So what is it you need from me?

I need some shoes for her, that's all. And maybe a wash and a brush down.

Yes, I believe she could use that. She don't look so hot.

Yes sir. I know it.

Well. What's your name, son?

Trude.

Trude? That's all?

Trude Mason.

The rancher swathed his hand across his pant leg and held it out to the boy. I'm Charlie Ford.

I know it. Some men in town told me to come see you.

They shook. The rancher lowered his head and rolled it and snorted at the ground.

Old cigar smokers?

Yes sir. That'd be them.

Charlie Ford swiped at his chaps with his hat and snorted again.

Sons of bitches always gettin in the middle of things to which they don't belong. I'm tellin you son, stay away from that pair. That is, if you want to keep anything of yours private. That town down there ain't but seven years old from the time they laid the first brick but those boys will have you believe it's Rome with all the stories they sling around.

I guess I figured them for that.

Then you done some good figurin. That's a sign of good character. It's good to have character, specially seein how scarce it is these days. Charlie Ford wiped the side of his face and looked out at the cattle which were plodding unthoughtfully about the paddock mud.

Well, the boy said. Is there a ferrier about?

Charlie Ford turned from the cattle and tilted his hat from his eyes as if to witness some improbability. Ain't enough money in the mayor's own pocket to rustle up a ferrier these days, he said. Around these parts at least. It's like everything else nowadays. I do it myself.

Who stands the horses?

When I'm puttin on their shoes?

Yes sir.

Hell, son. If I couldn't trust my own horses, there wouldn't be nothin left at all. I'd just as soon pack my bags and move to China.

They walked the horses to the barn. The air was crisp and the breath from all four noses rose to wind through the low trees like cotton twine. The rancher's gelding drew back and slowed and sidled over and sniffed Triften's backside and Charlie Ford scolded him, telling him not to be like them old men at the cantina and that the only business he needed mindin was his own.

He showed the boy to an empty stall where he put up his mare. The boy followed him to the back of the barn where they walked through a door into the grain room and then through another door which opened onto a small foldout table and two wooden chairs whose legs were cut to fit the table.

Damnation, the boy said, looking around, I ain't never seen a kitchen in a barn.

Charlie Ford looked around as though he hadn't seen the room in a long time. No, he said. I don't suppose you have. There's a story to it, though. When I was a boy, about the same age as you, I expect, I was constantly wantin to invent something new.

He walked over to a sink basin and took down two mugs from a cabinet above his head and took up a rag and ran it under the tap and scrubbed out the mugs. Ain't that a dandy, he said, turning to the boy. Somethin new's what I always wanted and now it's the last thing on earth I crave.

Charlie Ford went to a small oven range and lit up a fresh pile of wood beneath it and filled a pot with water and set it atop a metal range plate and covered it with an outsized lid.

I knew a rancher wasn't hardly new and that a rancher would always be a rancher, so I figured I'd be the first to feed himself and his horses at the same time. Turns out I think they like it when I eat with em. Eatin a meal together has got its own type of communication, I believe.

He looked at the boy, who was standing in the middle of the room watching the water heat, then waved his hand in dismissal.

Make yourself a seat, he said.

He dredged the coffee into the mugs and brought them to the table and offered the boy a bowl of sugar. The boy stirred a spoonful into his coffee. Charlie Ford held out a cigarette from his shirt pocket and the boy took it. Then Ford turned the other chair around and sat with his elbows on the backrest and they sat smoking and drinking coffee.

How come that truck's buried out front of your drive?

Charlie Ford looked through his coffee, then off behind the boy. Well, he said. I reckon I ought to have gotten used to bein asked about that but somehow I haven't. He shook his big heavy head at the coffee. It's a gravestone, he said finally.

The boy nodded unsurely but did not speak. Ford looked up at him. It seemed he wanted to inspect just what the idea had done to the boy.

It's the truck I bought for my wife when we moved up here, he said. She came up with me from Texas when Texas wasn't worth a damn. We was in Odessa where oil and booze were the only things that moved a

71

man out of bed in the morning, and that wasn't enough for me. Anne Marie, that was her name. She said she'd come with me if I bought her a truck. Charlie Ford chuckled to himself at that. Boy she was tough-minded, that girl. I didn't have a dime to spit-shine but somehow I was able to scrape together enough work to buy it for her. I'd of bought her the world, I was so crazy for her.

He lifted his elbows off the backrest and set them forward on the table.

One day she set off to town and didn't come back. I knew what it was before I could even think it. I rode out that night and found the truck overturned in a gravel ditch just outside of town. She was dead long before I found her. The roof had come down so hard on her head I wouldn't of been able to know it was her unless I smelled her perfume beneath the burning metal.

The boy looked down at the floor. I'm sorry about that, he said.

Well. You couldn't of done nothin for it.

I mean I'm sorry about askin.

Charlie Ford looked up at the boy. Then he looked into his coffee. He lifted the mug and held it to his mouth for a few seconds. Hell, he said. That's the one thing you should never be sorry for. Askin is about the one thing you can count on for gettin somethin in return. No matter if the answer's good or bad.

He leaned forward again and stubbed out the cigarette with his swollen fingers in the metal shell of an old curry brush.

Automobile, he said, drawing the word out slowly. You've only got two choices with them things. Either it gets you there a hell of a lot faster or it gets you there dead.

I ain't never been much for driving myself, the boy said. I wouldn't even know how to get it turned on.

Charlie Ford laughed. Son, he said, believe it or not, I think that may be somethin to be proud of.

He brought another mug of coffee for the boy and one for himself. In the barn the boy could hear the horses talking to one another between the stalls.

Now there ain't another ranch for twenty miles in any direction. So where'd you come in from?

Down south. Grant County.

Comin from far off. Making for cattle?

No sir, just movin away.

What ranch were you at down there?

Mason ranch. It was my dad's. Hatley Mason.

The name felt odd and cold on his lips and he set down his coffee. Charlie Ford leaned forward and tapped his cigarette ash in the curry brush and pointed a bent finger at the boy.

Hatley Mason, he said. I heard of you all. That was a hellfire of a ranch, I recollect. Now that was quite a long time ago but it sure was a fine one, I remember.

It ain't no more. The boy lifted up his coffee mug and tilted it to his lips. It sure ain't no more, he said.

Well. That is a shame.

Yes sir.

The smoke clogged the room and spun off in thin spindles where the rancher waved his hand through it. He coughed and waved his hand again. So are you lookin for work now? he said.

The boy shrugged. Depends on who's offerin.

Ford bent a thumb back toward the door.

You seen that old pile of sticks in town they call the barroom? That's standin where my first paddock was. Used to run a crazy old colt out there during the wintertime. Back then I had enough money for the talent but not the temperament. Never could break that sumbitch, so when they came and took my land off me I had to let him go. Didn't figure he'd soften just on account of geography. But there wasn't no way I was goin to leave him for them town councilmen. They'd of just turned around and put him to the auction pens. That horse's spirit alone was worth more money than all their characters combined. If I'd of known it would turn this bad though, I'd of held on to him. Tried him one more time.

Charlie Ford spread a hand out on the table.

I'd like to help you son, he said, but it can't be me who's offerin. I don't got the head I used to and I don't got the money to pay you right wages, and I know what it's like to be shortchanged, so I ain't goin to even start to do it to you.

He shook his head and drank from his mug and wiped his mouth with the back of his hand again. Ranchin is chancin, he said.

Yes sir.

They drank their coffee quietly for a while. In the stillness of the room the horse's voices came loud and from outside the boy could hear the cattle shouldering into the crossposts of the paddock. He remembered the day when his own family's herd was auctioned off, and how he had opened the door at dawn on that Sunday morning to the scarred face of the auctioneer who told him to get everything ready because folks were wanting to make church service after the sale. He recalled how they had sold poorly on account of his father's constant heckling of the bidders and the threats he unleashed upon the auctioneer who stood on a peach crate by the tree beneath the boy's bedroom window. He remembered how he had watched the cattle being driven off from the auction pen and en route to a rancher down in Bayard who nodded solemnly after his final bid and went to the auction stand and took down the papers from the auctioneer who had to grapple them loose from his father's clutch and signed them and folded them up tight and placed them in his breast pocket and turned toward the pastures without ever looking up again.

I don't know what to tell you exactly, son. Charlie Ford got up with a groan and cleared the coffee mugs off the table and set them on the sideboard under a mirrored cabinet. The loggers cleared out of here about a year ago, he said. It's too damn brittle here anyway to get good wood. You want any work that pays money, you got to go look in town these days. I don't know how you feel about the railroad business, but the way I understand it they'll be movin in right soon. Other than that, I just don't know. You got any school under your belt?

I couldn't say too much. The boy pushed back from his chair and pulled the corner of his vest up to reveal the dirk knife he had sheathed in his belt. He rolled back his shoulder to drive the old ache out of it. That's about all, he said.

Shit, Charlie Ford said. I swear to you we were the same damn person in some time or another, exceptin you're a mite quieter.

Well, the boy said. I hope not always to be that way.

The boy helped steady the mare while Charlie Ford set her shoes and they watered her down with the horse stomping on the barn floor. The boy scrubbed her mane and her neck and he scrubbed down her barrel and withers and combed her crest and brushed her thighs and cannons. Charlie Ford wrung a sponge with fly oil over her back and the boy dried her down and in the late afternoon he led her out of the barn and into the drive.

She looked like a new animal unshelved from God's rack with her brushed forearms flexing and the muscles of her shoulders rifling and twitching. The boy walked around her and regarded her with great pride and he thanked the rancher who stood watching them with a rag in his hand. When the boy finally mounted her, Charlie Ford raised the rag up and shook it at them.

Good luck findin a piece of work, he called out. You need anything else, don't hesitate to come a callin. I always like the sight of a galloping mare comin down over the hill.

I'll do that.

Charlie Ford lifted his hat and squinted against the sun and smiled curiously upon the boy. He pointed at the horse, her smooth glinting mane. You might want to try the same for yourself, he said.

Shit, the boy said, shaking his head. I reckon I'll have to do that too.

On the way back to town the boy rode the mare at a trot. Triften's hindquarters swept through the grasses to stir up old dead leaves from the outcropping trees, her shining barrel making her look as if she'd just recovered from some long waged war, or as if in sudden preparation for its coming.

HE STEPPED INTO the barbershop east of the plaza with the barber watching him through the mirror.

Well look here, he said to the boy without turning. I reckon you're just in time before you'd have to start wearin ribbons.

He sat for nearly an hour with the light going away and the barber cutting off his long brown hair and speaking affably to him, turning the chair from time to time to study his work with a grind from the chair's oilless swivel.

When he finished he brought forth a thick blue lather and a straight razor with a carved oak handle. The old barber shaved the boy's soft stubble with a shaking hand but his touch was smooth along his neck, as if he'd willed the trembling out when the blade touched the boy's skin.

In the dark of the night he went through the foyer and past the low leather chairs, running his fingers along the broad backboards and gripping the banister rail. Up the stairs he went down the dark hallway, past the low burning lamps and the pale flowers on the sideboard and into his room.

The room was walled with oak and the floor was oak as well and the wainscoting beneath the window painted white. He twisted the key on the desktop lamp and turned the desk chair to face the window. He set off his clothes slowly. It was the first time he had fully undressed in months and his skin was dry to the point of cracking. He placed the torn and mud-stained clothes at the foot of the bed, folding his overalls at the pant seam the way his mother had taught him years ago.

The thin brown muscles of his legs flashed up as he hopped down the hallway and into the bathroom. He pulled on the taps and scrubbed himself with a sliver of soap that was stuck to the tub drain. When he came out he tied a towel around his waist and went back down the hall, where from other rooms he could hear the high-pitched falsettos of whores not altogether different from cries of the injured house martins that as a child he sometimes found on the old barn floor.

From the closet he took out his saddlebag and redressed himself in his white-button shirt and took out his thick burlap pants with the heavy brown buttons his mother had sewn on and shook them up his legs and rolled back his shortly cropped hair with the fine-bristled brush from her old saddlebag. At last he pulled on his boots and got up and looked at himself briefly in the mirror that was screwed into the door of the hutch. It had been long time since he had seen his own face and there was little in it he recognized.

He went and laid upon the bed. From the bedpost he took down his hat and placed it over his face. Before long he was thinking of his mother again. How she had gone with him to buy that hat in their old hometown, and how she had straightened it for him with the shop-keeper standing by. He remembered how he had been embarrassed, but also comforted, and he lifted the hat and studied it as it was now, worn and sweat-stained and forked deeply at the center.

He awoke later in the evening and sat up at the edge of the bed. He pulled his pant cuffs down over his boots. Slid out of the saddlebag and resting beneath the dark varnish of the hutch he saw the corner of the picture frame and he leaned down and took it up. It was a picture of his grandfather taken during the early days of the ranch. He stood before the carriage house, in front of which two painted ponies were trotting by. In the far distance were the tiny skeletons of storefronts. In the picture his grandfather was flanked by the boy's young mother and father before they'd even been married. They stood with their arms locked about each other's shoulders and all three were smiling wide.

He set the picture down and smoked a cigarette in the night's quiet, the pale light of the plaza lamps fording the room to draw long shadows across the floor. He watched the smoke rise and darken at the ceiling. A bottle shattered on the thoroughfare. Car and truck horns blasted from the streets and people called out into the night, laughing at words he could not make out. He looked at the clock on the false mantle. He drew out his mother's red scarf from his back pocket. What world has become, he whispered into it. Mama, what world has become.

SEVEN

HE WOKE AND went down and fed his horse and mule and the proprietor's horse. Back in his room he worked open the remaining tin of beans with his knife and ate and slept again. In the early evening he woke to the murmurs of a crowd of people gathered by the willow tree outside. He dressed and took up his hat and went down.

Among the people in the street he saw the waitress from the cantina and she hailed him over with a waving hand.

You decided to stay? she called.

I don't know. For a little while, at least.

The waitress slapped her hands together. Well that's just fine, is what it is. What's your name anyways?

Trude.

I'm Jane.

She looked off to the willow tree where a man vested in black unleaned himself from the tree trunk and went and put his hands over a wooden podium that stood before the people.

Here he comes, she said.

The boy followed her gaze to the man.

Who's that?

That's the mayor. Ain't he just handsome as a rose?

The man held his hands up to quiet the people. The waitress tapped the boy's arm, then went walking toward the crowd. You make sure you come by tomorrow, she said. Tom's baking up some rhubarb pies.

The boy stayed outside the crowd with his thumbs hooked in his belt loops.

My dear ladies and gentleman, the mayor called.

His voice was as smooth and even as lake water. His hands went up again, this time in greeting. He looked into the crowd and briefly beyond them at the boy, then began again to speak.

It is by the glory given unto us by God himself that we stand together tonight and continue our shaping of this great town.

The townspeople clapped fervently. The boy inspected the crowd. He saw the innkeeper whistling with his fingers to his mouth and he saw children hugging the legs of their parents and the two old men from the bar sitting on fold-out chairs and smoking their cigars, but nowhere did he see the Englishman or the girl.

If we have grown toward a new future and if there is a design that so let us, it is His, but the hands that have built that design are our own.

The mayor held his hands forth over the crowd. Another cheer came from the people. They shook one another's hands. As you all must know, the mayor went on, a final step toward that future is soon to begin.

I can hear that train whistle blowin, someone shouted.

The mayor smiled. He nodded in the direction of the voice. That's right, he said. The railroad construction will begin in just a few days and before long we will no longer need call on the outside world. The outside world will call on us.

The crowd cheered again and the mayor spoke at great lengths about the coming destiny of the town, where outlaws would be broken and cast out and where goodness and economy would thrive side by side in that very place where the new West would be forged. He spoke about the completion of the electrical wiring and telephone posts being driven at that very moment along the rim of the town. He spoke about the path the railroad would take through the eastern mountain range and endless possibilities of import and export from which they would reap enough benefits so all could live in wealth and harmony.

The boy listened vaguely and looked around the crowd until something in the distance caught his ear. In the far east corner of the plaza he could hear the hollow music of an old guitar. He looked around once more, then wandered off toward the sound.

Under a porch at the music hall he came upon a group of young men and women. On the porch rail stood lanterns whose light made their faces look like sculptures. Some danced on the porch front where a number of bottles of port wine were scattered by their feet.

The guitar player sat crosslegged on the middle step of the porch rise, his white shirt hanging loosely to his body. On his breast the wine stained his shirt like blood. The boy crossed over to them slowly. Another boy stood when the guitar music slowed, taking up a pair of matracas and shaking them and summoning those who still sat to stand up and dance.

The boy leaned against a cherry tree. He watched them dance, the spinning of the girls and their sundresses flaring up, their patterns of flowers weaving into a sweet and liquid geometry.

Some of the eyes caught him standing there with his own eyes pinched hard and his fingers linked tight in the loops of his waist belt. Some of the girls looked at him over the shoulders of their partners. The boys who were still sitting watched him furtively, raising their lips to the wine bottles and drinking swiftly. After a while the young man with the guitar stopped playing and handed it to someone else and walked down the porch steps. He stood with the light heavy on his back and faced the boy standing in the darkness. You wantin to say something? he said.

No.

The young man nodded, considering him. The others watched them in the silence until the boy he'd handed the guitar to began to play again.

You lookin to be a dancer then?

No.

You want a drink then, is that it?

No. I reckon I don't.

You just want to stand there.

The boy kicked the ground absently. I suppose, he said.

The young man stepped into the darkness and leaned against the tree.

If you're lookin for something else, I expect you should remember I'm not alone here. You must think your balls are big enough to clear your way through all of us.

I ain't lookin for no fight. Nor do I think anything particular about my balls.

The young man leaned away from the tree and his face eased. You ain't from around here, are you?

No. I come up from the south.

You speak pretty good English for a Mexican.

I ain't Mexican. I come up from Grant County.

Well, I ain't from here neither. Not original at least. I was born here but my parents come over from Italy.

So you're an Italian.

The young man spat boozily to his side, some of the spittle enduring in a long strand down from his lip. He wiped it away with his shirt-sleeve. Yep, he said.

You don't sound Italian.

I reckon it's been bred out of me.

The boy watched him with a little curiosity, the young man's face slightly bemused, his knees unsure beneath him.

So you got a name, cowboy?

Trude Mason.

Trude? What the hell kind of name is Trude?

The boy kicked at the ground again. The kind I was given, he said.

The young man grinned.

Mine's John Frank. Changed from Franco if you have to know.

He leaned toward the boy, a half smile cocked on his face. You know what they say? he whispered in mock conspiracy.

No. What do they say?

Never trust a man with two first names.

I'll remember that, the boy said.

John Frank paused and scratched his head, tightening his brow to suggest as much gravity as he could muster. Don't you worry, he said. I aim to change that story.

I'm glad to hear it.

John Frank looked at him for a moment, then snapped his fingers in the direction of the dancers. Someone brought over a bottle of wine and he took it and drew long from its lip. He held it out to the boy.

I don't want none, he said. I told you.

John Frank raised his eyebrows. Easy cowboy, he said. Easy.

They looked out at the dancers. The light burned into the girls' faces and lit up their red lips.

My my, John Frank said. My my. He poked the boy in the side with the bottle. So what you doin here anyway? That's a long haul from Grant County, ain't it?

It is.

So why you here?

The boy studied his hands briefly, then looked down at the ground.

No reason I could say for sure. Just movin away.

To here?

No. Well. For a while. I'm on my way to Colorado.

Colorado, John Frank said. Colorado for the cowboy.

The sound from the plaza escalated into a clatter of hands. The boy looked over toward the wooden podium from which the vested mayor was now stepping away. What was all that about over there? he asked.

The Italian peeled his eyes from the dancing girls and looked toward the plaza. That was the mayor's first-of-the-month speech, he said. I work for him.

With this last declaration John Frank straightened up.

Doin what?

Frank slumped down again. He waved his hands pointlessly before them.

Doin anything he says. He's pretty much judge and jury around here. I just follow him around and make sure he's got everything he needs.

What were you doin over here then?

Same as you. I heard enough of them speeches to last my life and my children's, were I ever to have me some. He glanced back at the girls and shook his head. My my, he said again.

The boy turned back to the darkening willow tree from which the crowd had gone. You like that kind of work?

John Frank turned back to the boy and raised his eyebrows. I don't despise it, he said. It pays. And the mayor comes out a pretty good man. Does he?

Yeah. Good as we got, I figure. Smartest one, that's for sure. I reckon he'll be runnin this town until his dyin day. Ain't nobody crosses him cause they know he's smarter than they. Myself, I don't aim to run this town. I just aim to stay on his good side.

The boy shifted his hat down from his head and looked at it in his hands.

He's got a bad side then?

Frank looked at him queerly, then nodded. It's been said.

The boy held out his hand to the Italian and they shook. Then he reached out and took the bottle from Frank's hand and turned it and studied the damp label, then handed it back to him.

Don't we all, he said.

In the morning the boy sat in the same booth at the cantina. The waitress brought him a slice of the rhubarb pie she had spoken of and a cup of coffee.

You get that horse of yours all fixed up?

Yes ma'am.

She leaned over the booth and looked out the window to where Triften stood tied to the porch rail. Looking right fine, she said. And I see you cleaned yourself up too.

She rubbed the stubble of his sun-streaked hair.

Thank you Miss Jane, he said, moving away from her hand and patting down his hair. You got an ashtray?

He sipped his coffee and smoked the last of his loose tobacco. After a while the door swung open and the bell above it rang and John Frank walked in, his suit a fine gray and freshly starched. He saw the boy sitting in the back and grinned and sauntered over and slid into the booth.

Mornin cowboy. You followin me now, is that it?

The boy sipped his coffee and looked out the window. Mornin, he said. But I ain't no cowboy.

John Frank shook loose his coat from his arms. What are you then?

Nothin. The boy turned his head away from the window and looked at him. Right now I'm nothin, he said.

I believe whatever side of the bed you got up on wasn't the right one, John Frank said. He rubbed his hands together and took a long brisk breath. So you offerin me a cup of coffee?

Yep, the boy said, long as you're offerin me this here piece of pie.

John Frank reached in his stiff shirt pocket and took out a pack of cigarettes. That's a quick tongue you got, he said.

The boy thumbed out his own cigarette in the tin ashtray the waitress had set on the table and reached his hand across the table. And I guess you're offerin me a cigarette too, he said.

Sumbitch. Frank passed the boy a cigarette, grinning and shaking his head. Just cause I work for the man don't mean I feast like him too.

I'm sure you feast well enough.

How bout you? You seem to look pretty good yourself. Good enough to buy your own cigarettes at least.

Lots of things in this world are different than they look.

Is that so?

Yeah. It is.

So?

So you're lookin at one.

John Frank flicked his cigarette ash toward the ashtray. You huntin work then? he said.

Nothin like what you got. I don't aim to stay too long.

Frank leaned across the table. Well listen here, he said. It ain't cattle ropin but I got work enough to keep you paid for a stretch. It ain't much but I can probably get it. And I reckon you could leave it whenever you so desired.

I don't know, the boy said.

John Frank eased back as the waitress stepped up and leaned over the table to fill their coffees.

How was that pie? she said.

John Frank peered down at the boy's plate where only the crust of the pie remained. He pinched his nose and stuck out his tongue. It was rhubarb alright, he said.

Nothin was directed at you as I recall, Miss Jane said. And if you don't like it, you won't get none. Don't think I don't see you pickin at it from the case.

I guess I'm just what you'd call a glutton for punishment.

The waitress waved her hand in front of John Frank. You got the glutton part right, she said.

The boy looked up at her. It was good, he said.

Just hear me out, John Frank went on when the waitress had left. I'm always havin to run these papers to this house in the middle of nowhere for the mayor, and half the time I don't got the time. You hear me?

I reckon. So?

So I can put you on the old man's payroll. Tell him I need help. Shit, he's got enough money to buy Santa Fe if the idea struck him.

What kind of papers are they?

John Frank put his hand up in the air. I don't know, he said. Official-type papers. Nothin interesting. You'd just take the package of papers over in the morning and slip em under the door and that's it.

And that's it?

Yeah. That's it.

Who's door is it?

I think the old man's lawyer. But you never see him around. Some say he's the only one who knows the town's true business, and I myself believe it. I know a good piece and the mayor more than me, but I reckon that lawyer knows it all. John Frank passed his hand about the air again and hunched over his coffee. Anyway, it's an easy little dance. About a three-hours walk is all the trouble to it, lest you got a truck.

The boy turned the mug in his hands and looked out the window. I got my horse, he said.

John Frank slapped the palms of his hands on the table. Well well, he said. A cowboy after all. Ride on then, hombre. You can cut that time in half and the rest of the day and night you can spend in whatever way you fashion. Colorado ain't goin nowhere. Save yourself some greenbacks. Besides, I could stand havin someone around who in all likelihood dances worse than me.

The boy looked at Frank and blew smoke into the ceiling light then looked out the window. He ran his fingers along the table edge. I guess I'll give it a shot, he said. But just for a while.

John Frank slapped his hands on the table again. Some of the coffee from his mug toppled over and he grinned at it running down the table. Hot damn, he said. He fished in his pockets and brought forth a handful of coins and stacked them on the table. It's on me today, he said. You sorry-lookin cowboy.

The boy shook his head.

John Frank fingered a pocket watch from his vest. I got to get on, he said. Duty calls. You stayin at Abner's?

If I can muster the rent again.

Well how about you meet me out by the plaza tree tonight. We'll walk down to the barroom and have us a beer and figure it all out.

Figure what out?

The details, cowboy. The details. It ain't cattle you'll be movin.

The boy sat and drank another cup of coffee alone. John Frank tapped on the outside of the window as he went by, pointing to the pocket watch in his vest. Seven o'clock, he mouthed.

The boy stayed watching the aged vendors under the willow tree that was bathed in an orange husk of light. His eyes followed the sky above the tree and went out past the town to where the imprints of the foothills shone in shadows and the mountains sprawled irreverently beyond them to impale the sky.

He tried to imagine where she might have gone from there, where the Englishman might have led her and to what ends. Yet he knew there was nothing more he could do without any money, and at last he hefted himself from the booth and put a hand up to the waitress, then walked out the door and passed into the street, his eyes searching everywhere for a sign of her voice.

Before returning to the inn he stopped at the general store along the plaza lane. He bought a pinch of tobacco that the proprietor stuffed into a paper sack and a can of beans and a jar of milk. He paid the woman who watched him while he muttered to himself and fumbled through his trouser pockets to bring forth the change, her fingers along the rims of her eyeglasses as though to better tune in the sight of him.

When he returned to the inn the foyer was empty and quiet. He sat in one of the tan leather chairs and heightened the lamp's glow with the key. He pulled the remaining money from his billfold and counted eight dollars and a few loose coins.

As he put the billfold away he heard a creak of the banister rail and turned toward the staircase. A woman in a long black skirt and white blouse came stepping carefully down, her attention set on tucking the corners of the blouse into her skirt. When she looked up and saw the boy she put her hands to her mouth to feign surprise, then came and stood by his side. Her painted face shone in the lamplight. She leaned down and touched his hand.

You won't need that much for me, she said.

She batted her thick black eyelashes and turned her hands down upon her ribs. She leaned back with her heavy bosom thrust out to better study him. You sure are pretty enough, she said. And you ain't too young.

The boy regarded her for a moment, pushing the billfold back in his pocket. He turned the key on the lamp until just a small flare stemmed from the glass casing. At last he stood and looked down at her, a strange longing smile on his face.

No, he said as he stepped around her toward the staircase, I'm too old.

THE BAR AIN'T the first place you'd want to be if you were too concerned about your well-being. John Frank raised a finger as if to signify the exception to that rule. But you stick by me and it'll be fine. Them boys in there know I work for the mayor and if you're with me, they won't mess with you either.

They walked down the plaza to the east in a darkness disturbed only by the night lamps. John Frank looked down to where the boy was adjusting the Colt revolver under his waist belt.

They'll be havin that at the door, you know.

Yeah. I thought it.

The boy stopped and raised the cuff of his trouser leg to reveal the dirk knife strapped above his boot.

What in the hell is that for, cowboy?

He pulled the leather strap tight to his calf. You're the one said it was still dangerous in there, he said.

The room was smoke-filled and the bar itself was shaped in the manner of a horseshoe. All around men leaned up over their glasses, some leaning back against the polished wood and tilting their heads back and blowing thin streams of smoke into the already gray air. In the far corner of the barroom a white pine-box piano stood unplayed.

By the side of the piano a fiddler sat rocking in a three-legged chair, the music he bowed fast and Spanish.

At the antechamber Mexicans sat at slick dark tables and peered toward the bar. Every once in a while they called men over and talked in low voices, grim and knife-mouthed with their faces pitched toward the floor. Around the room were women of all sizes and dress. They glided about the tables, elbowing their way to the bar ledge to stop and converse with the men as they circled the room.

The boy shouldered past John Frank to examine the faces at the bar. All met his gaze with the same unwavering drunken lucidity. After he'd gone full around the bar he turned and motioned the Italian to an empty table near the fiddle player.

I told you to stick by me, Frank said, looking furtively about the room.

Let's set then.

John Frank sat down, flipping back the flares of his coat and drawing a pack of cigarettes from his shirt pocket.

So, the boy said blandly, here's where it all happens.

John Frank offered the boy a cigarette. Here's where what all happens?

Where men break themselves to pieces.

The boy took the cigarette and lit it.

You ain't some kind of cowboy outlaw, are you?

The boy shook his head without any animation at all. No, he said. Just sayin how I see it.

A waitress clad in high brown boots and a denim skirt and a purple blouse came and stood by the table. She looked at John Frank. You sure he's old enough? she said.

Her face was lightly painted and her lips glistened when she pursed them to size up the boy.

He's old enough, John Frank said.

He ran a hand along the hem of her skirt and she swiped it away. She turned to the boy.

You old enough?

For what? the boy said.

John Frank grinned up at the girl and she smiled down at the boy. Alright, she said. I reckon you are then.

John Frank ordered a glass of whiskey waterback. He winked at the waitress. She shifted from him with her lips turned down and asked the boy what he favored.

Just a soda, he said.

The waitress's eyes waited on him as though he would speak some hilarity but the boy only nodded to her and went to looking at the ashtray and the smoke rising from his cigarette.

A soda? she said.

The boy took up the cigarette and leaned back and drew on it. Keeps me sweet, he said.

The waitress smiled a long smile at him then went away, a fist balled up behind her skirt to ward off John Frank's hands.

Smooth-talkin cowboy you are, Frank said when she was gone.

He watched the fiddler and tapped his foot to the melody. After a while he turned back to the boy. Hey, he said. Don't go starin over there. Hey. John Frank raised his glass and pointed it meaningfully at the boy. You know what they say amidst such folk. A stare is a glare, and that ain't something you want to learn about firsthand.

I'm just lookin, the boy said.

Well don't. Don't just look.

The waitress returned with their drinks. Soda for the sweet one, she said.

Damn, John Frank declared when she had gone away again. He pounded his fist on the table. You ain't goin to say nothin? Woman like that make a man out of you yet. And not just any woman. No. He shook his head, his eyes wide with certain wonder. She got an ass on her like a sixty-dollar bill.

Ain't my way.

Ain't my way, Frank repeated woodenly. That's a girl no mama would be glad to see her son with.

Don't talk about that.

The boy set down his soda and pointed his cigarette across the table.

About what?

About my mama.

Shit, I wasn't sayin it like that. Any mama. Hell, it was just jokin. Well don't.

They drank. The boy had stopped eyeing the room and John Frank eased back in his chair. The Mexicans in the antechamber got up and left. The fiddle player stopped bowing and the bar took on a sudden stillness.

Now listen, John Frank said. Tomorrow at noontime you meet me at Garrets. I'll take you over to the mayor's office in the town hall. Just meet him and be grateful and polite and I'll give you the papers to deliver. Noontime, alright, bud?

The boy drained his soda glass.

You up at Abner's then?

No. Not no more.

Where then?

Yonder in the foothills, I reckon. It's plenty warm now. And the grass don't charge you for sleepin.

You're talkin bout outdoors?

No. I'm talkin about that big old hotel out there in the countryside that has grass growin for beds. Yeah I'm talkin about the outdoors.

But you'll be back at noontime.

Sure as the sun.

For a while longer they sat. John Frank's eyes fell fixed on a girl selling cigars behind a high counter near the door. A peach, he said. A genuine peach. He shook his head. To this day she won't look at me.

Well, you just goin to sit there or are you goin to get up and let her make a man out of you?

The boy smiled at the Italian for what was perhaps the first time since coming down from the mountains. John Frank grinned and slapped his hands on the table and ordered another whiskey.

You first, he said. I'll slide on in behind you.

The boy rose and crossed the floor. The men at the bar watched the boy closely. There was nothing about him that said he should have been there, neither age nor dress nor the lowered hat and hooded eyes. He stepped over to the girl at the counter. What you sellin? he said.

She glanced up at him, then went back to the journal she was studying.

What's it look like?

Like cigars.

Smartly done, she said. She looked up and gave him a cold smile. You want one?

No. I don't guess I do.

She looked down at the journal again. What then? she said without looking up again.

The boy glanced back to where John Frank was tossing back his whiskey. Just wanted to say you a goodnight, he said.

That right? Now why would you want to do that I wonder?

The boy shifted his hat up on his head. Well, he said. Seems to me you might be the only one round here that would appreciate it.

The girl smiled at him again, this time not coldly.

Evenin, John Frank called over the boy's shoulder.

He stepped forward in front of the boy and took down his hat and held it against his chest and pushed at the boy to step back. He winked at the girl. She shook her head slightly and looked down at her journal again. The boy leaned into Frank's ear.

Genuine peach, he said. Good luck with her.

He turned and walked off to the door with John Frank trying to hail him back to his side with a quick snapping of his fingers. The boy went to the doorkeeper and collected his pistol. He stuck it back under his belt, scanned the faces at the bar once more, then strode out the door to where Triften stood looking up at him from the empty street.

EIGHT

THE HAND HE felt on his shoulder was unfamiliar, yet in his half-conscious state he recognized a roughness he believed to be his father's. When he turned and rolled onto his back the man above him stepped forward. The boy squinted up at him and saw it was not.

It was an old man gathered loosely in his flesh and oversized denim pants. He stood shirtless over the boy with a rifle cocked in his arms. The boy braced himself with his hands. He looked closer at the rifle and saw that it didn't have a trigger.

Cronus or Zeus, the man called out.

His few teeth tilted toward his mouth. The boy rolled over to his knees. The sun darted through the trees beneath which the boy had slept, and he put a hand up against the light. The old man pushed the rifle's barrel into the boy's ribs.

Hey now, the boy said.

Cronus or Zeus, the man bellowed again.

His croaking voice seemed nearly comic in the morning quiet. The boy knocked the barrel away from his chest and propped himself to his feet with the other hand. What are you askin?

The old man spoke very slowly this time. Cronus or Zeus, he said.

The boy stooped over and began to roll up his bed linens. Zeus, he said.

Ah. The old man raised his hands like he meant to send the boy's reply somewhere above, all of the violence in his face dissolving into a wide gaping smile. Ah, he repeated. I knew you appeared sensible even sleepin. A shaking hand went to the pocket of his jean pants from which he drew the boy's knife. You can have this back now.

The boy studied him a moment, then reached out for the knife.

What if I said Cronus?

The old man shook his head. Ah, he said. You wouldn't of. Everyone sensible knows the Titans were nothin but greed. Olympians the ones who gave everythin back to us.

The boy walked over to his horse. The old man followed him, a curious hitch step in his gait. What are you doin out here in my country?

I wasn't aware it was yours.

Well it is. It's mine. I claimed it in '03 and I hold that claim to every last acre in this valley.

The old man peered out at the rocky hills and the thin trees. The boy recinched the saddlebag on the mule. The man turned back and watched him. He appeared suddenly stricken and earnest. You headed for town? he asked.

Yeah.

You hungry?

I reckon I'm alright.

You need to eat. You can come on down under my roof. It's the only one out here. Otherwise you got to wait till you hit town.

The old man turned a crooked shoulder and pointed between two foothills. It's down yonder, he said. Give me a ride down there and I'll let you eat and feed them horses.

The boy thought about it a moment, then helped the old man onto the mule, both of them heavy in the stomach and thin besides. His body tipped forward as he leaned his hands down on the mule's neck. The old man pointed the direction and they downstepped into a flat valley between the adjacent hill rises. The old man mumbled about Cronus and Zeus, and the man and the boy went down the hillside.

The air was pale and the land too. They rode through boughs of cherry and yellow grass which grew high by a stream that ran down the hill. They rode along the stream until they came to a cabin gilded by low-hanging saltwing bush. The house was an old creek cobble structure and from the side walls wildflowers sprang in garish colors. The two front windows were dashed on the ground. A vagary of rusted field tools lay about the yard. There was a chimney of red brick blackened by soot and a thin spindle of smoke rose from it to cross over the streambed.

The boy whoaed his horse and helped the old man down. He hobbled to the door and went in and waved the boy on behind him. Get yourself set in here, he called out.

Inside the one-room cabin was a strong smell of chili peppers. The boy looked around and saw the peppers hanging black and brittle like scalps along the wainscoting on long-staple strings. Toward the back of the room where the light peeled away from the window chute, a porcelain tub tilted to one side where the clawfoot was gone. The smell of alcohol rose out of it. Farther back was a box made from meshing and twigs. Inside the box crickets sprang up and clacked over one another. The old man glanced over at them and told them to be still. It was just a boy.

Set down, he said again.

The old man went to the sink basin. The boy sat at a small table cluttered with clay jugs and tin spoons. The old man huddled over the wood stove and waited for the plate to warm. Besides the table and chairs were only the basin and a thin cot cornered in the shadows. The old man sighed heavily as he heated a pot of beans.

You like beans?

Good as anything else.

They ain't no steak dinner. The old man turned to him as if to solicit his agreement.

No. I reckon they ain't.

He carried a bowl of beans to the boy and pointed to the spoons and sat across from him.

You ain't eatin? the boy asked.

No, no. I don't eat nothin till noontime.

The old man sat back in his chair and crossed his arms and scratched them. His chest was hairless and his skin was brown and wrinkled. Not till noontime, he repeated.

The boy ate. The old man scratched his arms and watched the boy. The clouds split the sky outside, and from the window a wavering strand of sunlight crossed their feet.

You live in town down there?

No.

The old man squinted at him. They send you boy?

Who?

The town.

No.

No?

No sir. I come out on my own.

What for?

I couldn't afford to stay down there no more.

The old man picked at his teeth with a gnarled finger and looked at it. One of them crossed me up here once, he said. One of them magnates with his slick suit and stupid little hat. Was last fall I recollect. He picked at his teeth again and resumed scratching his arms. I scared em off good with my rifle. But I imagine someday they'll be back. Try and claim my land away or some such nonsense they like to compose down there.

Well, the boy said. You might look into getting yourself a new rifle. Or at least a trigger.

The old man's eyes were silver. I ain't shot it in forty years, he said. Long as I can keep em at a distance they won't know. You just seen it cause I got too close, ain't that right?

Yes sir. That's right.

The old man leaned back. Why you come up here boy? Tell it to me true.

The boy shrugged. Looked pretty enough from town, he said. Warm and somewhat covered. That's about all for my reasoning.

You ain't much of a reasoner are you.

No sir. I don't guess I am.

Where's your mama and daddy at?

Not here, the boy said into his bowl.

You runnin from them?

The boy looked up, his eyes set hard. I ain't runnin from nothin, he said. I just come up and aim to stay out here for a spell.

Out where? This time the old man's voice was even.

In the hills.

You talkin bout my hills?

Any of these hills. I can't say which ones.

Why don't you go on and live in town?

Cause I ain't got the money is why. And I reckon I don't want to. I'm no good at it anyway. It's better for me out here.

Oh, the old man said, grinning again to reveal the dark teeth, is it? He straightened up in his chair and leaned into the table. You know what it's like to live out here, do ya? Out of town?

Yes sir I do.

And how's that?

I done it. I done it a long time.

The old man watched the boy's eyes travel to the window, then he collapsed back in his chair. He resumed scratching his forearms, looking at them as if to summon forth some explanation. You know about Melampus? he said suddenly.

About what?

Not what. Who.

No.

The old man struggled to his feet and walked to the glassless window frame. He turned his head back to the boy after a long moment of peering out.

Well, he said. If you're wantin to stay out here, you ought to know about him. One day this Melampus found out his servants had killed two snakes in the forest. This was long ago now. Well, Melampus. For whatever reason, he got fixed on them snakes. Ended up goin out into the forest and savin the snakes' little ones. Reared em up himself, he did. After the snakes done growed up they wanted to repay Melampus, for he'd come to them in the forest and he wasn't afraid.

The old man crossed back to the sink basin. He took out a tin cup with a warped finger loop and dipped it into the tub at the back of the room. He came forward sipping from it carefully.

He was sleepin one day. Melampus, I'm talkin about now. He was sleepin and the snakes he saved come up on him and licked his ears. Just licked em right up.

He made an obscene lapping motion with his mouth, his shriveled tongue writhing beneath the shoddy teeth.

Now when Melampus rose up from his slumber he all of a sudden could understand what two birds sittin on his window ledge was sayin to each other. You see it? The snakes had taken him to be like them.

The old man came back to the table and rapped his knuckles on the wood and leaned back down in his chair with the cup held loosely at his chest.

He walked into the forest and scooped up the snakes like they was his own babes. And so they made him to understand the language of all flyin and creepin animals. Some even said he knew the world better than anyone because he could hear all the words that passed on earth. He knew more than the gods, some say, and he lived his life alone by that forest and no harm to him ever did come because he could talk to all the world.

The old man held out his hands then lowered them, slapping the table to signal the close of the story. The boy pushed back his chair and rose up.

Snakes, he said. He pushed the chair tight to the table edge. I got to get on.

So you don't believe it, huh?

Oh, the boy said. Now you're tryin to tell me that story's a truth.

The old man shook his head scornfully. No, he said. That's the myth. From the floor he picked up a ribbed undershirt stained with an indiscernible filth and wiped its sleeve along his flaccid neck. But that's how life is to be lived out here, he said.

Well I don't care to hear anything they're sayin.

You can hear anythin you want, the old man said, his eyes skittish beneath the gauzy lids, what's matterin is how you listen.

And what's bein said that could possibly matter.

With this the boy turned for the door but the old man suddenly reached out and took his shoulder and pulled him back with little strength.

That's right, he said. I don't believe it's all meant for you to hear neither.

The boy tipped his hat and the man withdrew his hand. Before he mounted his horse the old man called out to him.

So you want to try my way of livin? You're probably right to figure this way's the best. It'll be the only one left come earth's end, and I don't care what fanciness they got down in that town.

He stepped outside, following the boy into the daylight with his hand upraised to his eyes. Come on back tonight, he said. You can rest here. Summer ain't so sure of itself and it might still take to a cold wind yet. Hey. Go on and leave your mule up here. Let him feed out here. Might even take him for a nice walk down by the water.

The boy examined the shifting mule. The mule's legs were scored with lashes from the mountains and still thin to the bone. Well, he said. I might do that then. I thank you.

The boy patted the mule's head, then stepped up into the stirrups and quartered the horse to where the man stood leaning against the door frame.

You just remember it's my valley, boy.

The old man gave his arms a few furious scratches and looked away as if another thought were coming, but he only turned back to the cabin and raised his hand as the boy passed out of the high grass and into the cold coming sun.

Stepping down from the hills and onto the flatland, the boy watched the sky as the last of the clouds shivered away. He looked back once toward the valley of the old man and could see none of its bounty, but only the plateland of detritus upon which he now rode. He downstepped onto the dirt road that led into the town. He slowed the mare carefully at the pavement, trotting through the morning flurry of the plaza and around the steaming cars and up to the portales of the cantina.

He could see John Frank seated by the window with one leg folded over the other thigh. He was tapping a pencil on the table when the boy came in.

Late, he called across the room.

The boy crossed over to the booth where Frank sat.

What?

You're late.

John Frank kept on tapping the pencil.

No I ain't.

Yeah, you are.

The boy slid into the booth. Didn't sleep too fair last night, he said.

Nor did I. Worried that you'd show late or not at all.

I showed.

You showed late.

The boy looked around the cantina for the waitress. He looked at the pencil tapping on the table. Then he looked out the window. So what then? he said.

So you're fired.

The boy shook his head and felt in his chest pocket for his cigarettes and rose.

Alright, he said. But just don't say it was on account of bein late.

John Frank grinned up at him and held his hand out across the table. You ain't fired, he said. He smacked the pencil nub against the table and let out a spurt of laughter. You're on time. Two minutes to spare actually. I was cartin you for a ride. See if you'd try to shoot me or some shit like that. Don't you carry a watch?

The boy sat again and motioned behind the bar and held up his coffee mug. I ain't never found a need for it, he said. Sun comes up, it's day. Day ends when it darks.

You can't tell the hours, though. What if you come to be needin them?

I needed them today, didn't I? And I'm here.

John Frank looked at his pocket watch, shook his head and grinned. You are, he said. You are.

They crossed through the weave and smoke of the rattling cars. John Frank pointed out the gray-togged Chinese streaming out from Abner's inn.

Here they come, he said. Bringin that new West. Be lucky if they even live to see the other side of the wick.

They passed down one of the lanes off the plaza. The boy rode his horse at a walk with John Frank on foot struggling to stay abreast of him.

Why don't you get on up here?

I ain't ridin no danged horse.

It's just down here aways, right? Ain't goin to hurt you.

I don't ride no horse.

I'm ridin. You just set.

I ain't gettin on.

Why not?

John Frank looked up at the boy. You plannin to comb that hair down, or is it goin to fly loose like a crow? he said.

It's goin to fly loose. Why won't you get up here?

It's an animal.

It is at that.

I ain't its kind.

Nor am I.

Well, John Frank said. I wouldn't be too sure of that.

The town hall stood deep in a cluster of two-story buildings on the west end of the town. Across the door was bolted a polished rapier of some foreign metal. It shone sugar-colored in the sunlight and underneath were hung letters of the same metal tacked up by wood nails. It read Capital of the West. Below a smaller title was engraved in the clay wall and written in another language.

What in the hell does that say?

Says Trude likes to fuck horses.

Shit, the boy said.

They climbed the stone steps to the oak door.

Where's that little cigar girl of yours? She the peach you thought she was?

John Frank nudged him with an elbow as they went in. Behind a desk set square in the middle of the rotunda a hulking woman sat with her arms folded across a yellow flower-printed dress. The boy leaned into John Frank's shoulder and whispered against his arm.

She sure has changed, bud.

Frank grinned and pushed him away. Morning Molly, he said. This here's the one goin to run the papers across town for me.

That right?

She looked up with disinterest while her hands fumbled along the neck of her dress.

Yes ma'am. I can't keep up with all this and that the mayor's got constantly goin.

The secretary shifted her heavy bottom in the thick-wooded chair she sat upon and lifted the blouse on and off her breasts with her chubby fingertips. Nor can I, she said.

Me and you, John Frank said grimly. He grinned at the boy again. Havin to run this town, he said. Make things right.

Down a long hall scripted by alabaster and shunted with doors closed and immaculate John Frank led the boy to the office of the mayor. Daylight flooded the hall from the slant-paned windows above.

You sure this ain't the church?

Hell. That's about the one thing I am sure of.

The lacquered mahogany door flowed upward like a forest gate. The two of them looked up, standing puppetlike beneath the door.

Good goddamn, the boy said.

John Frank motioned toward two clap handles of silver which were crafted into spindles of rosebush. At the bottommost thorn joint of each were knobs of ivory. Knock back one of them, he said. The boy gripped one of the knobs and took the silver loop back and dropped it twice. They waited. John Frank looked down at the creak of leather from the boy's boots.

Maybe he skipped town, the boy said. Maybe found an easier way to get his cigars.

Maybe you better.

John Frank fell silent with the sound of movement on the floorboards. They heard two distinct voices but could not make out the words. No one came to the door.

To hell with it, Frank said. Always locked up in there. Come on, I'll tell him later.

They went down the hall and through another door. John Frank walked behind a desk in the corner of the room by a window that opened onto a lane with the plaza in the distance.

This yours?

Yeah. And don't say nothin about it. I come to deserve it. Finally got moved up around here.

This is up?

John Frank grinned at him. Take this, he said.

He handed the boy a docket with a leather binder and leather straps that lay tied across it to where the straps were threaded through a gold hasplock.

That's what you got to carry every day. You can meet the mayor later on. Follow this little map I made. We still ain't got a printed one. He handed the boy a piece of torn yellow paper. The road you want to find the house on is Old 17, he said.

The boy studied the map. He pointed at the paper, then out the window. Is this that little thing down yonder?

Yeah.

He folded the map and put it in his trouser pocket. Alright.

Well. Good luck, cowboy.

The boy walked to the door then stopped and turned and looked at John Frank again. Shit, he said. I'm sure I'll need it.

THE PATH HE rode curved gently toward the north, bringing the boy back under the shadows of the mountains. He rode through darkened woodland. From time to time he looked out at the peaks, their shadows bearing down on him as if they held a weight as great as the mountains themselves. His mouth so dry, the air so quiet.

When he reached the fenced yard of the lawyer's house he bent from the horse and swung loose a sickle-shaped iron draw bar. The wooden gate flushed open onto a flagstone path. He hobbled the horse at the gatepost and twisted the docket loose from his saddlebag and walked up to the house.

It was a simple adobe structure. Two windows flanked a low door. The boy stood on the porch and looked around. He listened to the wind and the wind chimes that hung on the rear drain head. He could see nothing that would lead him to believe this place was at all occupied. There were no chickens or cattle and no shirts hung out to dry and there was no automobile or horse. No sound came from within, and though it was still day, the inside was dark. No dirt lined the porch. No tarnish upon the window or smoke staining the chimney. He wondered if John Frank had meant to fool him.

At last he bent and slid the docket under the door, shuffling his foot against it until it stiffened and flattened out and disappeared inside.

He rode back onto the thoroughfare sweating cold. It had grown night quickly, both clouds and dark snapping down like a drape. When he neared the plaza center he saw John Frank propped up against the willow tree by one shoulder and looking drunk with his knees buckling beneath him.

Cowboy, he called out when he saw the boy.

The boy rode up to him. In his haggard suit and ruffled hair John Frank looked like an attendant sent out to observe something he had long given up on finding. I'm drunkern shit, he slurred.

What the hell are you out here for?

I got a date, cowboy.

The boy studied him. Don't tell me, he said.

The cigar girl indeed, John Frank said, languidly wiping a sleeve across his mouth. Everything fly alright out there?

If there's somebody out there, they'll get the papers.

Good.

Yeah. But is there?

What?

Somebody livin out there. It don't look like it's ever been used even once.

Well hell. Course there is. What else do you think you were out there for? The wind in your hair? Shit. John Frank's mouth hung open and his eyelids closed and opened again whenever the wind kicked up. What time is it?

You're the one with the watch.

What time you think it is?

About a quarter and six.

Frank fumbled loose his pocket watch then dropped it and cussed at it and picked it up. Twenty and six, he slurred. Goddamn close, I must say.

When's she meeting you?

John Frank's brow tightened. He looked up and grinned. I got no idea when I meet her. No idea.

You sure it's here you're meeting her? You could be passed out for the balance of the night if she don't come on soon.

John Frank started up and stood straight and held a finger in the air. He dug about in his pockets and pulled loose a scrap of typing paper, picking it open roughly but trying at the same time to administer some delicacy with it. He looked down at the writing, his nose almost upon the page.

I's supposed to pick her up. Shit, I got to go.

You're one qualified certified and bonafide dumbass my friend. And your breath stinks.

But John Frank was already down the road, his coattails flailing behind him. See ya in the mornin, he called out in no particular direction.

The boy watched him until darkness covered all, then walked his horse down the road. Before heading out to the old man's hills he stopped at the general store. He went in to where a single kerosene lamp burned on the countertop. He looked through a collection of bedsheets against the near wall.

You need some help?

The boy looked up at the old lady behind the counter, her face tender and wrinkled in the lamplight.

I need a bedsheet lighter than flannel.

You want a cotton one then.

He paid for the sheet she brought forth in her tiny hands and folded it squarewise so it fit under his arm. He walked outside to his horse and stroked her mane. While he was folding the bedsheet into the saddlebag, he heard metal jangling from the far side of the plaza. The wind struck up and whistled through the trees. He took off his hat and scrubbed his hand over the bristle of his hair, listening. He stepped forward off the last porch step and toward the road. The clanking grew louder. He peered out. Then above the sounds of metal he heard rough voices. There was a sharp retort that rose above all other voices, then only the rustling metal.

His hands fell from the strappings of the saddlebag. He knew immediately the voice was hers and he went out into the road.

She was being led down a side street at the far end of town by two men wearing silver concho belts and silver pistols. They wore the broad hats of peacemakers and they eased the girl under the lights and back into the darkness.

He could see her only faintly. She wore leg irons and her hands were manacled likewise. He walked out under the plaza lights. Her dark hair flowed into the darkness like rainwater into a pool. For a moment he saw her clearly. In the last glow of the lamplight he could see her eyes fixed upon him. He stood still. She stopped talking altogether, her neck turned long and thin to better see him, her bare feet shushing upon the road.

The men gripped her shoulders when she slowed and jerked her down the road. There was a silver car parked along the roadside. The driver got out and motioned to the men. As she came abreast of the car she leaned her head back over her shoulder once more. Her dark delicate hands bound as if in terminal prayer and her eyes pitched out and burning, darkness unto darkness, collecting in him.

By the time he had mounted his horse again and rode up the plaza they were gone. He rode through the streets with the wind licking his face and the storefronts bolted and the shutters clamped back. He went along the edge of town, riding through no light from the town or even the sky. He went through the alleyways but could not find a trace of her anywhere.

Back upon the thoroughfare he stopped the horse. He quartered her around and around but neither saw nor heard anything more, the slick black of the paved road stretching out forever and empty and taking her with it.

When he reached the old man's cabin the boy saw his crooked form below one of the window frames. He was sitting on a tilted tree stump. A candled lantern sat beside him. In his soft mouth he worked a piece of briar root. The old man stood and squinted as the boy came on. You're back, he called.

He spat black onto the ground and put his hands on the small of his back.

Hungry?

No.

You wantin to sleep then?

Yes sir. I do.

Still want to stay out here?

Yes sir. For a while at least. I'd like to.

Mmm. What cause you got to be in town in the first place?

The boy looked off toward where the stream was running crisply down the slope. I got some things to take care of there, he said.

Well I ain't got no Lincoln bed for ya, but you can sleep on the floor if it suits you.

The boy made no response but gazed down at the dark water skirting along the bank. I wouldn't mind sleepin out here, he said. By the water.

The point of havin the cabin is most of all to sleep in.

It ain't too cold out tonight. The boy looked at his feet. Besides, he said, I reckon Zeus will watch over me.

The old man picked the weed from his mouth, then thrust it in the direction of the water. Go on then, he said. Just know that I rise with the sun and anyone wantin to stay around here best do the same. I don't want no driftage in my valley.

No sir.

Alright then, the old man said, patting his trouser pockets absently and turning toward the door. See you in the mornin.

The boy shucked the bedroll from his saddlebag as the man bent and hoisted up the lantern and disappeared inside the cabin. He walked down to the river and found level ground, laying out the bedroll with the new cotton sheet. He could hear tin pans ringing from within the cabin. He heard the old man's feet shuffling on the warped floorboards, the sound of them almost mimicking the water pass and the wind that moved it. The boy laid himself down.

For a long time he stared up at the sky. Later in the night he rolled over to face the bank so the cool breeze from the river blew on his face. He shifted once more, a thought of the girl, then fell off into a troubled sleep with the moon receding into the clouds and the face of the sky blackening still.

III

NINE

A LOST AND forgotten grove and her hair its black fruits. Standing at dawn in the rocky shoal of the stream, this new vision or delusion or idle journey of the mind had come to him for several mornings running. He kicked at the stones beneath his feet and breathed heavily in the thick air, all about him the smell of wood smoke and untold rains.

Inside the old man was hunched over the clawfoot tub as the boy had found him every such morning. He turned and glanced at the boy coming in and turned silently back to the tub. The boy stood by the table and drew the fresh pouch of tobacco John Frank had given him from his breast pocket. The old man rose and scuttled over to the worn shelving above the stove. He took down a cup and went back to the tub and filled it. Then he sat by its side with his coverall straps dangling loosely from his hips. He motioned the boy to sit at the table, and the boy did.

On the table was a bowl of buttermilk and a plate of corn mash. He motioned to the boy again, shaking a tremulous hand at the plate and nodding ambivalently to him. The boy slowly took up one of the dark glazed spoons and made no effort to speak but only lifted the gruel to his mouth and swallowed.

After eating the boy rose and walked down to the stream, dipping his hands in and squatting with his forearms around his knees. He removed his hat and thrust it in the water until it was soaked through. He placed the hat on his head again, beads of water dripping down his nose and cheeks, and watched the water. The current was slow and beneath the turning glass sheet he could see small fish riding swiftly over the green stones.

Once upon Triften the boy fixed his shirt collar and rode to the door of the cabin. The old man was still slumped by the tub, his head cocked down into his chest and his hands fumbling around the cup. He looked up when the mare's shadow peeled away from the floor. He half raised up a hand to the boy's back.

Come back, he said.

What false magic or unseen hand led the boy into his quietness he could not name, but he went on for weeks in a slow procession of necessity and no real thing besides. He rose into town in the morning and at the town hall Molly passed him the papers from behind her squat desk and he rode them out to the lawyer's house, then back through the town and into the foothills. For many nights the old man was unaccounted for and many mornings too, found only occasionally curled and rigid on his shapeless ticking or folded awkwardly on the back of the boy's mule, scouring the brush for berries at dusk. He saw John Frank few times during those weeks and avoided conversation. When he did agree to meet him one night at the bar, the boy sat and drank sodas for an hour until John Frank pushed back his chair violently and stared down at him. I'm leavin if alls you're goin to do is sit there. I could have me a better time with a stick and a rock to roll.

The boy said nothing and did not look up from the bar. You ought to get goin then, he finally said.

What was in him was virulent beyond his knowledge and he rode the days out with his eyes turned down and squinting as if startled by the light. When he ate at Garrets Miss Jane watched him more than she spoke. She emptied his ashtray and filled his mug with coffee and made his change when he finished eating.

Some nights upon returning to the old man's cabin the boy would walk along the streambank, kicking old twigs and snapping leaves from the overhanging trees. The animals of that country fell and rose before him on the landscape and he studied them hunched over with his faded bed linens draped upon his shoulders. To any unlikely onlooker the boy would have seemed as much a part of that place as the beasts who roamed it.

His hair grew long again and by the close of those weeks it brushed his collarbone when he rode his mare. The staggering sun had browned his face and his stubble goldened with the wisps of hair that cropped out from under his hat brim. He faded thin, the muscles surfacing stark and stunned upon his flesh. Only his eyes remained unchanged, a pale bottomless sealike blue.

During those days the plaza rocked and swayed with heat and peddler and passersby, the explosion of commerce settling only in the wan hours of dawn. The railroad men had arrived and at night they mulled about the streets and crossed the windows of Abner's in silhouette, smoking or drawing up their stiff and blackened overalls like custodians of some dark secret. Sometimes riding back from the lawyer's house the boy could hear music from the outdoor bandstand behind the bar, the soot-faced spike drivers and the hard-helmeted engineers and their haggling and laughing and coming down from the windows of the inn their sharp cries of desire. It was not the world that he had smiled upon with his mother when they sat by the edge of that mountain creek, nor was it the world at home in his bed he had once dreamed of, but what world it was he could not quite say.

THE FIRST MORNING of August brought a heavy heat. The boy woke in a pool of sweat. He rolled up and held his knees. There was no birdcall that morning and he sat listening to the quiet.

When he came out of the stream he looked over his makeshift camp and his dirty linens and the dusty spot of matted land where he had slept all summer long. A tin cup and his dirk knife lay beside it. His dull silver pistol and his grandfather's rifle were nearly covered in the fallen leaves of a cottonwood. One saddlebag was unstitched and loose with his extra clothing and wilting beneath them was his mother's old saddle.

With his shirt unbuttoned and his eyes boring down without fix on his trousers, he loosed the horse's headstall and saddled her and mounted. He did not don his hat or sit and smoke or stop to see after the old man but chucked the heel of his boot against the mare's flanks and rode on down to the town at a gallop.

At the town hall he went straight past Molly, who looked up and shifted largely in her seat to regard the boy passing. He walked down the hall buttoning his shirt as he went. When he entered the office John Frank was bending over behind his desk to relace his shoes.

He looked up for a moment when the boy came in, then leaned down to his feet again. Molly's got the papers, he said.

I know it. I was wantin to talk to you.

Frank looked up at him, his eyes just above the desk. Is that so, he said. He looked toward the floor and finished with his laces and sat up and leaned back in his chair. You in trouble?

No.

You wantin to quit the job?

No. I'm not.

What you want to talk to me for, then?

The boy cast a sidelong glance at John Frank then went and stood by the window. Well, he said. I ain't never been much for words.

No, you ain't. But at least in the past you've used them where they were needed. I reckon with me they're not.

I'm using em now, ain't I?

They were both silent.

You are, John Frank finally said.

The boy walked to the far corner of the room to where a lone chair stood. He dragged it across the room and sat in front of the desk. He rubbed his head and looked around again, as if something in the room might offer him reprieve. How's that little peach of yours? he said.

John Frank watched the boy stone-faced. Then he began to shake his head. She don't want to see me but sunk six feet underground, he said. He straightened up in his seat. I wasn't at my best walking skills that night.

The night I seen you in the plaza.

I'd say that was the one.

You ain't seen her since then, I take it.

I imagine if I'd seen her I'd be sittin here with a wind-filled skull.

What happened?

Well, at first I didn't have no problems. Then we sat down at the restaurant and I could barely keep her face in one showing. There were about three of her rotatin in front of me like I just stepped off a fair ride. She kept askin me why I was blinkin so much and I told her it was out of nervous habit. By the end of the night I thought I'd taken to feelin better. I asked her if maybe she wanted to take a walk for some ice cream and she said Alright. But when I went to stand, I couldn't. My legs was heaviern cow shanks. I told her I couldn't quite walk yet and that it was another of my nervous habits that was probably stirred up on account of bein with her.

You sweet-talked her, I guess.

Yeah well, the problem was she went to feelin bad for me and that's when it all went to hell. She stood and tried to help me up, believin it was all my nervousness, but when I leaned over and unloaded on her there wasn't nothin I could have said to make her believe it was just another habit of mine.

The boy's face grew grave. I don't see where the humor is in that, he said.

John Frank's grin went away. It's not like I'm tryin to make a habit of it, he said. One of those things, is all.

Is that what you call it?

John Frank threw up his arms. Ah hell, he said. At least let me finish the story. Jesus. You're the one said you wanted to talk.

The boy shook his head. Go on then, he said. I ain't stoppin you.

John Frank rubbed his hands together. He righted the legs of his chair so he sat square behind the desk. Alright, he said. This particular time, I did happen to throw up on her. Heaved a good gourd, too.

What did you do?

You see I wanted to help her, so I got up to my feet, but there it came again. I don't know why she hadn't stepped back by then. I reckon she was unable to think at all.

Shit, the boy said.

You said it.

And I suppose she did too.

That and a lot more. I stood there in the middle of the danged restaurant bein laid into by a girl drippin in garbage. The mayor didn't take too kindly to it neither.

He was there?

No. He wasn't there. John Frank poked a fingertip on the desk three times. But I came to work the next day and puked right here.

You were still drunk the next day?

I was drunkern a shithouse pig. Said one more strike and I'm out.

Shit if I don't know you from a travelin clown.

John Frank grinned at him. Hell, he said, even if I was a clown, I don't believe they'd want me gettin up to travel.

They sat. John Frank's mouth turned down. He took up a pencil from his desk and began to tap it and looked out the window. What's been tyin your fancy in such a knot? he said. You been like a goddamn ghost.

The boy did not respond. Frank kept tapping his pencil as he watched the boy. They been talkin about you, he said.

Who has.

People. Everyone. Damn, you ride around the plaza on that danged horse of yours like you was just waitin to fall off. You don't even look like you've eaten better than grass in the last month. I seen one little girl was cryin over you. Sayin, What's happened to the pretty cowboy, Mama?

Ain't nothin's happened. The boy stood. He folded his hands behind his back and walked to the window and let them drop. Maybe that's the problem, he said.

He came away from the window. He pushed his fingers through his hair then down his sides where he began to rub his hips slowly, as though in speculation of his own form. John Frank held out a cigarette across the desk and the boy took it and walked back over to the window and looked out to where the clouds had come low and ponderous into the valley.

Who's been penned lately? he said.

You mean put in jail? Shit. John Frank cocked his head back. Shit, he said. I don't know those things. Nobody does unless somethin goes down in broad daylight. That's the way the mayor's been runnin this town. Keep all the hell-raisers private. That way nobody's got to worry about them.

The boy turned from the window and studied him closely. So you don't know, he said.

No. Things around here ain't the same way maybe you know them to be. Here a man ain't asked to account for all things that occur around him like he used to. And one of them things is the criminals. So I don't know. That's God's honest truth.

I don't want nobody else's truth. I want yours.

Shit, then you have it. I don't know the first or last of any of that business.

The boy turned up the cigarette he had been holding in his hand and now lit it with a match. Who knows then? he said.

Somebody I reckon.

The boy pointed the cigarette at him. You reckon right, he said. Ain't nothin happens without somebody's knowledge. I reckon the wind and rain is about all. He walked to the edge of the table. So who is somebody?

John Frank's face clouded. He slumped down in his chair and hit the table with an open palm. What the hell is this about? he said. Why you want to know? Is one of your old buds in there? One of them outlaws?

The boy's face paled and he looked away from John Frank and out the window again. I ain't no outlaw, he said, and I don't got any buds except you and if you're not wantin to help me I'll be on my way and not botherin you anymore.

John Frank leaned back in his chair. He ran his hands down his face. He looked out at the boy through the gaps of his fingers, then lowered his head and linked his hands over the back of his neck. Ah hell, he gasped. The only one I know who knows about the jail is the mayor himself.

What about the lawmen?

They're hired out from the north. The town's too small yet to have our own peacemakers and we haven't had that much need for them. When we do, they come down and take care of business and then they leave.

But the mayor knows.

Yeah, he knows. And maybe the lawyer too. The lawyer probably for sure. But you'll never meet him, I doubt. Nobody really has since he come on.

The boy looked past him and nodded slowly, as though considering something on the wall behind him. Then he stubbed out his cigarette and went to the door.

Where you goin?

To do my job, the boy said. He tried to smile. It's hottern shit out today, ain't it?

It is. What about all this jail business?

I reckon it's about time I met the mayor.

John Frank looked him over. I guess, he said.

When can I find him?

He'll probably be over at the festival tonight.

What festival?

In the plaza. It's for the harvest.

What harvest they got here?

Not much anymore. I reckon it'll be more for the railroad. Either way, it's tradition.

Then I'll come back after supper.

John Frank snapped his fingers and pointed across the room at the boy. Bring him a bottle. Whiskey or something. He'll like that.

The boy put his head back into the threshold of the door. Whiskey, he said.

When he turned to go again John Frank called out once more.

Hey Trude.

What.

John Frank leaned forward on his desk and took his hands down from behind his head and folded them in front of him and squinted at the boy.

How many seasons you pass up in them mountains anyway?

I don't know.

You don't know?

There weren't no seasons in them mountains, the boy said. Only weather.

In the plaza there was already excitement for the festival as the boy rode onto the thoroughfare. Lights strung lengthwise across the eaves of the storefronts bobbed rhythmically in the breeze. The old Indian women crouched under the shade of the willow tree and tinkered with their wares. Children burst around the street corners winging wooden ladles of water at one another. The men stood smoking and sweating under the porch fronts. Around the base of the tree where the women sat, small lanterns stood unlit. Their crepe paper casings snapped and glistened brightly in the afternoon sun. A few yards off from the tree the boy watched a group of railroad workers hunched over a spit and cradling its ends to fit an iron post across two cherry branches that were forked into the earth and standing on opposite ends of the pit.

He rode the horse at a walk. Some of the Indian women waved faintly at him and he raised up a hand as he passed out into the foothills.

The old man was slouched in the same manner as the boy often found him, the cup loose in his trembling hand and his hand resting on the edge of the tub. He watched the boy with his gray eyes as he came into the room.

Cronus or Zeus.

The boy felt in his shirt pocket for his cigarettes and brought one out and sat at the table. Zeus, he said.

What for so early?

The old man's speech was little more than a drunken warble.

I need a favor from you.

Ah. But only the gods grant the favors. We only here to carry em out.

Then I hope the gods want you to pass over a bottle of whatever's in that tub of yours.

The old man lifted his reddened eyes. I reckon you'd soon need some relief, he said. That town'll kill ya.

It ain't for me.

Who then?

The mayor.

Oh no you don't. The old man wheeled around on his backside and held his cup out at the boy. The mayor my ass. Day that wretch gets a wooden nickel from me will be the day I die and go to Hades.

Well I'm sorry about that but I need it. He's got something of mine.

Unfair deal the mayor been handin ya boy? That ain't no surprise to me. No sir.

Can I have it or not?

The old man studied the boy. His face grew momentarily clear and he lowered his eyes and shook his head like he carried some foreknowledge that if he agreed bad things would befall them both. He sighed and put up his sickly hands, as if concession were an affliction. Straddle up here then boy, he said. I'll show you an old workin man's trade.

The boy pushed out his cigarette and rose and walked to the side of the tub. In that rear corner the room was almost gone to dark. The boy stood a ways from the tub with his head cocked back.

This here's the old peach brandy. Best drink this half of the Rio Grande in the bootleggin days. The old man rubbed his hands together fervently. Look here, he said. This is what you got. First you got some alcohol, he said. That'd be the most important. Then some water. Easy enough. But the trick here's the flavorin.

He stopped and put his hands across his forearms.

Danged if I could ever figure on why, but ya need raspberry flavorin, not peach. Most folks wouldn't know that. He looked up at the boy, his eyes nearly closed. Curious world, ain't it boy?

He touched one of his teeth with his thumb and nodded slightly.

The last thing I recommend, though some would say you don't need it. But with me you get the best. The whole service done up like they do in them big old cisterns now. The finishin touch here is the red ink. Some call it the dye. However you name it, the best kind is Carter's, if you can get your hands on it. It's the clearest and stays set the best in the liquor. Believe me, I know em all.

The old man leaned off the tub and nodded, across his face a twisted smile. The boy tried to thank the old man but his eyes were fixed on the tub and his mind on his father. All those days and nights he went across the road from bar to backroom while the boy kept up the ranch, the stained bottles of whiskey and rye filled by men not unlike his father and bought with the money of men not unlike his father and the passage of that money into their twitching hands no less than the passage of souls across the borderland that balances the world's polar natures.

Fill it up, he said.

The old man wrung his fingers and knitted his brow.

Give me that there colander, he said. Let's see what we can do. Alright, take it back. You hold it there. Right there. Steady now. Here's the pour.

TEN

BY THE TIME he came back upon the thoroughfare the night was black and the moon a smear of chalk in the deep vast sky.

Some flamenco music twisted through the air. He could see a ponytailed and blanket-wrapped man standing by the willow tree, snipping castanets with raised fingers. The band makers smiled and canted their heads to the music while the singer flared a bright frilled scarf with his outstretched hands. Around them many of the townspeople moved lightly to the rhythm. Most of the men appeared to be drunk and the women held fast to their shirt collars.

John Frank was leaning a hand against Garrets's porch post. He waved wildly when he saw the boy coming. Ho, he called. Cowboy. Over here. He pointed at himself. Over here.

The boy dismounted and hobbled his horse on the post.

Do ya got to set him right here, Frank said. He stinks.

She. It's a girl.

Whatever you want to call it.

Maybe she thinks you stink. And I don't know that she'd be wrong.

Maybe she thinks . . .

But John Frank was too drunk for crossing words. He shot the thin mouth of a bottle against his lips and shuddered and pushed it toward the boy.

Festival, he cooed.

Not for me.

Che no? Per quanto tempo farà così?

My Mexican ain't that good.

C'e italiano.

Then it ain't at all.

Porca miseria, John Frank said, grinning.

He made a slow sweeping gesture toward the stage where cones of minced red and yellow fluted from the paper-tinted lanterns.

The women here, my friend. You don't even got to look and you can see em, there's so many.

I guess you ought to look first. Specially in your state.

Look here, John Frank said. Every one. Soft skin. Smell of roses and talc. Red lips, tight hips. Eyes like a bedroom.

He shook his head with exaggerated slowness and they both looked out into the crowd, watching the people dance.

A tall lean man dressed in black stood elbowing over the hog roast pit with a butcher knife. He cut loose the entrails of the hog while the children stood by and cheered and the women turned away with amused disgust. Blood popped in the flames. With knives in hand some Mexicans stood and awaited their turns.

Someone was calling for the head. The tall man rose up with tears of blood on his cheeks and put up a finger and smiled. An instant later the hog's head came down. It rolled to the edge of the pit, then sunk to a stop. Its eyes were peached over and cross-tilted and the little mouth had taken on an unnatural crook.

The boy turned back to John Frank who was leaning against the porch post again and making eyes at the women who passed. He reached out once to pull the knot of a handkerchief a wide-hipped woman was wearing over her red hair, but his fingers missed it. The boy lit a cigarette and flushed out the match and dropped it and spoke.

Can I see him?

John Frank looked up from two women's backsides who were now going by. Him?

The mayor.

Ah. Frank looked at his pocket watch and fumbled for a cigarette in his coat pocket. What time you think it is? he said.

The boy shook his head. Just tell me, he said. Will he be here or not?

Ah hell. Just go on over then.

Over where?

Town hall. His office.

Right now?

John Frank lit up his cigarette and drew it in. Hurry, he said, and the boy was gone.

Outside the door of the town hall he fixed his hat straight and buttoned his shirt. He walked very slowly and he fingered the wall as he went. He listened to the dull clack of his boots on the stone floor and he turned the bottle of brandy with his thumb and forefinger. He paused a moment in front of the mayor's door, then lifted the ironwork handle. Soon after he dropped it a second time the door opened and the mayor stood before him.

The boy stepped back and brought his hat to his chest. Evenin, he said. The mayor looked him over casually and meticulously. He removed his spectacles and nodded and held his hand back into the room for the boy to pass.

Good evening, he said.

He was not much taller than the boy and he wore a long duster black and white at the seams and a bolo tie of polished silver. His shirt collar raced along his shoulders where it was still stiff with starch. He smelled of the leather of a woman's riding saddle and his eyes drooped slightly at the corners. He wore also a pepper-colored beard that bristled upon the pink of his lips. His boots were shining black, and even in the low candlelight they sprang forth from the floor like hand-rubbed coals.

Please, he said, sit down.

The boy put his hands on the back of the leather chair that faced the mayor's desk. He walked in front of the chair and the mayor tilted his head. The boy spun in the chair, raising up and sitting again and reshifting it to face straight forward. He put his hat on his lap and touched his hair. The mayor leaned toward him.

I am sorry about the lighting, he said. He made a gesture with his hands at the candles. I have read by candlelight for many years and I'm sure you agree that waste is a terrible thing. He smiled at the boy. Now, how can I help you? The mayor turned an inkwell under his fingers

121

and regarded the boy with unwavering eyes. I was just on my way over to the festival, he went on, raising his hands as though to mark this new thought. Would you like to join me?

Maybe in a while, the boy said. He lifted the bottle of brandy onto the table. I brought you this.

The mayor looked at the bottle but did not move to take it up.

Thank you, he said. I know that you are new to our town. I have seen you in the plaza on your horse.

Yes sir. That was me.

That's a fine little mare.

Thank you sir.

The mayor nodded, slowly and with circumspection. Not taking his eyes off the boy, he took hold of the bottle and set it in his lap and leaned back. He turned the bottle and lifted loose the corking and put his nose to the lip of the bottle. He raised an eyebrow.

Peach brandy, he said.

Yes sir.

But what kind, it doesn't say.

It's from the hill country.

It was all the boy could think to say.

You mean the bathtub?

Well. Prohibition's over, ain't it?

The mayor smiled obliquely and turned the bottle once more. The boy's eyes shifted around the room and fell onto deep oak shelving crammed with leather-bound books. His eyes stopped at a row of glass statuettes of train engines and caboose cars.

There is a man in Grand Junction who makes those for me, the mayor said. He is a glassblower. The mayor looked upon the trinkets in a manner that suggested he had not thought of them in a long time. Once I asked him why he liked working with glass and he told me because it is the closest a man can get to shaping the wind. You see, he believes the glass is a form of wind. That the glass is the wind captured.

I reckon it's a good thought, the boy said. But the way I see it, the wind can't be captured. The glass don't blow. You blow the glass. He pointed toward one of the crystal trains that held softly the candle's tapered light. The only thing that train and the wind got in common is the sound they make when they come.

The mayor smiled. This is your opinion, he said.

Yes sir. That's all it is.

It is a good one.

Yes sir. Thank you.

The mayor slowly turned the inkwell in his fingers. Why did you come here, to our town?

I just kind of rode into it.

Just rode into it, you say?

Yes sir. I came out of Grant County with my mother. He paused with his hands upon the crown of his hat that rested on his knee. When I came through the mountains I rode into the town and just ended up stayin. I'm on my way to Colorado. My horse needed some rest and I needed a bit of money is all.

He looked up from his lap. The mayor was still watching him.

And that's it?

The way he asked the question seemed oddly forceful to the boy. Yes sir, he said. I work for you.

The mayor leaned back. I know, he said evenly.

I do a good job, I think.

That is what I am told. But where is your mother?

The boy looked at one of the brass candle fixtures above the shelving. He turned and saw himself reflected in the window behind the mayor's desk. He straightened his shoulders, a response perhaps gathered from some lesson of manner she had once taught him. She ain't with me no more, he said.

I see.

The mayor stood and walked to a wheeled drink cart and took up a glass between his forefinger and thumb and held it out to the boy.

Thank you. No sir.

The mayor poured himself a small amount of the old man's brandy and sipped from it and studied the syrup behind the glass and turned it in his fingers and went and stood by the window behind his desk.

Perhaps I could lend you the money, yes? I know how it is to be without. It is quite a thing. Quite a thing indeed.

The boy looked down at the floorboards. They ticked darkly in the candlelight. Thank you sir, he said. But no. I reckon getting paid always followed work, the way I know it. I'd feel wrong about it somehow.

The mayor watched him with a curious smile. He nodded to himself and drank from the brandy. What's your name? he asked.

Trude.

Trude what?

Trude Mason.

Are you from Indian descendants perhaps?

My grandma. She was Navajo.

The mayor nodded. This is nice brandy, he said. He pursed his lips to the glass again. Yes, he said. I thought I saw it in you. The Navajo. They are fine people. Violent people.

The boy looked down at the floor again. Most are, he said.

The mayor raised his eyebrows again and nodded in agreement.

Sir?

Yes.

I have a question for you.

The mayor took his shoulder off the window and stood upright. He appeared suddenly formidable. What is it?

The boy lifted his hat from his knee and leaned forward in his chair. Have you got a girl jailed here?

A girl?

Yes.

The mayor eased back against the window again. He moved his fingers through his beard. What girl?

You see, the boy said. Well. He fumbled with his hat for a moment, then folded both hands atop it and looked at the mayor. A black-lookin girl, he said.

The words seemed to hang still in the room like something unwanted and waiting to be claimed. The mayor sat again and resumed turning the inkwell in his fingers.

You are a smart boy, I think. Do you know what respect means?

I reckon I do. Yes.

Yes. Here we have a certain kind of respect. The mayor withdrew his hand from the inkwell and pressed his palms together into the table. Respect is an elusive thing, he said. Some people think respect is about a person's etiquette around others. Do you know what I mean by etiquette?

Yes sir.

Well, etiquette is only a very small part of respect. Respect is deeper than etiquette. Respect is more important than courage sometimes.

With this he paused and regarded the boy over his spectacles.

Here I have made respect a way of life. I have made respect undisturbed by age or status. I have made it so the people believe in me and know I will bring them everything I can to help them up the long ladder to wealth and substance. I have made respect into a form of truth. And the truth here is that the world is not easy. The world is a complicated place and we must treat this world with respect, as we do one another. Here there is respect shared between our people. Day to day. On the streets and at home. But this respect is also necessary to keep us from trouble. To keep us from the troubles of this world. I have respect for all the people, and I know that I am making this town as strong as I can for them. In turn the same is expected of the people. They must respect me. The mayor brought his hands from his stomach and held them out toward the boy. And you, he said. You must respect me too.

The boy glanced down at his hands. I do, he said.

Good. I believe you. So you must understand that some things that make the world difficult should be left to those who can deal with it. You must respect those people who can deal with it.

Does this mean I can't ask you about who's been jailed?

The mayor moved his spectacles back against the bridge of his nose.

If you are at home and you curse your sister, do I come and ask if it is so? Do I come and say, Trude, is it you who cursed your sister inside the walls of your home? No. I do not ask you that. I must respect you. Your position. If you do not respect your sister it is not my business, unless for some reason it becomes so. But if you damn your sister, it is you who ultimately suffers, regardless of whether or not I am called upon. It is again about respect.

The boy fingered the rim of his hat and moved it to the other knee. Well, he said. I have a different way of lookin on it.

The mayor tilted his head back. He ran his fingers through his beard. Oh?

Respect don't always come to all of us, the boy said. Some people who aren't respected have no one to help with their problems. Some people just plain don't have no handle on respect. Excuse me sir, but some people would just as soon knock their wives out as take dinner with them. It ain't that simple. If the world is as complicated as you say, so are the things that happen and don't happen in it. And when they don't happen or they happen wrong, who's there to say? Who's there to deal with it?

The boy's eyes fired and the mayor watched him with deference and caution. This is your opinion, he said flatly.

This is how I've seen it to be.

I see. Maybe so. But we must try and keep things in order. We must make some sort of order or else there is no cohesion between us. Rules are rules are rules and they come in many forms, but they all come for a reason. And that is to keep order. These rules, my rules, they must remain. As long as I remain, they must too.

So I can't know.

The mayor shifted in his chair, then pulled the shirt cuffs under his duster and stood. With respect, he said. No. You may not.

The candles faltered in their wax pools. Through the warbled light the boy looked at the mayor a moment longer, then rose and took up his hat.

Well.

Well, the mayor said. Go on to the festival. Be easy. You are young. You don't need to be spending your time with all these grave questions. Enjoy yourself. Though you may think otherwise, this is a fine town. And a fair one.

Yes sir. I guess I'll wait to see it.

The mayor pressed the boy with his eyes. Ah, he said. You will see.

The boy took one last look around the room. His eyes lingered on a glass caboose that stood molded in the blue light.

You like trains? the mayor asked him.

The boy was standing at the door now with his back to the room. He turned around.

I couldn't say. I never been.

The mayor folded his hands in front of his belt.

You know it is coming here, he said. The train. You will see how fine this town becomes very soon. Perhaps by then we will find some better work for you. Something to better suit you. But you see, the train, it is very exciting to me. It is what I imagine your horse is for you. It is like the child you do not have, the child who goes with you and loves you without condition and will never leave. But it is my way that is in advancement and yours that is in passing. We are not so different though, you and I. Only the pastures you wish to travel through are of grass and mine are of steel.

The mayor took off his spectacles and peered at the boy through the dim light.

It is no matter, though. How we go. Where we are going. There is only one thing you need remember. You will never become lost as long as you follow the straight tracks.

He made a slight bow to the boy, then turned back to his desk.

But you don't see the same things as when you follow the crooked ones.

The mayor half turned at the boy's voice. He paused there and straightened the papers on his desk.

Keep up the good work for me, he said.

The boy sat silently with the old man late into the night. He pulled to right the battered tines of a fork. The old man sipped at his cup. The moonlight collapsed half shorn from the clouds and onto the legs of the chairs they sat upon.

Eventually the boy rose from the table and walked to the door with a dead cigarette crushed between his teeth.

Don't pay them no nevermind, the old man said.

The boy turned. The old man got up and walked toward the stained tub, his delicate birdlike legs buckling under their own weight, as if salvaged from the wreckage of older bones yet.

They got their own designs.

ELEVEN

THE MEXICAN LEANING forward over his steering wheel as his truck bounced past the boy and down the lane rubbed a hand across his chin, perhaps pensive of what type of mind worked beneath the lowered hat and the dark squinted eyes. The boy went solemnly through the truck's dust and came down from his mare at the porch of the cantina. He had not slept at all the previous night and the slow roll and drop of the river which he had watched through the early morning hours seemed still to possess his eyes, as if those waters might carry him someplace far from where he now stood.

Through the storefront windows of Garrets he saw the two old men sitting at the bar, their figures warped in the glass. When he came through the door he tipped his hat up at them. One nodded. The other smiled ruefully and spat down between his legs. He sat in the back booth by the window and thumbed loose the wage envelope from his pocket. Miss Jane came swiftly to his table and thumped down a heavy mug in front of him.

Coffee?

Yes ma'am.

Thought so.

She turned away and the boy watched her shuffling into the kitchen. He made to call out to her but stopped himself and leaned over the adjacent booth and took up an ashtray. He lit a cigarette and set down the emptied envelope, working the few oily bills over and over again in his hands as though through repetition they might multiply. Though the money he had saved was still not enough to get him to Colorado, he knew, looking out the smoked glass of the cantina window now, that even if it was he could no longer leave.

Miss Jane returned after a while and he ordered honey ham with red-eye gravy. A radio hummed from behind the kitchen doors, its melody lost to him among the clatter of glasses and plates. He blew on his coffee and looked out at the plaza.

All about were the remains of the festival. Paper lamp casings lifted and slipped along the road. The remains of the hog-butchering pit lay in piles of pink slag. No one crossed the willow tree save a few Indian women who walked hunchbacked and stooped to pick up the crushed paper cups and empty bottles of beer.

Not long after his breakfast arrived, the doorbell chimed. A short squat man the boy had not seen before walked in and stopped still and looked furtively around the cantina. He was wearing a heavy flannel suit of brown. Beads of sweat balled up on his upper lip. A gold chain hung limp from his hip pocket. He wiped the dust from his glasses with a handkerchief he withdrew from his suit coat. When he pulled his glasses back behind his ears he caught the boy's eye. The boy lowered his head back down to the plate but the man had already begun to move toward his booth.

Do you mind if I sit down? He spoke with a gravel voice that did not seem to fit the sight of the man.

The boy looked around the cantina which was empty save the two old men at the bar. I don't guess, he said.

The man nodded with what seemed to be great pleasure and relief and lowered himself into the booth. He straightened his vest with his thick fingers and watched the boy nervously. The boy had begun eating and he kept his eyes on his plate.

I just arrived in town, the man huffed.

The boy looked at him a moment, then took up his coffee.

Where from? he said.

Connecticut.

The man righted his vest again and put his elbows on the table. He moved one hand over the other. The boy went on eating.

It's back East, the man muttered. Right around—

I know where it is.

You do. You do, of course.

The man glanced at the old men at the bar who met his gaze coolly. He turned back to the boy and pinched his nose where the bridge of his glasses had turned it purple.

Yes, he said. I'm a writer, you see.

A writer, the boy repeated.

Yes. Actually a reporter. A newspaper reporter. When I heard about your town here, I just decided right then and there to come out and do a story on it. They say it's going to be a western metropolis.

A what?

Oh yes. Well. A metropolis. It's like a big city.

The boy drank back the dregs of his coffee and motioned the waitress for another. I know what a metropolis is, he said. I just didn't hear ya.

Of course. So I hope to record how your town here grows. Have you a newspaper yet?

I couldn't say.

That's alright. I was planning to go to the town hall anyway. Got to meet the mayor, you know. He smiled meekly across the table. Meet the engine that drives the train, so to speak.

The boy spooned sugar into his fresh coffee. So to speak, he said.

My name is Trewitt, by the by. Thomas Trewitt.

The man reached his short flabby arm across the table. The boy looked up and stared at the soft little hand for a moment. He set down his spoon and they shook hands.

What kind of name is that? the boy said.

Oh. Yes. It's a pen name. It's my name for writing. Trewitt leaned back and looked nervously out the window. He was studying the boy's horse. You still ride horses out here too, he said. That's dandy. That's just dandy. The real West. Is he yours?

She. Yeah. She's mine.

Beautiful. Really beautiful.

The boy pushed his plate away and swung his mug up by the handle and sipped from it. Thanks, he said.

They have good fare here, do they?

It does the trick.

Trewitt giggled and put his hand over his mouth.

It does the trick. That's just dandy. Yes, that's the one. He nodded and pinched his nose again. That's just the one, he said.

The boy finished his coffee and inspected Trewitt who peered back at him from behind his small wire-rim glasses as if in great anticipation of what the boy would say next. The boy said nothing but only turned and looked out at the plaza. The Indian women were squatting once again beneath the willow tree and laying out their wares.

At last the boy gathered up his money and cigarettes and stood. Pleased to know you, he said.

Trewitt looked up at him and then around the cantina. He seemed unsure about what action to take next. Yes, yes, he said. Grand to have made your acquaintance. I'm sure I'll see you again. It's still just a town yet.

I wouldn't worry, the boy said. I'm pretty well sure when the engine gets done with it, it won't be a town no more.

He stood by the window with his hat cupped in his hand and his forehead pitched against the glass. When John Frank came in he turned around and put his hat back on.

How'd you get in here?

Door was open.

John Frank's hair was oily and standing on end and his shirt flap fell untucked from the rear like a tail. He rubbed his eyes and went and sat at his desk.

How was the dance?

There was dancin alright, Frank said. You should have come along.

You just gettin back?

John Frank licked his fingertips and matted his hair down with the palms of his hands. Yes sir, he said. And I ain't all the way here yet.

Find yourself any new friends?

I sure did cowboy. No one I'd know by name, but names don't always tell the tale, do they?

I don't know, the boy said. I don't know what tells what no more.

John Frank grimaced at the boy a moment, then slapped his hands and rubbed them together. You want some coffee? he said. Got a new brewin machine down the hall. You want some? I'll get it.

When John Frank came back the boy was sitting in the spare seat with his elbows on the desk and his head in his hands. Frank put the coffee in front of him and sat.

I put some sugar in it. Sugar, right? For the sweet one.

John Frank blew on his coffee. He leaned back in his chair and watched the boy who sat in the light that fell across the room from the window. After a while Frank said, You don't much like my drinkin and carryin on, do you.

The boy did not raise his eyes from his lap. No, he said. I guess I don't.

Your daddy was a drinker, wasn't he.

Yeah.

I thought it. It can tend to skip a generation on account of what the next of kin sees. My daddy was a drinkin man himself, but I guess I just took up after him. Course he probably wasn't the same man your daddy was on the drink. Not from what I can tell.

I'm sure you're right about that.

He messed you up when you was younger, didn't he.

The clouds came over the sky and the light drew away and the boy raised his head from his hands and looked vaguely out the window as though to turn his gaze that way was nothing more than a thing of function.

My mother said to me not long before she died that he could never settle on happy. I don't know if that's true, but it's the best way I've heard it said. And back home it'd been said quite a few ways.

John Frank stared down at the desk. It appeared he believed that to look upon the boy would be to betray him in some way. He still alive, your daddy? he asked.

I imagine so.

You run off from him then.

Yeah.

With your mama.

The boy took off his hat and pushed back his hair and set it atop his head again.

I guess I could never talk to him right is what it was, he said. People say when you got a problem with another you just need to talk at it and it'll go away. Well there's a lot more to it than that. Lots of ways to talk at something and lots of different results in them ways. I guess I just talked wrong. At least not the way I wanted to. But the stare he'd put upon you was enough to make cattle turn heel and run for pasture. The boy paused. He laughed without heart. I guess in a way I wanted to help him then, he said. But not no more. Truth of it is I hate him. Hate him worse than poison.

John Frank stayed his eyes on the desk. After a while he made a slight shrug of his shoulders. Well, he said. You got to remember, though. Blood's blood, same way dirt is dirt. You can't change it.

The boy shook his head slowly at the window. I don't know, he said. I don't know what's more in him. Blood or dirt.

You think he's huntin you?

No. At one point in time I thought he might keep comin after me, but not now. That's one face I know I'll not see again.

How can you be so sure of it?

I don't know. It's not that I believe he's quit the idea. But I imagine he's had lots of ideas in his days, just not too many he's seen through. Anyway, he never seemed to be a man to give too much thought to the past.

You tellin me you ain't even afraid for it?

The boy turned back from the window and looked at John Frank, then looked out the window again. I didn't say I wasn't afraid, he said. Just less afraid than before.

On his way back from the lawyer's house the sun clamored free to shine upon his dark and folded shape. His mare had come to a path of her own liking and the boy half guided her through the bramble while the horse snorted and footed her way to the old man's cabin.

When they came into the clearing by the river's edge he saw the old man sitting flat and nude just outside the water's current. He was holding a small pot in one hand and balancing himself upright with the other. He saw the boy coming. He smiled wide and toothlessly. The boy raised a hand and the old man grunted something as he poured a potful of water over his head. The boy dismounted and led his horse to the river and dropped the reins and let her down to drink.

What happened to you?

The old man tilted his head back and swept the pot of water over his hair again. I got too drunk's what happened, he said. I'm sobering myself back to health. Can't remember when I last bathed either. I reckon it was all and all a good venture to come down here. He wiped the water from his face and looked at the boy. And what about you? he said. Lookin like a bad check back to haunt me.

The boy kneeled down by the bank and sipped the river water from his cupped hand. He shrugged. A single bird called out from the forest's dark.

Whoowhee, the old man declared. I thought my legs numbed up for good that time. You'll have to start watchin over me, you hear? Keep me clear of the white devil.

The white devil?

The tub, boy.

The boy nearly put up a fist to him. I will not, he said. You're old enough to know what you need to be doin and what you ain't need to be doin. It ain't my fault you're wrecked.

The old man smiled demurely. Well you're still feisty at least, he said. You hungry?

No.

The boy leaned back into the high grass by the river's edge and the old man watched him a moment longer, then fell silent. He swanned his fingers through the water and seemed entranced by his white toes which bobbled before him.

The boy watched the light jog down the cut path of the river. He put his head back and his breath pacified and before long his eyelids slipped shut.

In the winding tunnels behind his eyes he watched her hair spiral downstream. Her face gleamed and rippled past in the sheets of water. Her eyes appeared crossed and backstitched to the muddy banks and he watched as his vision of them bloomed and crumbled, wondering vaguely if always and everywhere the world's body would be perishable. Then he heard his mother's voice coming once again from the deep forest, distant and resolute and rising and falling with the tumbling water. There were no words in her voice but he felt an emptiness there that he imagined she named Pity and it was abreast in her calling and nowhere was there a sense of redemption. Nowhere was there a sense that all could be whole, that all could be forgiven.

For a long hour neither the boy nor the old man spoke but only laid their heads back. When the boy woke the old man was still sitting in the water. His lips were smeared with the red juice of chokecherries and he smiled at the boy like a demented whore. The old man rose to his feet. He slicked back his few matted strands of hair with his pruned hands and wiped his face. Hungry now? he said.

Inside the cabin the old man cradled his legs into his coveralls and clasped the side buttons and rose and stood barefoot by the stove. The boy sat at the table and rolled a cigarette and watched the old man over a rusted timbal that held a seething parboiled mixture. The old man put a wooden spoon down and turned to the boy, his face ruddy and his eyes strangely healthy. The boy turned away from him to where the trees were blackening and growing stark in the night shadows and he regarded them with heavy eyes.

What's her name?

The boy turned back to the old man. Who's name? he said.

The girl. The old man picked up the wooden spoon and shook it at the boy. Old don't mean stupid, he said.

A breeze blew in from the empty windowpanes. The boy watched the cigarette smoke roll over his hand. I don't know, he said.

I'm supposin they ain't sayin neither.

No. They ain't.

But they takin my booze just the same.

The boy nodded. From the kettledrum the old man ladled out a chicken breast with one half of it hanging on by its pink skin. He set it on a wide tin platter and salted it and brought it to the table. He searched the shelving for plates and brought two forward with two knives and a pepper mill and sat across from the boy. He portioned their meal onto the plates and pushed one in front of the boy and pushed the pepper mill forward and the knife and one of the forks lying on the table.

Might as well eat up, he said. This chicken you bought don't look that bad after all.

The boy stubbed out his cigarette in the stone bowl by his elbow. Not long after they began eating the old man set his fork down. Did I ever tell you about Sisyphus?

He paused and waited for the boy to answer. When he said nothing the old man cleared his throat.

He was a king, Sisyphus was. King of Corinth. And he was much loved because he was a gentle man. A man whose powers came from his actions, not his words. Now one day Sisyphus, he was just walkin through his gardens, no reason to it really. Just walkin along, maybe havin a drink or maybe just plain old walkin. Wanderin the land.

The boy looked up. The old man pushed his plate aside. He folded his hands on the table.

Gone out there this particular day he's lookin up at the sky when this big old eagle comes a flappin out of nowheres. Now this wasn't no jay-hawk or bluebird type. This was the biggest, most mighty and fearsome bird the king ever did see. So this bird comes across the sky, glidin head-long toward an island not far off from them, but when it comes out of the sun's glare the king sees the bird clear and he knows right off he seen somethin he ain't supposed to. Now I bet you wonderin what it is.

The old man cut into his chicken and held up his fork.

What he sees is the fairest maiden his eyes ever known and she's caught in the eagle's claws. He seen her face beneath them great wings beatin the air and he seen her face stricken and then soon after they was both gone. Disappeared right into the wind. Like the sky opened up and they went through some unseen door. After that the king he tries to go on about his business but she keeps stealin into his mind. Commences thinkin about her all night and day. And not long after, when the king didn't know what he was to do about it, Asopus, he's what was called the river god, he comes ahollerin into the king's palace all teary-eyed. The king he wants to help Asopus, seein him so bad off. That's just the way he was. So he sits him down and Asopus goes on to tell him that his daughter's been taken, and what's worse is he suspects it was Zeus that did it.

The old man stopped and put his hand forward with his palm turned up as if to make the boy understand.

Zeus in the form of an eagle. Now when the king hears that, he knows he can't deny it. He seen it and he seen that it weren't no common lark that carried her. But Sisphyus was caught, you see, cause he knew what it was to go against a god. Especially Zeus. He knew that if he told Asopus they was headed off to that island, he would be punished by a hand greater and more cruel than any on earth. But because of that love he felt for the girl, because of the way she stayed with him, like she was a disease he'd caught, he told Asopus his story. Asopus, he don't know what to do neither, cause he knew about challengin the gods too. Especially Zeus. But the king helps Asopus resolve himself to it and he goes out huntin.

The old man made an expansive gesture, his bony arms and their black shadows like wings upon him.

The river god stretched his body all across the land but every time he come close to the island Zeus drives him back with his thunderbolts. Old Asopus, he never could get to her, no matter what force he called up from within. And when Zeus found out it was Sisyphus who told the girls' father where they'd stole off to, he was felled straight into Hades. He was cut down into Hades where he was punished on terms you could scarce imagine.

The old man leaned forward and put his eyes on the boy.

He was punished in Hades by havin to forever try and roll a rock up a hill which forever rolled back upon him.

The old man stayed still a long moment, his eyes wide upon the boy, then reached across the table and took up the boy's pouch of tobacco and began to roll a cigarette. The boy put his knife down on the table and looked out the window at the night's dark. I can't just quit her, he said. Besides. The mayor, he ain't no Zeus.

The old man lit the crooked cigarette he had rolled and jabbed toward the boy with it. No, he said. He ain't. He's small brass but around here small brass is all we got. But he don't quit neither. I'm tellin you, I know it.

The old man set the cigarette in the bowl and wrung his hands together like he was trying to work some history from them.

I known the man, he said. Known him from when he was just a pup. His family lived down by Las Cruces where I was workin masonry. Fore I came here. Then I came on and soon after he did. All growed up. He come from good folks but there's somethin about power can turn a man clear to stone. Can put his nose so high only the birds can see it. That's what happens. That's how it is with him. You know why he wears that beard, don't ya? Wears that beard to hide his face. And not just from other people. He wears it to hide it from himself.

The old man shook his head solemnly.

And it ain't just him neither, he went on. They's others to be named but there ain't no namin to be found. He's got ghosts workin behind him. Ghosts who also got the power but you'll never see them. Like that lawyer you go to. You seen him ever? No, you ain't. You said it to me yourself. And you won't. And the mayor knows it and he knows you know, just like everybody else knows. It's like workin against the devil. Or Zeus. The hardest kind of power to fight is the one you can't see.

The old man set his hands in his lap and looked across at the boy.

You'll not likely break him, son. He's got interests of the political nature. He's got Washington interests. He's got strong interests in the future. And to him the world affairs ain't the affairs of the world. They's the affairs of government and they's the affairs of his town and its progress. They ain't got nothin to do with us.

He held a trembling hand out toward the foothill dusk.

They ain't got nothin to do with this place, he said. Least of all to those who set in it.

The boy rubbed his hand over his head and shook it slowly. But he ain't rockhard, he said. Every man got a place where they can be broke. Or at least bent.

He's the highest power in that town, son. And he's had it from the get go. When you been swingin the hammer as long as he has, everythin starts to look like nails.

The boy turned again to the window and closed his eyes. I don't even know if she's down there anymore, he said. I don't even know her name.

Some things you got to let pass on. Some things you supposed to see and you supposed to want. Maybe even you supposed to need, but for one reason or another you ain't supposed to get em.

With the dark so heavy and the night grown so still, the boy was called back to the great sweeping horizon of the plains on which he once lived. His mind lapsed to a night he sat with his mother on the pasture fence of their ranch at dusk when she had told him that the place where the sun hits the land was not just the horizon but the place where the world sprang from. He remembered her eyes and that strange way she looked out at the pale and endless landscape with a longing so complete that he could not understand how it was that she was smiling. He recalled how she had then said that the place was where everyone strove to be, whether or not they knew it, for only there was the world without history, without name or need, without voice or hand that could steal one's freedom.

I just want to see her once more, he said. I just want to know why she's in that jailhouse if she is at all. Somebody's got to know. Somebody can tell me.

The old man sighed and flung his cigarette onto the floor.

Now listen, boy. You ain't got no cause to be this way. You just a boy. You ain't no goddamn god nor are you the mayor. Nor are you the hand that comes down to say right or wrong. You see what they doin down there? They don't want no problems. They got a new world comin to settle down there. They don't want some kid stirrin up things that'll slow em down. They ain't goin to let the people see that the town ain't no more than a bunch of half cowpoke half idjit country boys who come into a bit of money when they selled off their ranches. Don't you see that boy? Why don't you see that?

The boy looked down at his plate. The old man gazed out the window to where the boy had been looking.

Son, he said. This country here. This country here is gettin old and I'm just tryin to get old with it.

They sat. After a while the boy said, Somebody must know.

When he turned his eyes from the trees the old man saw the boy looking at him. A slackened stare without thought or feeling that almost frightened him.

Well then, he said, I don't know what all else to say. There ain't no reasonin with you. If I had to guess, you ought to be lookin in after that bar crowd. Them Ralston boys. I'm sure you know em. Them burly mustached brothers. They carry some kind of contract with the mayor. I'd say to sniff around them. They may know a thing or two. Only don't sniff too hard. They'll likely tear your nose clean off.

With that the old man began again to pick at his chicken. He sighed once more and set his fork aside and took up the plate and got up and set it untouched by the sink basin. I believe the appetite's gone out of me, he said.

The boy walked around the table to the old man and put a hand on his pallid shoulder and would have spoke but instead walked off out the door.

Hey boy.

The boy turned. He came back through the threshold and stood with the edge of the lantern light touching the tips of his boots and no more.

Just remember.

Remember what?

With one wind cometh another.

The boy smiled slightly. Is that the myth? he said.

The old man did not smile back. He turned away from the boy and picked up his cup and sidled over to the tub. No, he said, leaning over the edge of the tub and not looking back at the boy. That's the truth.

THERE HAD BEEN a rainfall in the lowland and the dirt path he rode was thick with mud. When he reached the thoroughfare he passed a few railyard workers still dressed in their work togs and leaning against a pickup truck and smoking wordlessly. Black viscous puddles lay like serpents in the undercarriages of the storefronts and the drip and splatter of gutter water broke apart the music coming from the bar. Fine rivulets of water ran wood-colored from the outcropping vigas he rode beneath and they fell upon the sleeves of his jacket. He shook them out as he went. In the near distance a woman was shouting at someone or something from her porch, her voice wildly rising and caving with the wind.

The boy got down from his horse and fanned the dew from his hat and hitched up his pants and hitched the mare at the porch rail and went up to the bar. He stepped aside to let a couple pass. The man tipped his hat at the boy and the woman looked down at her shoes and gripped the man's arm.

When the boy walked in he had to sweep his hand at the smoke-filled air to see his way. Railroad men with harrowed faces lined the bar. Many waved urgently at the barkeep's back, as if they longed to order some antidote for the burdens they carried in their mauled hands and dark blood. Around them women sidestepped unattended, their breasts plumping up against the crude field jackets of the men and their hands skillfully light upon their waists. Those who spoke to the women did so without turning from their tumblers of whiskey and in voices so low it seemed they were mouthing words they could not figure a way to bring from their throats.

The lively melody from the piano did not stir many of the men from the bar ledge. The boy walked slowly past the bar to the back of the room. He stood against the far wall and lit a cigarette and watched a quadrille swinging on the makeshift dance floor. The men who danced seemed to be inclined by some power outside their own reckoning.

When the song ended the boy heard a voice rise from the inset of the bar, a thin wire low note which he knew he had heard before. He moved around the dancers who were now breaking up with the men speaking desperately to the floor. He stood at the end of the bar. He saw the brown sleeve of Thomas Trewitt reaching out to take up a glass of whiskey.

John Barleycorn all around. Hey barkeep. Doctor. You hear me? A little sip for all my friends.

The boy came around, all eyes still on the bar or quietly studying the silver bottles on the shelving as if their own bones set out for display. He stood a distance behind Trewitt whose waistcoat was open and shirt untucked with his potbelly bulging from the belt cinch. Around him sat three tall men with identical handlebar mustaches whom he had seen before with John Frank and whom the old man named the Ralstons. All three watched Trewitt with malevolent amusement. Thomas Trewitt drew back the whiskey glass and caught the boy off guard when he whirled around from the bar and saw him standing there.

Hey, he called out. Another of my friends. I told you I'd see you again. Come on over here, young mister. Hey barkeep. Another for the young mister. That's the one. Oh yes. That's just the one.

The boy stayed his ground and only made a slight gesture of recognition with his lowered head. Thanks the same, he said. Nothin for me.

The boy could tell from Trewitt's eyes that he was drunk, and he looked at the boy and smiled vacantly. He shrugged and drank back the whiskey himself. Ohh, he shuddered. That's just the one.

One of the mustached brothers leaned over and took the tumbler from Trewitt's hand and finished the whiskey where he had not. None of the Ralstons paid the boy any mind, or if they did they made no sign of it. Trewitt turned away from the boy and leaned into the Ralstons' conversation, acting as if the transaction being made among them was of grave consequence.

So this old boy goes down to San Antone, one of the Ralstons was telling. In the middle of the goddamn summer with a fur coat on. Now he's drivin this stoled truck through Dallas with a fur and about two thousand dollars of jewels in the pockets. And expects he's just goin to drop right into town and give them over to this old fur buster and get paid.

The brother telling the story shook his head to suggest the impossibility of it.

Well, I'll tell you all. Them Texas rangers ain't no goddamn yearlings. They seen every scam in the book from the wetbacks tryin to cross the border. This old boy all of a sudden sees one of them rangers come riding out of the desert like he was just borned there. That's right. Comes pounding out onto the road and cuts across the path of the truck and starts after him a horseback. I mean to say he's tearin down the road chasin a goddamn truck. Now don't ask me how, cause I can't say. Alls I know is that he catches him.

Bullshit, one of the other brothers cried.

The one telling the story glanced at the other briefly. Oh he does, he replied with raised eyebrows. Oh hell yes. Catches him on the dead run not ten miles from San Antone. Damn fool even wrestled with the ranger, screamin that he'd bore them jewels out of a coal mine in Silver City. They done locked him up for the better part of his life. The way it came back to me was that by the time he got out he couldn't even remember why he was down in that damn city in the first place.

The boy watched Trewitt who seemed suddenly lucid by the gravity with which he took the story. All three brothers appeared equally stilled, their heads hung and slowly shaking.

After the story had settled Trewitt's eyes grew bright and scattered and he leaned up on the bar ledge. They're going to hang someone here, he said.

The Ralstons and the boy alike turned and faced Trewitt who took a small step back and looked about their faces apprehensively.

What?

Yes. They're going to hang someone right here, he said with resolution now. I heard it. To make an example for those who come to live here. To show that nothing will be tolerated that is outside the confines of the law or in direct opposition to the town's well-being.

Who told you that? one of the brothers said.

Trewitt offered up his chubby hands as if he could give no help. I just heard it, that's all. Someone in jail is going to hang at two months' end.

And who the hell is goin to hang?

That I do not know.

When they saw he had no more to say they turned back among themselves. Trewitt looked after them with a certain desperation in his eyes. And you know what else I heard? he said.

One of the brothers turned back to him.

No. What the hell else you know, fat man?

Trewitt leaned into the bar again. The boy stepped up behind his shoulder to better hear him above the piano which had begun to play again in the back of the room.

They have a Negro in there.

A nigger?

Trewitt nodded.

Here?

Yes sir.

Bullshit. Must be one of them half-breeds. A quadroon or whatever. Naw. That's bullshit.

No sir. Not a quadroon. Not bullshit. A Negro. And do you know what else? It's a girl.

A black girl, you're tellin us now? They don't tip the bottle much back wherever it is you come in from, do they.

Sir. No. It is a truth.

Where the hell is she from then?

I don't know.

They goin to hang her?

Well no. No, I don't imagine they'd do that.

What'd she do?

I believe she may be a thief. But this I am speculating on.

So they goin to hang her?

No. I don't know. I don't believe they do either.

They ought to hang her. Nigger girl stealin.

Naw. They got worse in there, Adel. They got Wingless James in there. I reckon they ought to kill a killer. It ain't reasonable.

I ain't talkin about reasonable, I'm talkin about right. I vote for the nigger girl.

It was the tallest brother who now spoke. He appeared to be the oldest of the three. He pulled at his mustache with his teeth and watched Trewitt.

How bout you, Mister Newspaper?

Thomas Trewitt turned to the boy in hope he might offer himself in relief. The boy stood unmoving with his hands clenched together behind his back and his eyes drained of color. Trewitt turned back to the Ralstons and gripped the collar at his fleshy throat.

Oh, I couldn't say. I don't know the details of it. I vote for the worst criminal, I suppose. The one who has done the worst to society.

So you vote for the nigger, right?

Oh well, yes. Well yes. I suppose.

Alright then. What say we raise em up?

The three brothers lofted their whiskey glasses above their heads and Trewitt watched them and followed.

To the nigger.

To the nigger.

Mister Newspaper?

Oh yes. To the Negro.

Put that glass down.

Thomas Trewitt turned and looked incredulously at the boy. He hesitated, then set the glass on the counter. The boy made to step up to the bar but stopped. Four other men who stood not far off were staring at him as if he were all the barroom held. They wore the same mustaches as the Ralstons, as though they were every one kindred to the same interminable bloodline. All of them, even as they upheld their glasses silently with the others, kept their stares upon him. And what the boy noticed first and above all was the shared rile in their eyes.

As he turned and walked toward the door he heard another toast float up above the piano and he heard the tumblers smacking wet and hot upon the bar top and the clipped laughter of Thomas Trewitt rising nervously above it all.

He stepped out into the crisp night air. The door slammed behind him and the piano fell muted and the laughter of Trewitt rang hollow through the walls. He mounted his horse and rode off toward the old man's cabin with the voice of the woman in the distance going on tirelessly and without answer as if maddened by the night.

TWELVE

HE FOUND THE Italian at the old nickelodeon on the south edge of town. Outside hung two posters flanking the blue iron doors which advertised Wallace Beery in *Old Ironsides*, and though they seemed to have been hanging there for a very long time, when the boy paid his quarter to the old woman behind the wire window and went past the concession of soda pop and black cows and paper cones filled with peanuts and walked through the brass turnstiles and into the screening room it was still the picture being shown.

A single shaft of light from the projection room came looming down the high darkened ceiling. Beyond its dusty silver glow the room was pitch dark and the boy steadied himself on the low velveteen chair backs as he descended the aisle. The air was hot and the room smelled of sweat, and from the vaulted balcony the boy could hear the dampened exchange of tongues and whispers and the dull whirling of the ceiling fans.

John Frank was sitting still and low in the fifth row with his arm stiffly placed around the shoulder of a young woman. His hand was raised to the back of her head and he was twirling his fingertips through her hair.

Hey.

Both John Frank and the girl jumped upright in their seats. The girl withdrew her hand from Frank's leg. The boy sat himself down next to them.

What the hell you doin here? John Frank brought his hand down from the girl's hair and pulled the lapels of his jacket across his breast as if to suppress some indiscretion beneath it. How'd you find me here?

Jane told me. At the cantina. Said you was on your way over here.

Well hell, John Frank whispered sharply, I know my company's the best thing goin around here but couldn't it wait until I was back in the office?

No. It couldn't.

Shit.

John Frank put his arm around the girl again and leaned back and pulled her gently in front of him. This here's Salva, he said. This is Trude. Apparently he don't want me to go off and have a good time without him.

The girl blushed and said a soft Howdy and the boy tipped his hat to her, then turned his eyes back to John Frank. I need to talk to you a minute, he said.

Well go on then.

I need to talk to you alone.

Frank shook his head. Ah hell, he said. Alright. Come on.

He kissed the girl lightly on the forehead and told her he would be right back. He and the boy rose and ducked their heads under the projector light and walked back up the steep aisle and slid into a side row near the back of the room. From where they sat they could hear the projector ticking out the frames over the actors' conversation. The light was so dim that all the boy could see of John Frank was his eyes and all Frank could see of the boy was the battered crown of his black Stetson hat.

What in God's green earth is this about? First girl I meet who's taken a genuine liking to me, and you got to come and bust it up.

Sorry about that but I got to ask you something.

The boy could see the slow shake of John Frank's head in the shadows and he saw his teeth shine brightly when he grinned.

She sure is something though, ain't she?

She is at that.

Damn straight. So what is this about you got to drag me away for?

The boy put his hands on the back of the chair in front of him and clenched the damp wood in his fingers. Well, he said. Say the mayor asks you to find something for him. Like some record of purchase or law. Where would you find something like that?

John Frank lowered his head and tried to look at the boy through the backlight. What the hell's goin on here? he said.

Just tell me.

John Frank hunched his shoulders and looked around and leaned toward the boy. Damn it. I want to know what's goin on first, he said. You come in here all lowdown and harried and asking me about law and papers and the mayor's business and such. Don't you reckon if I'm your bud you ought to tell me what it's about?

The boy looked off to the movie screen. The heroine was down on the ground with her arms wrapped around her chest and she was speaking into the sky but with what words he could not tell. He thought for a moment of the one and only time he had been to such a place, when his father had tore up the kitchen with a field hoe and his mother had whisked the boy silently into the open road and walked him into the town.

The feature they had seen pictured Tom Mix and his horse Tony and he remembered how for that long hour he had lost himself in a world as foreign to him as any of the others that he had read about in books, yet there was something in the actor's determined face and the way he held his elbows tight against his sides when he rode his horse onto the plains and into a gallop that had made the boy feel closer to him than he had ever felt to his own father. He remembered also how they had returned that evening to find the kitchen plates broken on the floor and his father gone and how for many days after when his father would leave the house he would close his eyes and make silent prayer that when he returned he would return on that shiny stallion and with those clear eyes of the hero that seemed to know always and everywhere the purpose of his travel and the treasure that was his long lost home.

They got a girl in there, he said finally.

In where?

In the jailhouse. They got a girl I know in the jailhouse down there.

John Frank squinted at the screen as though it might make clear for him what the boy was talking about. Some girl you know, he said. More of this jail business? What girl you know up here anyway?

Just a girl.

What girl?

A black girl.

John Frank turned back to the boy. You mean a Mexican?

No, I don't mean a Mexican. I mean a black girl.

A black girl? Where's she from that you know her?

I don't know.

Hellfire. You know her but you don't know her. Which is it?

I don't know. I guess it's both.

You are one stubborn sumbitch, you know that? And what the hell does some law records have to do with it?

They don't. But the jail records do.

And for what purpose?

To find out who she is exactly. Where she's from. The boy paused and looked over to where John Frank's girlfriend was sitting with her white-gloved hands folded in her lap and her head turned back up the aisles toward them. What her name is, he said.

Jesus Mary and Joseph. A black girl. John Frank shook his head again. I seen a bunch down by Albuquerque one time, he whispered. Out there workin on a ranch I was drivin by. But they was men. I ain't never seen a black girl out this way, or a woman for that matter. It's rough enough around these mountains for a man out here and I don't care what color he is.

Well, there's one here now. At least I think it.

I still can't see what you want me to do about it.

Why don't you start by telling me where such records could be found. I might be able to find something on her.

I wouldn't know nothin about the jailhouse, bud. I told you that. I'm not even allowed to go in. But I reckon if you want to find some papers, only place I know is the old refectory down the alley behind the town hall. That's where all the records I know about are kept. But that place is all bolted up with locks and drawbars and the like. And it's just a big old room stacked floor to ceiling with papers. I can't see how you'd find anything even if you could get in there, which you can't.

I reckon I got to try.

Try what?

Get myself in there. Locks are made to be broken, ain't they?

John Frank started up from his chair like he meant to unleash some prophecy upon the boy. He pressed the palms of his hands together. Then he sat again and began to speak rapidly through his teeth.

You can't do that, goddamn it. It's crazy. You can't.

I got to.

No. No you don't. You ain't goin to be stupid. I won't let you.

You won't let me what? You goin to arrest me yourself?

Well shit. No. But goddamn it, listen to me. They throw you in jail yourself if you get caught. Or worse even.

Jail ain't far off from where I stand now, the boy said, and walkin away ain't goin to help it. Seems to me all I've ever been around to see is endings. And I know that it ain't supposed to be that way. Not for nobody. I ain't sayin I deserve better but I'll be damned if I don't try for it. This girl. He raised his hands briefly, then let them fall. I'd just like to see the beginning of it, he said. That's all. I'd like to know how it is that something begins. That it could.

The boy leaned back in his chair. The movie was reaching its climax and a brooding anthem of heroics rumbled up the aisles. The boy put his head on the wooden chair back in front of him and held it there a moment before he sat up again and faced John Frank. They're goin to kill her, he said.

What the hell? Now how do you get to thinkin something like that? They ain't never killed no one here. That's downright ridiculous is what it is. And I can tell you as sure as we sit here now, if you try and break into that place in a week's time you'll be sitting in that jailhouse yourself.

I don't care about any of that. Didn't you hear what I said? They're goin to kill her.

Alright. They're goin to kill her. Which they ain't. But what you goin to do about it?

I don't know. But somethin. I'll do somethin.

The lights began to come up and the girl called out to John Frank. He put up a finger pleadingly and then turned back to the boy. In the white light the boy's face appeared suddenly very old and featureless and even his eyes seemed to have no fix about them but only a curious glass sheen.

John Frank put his hand upon the boy's shoulder, then took it down and looked at him. He raised both hands in apology.

I can't be a part of it, bud. I just can't.

I know it. I ain't askin you to. What I wanted to know you told me, and I thank you for it. I don't need nothin else.

They looked at each other in the bright and ugly light and at last the boy rose and tipped his hat. You best go on now, he said. Don't want to leave that peach all alone.

IN THE GENERAL store the boy bought a bag of oats for the horse and the mule and he bought a new razor and a blue cotton washcloth. He bought bread and a pound of cheese and five tins of sardines the old man had asked for. He bought a new pair of cufflinks fashioned from stones and displayed in a cracked fishbowl to replace the pair he had lost by his riverside camp and he bought a soda with his remaining dime. The old woman behind the counter carefully placed all of his purchases in a paper bag. She looked up at him each time she pushed an item into the bag and she offered him a soft smile from the leather jowls of her thin face. She took a very long time and seemed to be trying to place the boy in her memory.

Finally she tilted the bag upright and folded it over twice and held it out to him.

Aren't you the nice boy who came in and bought those sheets? she called out to him.

The boy, who had taken up the bag and was halfway out the door, stopped and turned back to her. Yes ma'am, he said. I think I am.

The cotton ones, right?

Yes ma'am. That's right.

Oh, how nice that is.

Ma'am?

I just find that to be sweet. Goin out to do the shoppin chores.

She wagged a long bony finger at him.

Your mother must be very proud.

Thirteen

IN THE NIGHT it grew very cold and he woke from a dream of the bears disbanding along a purple ridge and lumbering soundlessly into the knifing snow and after that he could sleep no more. He pushed off the bedroll that had gathered a light dusting of dew and pulled on his boots and rode out upon the foothills in the last hours before dawn. The moon was sickly and disfigured behind the clouds and the light it cast upon the earth was without substance.

Out on the mesa it was profoundly dark and the boy's horse lost her footing and went down on her front legs and pitched the boy into a gravel ditch from which he emerged bleeding above his left eye. The mare swung her head around and staggered up and stepped backward, panicking with her nose high in the gusts of wind and her eyes drained white and spooked on the boy.

The cut was deep and long across his eyebrow and he wiped the blood away from his face and ran a glove along the back of his trousers. He collected the reins and crawled out of the ditch and soothed the mare down and stroked her mane with his gloved hands and told her it wasn't her fault.

From where they stood the boy could see off to where the railroad tracks were forming out of the bleak horizon. Below them on the foothills the singed brown conifers were beginning to forest green. Just as he knew there would soon be skeins of dark weather and whorls of blue rain, he knew his own chance for setting out to Colorado would soon pass him by for another season if he did not hurry.

He went on riding long into the remaining night, up along the mesa above the edge of town and down into the mud slicks and crabgrass. Such sparse trees rose before him he took them to be corpses of trees, and soon he found himself galloping the road that stretched out to the lawyer's lone and silent home.

Though he had figured how to pop the lock on the docket with his knife, all he ever found was news about such things as the water table and a new car for the mayor. He had read fragments of a letter addressing the portioning and zoning of the lands and a bill being drafted that would tax the Indian women for using the space around the willow tree to sell their goods. He read about a number of business transactions and the purchase of pressing machines for a new metal company. He read countless figures that calculated earnings and percentages but never in his search did he find even a single word about the girl.

He slowed the horse at the gate and came down and drew up the latch quietly and stepped into the yard to find the house as he had found it every day. No hand seen through the window nor foot upon the floor. No voice left trailing in the wind, and no words that he could give to beseech it.

He went up to the window and wiped his sleeve across the hoary frost that had formed upon it and peered into the room. A chair and a standing lamp. A pale brown loveseat. An empty mantle. In the corner of the room a coatrack stood unadorned but for a single white shirt that hung from one of the wooden pegs. Below the collar was a golden chevron. There was an inscription upon it but the boy could not make it out. He ran his hand over his hair and walked around the house to where a cobblestone water well stood with its bucket creaking forlornly on the hook. There were no windows in the rear of the house and after a while he went back to his horse and swung his leg over her and swiped at the fresh blood on his cheekbone and walked out onto the cold hard road.

———————

Traveling back into the foothills he downstepped the backside of the mesa wall and trotted the horse into a gravel pass. In the distance a fire burned fiercely behind the timberline and crudely shaped tents worked themselves out of the firelight like broken fragments of some failed greater contraption.

He slowed the mare when he came upon the tents. Through the fire he could see to where a great many men sat crosslegged or stood crouching in gray-and-black overalls with gray blankets upon their shoulders. They were about twelve in number and all were talking at intervals and over one another though none raised their heads to any of the voices, as if speech were as trifling as scrubbing their hands.

The shadow of the mare fell long and dark upon the congregation and some of the men turned to the boy. He was wearing only his ranch jacket and undershirt and on his legs he wore his burlap-sack pants one leg of which was twisted inside the top of his boot and he wore no hat at all. His hair fell thick and stiff across his face from where he momentarily pushed it aside to better see them with his good eye.

Howdy.

The man who spoke out was of mild build and middle age and his own face was cut along the jawline.

Where you headed to at this hour? he called out.

He held a bottle of cutthroat whiskey in his hands which were cradled between his crouched haunches. On his left eye he wore a black leather patch and he nodded slightly at the boy as if to make kinship over the common ruination of their eyes.

The boy looked around at the tents and then at the fire and then at the man who spoke to him. He put his hand up to where his hat should have been, then put both hands down into his trouser pockets. I seen your fire, he said. I wasn't headed nowhere.

You look rightly bad off.

I'm alright.

None of the other men seemed to pay the boy any mind. The firelight danced upon their faces and spent itself, with the wind guiding it one dumbstruck face to the next. The man drew on his bottle and handed it to a bald man sitting beside him without ever looking at him. That so, he said.

He motioned the boy to a place across from him where another man had pushed back away from the fire and laid his head down and was now snoring indelicately with his legs curled into his chest.

I was about to commit myself to story. Set on down.

The boy did not agree but only let down the horse's lead rope and came and sat by.

My ears is too tired to listen to your jawin tonight. We was talkin about Roosevelt.

The bald man was small and wiry and the hand he held raised in protest had only a thumb and a pinky finger.

Ain't no more to say about Roosevelt, the first man said. The man hunts in his Sundays.

We ain't talkin about his Sundays.

Well, what I'm talkin about is if we goin to waste the last hours before we head back to the tracks, we ain't goin to waste em on somebody who wears his Sundays to sight a buck.

Let him go on, someone rasped from outside the firelight. Ain't a gun in Texas that'll stop him anyhow.

It just so happens I got myself such a gun.

Shut up Franklin, someone else said. You ain't got no gun.

Looking around the boy saw a deck of playing cards by one man's side and he saw the many bottles clenched in their hands. He saw that the fire was girded by spike irons that were toed out and rusted and he saw the sledge handles leaned against the tent posts and he knew the men to be railroaders come to bear witness to the mayor's new city.

No one asked him his name nor did they give theirs but only looked at him briefly, then looked back at the fire and drew on the bottles with hands as black as the liquor they drank. His eyes dark and low upon them, the boy himself seemed to be pondering why he had come to sit there and now what to do. He snapped off his gloves and felt around in his jacket pocket and brought forth a crumpled pack of cigarettes. One of the men offered a swig of his bottle in trade. The boy declined the bottle but gave the man a cigarette. He asked the man why they hadn't put up at the inn. The man only shook his head and said they weren't never allowed to stay the night but he did not say why.

Now what was I talkin about?

The man went down from his haunches and sat with his legs drawn out before the fire and his hands cupping the bottle on his belt buckle.

Diggin tracks, someone said.

That's right. Diggin tracks.

He turned the bottle down from his belt and tipped the nose of it across the fire at the boy. You ever seen a fire in the desert? he said.

Not this one again, someone called out. You don't never tell nothin but this.

The storyteller looked as though he'd been wounded and he balled his lips up at the man who had called out.

I ain't talkin to you no more.

Go to hell, someone else called.

I ain't talkin to you neither. I'm talkin to the boy.

I'm sure even he's heard it before.

For a moment he kept his working eye on the place from where the last slur had come, then turned back and looked across the fire to the boy. He had to tilt his head to ballast his sight which made it seem it was not only his eye he had lost but his equilibrium too.

You ever seen a fire in the desert, son?

No sir.

No. Not likely. Not likely any of you all have.

He looked around the fire defiantly. None of the men answered except one who was very drunk and all he said was, She ain't nothin but a two-dollar whore.

Exceptin William over there. He was with me.

The man he named William sat with his tattered blue hat pulled over his eyes and he raised his bottle gravely at the sound of his name, though he did not seem to know for what purpose it had been called.

We was with a crew down on California, the man went on. This was before the Chinamen come and brought the wage down. We'd meant to replace some track line been run thin by the heat but we ended up spendin most days that summer diggin tracks. I'll tell you that line didn't run but a fingernail into the desert. And I'll tell you another thing.

He stopped and took the bottle to his lips. He looked at the boy across the fire.

You get yourself a fire goin in the desert, you best send a telegram quick as you can to your next of kin. They talk about these steep-grade trains run up through the mountains bein most dangerous, but let me tell you son, you don't clear them tracks of sand and the train come on over them, step back. Even if the bumps would ride there's the hot coals from the furnace can bust open, and that's what this here story tells.

The man got up on his haunches again. Some of the men reclined onto their sides like the one whose boot was now pressed against the boy's back. The others stayed drinking and watching the fire, their shoulders slouched into their chests, their eyes so oblique and tamped they appeared to have been the subject of men's wrath as equally as the steel tracks they pounded.

There was a man down on the Pacific line back then by the name of Dupree. Fred Dupree. Was a coal shuttler. Was a friend of mine, too. Worked on that line since the first day they burned the tracks. One day his train was ridin down there by us. Time of year wasn't much different from what it is now, but down there you near inside of Mexico and this here month is the worst for the sandstorms. Way I remember it we was short on account of some paper mill openin up and takin three boys off the crew. We got put out to clear some track been blown over and they pushed us out there real fast because the 212, that was Dupree's train, the 212 wasn't receivin no messages off the line and the tracks was duned up bad.

Across the fire the boy smoked silently. The man sitting next to him nudged him for another cigarette. He shucked one from the pack and held it out. The storyteller stopped to watch this exchange and waited until it was over, then tilted his head again and went on.

So we was out there frantic diggin, still couldn't get no message over the wire to slow em down and that sand seemed to blow back over us two spadefuls for every one we throwed. And sure enough, before long that strand of smoke come spinnin up from the horizon. I always remember that. It was clear blue that day and all besides us men you could see was that pile of smoke come off the land like it meant to set the world afire. Now I ain't one for omens or witches' tales but that was the first day it come to me that the world ain't no more ours than it was that little wire of smoke driftin off to nothin.

The man held his bottle cupped before him and turned it slowly in his fingers as though considering its weight.

Well. There wasn't nothin we could do then but wave our arms, which we knew wouldn't make a damn, and watch it come on. And sure enough it come without the slightest touch of brake, come on like there weren't nothin that would stop it even in the span of forever. But it did stop. Made it about halfway up where the joints was laid under, then one of the couplers gave loose. Back end sort of groaned off to a stop, just sat there upright on the line. It was the front end that tipped. It'd slowed a good bit afore it went over and then even when it went over on its side the smoke kept pourin out of the hull like a child's windup. Didn't look to be that bad in the end at all. To tell it straight, only one passenger took hurt. Broke his ribs, maybe, I disremember.

The storyteller looked across the fire to where William sat with his eyes on the flames.

Broke his ribs?

Yeah, William whispered into the fire. Was his ribs.

Right. His ribs. Old Dupree, though.

The man set the bottle now nearly empty by his side and juggled it to stay upright. He looked after it a moment until he saw it wouldn't fall over. Then he looked across at the boy.

Old Dupree was in there loadin up them coals. The way it was said later was that he didn't break a single bone, but nobody could of rightly knowed that. Engine just went over on its side and Dupree he fell straight back against the engineer door, just alayin on his back. Stunned was all his trouble, I reckon. But that old iron door had broke off at the swing bar and come open. Come down on Dupree a whole armful of red coals. Right on his belly.

He paused and looked off into the distance. He seemed convinced that the scene he spoke of had been laid out for them on the black hills.

Time I got there he was lit up like a brush fire, he said. When he finally come crawlin out, he commenced to rollin around in the sand callin for water. Water, water, he was callin. Way a boy calls for his mother. And you couldn't of stove off the people comin from the rear of the train with their tumblers filled up. Twenty, thirty people, women too, all tippin them thimbles of water upon him. Was a portrait, it was. I've not seen its like since and I don't guess I ever will. All of us boys, we was froze. Just gawkin down at him. I even recollect stuffin my hands in my pockets. And I knowed that man more than ten year. I come to wonder what he was thinkin when he looked up to see us boys standin there like we was made of wood. Would have made him consider the nature of man, I reckon. Seein we was the only ones who knowed him by name and the only ones who weren't doin nothin for him. But standin in the middle of the desert there was these people all bent over Dupree, whose clothes had caught and was flamin on and on, and they was blowin on him. Damndest thing I ever did see. Callin at the flames to quit. But it was Dupree who quit first. When he'd finally stopped breathin them flames just went on lickin at his shirt collar where his neck had gone black and bony. Them flames goin on like it didn't make no difference he was already dead. Finally I looked over at William there and couldn't think of nothin to do but just come up on his body and put a boot hard on his chest. Time I was done stompin out the flames, Fred Dupree was as flat as the land he lay on.

The man took up his bottle and seemed he would speak more but he only slung back the dregs of the whiskey. At last he spoke again and as he did he kept his eye pitched down at the ground between his boots.

Only thing left of Dupree was his brown briefcase. Carried that briefcase to work every day. Strange thing it was. He was the only one. Nobody ever heard of no coal shuttler carryin a briefcase and we was forever ridin him about it. He was always congenial about it, though. Just smiled and didn't say nothin. When they brought it out of the furnace room it was more likely a snakeskin than anythin else. All burnt up and flaked to pieces. We laid it out on the ground and since I was the one put out the fire it came to pass that I was the one to open it. Them boys I was with were real curious to see about it, seein as we was always laughin and makin bets on what it held. Nobody laughed when they seen what was in it, though. The pictures was all curled around the edges but I knowed right off who it was on account I'd heard him talk about her once. The thing I didn't know was Fred had himself some kids, too. Three in number, all little ones. Two girls and a baby boy. I never even knowed it. And what was worse was nobody knew who they were or where they was. And I never did find them. I asked around but the man who'd hired him on those years ago had died himself, and there weren't no papers to show the way. In the end I throwed them pictures in the fire. I don't know why, but that was the only way it seemed right. Was the only way I could think to tell him we was sorry.

For a long time after, no one at the fire spoke. It was as if although they didn't seem be listening to the story, they knew that when it was over the only thing it was to be remarked upon with was their silence. The storyteller looked across the fire at the boy and when someone finally rose and walked off to the tents he asked him what he thought about all that.

I don't imagine there was much else you could've done for him, the boy said.

The man nodded his head slowly but said No, he didn't think there was either. But who could have? he said after a moment. Or what? I reckon there's a force for everythin. What force could've changed such a scene? There was a door and the fire it kept inside. Then that door opens. Just like that. Twenty years Fred Dupree worked that fire like he was feedin his own child. The one thing he'd built his livelihood around had become his death in a single instant. An open door. That's all it was. I think about that from time to time. And then there were other things could have been different, too. A stronger wind, maybe? A sudden rain? Faster hands? I imagine. I imagine them forces was out there too, could have come just as likely as the fire that did. But that door. That door was his. How does somethin you count on do you like that? Who owns that which you for so long thought had belonged to you? And where does it steal into your life? That's what I'm always wonderin. Every story got a beginnin and an end, but when you look close, what is it that makes them stories turn one way and not the other? What force is it lies behind that act?

I don't know, the boy said. I don't know that anyone does. I reckon all there is to do is try to make it go the way you see it should.

The man studied the boy for a long moment. His eye grew circumspect as if for the first time he was curious as to where the boy had come from to find them that night and why. At last he rose with a grunt and steadied himself with his hands on his knees.

One thing I learned that day, he said. Don't never bet on a man against nature. It ain't no fight he could make. The storyteller leaned down and took up his empty bottle and staggered back a few steps and pitched his head back up toward the lightening sky. It's goin to break soon, he said.

He pointed the bottle across the fire at the boy.

You go on and sit here as long as you like. Any of them boys wake up and ask you who you are, you just ask em the same. In the end the difference, well, it just don't make a damn.

The man turned from the ruined fire and flung the bottle into the trees and tromped back off through the crushed brown grass. The boy watched his tiny shadow fold into the dark. When the man reached the tent flaps he turned back to the boy who was still watching him.

Tell em you're Dupree's ghost, he called out in a drunken slur. Tell em you come back to put a burn on their souls.

THE FOLLOWING DAY brought a sky filled with threats of rain though none came. By the time the boy arrived at Garrets it was night and the sky had cleared. He went up the porch fingering the stitching where the old man had closed the gash with a hemming needle. His eye was swollen to nearly shut and when the old man had taken down the looking glass from above the sink basin and handed it to the boy, he had looked at it only briefly, but long enough to know that he still did not recognize the darkly creased face nor the glazed eyes he saw looking back at him.

John Frank was waiting for him in the backmost booth. He was leaning his head against the window frame when the boy walked in. He looked up and watched the boy as he slid into the booth.

You eat yet? the boy said.

Nope. Just waitin on you.

They both laid out their packs of cigarettes on the table. When the boy made to motion the waitress for coffee John Frank told him it was already coming. Miss Jane brought the handles of coffee and set them down on the table. She looked at the boy but he turned his head away from her. She put her hands on her hips. You boys ought to try drinkin some water sometime, she said.

John Frank ordered eggs and tortillas and a bowl of chili peppers and a plate of fried potatoes. The boy asked for two slices of mincemeat pie. The waitress nodded slowly and scratched it all down. Up in a shake, she said.

The boy lit a cigarette and blew smoke at the window which was fogging up with the heat from inside. Outside on the rim of the horizon the clouds were gathering up again. Listen bud, he said.

No. You listen to me.

John Frank straightened himself full and cleared his throat. It appeared he had suffered long preparation for what he now wanted to say.

Ever since yesterday I can't put my finger on what it is you're after exactly but all I know is that it don't make no sense. I walked down by the refectory today, bud. I figure you'd be lucky to get five minutes in that place before someone heard you. And that's if you could get in. There's people livin right beside it and they'd just as soon believe you was sneaking in their houses as anywhere else. Frank lit his own cigarette and pulled on it and set it down in the ashtray. Besides, he said. It ain't right.

The boy pointed across the table with the spoon he had been stirring his coffee with.

Don't even, he said. Don't even try to be sayin what's right and what ain't. I heard enough of that. He lowered the spoon and shook his head at his knees. I know I ain't no authority, he said. I know I ain't the mayor of this town. But I also know right or wrong ain't got nothin to do with me finding out about her.

John Frank glared back at him but said no more. Miss Jane came back and set the heavy blue plates on the table. The boy set the ashtray on the windowsill.

Let's eat, he said.

He took up his fork and cut into the pie. John Frank looked at him.

What happened to your eye anyway?

The boy swallowed. Fell off my horse, he said.

They remained quiet while they ate, watching out the window to where the night drifted slowly by. Now and again came the jar and clatter of gear shafts working down the road. A bell rang out from the kitchen window and Miss Jane rose from where she sat reading a newspaper and went through the doors. A voice called out in the plaza but there was no reply.

The boy pushed away his second piece of pie and took the ashtray down from the sill and set it in front of him and shook loose a cigarette and struck up a match. The smoke he exhaled rose blue and unbroken above the table. John Frank stopped picking at his potatoes and set down his fork and looked to where he had set it.

If it happens to turn bad, he said. If it happens you can't

He put his hands flat on the table and stared across at the boy.

If it happens you go to jail, I don't know what I can do for you. I mean, if the mayor sets his mind to it, I don't know my word would carry anything against it. Some things he don't pay much mind to. But when something grips him, it grips him like a vice. And if that happens then there ain't no one to change it.

The boy tried to smile but winced from his broken eye when his cheek went up. Don't worry about it, he said.

John Frank's face darkened. He frowned at the boy.

You in love with her? Is that what it is?

The boy's mouth froze half open. He leaned back and took up his cigarette and held it to his mouth but did not draw. Then he set it back in the ashtray and turned his face to the clouded window. I don't know, he said.

John Frank watched him. The lights in the cantina flickered dully from above the counter and fell pale and weak upon the table where they sat.

Yeah, he said at last. I guess I do.

But you don't even know her, John Frank pleaded. Not even her name. How you think you could tell something like that?

The boy fumbled with the remains of his cigarette then looked at it with annoyance and pushed it out in the ashtray.

I don't know. I ain't never known it before. I know how it's said. Warm feelings and dizzy in the head. Some kind of calm comin over you, but I ain't seen it. But the dreams. He spun the ashtray beneath his fingers. In the dreams, he said. Well. I seen her dyin, and I feared it. The boy let off the ashtray and made fists of his hands, then opened them again. Every time there's this great light pourin out of her, he said quietly. Then all of a sudden it just bleeds out. And I was scared for it. I guess that's how I know. I guess you know you love someone when you're afraid of them dyin.

The boy drew out another cigarette and lit it but did not take his eyes from the window. He looked out at the empty road as if it were something he had seen a thousand times and was condemned to look upon for a thousand more.

Well, John Frank said, I don't know nothin about that. What I do know is that I'd be damn sorry if you got put up. I know you're alone, and I know it may not seem it, but I ain't got that many myself.

I know it.

Well, just don't forget it, John Frank said. That's all I'm askin.

The boy turned from the window and a small sad grin drew across his face. His cheek shuddered and a long tear ran down from his bad eye. Forget your sack-of-shit person? he said. Never.

Fourteen

UNDER THE FIRST full moon of autumn the boy packed his saddlebag by the river. He packed the cotton rags the old man had given him to dampen the sound when he cracked the locks on the refectory door and he packed the two-foot iron bar he had pulled from the wreckage of an abandoned bridge downstream. He packed his bedroll up high on the mare's rump. He strapped a lantern at the concha of the saddle and tied it on with his mother's old lead rope. His hair which had grown long enough to sting his neck when he rode was now drawn back with a frayed piece of cottonweave he had cut from the same rope. The hat he still thought of as new was dirt-crusted and side-clefted from his constant fingering and it sat upon his head like a crushed bird.

At the door of the cabin the old man looked on quietly and without protest. He stood knobby-kneed and drunken with his hands working back and forth over his arms.

Once the boy had mounted Triften he walked her to the door and sat looking down at the old man. The old man asked the boy why he was prepared to give so much to someone he didn't even know and he asked him half seriously what it was that he himself got for putting the boy up. The boy worked the reins in his hands and the light from the moon was bright upon them and he said that for once he would get to see some justice in that town. Maybe not the kind writ in books, he said, but justice just the same.

When he got to the outskirts of town he dismounted by a thick cedarwood that stood alone in the scrub. He laid out his bedroll and pinned it down with some loose rocks. For a while he sat under the tree and turned the equipment over in his hands, gripping the iron bar in his fist.

Before he got up to his feet, two men came riding horseback on the road beneath him. As they came nearer he could hear them talking and saw that both stared ahead at the road. At first the boy thought they were arguing about a woman but then it was clear that it was a horse they spoke of and that one or the other had misplaced or wrongly sold her. When they came abreast of the boy he could see their heads bobbing sharply up and down, with their eyes still looking ahead and one man pointing and poking his cigarette toward the sky, and then they were gone down the road.

He walked into town with his horse trailing on her lead rope and quickly stepped into an alleyway that led back toward the refectory. He passed the squat adobe houses and he passed dimly lit rooms where shadows fell out of the windows and onto the road. Each sound caused the boy to stop and listen. A tick or rap or clutter of bush froze him and by the time he had arrived at the records building he was exhausted.

The refectory was long and low and without moonlight upon it, the red clay bricks of the door dull and dark as a stall gate. He walked the horse down the road a little farther, then came back and leaned against the wall and got his breath and let the saddlebag off his shoulder. He set it on the road. After a moment of looking out and listening with his hat cupped in his hand and held at his chest, the boy squatted down and untied the saddlebag.

The locks were three in number and he wedged the iron stake through the lock cuff and with his other hand held the rags over it. He leaned down with all his weight and when the lock finally cracked open he spun around and pressed his back to the door and sat on the road.

He pulled his hat lower as though it would better conceal him. He sat still and listened. Nothing came. When he'd broken the last lock he slid the cuffs off and set them in his saddlebag and sat against the door for a long while.

When he finally rose and pushed the door into the room he brought forth a single match from his breast pocket and lit it on his zipper. He put the match to the lantern and closed the door behind him. There before him stood a mountain of boxes and crates. Along the walls stacks of paper were packed into the shelving just as John Frank had told him. There were no light fixtures he could see and only one barred window, high in the back corner of the room, out of which the moonlight spilled so mildly it seemed only a different shade of dark.

He held the lantern by his neck and carefully stepped over the boxes and into the middle of the room. He turned and circled slowly round, each direction out of which he could not see any type of order. He took down his hat and wiped the beads of sweat from his forehead and wiped his hand across the leg of his trousers. He set the lantern on one of the high crates and got onto his knees and began to thumb through the papers in the box closest to him. With only one working eye it all seemed almost another language, tiny scribblings of red ink faded by the years and without clear notation as to what history they meant to keep. He worked quickly through the first row of boxes, most of which he could not decipher. He had allowed himself a half hour until he would have to leave for fear of being discovered and now that time had passed and he had not searched a third of the boxes on the floor.

He took up the lantern and straddled the row that stood in front of the shelves and began to flip through the papers. He went so fast now he barely made an effort to read them. A voice spun in from the plaza and the boy stood still. He listened as the voice grew harsh and he heard the Spanish inflections of it though he could not hear the words, and he waited a long time until it had fallen away. Then he went on furiously, his hands brought to such shaking he could not separate one page from the next. He let the papers he looked at fall to the floor and his arm swept others which he had not studied off the shelf. At last he came to a thick folder across which a great smearing of black ink spelled out the name Delilah. He stopped and squared it before him and held out the lantern and set it on the highest shelf and opened the folder.

There before him she lay. In bold letters at the top of the first page he read, Delilah Jones. Black girl. Brought to county July 7 on one count of theft. Rendered guilty and incarcerated. Held in #12 of county prison. Sentence pending.

He flipped the page. The same indecipherable scribblings appeared again and beneath them in typed letters were her height and weight and age and birth state but before he saw any of those things he was up and out the door with the lantern held up to his eyes as if to burn from them the words he had read.

He shut the door and stood with his back pressed to the wall. His breath pounded in his chest. He listened as it faded off, listening long and long into the black until all he heard was the sound of his feet clapping down the road and the rustling of the branches from the distant treetops which the moon held captive, bright like candles on the brown and barren hills.

Morning wind blew the boy awake at dawn. Triften stood tethered to the cedar tree with the lead rope twisted about the trunk. The boy looked up and saw her rubbing her nose in agitation against the bark and he shucked off the bedroll and sprang up and led her around the tree, speaking softly to her. When he had her standing free he stepped over the rocks and pulled on his boots and pushed his pant legs down, gripping his hands together to take away the trembling that had not stopped since he first read her name.

At Garrets he sat in a booth near the back, nodding to the barstools where sat the cigar smokers with Thomas Trewitt who held a wet rag to his head. No one else was in the cantina save Miss Jane who brought him coffee and an ashtray. The boy studied the old men at the bar to see if they knew anything of the night before. If they did, they did not show it but only smirked and nodded dully as Trewitt mumbled some fable of debauchery across the counter.

Early start this mornin, Miss Jane said.

Yes ma'am. He made a glancing gesture toward the bar. Looks like they found another to suit them, he said.

The waitress looked over at the bar and shook her head.

I prayed those two would be somehow split apart, but it looks like they've multiplied.

He ordered huevos machaca and two glasses of buttermilk and a stack of blue corn tortillas. The waitress penciled it down. She shook her head at the bar again, smiling back at the boy, then went away. The boy smoked and watched the men talking from the corner of his eye.

He ate very slowly. He moved the tortillas in his thick jaw and drank his coffee and out of his good eye watched the daylight streaming pale and cold and wintry across the hills, and he watched it intently as he had once done but had not for a very long time.

The sight he saw when he looked up again as Trewitt twisted in his stool and turned away from the bar made him put down his fork and stop chewing. High up on the lapel of his coat Thomas Trewitt wore the same golden chevron the boy had seen pinned to the shirt inside the lawyer's house. He swallowed hard. When Trewitt made to stand the boy set his money on the table and turned his head away until he heard the doorbell chime. When the door rang closed he rose and went out and followed him down the street.

Trewitt walked with his hands in his pockets and he whistled and bowed his head to the people he passed. The boy stayed at a distance until Trewitt turned down an alleyway and into the morning shadows. When he caught up to him the boy was in a full run, and before Trewitt could turn to see what was coming the boy had his shirt gripped at the throat. He spun him around by the shoulder and pushed him up against the west wall of the general store. Something like a shriek came out of Trewitt and the boy closed his hand over his mouth and stood up close to his face.

Who are you?

Trewitt's eyes were frantic, rolling back and forth like a wild horse's at its first sight of a rope. Newsman, he mumbled.

Where'd you get that pin?

Where'd I get what?

The boy gripped him tighter by the collar. The flab of his neck rolled out over the boy's finger. The goddamn pin, he said.

The mayor. The mayor gave it to me.

Trewitt's mouth was hot and wet under the boy's hand. The boy shook him violently. Trewitt's eyes welled up.

Are you the lawyer?

At this Trewitt's eyes blinked in confusion and he raised his head as much as he could from the wall. Who? he cried. What lawyer?

The mayor's lawyer.

Trewitt shook his head more emphatically now. The boy moved his hand from Trewitt's mouth to his throat.

I ain't afraid to do it, he said.

Trewitt's eyes were wild. His breath got caught in his throat and his neck fell limp in the boy's hand and he whined something about going home.

Oh Christ.

The boy dropped his hand and stepped back. Trewitt moaned and ran a hand over his reddened throat. Why the hell did you do that? he said.

You say the mayor gave you that pin?

Yes. Yes, that's what I said.

Why?

Trewitt shook his head and clenched at his throat. I don't know, he said. It's just an honorary thing. Part of the establishment, I suppose. He pulled the collar of his shirt down his chest and fanned it up and down. Look at me, he said. I'm supposed to meet the mayor in ten minutes. He looked up at the boy. You know what I could do?

The boy stepped closer to him again. What could you do? Kill me? Go on then.

You're crazy.

Tell me what the pin says.

It's Latin.

For what?

United we stand, Trewitt rasped.

Divided we fall, ain't that it?

No. Yes. That's it. But it just says the first part. Jesus, look at me. He swathed a hand across the sweat on his chest. What do you care about it to make you like this?

The boy looked down the road and shook his head. He pressed his fingers to his eyes. Then he looked off down the road again.

Trewitt peered up from his chest at the boy. You're in suspicion of something, he said.

The boy kept his back turned away. Forget it, he said.

Wait. Wait a minute, Trewitt called out. I know what you're after.

The boy stopped and came back and collared him again.

Hold on now, Trewitt said. Just hold on. I'm looking for the same thing you are.

Oh yeah? And what's that?

Well, you know. News.

The boy turned and started off again. Stories, he said. Stories is all you're lookin for.

Thomas Trewitt watched the boy walking away. Then he said, She shouldn't die.

Once more the boy stopped and turned. He looked at Trewitt. Then he made a jump step forward and took him by the neck.

Look, Trewitt wheezed. I know about the girl and I know about you. I could tell by what you said to me that night at the bar. The look on your face.

The boy tightened his grip on Trewitt but did not speak.

I won't say anything, the newsman throated. I swear it. I'm on your side. Now please. Let go of me a minute, will you?

The boy stared Trewitt in the eye, then let his hand down. Trewitt felt around his neck and took a step backward.

Why then? the boy said.

I don't know, Trewitt said, still fumbling with the shirt at his neck. There are many possibilities. I'm trying to find out but I cannot press him too hard or else I risk losing his faith in me. I have to be careful with him, you understand. The mayor is very good at guarding the happenings of this town.

The boy looked down the road again. I know it, he said.

Trewitt fanned out his shirt. Look, he said. I will say nothing about this to him. I will try and you will try. That's the best I can do.

The boy studied him a moment longer. Try, he said. Then he righted Trewitt's twisted collar and stepped away. Try.

He went up the road and into the town hall where he took up the papers from Molly who stared sullenly at him, then went down the hall to John Frank's office. Frank was standing by the window and frowning down at the road when the boy came in. He turned from the window and looked at the boy. The boy stood in the doorway, breathing heavily. John Frank went around and sat and kicked his feet up on the desk. He inspected the boy's shabby dress and his untamed hair and his hands which were clenched around the loops of his belt. He made his frown tighter. Why are you sweatin? he said. It's cold out there.

The boy only looked steadily at him and nodded.

You ain't done it, have you? John Frank swung his feet off the desk and sat upright. Jesus, he said.

Then I reckon nobody knows yet.

John Frank shook his head absently and with some bewilderment. No, no. I don't think, he said. It's not too often anyone goes in there. Maybe a few days. He folded his hands before him and leaned over them. So you got inside?

Yeah.

Did you

The boy nodded his head meaningfully before John Frank finished getting the words out.

Good lord.

The boy took his hands out of the belt loops and went and leaned down over the desk. She's in number twelve, he said.

Number twelve?

In the jailhouse. Number twelve. You know where it is from outside?

Christ on the cross. Let's see. Cell twelve. Well. I know that's the last one.

Frank rifled through his desk, still looking up at the boy from time to time and saying, If the mayor knew about this, and shaking his head. At last he brought forth a folded sheet of paper gone yellow around the edges. I don't know why I got this but I do.

He handed the paper across the desk to the boy. It was a layout of the prison.

Here it is, the boy said. He pushed the paper back at John Frank with his finger pressed down on it.

Yeah, Frank said. You got it. That's it, alright.

Does it have a window? That's a window right there ain't it?

John Frank looked at the paper, then up at the boy. He nodded his head very slightly. It is, he said.

On the north side.

Yes.

What's the guarding like?

171

Outside? Nothin, I don't think. Inside, of course. Ain't no way but that window if you was wantin to see her, which I reckon you'd already figured. You go around quiet enough, you just might make it. Frank shook his head at the window. Jesus, he said. But it'll be up high. Whole thing is built on a slope.

The boy studied the paper a moment longer and then folded it and pushed it into his back pocket. He held out his hand. John Frank took it circumspectly and frowned at the boy again. What are we shakin for, he said.

I got to go.

Stay on awhile, why don't you? I could tell you about Salva some more.

I got work to do.

Work can wait.

The boy smiled strangely at him, then walked to the window and leaned against the frame and looked out at the willow tree. Well, he said. I don't reckon she can. He paused and held his hands to the window glass and then he said, I'll go tonight.

Tonight? John Frank put both hands up. Bud, that ain't a good idea.

Why not?

Cause maybe they find out about it and be on the lookout. You ought to wait a while. A week or two at least.

I ain't waitin any longer, the boy said. Seems that's all I've ever been doin.

Then he hefted himself off the window frame and walked to the door and turned once more to John Frank who looked like he would argue it more, but the boy only shook his head to tell him not to waste his words.

Anything happens to me, he said, you'll know where to find me.

THAT AFTERNOON THE boy found the lawyer's house as absent as always. He rode swiftly back to the cabin and watered his horse and mule and fed them with oats he had bought at the general store. For a long while he sat by the river's edge while they drank. The cabin was silent and at length he got up and walked through the door to find the old man sleeping in one of the chairs with a single tooth straggling loose from his open mouth. The boy put his hand on his shoulder.

Hey. Hey now.

The old man's eyes blinked rapidly, then opened.

Ho.

The boy leaned into his brightly veined ear. Delilah, he said.

The old man opened his eyes wider and raised his eyebrows. Then he closed his eyes and smiled. Like the Bible, he muttered.

The boy looked after him a few seconds, then nodded and put his hand on his shoulder again and patted it and turned to go.

Hey, the old man coughed.

Yeah?

It's getting cold out there.

Yeah?

Best make yourself a fire.

He followed the old man's wishes and while the night came on the boy collected brush for kindling and he collected a few splintered one-by-threes from the old bridge and piled them near his camp. He straightened up his gear and tidied the saddlebags. For a while after he sat and thumbed over his mother's old saddle. He smoothed the cordings flat and caressed the swells and the crusted seat where she once sat. He leaned an elbow on the cantle and watched the river as it blackened with the coming night. He thought about his mother gone and for a moment he thought very clearly that she could not have been saved and he felt a great burden lifted from him.

From the saddlesack the boy removed his razor and he took with him a towel and a bar of soap and walked into the cold river. He undressed in the water and plunged his clothes and scrubbed them with the soap and plunged them again. He hung the heavy linens on a broken tree branch to dry in the wind and then returned to the water and washed himself and shaved blindly and came out of the water clean and naked. He stood still and shivering for a long time, looking up at the black stars pulsing atop the great plate of the western sky.

At last he slung his jacket over his shoulders and wrapped the towel around his waist and hepped back into the cabin. He heated a cup of coffee on the stove and set it in front of the old man who looked at the mug as if it were poison. Drink that, the boy said.

The old man took up the mug grudgingly and sipped at the rim. The boy sat across from him at the table and held his shivering arms across his chest.

Where's she at then? the old man said. This Delilah.

The boy gripped his arms, then let them down from his chest and onto the table. In the jailhouse, he said.

Mmm. That where you're headed, all duded up like that?

Yes sir. That's right. The boy looked out the window where the last of the sun had fallen away. You got any more stories for me before I go? he said.

No, I don't guess I do. You don't rightly listen anyway.

I listen.

Well. I don't know I got the strength right now.

Where do you get em from anyways?

They was given to me. Passed down by my daddy.

Where'd he get em from?

Him? I don't know. Alls I know is when my mama died we didn't hear no more from the Bible. I guess maybe he found more comfort in a whole bunch of gods than just that one. Maybe he saw our chances bettered by the numbers.

Have they been?

Been what?

Made better.

I don't rightly know that either. What's better? I guess I'm still happy to be alive, if that's what you mean to ask.

I don't see how you've made it all these years on your own, he said.

The old man raised his eyebrows.

Alone? Son, I was young at one point here myself. And I ain't alone. Even now.

I know it. I'm here.

I ain't talkin about you. I'm talkin about the space you occupyin. That chair your ass is sittin in. Was my daddy's. Built it out of ashwood. And the table too. I reckon I've spent half of all the years of my life at this table. I wish you could play it out like a picture, see the way things have altered. Nine presidents of this country has come and gone in this table's days. Soldiers from two different wars sat right here. Girls was courted here. My brothers and me all four sat here together. Two of them chairs is gone now, burnt for firewood in the winter of

'11. Them two brothers is gone too. And the other may as well be for all I know. Only this old dinin set's left. But they're all here. Here at this table. Here in this wood.

The boy set his hat right on his head and pushed his chair out and stood. I don't see the comfort in that, he said. Seems more like pain to me.

The old man drained the mug of coffee and shook his head woefully at it, his hands working over the table's grain as if to soothe away the years he saw there.

You're right about that, he said. He shook a finger at the boy's back as he went out the door. But what you think pain is, son? he called. Pain ain't nothin more than the memory of comfort.

By the time his clothes had dried it was past midnight. The late hours had brought a new showering of cloud and the boy gathered his clothes and dressed quickly. He blew the fire down and kicked it dead and drew back his hair behind his jacket and called out for his mare.

A wicked rain fell across the landscape in the last quarter mile of his descent. The raindrops popped off his hat and the mare snorted nervously until at last they crested the hard paving of the thoroughfare. The surrounding lights of the plaza were washed near to nothing in the rain. He looked down the road to where the bar stood but did not see anyone outside. For a moment he paused, looking around in all directions, then turned the horse up the north road to where the prison stood.

He put a hand up to the brim of his hat when the facade of the jailhouse came into sight. It towered above him in the rain, gray and sand-colored and without light. The vigas that were laid through were thick and black as steel. A hundred yards away he walked the horse to a terribly bent acacia on the side of the road. He stood the horse under the tree and withdrew the layout John Frank had given him and looked back and forth between the paper and the prison. Then he swung down off the mare and lifted his hat and pushed back his wet hair and hobbled the horse at the tree, telling her softly not to worry, not to worry for him at all.

He could see her hair coming down thickly off the crushed pallet where she lay. Through the barred window the raised ticking outlined the sad curve of her shoulder, and for a long while he stood breathing and watching her from the rain below.

The window was cut out of the clay several feet above his head. He watched her head shift in sleep. There was a light affixed to the outer wall of the prison in a white porcelain dome. The boy stood just out of its reach which had been greatly diminished by the black night, the spools of rain. He wiped the water from his face and began to whisper her name up the wall.

Though he could not see her moving he heard her breath, heavy and deep beneath the rain. Then from behind the window bars he saw her eyes. She was standing blankly and suddenly before him with her hands around the iron posts. Through the darkness he saw her eyes and her eyes only and they appeared to him like coal smote from the slate mountainside where he had first seen her, yet still they held that wheeling light.

Delilah, he called.

At last she looked down and saw him. She remained silent for a long minute and they watched each other through the cold sheets of rain. I know you, she whispered at last.

I know it.

For a moment she went away. Then she appeared at the bars with a piece of cloth held between her fingers. I know you, she said again. She extended her slim dark arm through the bars and held forth the cloth. It's your blood, she said.

He recognized the scrap of shirt as the one he was wearing when the Englishman had cut him.

I found it in the mountains, she said. After I saw you. After . . .

She paused and then recoiled her arm and did not go on.

What happened? he said.

Tell me your name, she said.

Trude. My name's Trude Mason.

Trude, she said. I didn't think . . .

She stopped again.

I know it, he said. But I am.

She lowered her head again and he could see her hair rustling through the bars.

How did you know my name?

I read it. On the jail papers. The ones that said you were a thief. What did you steal?

The girl lowered her head to the window again. The breath in her raised chest paused so long it seemed to the boy that it might never come down again.

A rake, she said at long last.

A rake?

She nodded. From one of the builders in town, she said.

He could tell by her lowered voice that she was beginning to cry. What for? he said.

She shook her head.

For my baby.

He recalled when he had seen her in the mountains. He remembered the river and the Englishman and the cloth bundle he held before him and the purple stain upon it.

Yes, he said. I remember.

I wanted to find her. Even though it was him that done it.

She began to sob. He watched her with his hands held at his sides.

But she's gone, she said. And here I am.

The rain kept coming and he raised his squinted eyes to where her head rested against the bars.

He killed her?

Yes.

That man you were with in the mountains?

Yes.

He was your lover?

She raised her head to him and looked down with a sudden pity in her eyes. No, she said. He was not.

But they put you in jail.

Yes, she said.

Where's he now?

I don't know. I woke up one morning and he was gone. Then two men came out and dragged me up and brought me down here. The night I saw you. I'm eighteen and in jail and forgotten.

The manner in which she spoke, so forthrightly and with such bitter clarity, seemed a thing of wonder to him. You ain't forgotten, he said.

The girl leaned her head against the bars again and outstretched her hand into the rain. Then the boy called out, loud and heedless, his voice like a child's again. It ain't over, he said. I'm goin to get you out. I promise. I got to.

I can't hope for you, Trude. She stood back from the window. Look at me, she said. I can't.

I hoped someday I'd know your name.

The girl breathed heavily and watched his eyes. The boy could hear her chest heave above the splattering rain.

Hope for it, he said. It's the one thing left I know.

Then he was quiet again. The rain slowed. After a few minutes it surged again with a loud ripping wind across the landscape.

I wanted to, he started, but stopped himself abruptly.

He wanted to tell her everything. He wanted to tell her about his mother and his father and he wanted to tell her about the mountains and the reason why he could not name but it was in him and he wanted only to tell her if he did nothing else ever. He wanted to tell her that he had dreams about her and her dying and he wanted to tell her that he loved her but when he opened his mouth he could say nothing at all.

You better go, she said.

I'm comin back.

No, she said. You can't.

Why?

She looked down at his face and spoke very softly to him now. Trude, she said. Look here at me. Who I am. In this place. I'm never comin out.

You are, he said. He spoke out louder. You are.

Her hands tightened around the bars and she called to him as he began to walk away. Trude. Please.

He turned back to her. Delilah, he said.

She crooked her long thin neck to the side and called back to him. Yes?

He looked up at her through the hissing rain and once more he spoke her name, then turned and was gone.

Fifteen

AFTER A LONG night of rain the boy leaned up and shed the wet flannel bedroll he had reclothed his camp with and sat facing the river with his arms wrapped around his knees. The river was fast and swollen and he watched it going by. He could hear the old man stumbling somewhere downstream. He was singing a song about a girl named Sadie. The sun was gone and the moon high and the morning winds blew his hair across his face and after a while he lowered his head to his chest and watched the white of his breath rise between his knees.

Many days had passed since he had seen her. He'd spent little time awake, and he rose from dreams he no longer wished to recall. She was locked away and there was nothing he could yet think to do.

He rode the papers out to the lawyer's house but no longer looked inside. He saw the Italian only twice and both times what passed between them was no more than a nod and once a sideways smile from the boy from which John Frank quickly turned away.

A few times he rode through the town, speaking briefly to those who would speak to him. New storefronts were going up and the foundation of the metal press he had read about was being laid behind the inn. Wagons and trucks wobbled into the thoroughfare loaded with machinery and foodstuff. Around the plaza women sat on porch fronts, ogling and putting their hands to their mouths when deliveries from the East brought crates of clothing from New York and Chicago and paving tools and pipelines for the engineers. Sounds of hammers and nails and the groan of saws moved across the town like echoes of voices from a land far off. On the occasion when the sky was clear, he could see the path of the railroad snaking along the mesa and down through the foothills and sometimes back at the cabin at night he could hear the rails being driven and sometimes in his dreams it was he who swung the mallet, heavy and lifeless upon the earth.

During the evenings he sat as he had always done, by the river, looking out at the great and dark expanse beyond. He thought often about his old wide dreams of Colorado. He imagined his mother awake before him and he thought about the land he had roamed in the days after her death. At times in the slash of wind and cloud he even conjured his father, his figure a mere shadow in the bleak and tired fields.

And then in the darkest hours, he rode the open country. She had made him love the night and all of its colors. The tree branches became silhouettes of her hair and the ripple of stream or brook became her eyes and all of the hard brittle stone beneath them her heart.

One night he took a high trail above the prison house and looked down. He could see the lights from the guards' quarters and he counted out the windows until he was sure he was looking at hers. He stayed there for over an hour, his hands folded tensely over the saddlehorn, looking down at the bars which in his heart felt not like bars of one window in one small jail but bars slammed down into the mortar of the world.

He sat on the porch steps of the general store and watched the road. The weather was coming down in great heaves from the mountains and the wind slushed through the streets and raised the dust around the legs of the townspeople. Beneath the willow tree a young girl wearing a heavy twill skirt that fanned out at her ankles was peering over a wooden box filled with silver rings and clap bracelets. All of the Indian women wore their hair long to the small of their backs and wound and braided in thick ropes and studded with beads. They circled around the girl very slowly, looking out into the distance as if it were the mountains themselves that were coming down and not simply the cold. The boy stared down at the steps and wondered where their men were. Their eyes reminded him of his own, as if they belonged to other scenes. As if the world they looked upon was not truly their own.

After a while he rose and went down the road and sat in his booth at Garrets and ate with his head down. He drank a mug of coffee. When he finished his eggs he leaned back to smoke. A car passed. Smoke and dirt blew up to obscure his view. A woman came stumbling out of the inn across the plaza. Her face was screwed up in anger. She spat onto the porch but seemed to be dancing all the way out. No one else appeared in the doorway save a small dark wren who settled down on the porch floor, then flew off when the woman spat again. The boy ground out his cigarette in the ashtray and rubbed his shoulder where the Englishman's knife had gone in and drank another cup of coffee.

Miss Jane came and sat across from him. She asked the boy if he was still staying up in the hills and wasn't it cold out there and was he still working with John Frank. She asked him if he had heard about the break-in at the records building and she asked him then and more quietly if he had heard about someone being hanged before the new year. On this last question the boy stopped and put down his mug and asked her civil as he could if she knew who it was, but she only shook her head and shrugged her shoulders and said she wished it wasn't nobody at all.

It don't seem right, she said. I mean, I can't imagine the mayor allowing something like that. He's such a gentleman. And such a soft voice.

The boy pushed away the ashtray with his matchbook and then pushed the matchbook into his shirt pocket. I wish the same, he said. But he wants the town a certain way, and if fearing it out of the people is the way he thinks to do it, I reckon he will. And I doubt when he does you'll hear that soft voice you come to expect.

He nodded to himself and closed his eyes briefly, as though he had just made clear what had been in his mind by speaking it aloud, then rose from the table. I got to get on, he said.

Miss Jane got up and put her hand on his shoulder.

No more coffee? You look bad tired, Trude.

Well, he said. I don't imagine there's enough coffee in all of New Mexico that would make me feel otherwise.

He went toward the bar as the last light went away. The sky he and his horse walked under was black and clear and cluttered with stars. He could feel the earth hardening beneath him and he knew the colder nights were coming soon.

John Frank was sitting at a table near the back of the bar. He was blowing smoke up at the ceiling and watching it spread and fade. The bar was nearly empty and there was no music.

What'll you have, the boy said. I'll buy it.

He took out his billfold from his back pocket and set it on the table.

John Frank looked up at the boy and quickly around the dark smoked room. He leaned across the table. What the hell's happening with you? he said.

Just leave it, the boy said.

Your hair don't look much more than a mop and your body the handle.

Just leave it. What do you want.

Frank tried not to smile but could not stop himself. His face was red and heavy under the eyes. Bourbon and ice, he said.

The boy sipped at his soda. Two of the mustached brothers lingered around the bar, bending over each other's shoulders like medieval monks in mute prayer. The cigar counter was locked back and a tattered flower-printed curtain was drawn across it. After some time John Frank straightened up in his chair.

Things ain't good, bud.

The boy turned back and looked at him. You don't have to tell me, he said.

The mayor won't cut this one loose.

I didn't expect he would.

He knows about the break-in.

I heard it.

But it's worse than that.

How?

I heard him talkin about the girl. The black girl. I heard it said she's too pretty for her kind. Seems some of them boys like them up at the bar right now think she's a witch or something. I imagine it's the same one.

Delilah.

Yeah. That must be her. I also heard him talkin to that fat newsman. Talkin about layin down the law the right way so when the town gets under way there won't be no questions as to who runs the place. Said he'd have to put his foot down soon or else there'd be no place left for him to stand.

Well now, the boy said heatedly, why don't you just go ahead and tell me what you're tryin to say.

John Frank pressed his thumbs together and kept his eyes on them. Then he said, She may be the one they'll hang. He spread his thumbs apart. Then again, I heard the one who broke into the records building would be the one that goes.

They can't do that. Not either way. There's laws in this country.

John Frank shook his head very slowly.

Have you looked around at all? he said. Have you? There ain't even no courthouse here, Trude. Ain't no judge. The one judge that was here was sent up for undoin some girl. And you know who her mother was? The mayor's cousin is who. I believe that right there about says it all when it comes to what's allowed in this town and who says it is or isn't. Law in this country? Not here, he said. Not in this country.

They goin to hang her. I knew it anyway.

I think you ought to get out of here, cowboy. For a while at least.

Out of where?

Where? What do you mean where? Out of town. Do like you was goin to anyway. I hate to say it or see it happen, but I got to advise you to go on to Colorado.

Now you're my adviser? The boy waved a hand across the table. Well, I can't.

John Frank leaned into the table. You're a damn fool, he said.

I ain't goin to try to explain it again to you.

Alright then, bud. But you're goin to have to quit tellin me about what you plan to do. I mean, I don't reckon I can be a part of it anymore. Really this time. It's too goddamn tight now. And I wouldn't go quietly like I imagine you would. I'm not like you. You understand that.

The boy nodded at the table.

I just don't know what would happen were it to come down to you and me and no place left to hide. I'm not sayin I'd hamstring you. I'm only sayin that jail ain't for me and I don't think I could take it.

I'm made for jail? Is that what you mean to say?

No. I don't mean that.

And she ain't neither.

All I'm sayin is you might could handle it better. Maybe not the walls so much, but the silence.

They sat. Across the bar two of the Ralstons were pinching their mustaches and speaking under their breath to each other. Then they walked to a table where three Mexicans were reeling from drink with their arms slung over the backs of their chairs and their heads slumped onto their shoulders. A few words passed between the five men. The Mexicans' faces reddened and their hands came off the chair backs and onto their laps and then onto the table. One of them stood but sat back quickly when one of the brothers stepped back and drew open his coat to reveal the two pistols in his belt. The Mexicans stared at them a moment, their eyes red and wide with the bewilderment of the drunk. The Ralstons smiled down at the table and the Mexicans one by one rose and stumbled back from the table and filed out. The brothers watched them pass, pressing their faces close to the Mexicans'. When they were gone the Ralston brothers leaned down into the chairs and pushed back the flaps of their coats. They smiled at each other and one of them called for the waitress.

John Frank watched the boy who was watching the scene.

See, he said. Boys like them. They're made for it but they'll never go. Too many of em. And they ain't all dumb, neither. They always side with the mayor. And if they don't, they always seem to reach an agreement. Hell, he said. It ain't like I'm sayin we can't talk no more.

The boy gave a dry smile across the table. Yes you are, he said.

John Frank shook his head at the floor. For a while at least. He rapped his fist against the edge of the table. Sumbitch, he said.

Don't worry about it. It'll be good yet.

Frank downcast his eyes. The boy laid two coins on the table and slid out of his chair. John Frank reached out across the table and took the boy's arm and made him sit again.

One more thing, he said. Them fellas over there.

The boy glanced over at the Ralstons who were turning back tumblers of whiskey and eyeing him over the rims of their glasses.

I don't think they like you too much.

SIXTEEN

COLD AND DARK as it was within the austere gray walls, cold as the rapping of the wine-colored club across the bars of the cell, the girl stood in the dull blue shirtsleeves she had been issued with her hands limp over her pelvis, and even when the key clanked and the lock ran out she did not raise them across her breast but stood silent and without expression until a guard called her out into the hall. One of the two guards who attended to her clamped a pair of rusted handcuffs on her wrists and looked her briefly in the eyes before calling her to walk again.

Twin bulbs lit the narrow corridor she stepped into. Their poor light fell in flat ovals upon the limestone floor. She walked slowly beneath them. She wore the same plain shirt-and-pant outfit as the men and on her feet she wore a brown pair of woolen slippers. The only things left to her keeping were a bloody old rag and a creased photograph of the ocean, which she held pressed to the hollow of her slender throat and had thrashed for and bit hands to protect like a madwoman risen from sleep to in her unformed state between wake and dream reproach the world tenfold.

The guards held her at the elbows. They tugged her along not gently and each in turn eyed her breasts. They led her through a door to another hall of cells where figures rose with the sound of the unlatched lock and stood at their bars and looked out faceless and shadowed and hissed and made catcalls and reached their hands through the bars. One even called her name. But never did the girl turn nor speak nor did she change face, but only went on with her elbows like wings before her and her lips slightly parted to make room for her scattered breath.

They went through another door. One of the guards turned her to the left and through yet another door with his arm across her breast. He held his hand there a moment and smiled viciously at her and pushed her into a room where a small wheel of light spun from a tiny window above and painted the shabby table and chairs and davenport. The guard shut the door and she turned and looked at it. She stood motionless in the room for a long time and regarded the window and the patch of sky it held. Her hair spilled over her smooth face, her black skin made whiter by the cold.

After a while the door opened again and a man came in the room. He studied the girl briefly but intensely with his hand still on the outer knob, then he turned back to the door and closed it and stepped into the room and sat on the olive-green davenport. He rested one hand in his lap and the other on the torn arm of the sofa. She watched him with widened eyes.

The man wore a beige suit and black loafers and he wore a knot of black silk in his breast pocket and his dark brown hair was slicked straight back. He reached inside his suit coat and kept his eyes on the girl and withdrew a pipe and a gold snuffbox. He set the snuffbox on his lap and took a pinch of tobacco from it and thumbed it into the pipe chamber. Still looking at the girl he asked her was she cold, but she said she was not.

He raised the pipe to his dainty lips and from the snuffbox brought forth a gold lighter and began to pull on the pipe. Between puffs he asked her if she thought things could be different than how they were but she only lowered her head away from the window and said No, she did not. She said they never were.

The pipe he smoked had a brown lacquer with a stilettoed mouth-piece and he pulled out thin jets of white smoke that rose from his ruby lips and passed over his face.

I see you are still holding on to old memories, he said.

The girl looked down at the photograph in her hands. Yes, she said. I am.

The man tilted back his head. You are far from home now, he said. And do not think you will return again.

The girl kept her head lowered but did not speak.

Very well then, the man said. Perhaps it is better that way after all, because we all know how empty memories can be. The eyes behind the drifting smoke regarded the girl more seriously now. Sit down, he said. Sit down here. There is no such comfort in your cell. You may as well take it now.

The girl brought her hands together and looked at her wrist. The man raised his eyebrows at her and stood and walked across the room to her with a slight slouch in his shoulder that made him look like some infirm country gentleman. He reached in his pocket and took out a ring of keys and fiddled with them and finally released her from the handcuffs and tossed them on the table.

Better?

She did not say if it was better or not. She wrung her hands over the bones of her wrists and stepped back quickly when the man's own hand went up to her hair. He let his hand down as though she had caused him some grave disappointment. Then he drew on his pipe and blew a soft stream of smoke across her face and told her again to sit down. She raised her eyes to his and he smiled painfully at her and at last she stepped across the room and sat on the edge of the davenport with her knees together. She pushed her hair behind her ears and cast her eyes into her lap. The man straightened his shirt collar and leaned back against the table that stood before the davenport and folded his arms and faced her.

I don't have to tell you how stupid you have been, he said. How thoughtless. His hands went out and his brow tightened and his unanimated eyes squinted, and then he pressed his fingers against his chest and held them there. How thoughtless of me.

The girl composed her hands in her lap again and still she did not speak.

Silence, he said. Always silence with you. He let his hands down. Just like your mother. You are no different.

He lowered his head to try to meet her eyes. He grinned at her.

Silence to the end, he said. But don't think I don't know you. Your silence does not fool me. Were I to let you walk away from here today, you would go right back to the river. You would walk right into the mountains and all the way there you would call out my name in accusation. You would plead against me. No matter how fruitless you know it would be. Isn't that right, princess?

He tilted his head lower and his grin grew both wider and more malicious.

That's what your mother called you, isn't it? Your mother the whore. Princess? You would point and scream out against me.

Down from the window the light fell over the girl's dark hair and onto her lap and she could hear the rain beginning to slap against the walls and she further lowered her head into her chest to hide herself from the light.

Yes, she said quietly. Yes, I would.

The man raised up at the waist and stood and watched her a moment with the pipe held just off his lips. Then he began to pace the darkening room.

Not even able to lie, he said. Not even able to try. You are so noble, do you know that?

His mouth tightened and he spoke to her through his teeth.

So noble indeed. Did I not take care of you? Did I not bring you away with me? All of that poverty and hate. All of that unfortunate death among your family. And still you remain righteous. To me. Even to me. As if you had any right to it. You do not have a right to such a thing. You never have. With or without me.

He paused and for the first time he looked almost longingly upon her, yet even in his longing there seemed to be a disgust for the small shivering figure before him. He crossed the room again and sat very close to her on the davenport and spoke into her ear.

Are you thinking you will be saved? That you will be avenged? Ah, of course you are. I can hear it in your silence. I can see the act in your mind. Perhaps the little boy on his little horse and their country ruggedness.

He studied the profile of her face for any movement but she only turned away from him, the slim bone of her cheek caught in the yellow light. The man put a finger to the bone, a small slow wanting gesture that ran coldly through her fragile body.

The child was not possible, he whispered to her. In this world or any other.

The sudden movement of the girl's head made the man pull back from her ear and she looked directly at him now and her eyes were full of dark fire.

What world is this, then? she said. Yours? She lowered her head again and all sharpness in her features fell away. Yes, she said more quietly now but with the same determination. Yours. Not mine. And I never wanted it either.

The man drew on his pipe. Purposefully. As if to once again right his strict demeanor. Then he leaned forward and slammed it down on the table with a loud clack. The ashes spilled over onto the floor and he watched them for a moment. Then he faced the girl and took her head roughly in his hands and turned her to his pale green eyes.

And so it will be that way, he said.

He held her gaze for a long moment, though her watery eyes looked so deeply past him they seemed not even upon the wall but even farther to where the rain was hailing down from the clouded night. At last he clenched his small palm over her face, as though to hold it or perhaps to obliterate it from his sight. Then he rose and took up his pipe and walked to the door and rearranged his suit coat and breathed deeply and smiled benignly at her.

Just like your mother, he said.

Then turned the knob and went out and did not look back again.

She sat as she had before, with her hands folded in her lap. She listened to the rain pelting off the tiny window ledge and she heard the Englishman calling for the guards to take her away and she thought of the boy out in the world who had seemed as helpless and alien there as she was, and finally she raised the photograph in both hands and pressed her mouth to it as the door opened again, the tiny pulse of his name running out from her cold and bloodless lips.

THE FIGURE THAT lay beside his camp was curled fetuslike by a weak fire. In the dim light the boy saw the gaps where the old man's teeth had been and he shook his head to himself and came down and hobbled the mare by his mule and fed them both from a fresh bag of oats he had bought.

A metal cup tipped from the fingers of the old man's outstretched left hand. All of the liquor had dribbled onto the earth. His meager legs poked out from the boy's flannel blanket. The boy sat himself down and rolled a cigarette and smoked and watched the old man's face until he opened his eyes. He moaned and rolled over.

What you doin boy?

You still sick from yesterday?

No sir, the old man said. Still drunk.

He shifted again and rolled to face the boy and regarded him. He sat up and held the blanket over his chest like a prudent maiden. That old mule of yours has still got some leg, he said.

Yes sir. I hope he does.

Got me upriver to where them good berries are yet to be had.

Yes sir. You want me to bring you some coffee?

No, no. I'm all filled up with liquids. He grinned toothlessly at the boy. I ain't the same I used to be, he said. Used to call me the Lake, you know. Back when I was in the business. When I got out they said it was on account I drank up all my profits. He whisked his hand over his nose and stopped grinning. Besides, he said. That damn slag smell been creepin up from the tableland. Railroad getting close enough so's to set the cabin to rumblin once the train gets put up.

How about some of that chicken you never touched then?

No son. I don't need nothin. I was just watchin the river go by. Must of dozed off.

The old man rubbed his eyes with his swollen knuckles. Lots you can see from the river, you know, he said.

The boy poked at the fire with a cherry branch. Like what, he said.

The old man patted down the blanket and drew it high up on his chest again, and then leaned back and looked into the sky. Did it rain? he said.

Yes sir. I think a bit.

Well hell.

The old man shook the blanket out but he only raised a few drops which fell back upon the blanket again. He looked off behind them at the river. The river, he said. I guess what you see from it is dependin on how you look at it. He paused and coughed violently. He spat a thick yellow yolk into the fire. Some say you can see the way time moves by watchin it go by. Others say what you can see is power when it goes by.

I imagine you got your own opinion about it, the boy said. So which is it?

The old man screwed up his face. Both, he said. But I don't put much stock in neither of them. Them's the easy ways to look at it. I think the river be showin a person the way his mind's supposed to work.

The boy buttoned his jacket to the neck. The old man watched him and picked at his teeth and straightened up again and bent a finger to the fluid black current behind them.

You ain't never seen a river stop and think too long about nothin. It don't never twist and squirrel around what lays in its path, exceptin when the thing is too big to go rightly through it. Then it goes around. Gently. But otherwise it just goes and keeps goin. Over and under and through all things again like there ain't no need to lay mind to it. Like it knows they's always to be there at some point. There ain't no dallyin for the river, you see. No steppin back to observe. Just pure flowin and goin and never thinkin twice.

The old man nodded his head thoughtfully, his face a cave of shadows in the firelight.

That'd be what gets me most about it. Never lookin back and never steppin aside but always comin out changed in some way. But never worried about them changes. Like it knows they's to come. It may look the same to us. Out here. The first thing a man's most likely to think lookin on a river is that it don't never change. But it does. It sure does.

He eyed the boy across the fire purposefully.

Cause you know son, you can't never step in the same river twice. The old man's face twisted into a strangely youthful grin. I reckon the river's got the finest mind there is, he said. The most peaceful at least. You don't believe me, go on and look for yourself.

The boy eased back and turned so they both regarded the river that was flickering brightly in the new moon glow. The boy watched it dance past. Trying to follow one strain of water all the way to the eye's end but each time he tried he lost it among all of the other waters. Soon he grew weary and turned back to the fire and stoked it with the cherry branch. The old man watched the boy move the charred stick through the embers.

You know, boy. You don't got to live like this.

Live like what?

The old man made a gesture with his hands across the campfire. They got easier ways of livin now, he said. Get yourself a nice room. Hot water from the taps stead of haulin it up from the river like we always have to be doin out here. Electrical lamp on your bed stand. Get a nice suit like you see in them papers. Ride the girls around in a pretty car. They don't make your ass hurt no more than a horse and they go a hell of a lot faster.

You don't believe that.

Well. The old man paused. He shook his head with a look that seemed to be gathering some grim recognition of an idea long pondered. It's a new time, boy. It is. Has been for a while now. What I want to know is why you still livin in mine.

The boy looked into the river, then turned back to the fire again. His eyes hovered above the flames like clouds of blue smoke. Not where I come from, he said. What I known. It ain't what I was born to. Not like this town. Couple ranchers had their trucks to ride to the auction pens. A few bars and a general and a hotel. A post office. Five-and-dime, and that's it. Rancher named Larry Bowles cut everybody's hair. Even the missus. Besides. You said it yourself. They got it all wrong down there.

The old man nodded at him. For a moment he seemed he would press on but he did not. They listened to the wind and looked out at the bent timberline on the mesa and the grackles that shot from bush to grass and they listened to the voice of the river beneath it all.

Look at them stars, the old man said after a while.

They look far off, the boy said.

Reminds me of my favorite myth. Bout a girl named Callisto. You got an ear for it, boy?

The boy looked down at the river, then up at the stars again. Yes, he said. I reckon I do.

The old man thrust his head back and breathed deeply in that same manner he always did when about to recite his stories. He pushed away the strands of hair that the wind blew over his gray eyes.

She was the daughter of a king named Lycaon.

They was in plenty back then. Yes. Lycaon weren't the good man Sisyphus was. But like Sisyphus he ended up bad off in the end.

They always seem to.

But it wasn't straight him this time. The punishment not only went on him but went down to his daughter, too. Callisto. And that punishment I ain't even sure how to figure on yet and I thought it around many a time.

The old man scratched his arms beneath the blanket and squeezed them tight against the cold. Lycaon did one of the worst things a man could do in the days of the gods, he said.

Crossed Zeus, I imagine.

The old man grinned at him.

You're catchin on, boy. Zeus came to dinner with Lycaon one night. No small thing for a mortal. In fact, was about the biggest thing a man could hope for in them days. But what does Lycaon do when the great Zeus is guest at his home? Serves him up a sup of human flesh, that's what.

So Zeus kills him.

No. No, he doesn't.

The old man peered through the fire and pointed a finger at the boy.

He turned him into a wolf for his wickedness. Sent him out to roam the world and hunt each day and night for food to fill himself with.

The old man was silent for a moment. He gazed into the fire as though the structure of the story were taking root there.

Later on now, Zeus falls in love with Callisto. Lycaon's daughter. Not a strange thing, cause that Zeus was a buckshot of love. Loved a good heap of women in his day. But what he does with Callisto didn't sit well with his old lady. Gets her pregnant is what he does. Course it weren't too long before Hera found out. That's Zeus's wife. Foul woman.

He put a finger to his lips as if to make himself silent.

Still shouldn't say that, I reckon. He looked around the sky. You never do know. Anyways, after Callisto bears out the child, Hera comes down from the mountain and changes her into a bear. Like her father she's sent out to wander the world herself. But that weren't enough for Hera. Havin a man like Zeus stickin his lightnin in all them young beauties got her blood up. So then, again this is later on, Callisto's son, who's named Arcas, he becomes the bull's-eye of her fury. At the time Arcas is growin up in the woods with Artemis. Artemis bein the goddess of huntin. Is this too much for you, boy?

No. I think I got the handle.

Alright. Arcas, he gets up to be a good hunter, but it's just as Hera had planned it.

The boy set down the cherry branch and watched the old man's face flicker and wane and rise again in the flames. He held the collar of his jacket up against the wind.

One day when Arcas has grown big and strong, Hera sets his mind to killin the bear. The bear that's really Callisto. Of course the boy don't know it's his mother. Don't know she's been watchin out for him even though she can't say it or tell him or hold him like a mother should. So he goes off ahuntin her. All day and night, Hera's made him so crazy for it.

The boy sat up and crossed his legs.

He sees the bear and she flees him. He follows her here, then she's gone to there. Imagine her heart, like that. Runnin from her own son. Well, one day he traps her. Corners her in a big gorge of rock. She tries to climb the damn thing but them rocks is all wet with dew. It's an early mornin, you see. But just as Arcas raises his bow and sets his arrow, she's suddenly gone.

The old man's eyes widened upon the fire. He made fists with both his hands, then opened them as if to release some crucial invisibility into the air.

Gone, he said. Disappeared. Why? Cause Zeus come back to save her. Snatched her right up from the earth and set her in the stars where she's called Great Bear. Later on, Arcas, he's raised up too. Called later by the people Lesser Bear.

The old man leaned back and folded his arms under his head and pulled the blanket up to the sagging flesh at his chin.

But one last time Hera sticks her nose in it. All riled up about the honor Zeus bestowed on them. So she sets the only curse she can upon them. She persuades Poseidon, god of the sea, to forbid them two stars from fallin into the ocean like all the others. So them two bears, them stars that is Callisto and Arcas, they's forever and always the only ones never to be settin below the horizon.

The old man's voice trailed off on those last words and he coughed and shifted under the blanket. The boy leaned in toward him to better hear what had now become a mere whisper from his sunken chest.

That's my favorite, he rasped. Cause it ain't one way or the other. It ain't good nor bad alone. It's both. Sometimes I'm rollin that over in my head. When I'm thinkin clear. Did Zeus win or did Hera? Are Callisto and Arcas livin good up there or do they pine for the sea? Do they want to disappear under the horizon and get a rest for a while? Do they miss all the other stars when they're up there alone?

The old man stopped and breathed long. His mouth opened and closed again and his breath settled into a dim rattle that passed out of his nose. The boy watched him from across the last licks of the fire and he turned his head back and looked up at the stars that were going slowly covered by a host of dark clouds.

What did you decide? he said.

The old man groaned and shifted under the blanket and turned away from the fire. The boy looked back down and over at him.

Who won?

He leaned over the fire and nudged the old man but in the darkness away from the fire he did not move and the night crept over both boy and river as blind and faultless as the old man's sleep.

The following day he rode out to Charlie Ford's ranch to have Triften's toes clipped. The air was very cold but still. He found the rancher oiling his saddle in the barn. He came down from his horse and rapped the barn door that was cast open and shedding a thin rictus of light onto the dirt floor. Charlie Ford turned with a rag in his hand and his shirtsleeves rolled up on his bulging forearms. Trude Mason from Grant County, he said, his eyebrows raised in genuine surprise. Just the man I was lookin for.

They sat in the tiny kitchen in the barn and the boy made a pot of coffee while the rancher scrubbed the grease from his hands.

What were you lookin for me for, the boy asked.

Charlie Ford turned from the sink basin, shaking off the water that was dripping down his arms.

Like mind, son. On a day like this it's nice to be around a like mind.

Yes sir, the boy said. I was thinkin the same thing.

He poured out their coffees and both sat. They spoke at great lengths about the rancher's horses and his sale of twenty head at an auction in Albuquerque. He told the boy that he had done well and cleared up some old debts and that maybe in the winter he would have some work for him if he planned to stay on.

I don't know if I will. I hope to be on my way.

The winter ain't the best time to travel in this country, son. Specially where you're headed.

I know it. But I may have no choice in it.

Charlie Ford sipped at his coffee. Has that office job got you down?

It's insubstantial for sure, but no. That ain't it.

What is it then?

The boy looked at the rancher and the rancher handed him a cigarette across the table and said, Go on and tell me, I ain't goin to judge you for it.

The boy nodded a little into the mug. I would like to tell you about it, he said.

Charlie Ford straightened up in his chair and folded his arms across his chest. Sure, he said. Sure.

I feel like I can talk to you is all.

Alright.

I mean between just us two.

Charlie Ford reached across the table and gave the boy a stiff pat on the shoulder, then recrossed his arms. Only others I seem to talk to these days is my horses, he said. You go on and tell me anything you want.

The boy lit his cigarette and set it in the ashtray and blew on his coffee and told him about it. He told him about the old man he was staying with and John Frank his friend who was trying to help him and he told him about the mayor and at last and into the steam of his coffee he told him about the girl. He gave a brief account of the situation and both shook their heads as the story came forth.

When he finished Charlie Ford rose from the table and poured them more coffee and stood by the sink basin. For a while he studied his mug. Then he told the boy that he shouldn't be so sure of what the mayor was planning, but that the way the town was now was the way it would always be. He said he wished he knew what to tell him but there was little to say. He told him that he knew little about the mayor and truth be told he had left town when the organizing and expansion began. All the ranchers had, he said. And he said that no wind or wet had ever set them back the way that the mayor and his newfangled town had. They had all gone their separate ways, and the spring roundups that had once been the finest and toughest and sweetest days of their lives were lost and what's worse was that they were no longer even neighbors. Can't even sit around and chew the rag no more, he said.

Finally he shook his head and set his mug in the sink and told the boy that he once had a say in the way things went in that country but that those days had changed altogether. That they had changed once, and forever.

So there's nothin for me to do?

Oh, there's always things you can do. Charlie Ford smiled evenly at the boy. But right here I think they're things you got to figure on your own.

In the evening the boy helped the rancher bring in some strays that had drifted out along the fence line and he rode with that old swell in his heart. Both rancher and boy smiled at each other across the misty landscape and late at night when his horse's toes had been clipped they sat once more at the kitchen table, and in that stable room of Charlie Ford's in a country far from his home the boy passed into his nineteenth year without mother or father, or even a single candle to blow out.

When he came to the wall she was already standing there with her fingers wrapped around the iron bars and her eyes dark and swollen. The domed light from the prison wall wafted in the breeze and settled across his boots and after a while she looked down.

She saw him standing there, thin and pale and slightly shivering from the cold. His hands were stuffed deep in his jacket pockets where he was trying to stave off their shaking. Her face turned away almost fearfully. Then she began to cry. The boy stepped back and took his hat down and held it at his chest. He withdrew his other hand from his pocket and raised it up in supplication.

After a few minutes she lowered her face to the bars. She began to shake her head against them, slow and deliberate. One hand came up and pressed the photograph against her throat and still the boy did not call to her nor did she speak. He could see her face more clearly without the rain present and it seemed to him even thinner and more fine than he had remembered.

She went on shaking her head and at last, low and quiet beneath her breath, he heard her voice. No, she was saying. He stepped forward, her hair above him swinging across her face like a flag on the mast of a ship lost under the sea. He could hear her clearly now. No, she said again, but the boy knew she was telling him something else.

The wind stirred up and rustled in the outcropping trees and he felt it acute on his face as he had the first time he had seen her wide soft eyes, and he suddenly sat on the damp ground and put his hands over his face. For a moment his mouth opened wide but no sound came and he lowered his head until he was as still as she. When he rose to his feet again he looked up almost timidly at her. She was smiling down at him, and her smile seemed to the boy wider than all the dark folding sky and deeper than it too.

I'll be right down, she whispered.

She tried to laugh but for the boy there was no laughter to be had. He knew that when a man is reduced to all but nothing he cannot laugh at it for there is no laughter in worship and worship is all there is when there is but one thing that remains.

They talked past the night and into the first hours of morning. This time she did not try to make him go and for a long time she told him about her home in Ansley, Mississippi.

I was born in the water, she told him. She laughed sadly. The ocean ran right up to our house and my mother would take her bath in it. Purest thing in God's whole world, she'd say. When I started comin out she didn't have the strength to get back up to the house. My daddy's brother came running down and brought me swimming into the world. He laughed about that all the time. You came swimming right into life, Delilah, he liked to say. To this day I still love that water. She paused with her eyes down and then she said, I wish you could see it.

I never been to the ocean, the boy said. I don't even know if I've ever seen it. Not even in books. He smiled up at her. Where I come from everything's dry. Even the rain. He smiled slightly again, then lowered his head and frowned at his boots. But I will, he said. I will see it. And it'll be you that shows it to me.

The girl made her grip tighter on the bars and pressed her head against her hands. She looked down at him for a long time. Trude, she said.

Then she told him about her mother and the Englishman her family had worked for and whom she named Roland James, and how he had taken their poverty beyond money. How he had raped her mother and then later how he had raped her. How it came to pass that her father found out and one night gone with knife in hand to the main house where Roland lived, and never returned. And she told him how soon after her mother too was gone, the only thing left of her a photograph of the ocean she found in the weeds on the side of the road. She told him how she was then left alone with the man who raped her before she had ever bled down there and who had also probably killed her mother and father. No one stood up for her save a few old women from down the road but their hands were as empty and black as her own.

Later on with the moon high and the boy sitting again she told him of better days, of the ripe fields and the slow summer nights. The way the dirt road warmed her bare feet. How the ocean went on and on for miles and how on days when there weren't any clouds the whole world ran on like one big sky. She told him about the kindness of her father and how he never took to beating or cussing but was always tender to her. She said for a long time she had asked why others were not the same way but now she did not.

The boy took off his hat again and placed it on his lap. The wind went away and the trees behind them stood silent as fence posts and she began to speak more slowly to him. She told him of the first time she had seen him and how crazy she had been and how she had hoped that he was a god come down from above to save her baby. Something in his eyes had told her if she could bring him close enough she would never again need fear or suffer the company of men. She said that she had seen his eyes very clearly even from that great distance and they had appeared like tiny bits of sky held in his face and then she remembered the blood suddenly across his shoulder. She remembered for him with her dark face pressed earnestly to the bars how her heart had sunk so deep and how she had believed he was going to die.

She watched his serious face below her and told him what her father had always said to her. That only the best things and the worst things that happen in the world are the ones you can never explain. She paused at this and smiled, so pure and pretty to him upon her tear-stained face, saying finally that it was not, of course, the worst of things she imagined in him.

He listened silently and he waited until she stopped crying and then he told her about his own family. He spoke with an uncommon swiftness and at great lengths, passing his hand across his chest from time to time as if to wipe chalk from the slate of his heart. Telling her about what had been, what was now.

When the first full light came she told him he had to go. He rose slowly and told her once again that he would return. You're not forgotten, he said. Then he set his hat on his head and looked up at the lightening sky and before he turned away he told her that she would be free yet and he told her quietly, just above the shrill of the returning winds, that he loved her.

By the edge of town he caught up his horse and turned her out toward the upcountry. They stepped into the bramble with the light pooling over the hills. The boy leaned down into the neck of the horse and as they went he told her about the girl. With the mare he used words he never had in the open world, and in the cold quiet of the coming morning he told her the ways of his heart.

IV

SEVENTEEN

WHEN THE BOY opened his eyes he glimpsed a tall luminous shadow clinging to the cabin wall. Out in the frosted dawn the shadow sparkled almost white on the earth. He reached for his pistol and collected it with a slow hand as he watched the door. He could hear a hushed voice from the empty window frames and could see in the bobbing lantern light the shape of his horse in the distance.

The boy eased his chin over carefully to find the old man in the darkness. He had climbed off the mattress and was down on his haunches with his back against the wall and he held the boy's rifle aloft in his wizened arms. The boy made a quick low hissing sound and the old man peered across the room at him with surprisingly calm eyes. The old man tilted his head minutely, then both turned back to the door.

There was silence for a moment and then they could hear boots shifting in the yard. Then they heard the mule bawling from the darkened trees. When the door came open the boy and the old man set their guns. A lone figure stepped into the cabin and pressed up against the wall. All the boy could see was the man's belt. He rode the hammer back with his thumb and took aim. Before his finger was around the trigger the warped floorboards whined and creaked and when the lanterns came up from the raised hands both the boy and the old man saw that it was already over. The men at the door numbered six, all slightly crouched with rifles cocked in the pits of their arms, all wearing the distinct mustaches of the Ralstons.

The men found the two hunched figures at the back of the room, their eyes squinted against the flickering lantern light and their hands cupped against their brows. The Ralstons split silently into threes and approached. The old man let down the boy's rifle like he'd been crestfallen by some distant truth he had long tried to forget. He looked across the room at the boy. The boy set his pistol on one of the chairs and when the Ralstons saw their weapons down they came forward.

The boy was thrown against the moonshine tub. His head hit the porcelain rim and blood ran down his face. He heard voices distantly and his eyes dimmed and relit to find the old man curled up on his tick and calling down the gods. He felt metal upon his wrists and he felt the clamp of handcuffs run tight to the bone. The blood ran over his eyes and upon his lips. He heard cussing and laughing and he heard some remote announcement of his arrest for breaking into the records building.

The hands upon him one by one recoiled and his head slumped against the side of the tub. Then the hands gripped him by the shoulders. As he was lifted to his feet his eyes opened again and through the blood he saw the old man being slapped. He appeared to be unconscious. The boy's rage came out in no more than a limp flailing of his arms. His head swung down against one of the men's chests as they dragged him out the door. Next to his eye he saw a blurred golden chevron on the collar of one of the assailant's jacket.

They walked him to the edge of the river. The voices around him grew silent. One of the brothers was directing the others. He was pointing at the boy's camp. The men who were carrying him set the boy against the tree trunk from which his horse had fled. He watched as three of the Ralstons kicked through his belongings. One of them held up his dirk knife and laughed and lunged at another. The leader told them to stop fucking around and bring the kid to the river.

He could see the blisters of dawn's light on the river as they hauled him down the bank, and across the water he could see the trees shivering in the breeze. The same trees he had woken to and slept with he did not recognize now. They seemed strangely thin and small. He tried to raise his hands over his head but one of the men slapped them down and told him not to move.

The leader came around with his arms folded over his jacket and stepped in front of the boy with his back to the river. He smiled at him. The boy closed his eyes. The leader spread his arms out and held them forth. Mornin, he said.

The boy opened his eyes and tried to lift his head from his chest but could not. The man leaned down and took him under the jaw and raised him up.

Better? he said.

He kept smiling. The boy made to spit a clot of blood from his mouth but it only bubbled and dripped down his chin.

Look us here, boys. Got ourselves the lonesome outlaw. Little pisspot he is.

The leader leaned down again and put a hand against the boy's chest and pushed him backward. His knees buckled and he tumbled back into the shallows of the river.

Cool as the breeze, the leader said.

He regarded the boy a moment longer, still smiling at him, then stepped aside and nodded to his brothers. Then all five came forward and walked the boy out into the water. He could feel the cold currents rushing around his ankles. The chill of it pricked his mind and for an instant his eyes widened to see the river and the grass bending on the opposite bank. The wind moving through them both felt like liquid metal across his face and everything around his eyes thick and heavy.

Suddenly he was on his back again with the water at his chin and the blood unfurling from his head like a flag. He tried to brace himself with his bound hands but they could not manage his weight. The leader followed in behind them and pulled up his trousers disapprovingly and straddled the boy's chest. He leaned over him and whispered close to his face while the others converged around them.

You broke the mayor's locks, didn't ya, boy?

Before he could answer the leader closed a fist around one of the bloody ropes of the boy's hair and sunk his face into the water. He held him under for several seconds and then jerked him out.

Didn't ya, ya squirrelly son of a bitch.

He pressed the boy's head down again. Under the water the boy felt the silt and rocks grinding against the laceration in his skull. When he reemerged his mouth gasped open. He drooled and sucked at the air. The leader held the boy by his shirt collar and leaned his head up to look at his brothers, nodding with a fierce ambivalence.

Boy, he said facing him again, you most lucky the mayor wants you alive. He let go of his shirt and the boy fell back into the water. Now confess.

The boy's eyes slid open and locked as well as they could upon the leader but he did not speak to him. He watched the man's teeth move across the bristling mustache.

You think you can stonewall me? You got the saddle on the wrong goddamn horse, kid.

The leader stepped back and booted the boy in the side. Two others stepped forward and did the same. The boy lowered his forearms over his ribs. A rib had cracked and he tried to cover it with his hands.

Confess to huntin the fuckin nigger girl thief. Confess to crossin the mayor in his own goddamn town.

They kicked him again. Then the leader stepped back and commanded the others away with outstretched hands and huffed for his breath. Confess it, he sputtered, wiping his mouth with the back of his jacket sleeve.

The boy looked up at him once again but all he could take in now were the trees and the sky, silent and brightening above him, and the last thing he remembered until they hit the thoroughfare of the town was his own voice lifted out of the last of his consciousness.

It was me, he kept calling. You damn right it was me.

He was led through town the same way in which the girl had been. People stood in small circles in the blousy morning light, watching the Ralstons pull the boy along with fifths of whiskey rocking in their pockets. On the faces of the townspeople they passed there were no clear expressions. Some crossed their hands behind their backs and spat and nodded or merely shook their heads. One of the Ralstons went before them waving his hands vigorously and exclaiming Justice over and over.

When they came into the plaza the boy's eyes rolled open again. What he saw was what he saw in his dreams. Dark colors and long slow sweeping motions. He could taste the blood in his mouth and each step seemed to further split open his side. He held his ribs as they went. The feet beneath him could only walk a few steps at a time before they could only be dragged on behind him. He saw a wash of faces and upon them he saw the mouths of the townspeople moving vague and deliberate.

In the hallway of the town hall the boy made out the Italian through the trembling slit of his eye, and though the blood now blocked most of his vision he saw clearly the terror laid upon his face. John Frank made to raise a hand but it stopped at his waist and dropped again to his side and he watched as the Ralstons led him away.

When they reached the mayor's door the men stopped and huddled around him and held him up under the arms. Before the knock was given, the brother who had been chanting Justice slurred out again at the boy, raising a finger to his nose and saying, Damn lucky, and hit him square in the jaw with the black stock of his rifle.

THE ROOM HE awoke in was cool and bright. A breeze loitered around a half-open window to agitate the pale white drapery from the wall. When he tried to move he found he could not without a tremendous pain in his head. He was sweating and had sweated immensely through the night, the sheets stained yellow and wet upon his legs. The same eye that had been cut in the fall from his mare was now completely shut. He did not know how long he had been lying there, in the quiet of that white room. He stared up at the ceiling for a long time until at last he struggled to his side and looked out the window.

The window gave way to a back alley littered with broken clay pots and baling wire. Strung across the buildings a clothesline sunk under the weight of a blue twill blanket and three woolen stockings. The head of a child's doll looked back at him from the mud with painted eyes that were washed out and grotesquely still.

He rolled onto his back again and managed himself upright against the headboard and looked around the room. There was a dresser and a bed stand. A small serving table standing in the corner. There was a bathroom to his right with a cotton partition and a light fixture screwed into the ceiling and glowing palely in the noonday sun. On the wall opposite the bed was a portrait of Christ on the cross. His face was near Spanish and those who stood around him were too, all standing against a background of flaming red.

He woke and slept for several days without a clear thought in his head. The clock on the wall ticked with the rhythm of his breath but was of little use to the boy otherwise. He woke both morning and night to find his eye open to the Christ figure's pegged hands and in his clouded mind he reinvented the torture and loss and the divinity his own mother had long ago spoken to him about, and oftentimes in those formless hours he wished he had been sent to a place where the walls were bare of anything at all.

Late in the day he woke and sat up to the sound of the window closing. A woman turned to him from across the room and saw the single eye wide upon her. She put her hands to her chest. He studied her for a moment, a girl not much older than he, dressed in a long white coat with her hair brought up behind her head.

Mornin, he said.

The nurse rested a hand on the window ledge and tapped her fingers nervously, then pointed out the darkened window.

Seven in the evening, she said.

A few days later he sat up in the bed and fingered the bandage where it covered his ear and rubbed his eyes. The clock ticked formally from across the room and he swung his feet over the edge of the bed and onto the floor. The light in the bathroom was off and only the first glints of sun caught his bedsheets. There was a plate of sliced apple and a glass of water on the bedside table. He drank the water in one flush and pressed the glass against his forehead. The picture eyes seemed to watch him in the silence of the coming day.

After a while the nurse came in and stopped short at the door. The boy was standing by the window. He turned with the sound of her feet and gazed vacantly upon her.

It was gettin a mite chilly, she said.

What was.

You stopped sweating. It was gettin chilly so I closed the window. The nurse wrung her hands together and stepped timidly into the room. Your head's healed pretty good since the fever broke, she said. You broke some ribs too, but they're on their way to whole again.

The boy came away from the window and lowered himself onto the edge of the bed. I don't know how to ask but I can't figure it out, he said. Where are we?

Why, we're in the town hall. The nurse gestured with a closed fist she brought from her chest and lifted toward the door. Mayor's office is right down the hall. He sleeps here himself some nights.

The boy leaned up again and sat with his bare feet on the polished floorboards. He smiled coldly to himself. The sun began to push its way into the room and the boy closed his eye against it and when he opened his eye again the nurse was gone.

In the evening she returned with two envelopes in one hand and a pitcher of water in the other. She placed all three on the bed stand while he watched her from the bed.

These are for you, she said.

She walked to the end of the bed and tucked the loose corner of the blanket under the mattress and did not look up at him again but smiled falsely when she bent to raise the mattress, then went out the door.

The boy moved the pitcher away and took up the envelopes. They were already open. He laid one in his lap and fingered loose the contents of the other. In it he found a photograph of himself that Jane had taken when he first arrived in town. He was sitting shoulders back astride Triften, not quite smiling and not quite at ease, but in his unstudied pose he remained somehow imponderable to himself. On the back of the picture she had written, What have you done? I'm saving a pie for you. Get better. He looked at the picture a few seconds longer, then set it aside and picked up the other envelope.

It was a letter from the doctor. How he had come to find him there he could not imagine. There were forwarding stamps from six towns and two counties, and six times the word Urgent had been scribbled on the envelope. The paper was worn so thin it seemed to have passed through a hundred hands. The ink was faded and drawn down the grain but the precise lettering of the old doctor's handwriting was still legible to the boy's working eye. He held the paper up to the light and leaned into it.

There were a few lines about the town and the goings on there and another about Larry Bowles losing his hand to a renegade bull and something about everyone's hair grown so long it looked like a town of women. The remainder of the letter was about his father's death. The boy read the lines over and over until nightfall came. In the middle of the night he woke and stumbled into the bathroom and pulled on the light and read them again and somewhere in between he wept.

Your daddy seemed to fall to pieces after you all left. He cursed your mother endlessly but I could tell his heart wasn't in it. I think he missed her beyond the possibility of his own words. He was like a can of worms, your daddy was. Wriggling and wriggling inside but nowhere to go but back down to the bottom. He fell off New Bend Bridge second Tuesday of September. Some here say he jumped off of his own accord but I reckon he just fell off drunk. Your daddy was never one to quit. I think you know something about that. But he never did have too much luck succeeding in the end neither. Hope you're finding it better for you and your mama. Doc.

In the morning there was a knock at the door. A voice called out and the door opened. The boy was sitting upright with the pillows beneath his back. The mayor came in and crossed the room and stood by the foot of the bed. He outstretched his arms and gripped the bedposts.

I am sorry about your father, he said.

He looked at the boy with surprisingly sad eyes. The boy straightened his back against the headboard. I'm sure he appreciates it, he said.

The mayor acquiesced with a bow of his head.

Yes. I hope so.

They looked at each other from across the crumpled bed linens. The swelling in the boy's eye had gone down, but his eyelid still remained low upon it.

This is something I do not like, the mayor said.

He looked out the window, at the gnarled light staining the drapery. Then he began to pace the room.

You are just a young man, you see. Just a young man. He turned back and studied the boy with the same troubled eyes. A simple error is all it was, he said. That is what I like to believe. No different from the way the sound of wind rustling through a bush can sometimes be mistaken for water being poured out on the ground. You only mistook the deceitfulness of your actions for nobility. But a young man should be given chances. A young man does not need to be stricken down for faltering. He needs to be helped back up and shown where he has diverged from his path.

The mayor's face clouded and he shook his thumb across the room at the boy.

But there are some places and some people with whom a young man should know not to seek out a conflict. People he should know better than to cross.

He paused and stood in front of the window and looked out, with the boy watching him from the bed.

I am sorry for what the Ralston boys have done to you. I did not wish this.

The mayor turned his hands one over the other.

I did not wish this, he said deliberately. I explicitly ordered against it and they have been reprimanded for the way in which they handled the situation. The mayor nodded only to himself, then turned on his heels again. They did not handle it well at all, he said.

He pulled a chair from the corner of the room and set it by the side of the bed and sat down and crossed his legs and pressed his hands on his knee.

I want you to listen to me now. I want you to hear me. I do not intend to keep you in here. I once told you it is a fair town and I must not make a liar of myself. You have done wrong, but I believe it was commanded by the whim of the young, and this is not a thing you can be expected to help. Truth be told, I did not wish to believe it was you. That is why you have been untouched for so long. But it was you, and it is a thing you will learn from. A thing you must learn from.

The mayor made like he would stand, but he only resituated himself in the chair and raised up his laced hands.

When you are young as you are, you believe you hold autonomy over your life. Over what occurs to you and around you in your life. I know this feeling. But there is nothing more to it than that. It is a feeling, and feelings are not what we should proceed by. The code of your life is no different than the code of mine or any other. We are many. Even in this small town we are many. And we must balance ourselves within one another. We must follow in a code that is common to us all, and that code has no rulers. That code is a house for all. You cannot flee from it to satisfy things to your own liking. You cannot burn it down.

The mayor's face grew serious. He put a hand across his beard.

Choices that concern your life are constantly about nor can you make them all. Here is an example of one such choice and you are lucky to have the opportunity to make it.

The boy at last turned his head. He inspected the mayor through his half-shut eye. The mayor turned uncomfortably and stood and began to pace the room again.

A payment can be made for your release, he said. A payment of two hundred dollars can be made to the town hall and you will walk with impunity. You will be free to go on to Colorado. Where you are headed. Where the choice you have made is now common with mine. You will leave and not cross me again.

The mayor stopped pacing and looked out steadily at the doleful light falling on the alleyway mud.

If you do not leave, I'm sure the Ralstons would be eager to visit you again. This time without orders of restraint. And if you choose not to pay, you will remain here. With me. Let us say indefinitely.

The mayor came and sat again and his face hardened and the sad eyes now sparkled fiercely.

With the wages you have earned from me. From me, he repeated emphatically. You should have no problem with this.

The boy shook his head slowly on the pillow and turned away toward the hard glow of the bathroom bulb. The mayor stood and placed his hands behind his back. When the boy did not respond he went to the door and held the knob and paused and turned back once more.

Either way, he said evenly, you will not see her. To kill her or to love her, for in truth I know not which you seek, though I have my ideas. With respect, he said, making a deep bow toward the bed, you will not.

The mayor tugged the bottom stitching of his waistcoat and straightened his glasses and flattened his beard with the back of his hand and went out into the hallway where behind the closed door the creak of his polished leather boots trailed off into nothing.

Eighteen

JOHN FRANK STOOD with his shoulder leaned against the door frame and his arms folded across his chest. He looked dumbly across the room to where the boy sat with his legs folded beneath him on the bed.

You comin in or holdin up that wall?

John Frank smiled at the floor and pushed himself upright and came and sat in the chair beside the bed. How you feelin, he said.

The boy drew the covers up to his waist and raised an eyebrow.

Your head got busted up pretty good, John Frank said.

He leaned in and took the boy's head in his hands and turned it right to left.

Get them sweaty paws off me.

Hold on. Let me see it.

It's all mended.

Jesus. That's a mighty stretch of scar.

I guess it is.

It is. I'm tellin ya.

John Frank took his hands away and the boy regarded him, the pressed clothes, the slicked back hair.

Look at you. Went and got yourself all jellied up.

He reached out and flipped the lapel of Frank's suit coat.

I figure someone ought to look halfway good between the two of us.

I don't know, the boy said, fixing a shirt button Frank had missed. Halfway might be a stretch.

They sat quietly in the soft morning light. John Frank got up and went to the window. Heat's still hangin on today, he said quietly.

Did we clear through September yet?

John Frank opened the window a crack and looked over his shoulder at the boy, then came and sat again.

It's the middle of October, bud.

He righted the chair so he sat square to the boy and folded his hands and set them firmly in his lap. Lots of things have happened, he said.

Like what.

First off, the mayor told me you weren't biting on his offer. Says you'll stay here until he sees fit to let you go. Ain't nobody really standin up to say otherwise. I think the people round here figure you've finally become what they suspected in you.

And what's that.

John Frank opened his hands. Look where you are, he said.

The boy unfolded his legs and pushed down the bed and sat on the edge. How'd he find out it was me?

I don't rightly know. But I can guess the way you've carried on since you came to town might have helped in his figurin.

Well. I don't got the money he wants, and probably wouldn't give it to him if I did.

I can help with that.

No. I'll be alright.

No you won't.

The boy turned and regarded John Frank, whose hands were clenched tight and his face reddening.

Why's that, he said.

John Frank made to speak, then let off and rose again and crossed the room to where the dresser stood. He ran his fingers up and down the side of it. It's her, he said.

What's her?

Delilah. They picked her.

All of his breath seemed to go out of him yet on his face there was no surprise.

They're to hang her in the plaza, Frank continued with a forced steadiness. This Saturday coming.

What's today?

Monday.

Five days then.

Yeah, five days. I don't know what to say exceptin sorry.

The boy rose with a grunt and held his ribs and stood across the room from John Frank, looking out into the deserted alley. John Frank studied his face but it no longer gave change nor did it even reveal a sense of it.

Mayor said it was done by random lot, Frank went on. Says it's the only way to keep all types on their toes. Murder or misdemeanor, they're all the same, he said. No one is above the law. That kind of thing. That's what he said.

At random he said.

Yeah.

Don't the state got something to say about that? It don't quite fit the average American law, does it?

John Frank looked at the boy like he wasn't altogether sure who he was. Then he lowered his eyes to his feet and shook his head. Then he looked up at the boy again.

Get this through your head, Trude. The state don't even recognize this place yet and the country barely recognizes the state. You sure won't find this town on no map. And New Mexico, it might as well be Mexico itself when it comes to average American law. I guess that's what the mayor's tryin to change. They might not yet know he exists even.

John Frank walked across the room and put his hand on the boy's shoulder and whispered gravely to him. Look, he said. Your name was in the drawing too.

They stood shoulder to shoulder at the window. Outside a dog sniffed through some paper debris. They watched the wind going through the stick trees on the mesa. In the distance there were children crawling around on the ground and eating raw squash and carving their names in the dirt with their knives. An old man hobbled out of a back door with a whittled walking stick and crossed the road into another alleyway where he tapped twice on a door with the branch and after a moment ducked his head and climbed down the steps.

I got to get on, John Frank said. I ain't supposed to be here. Only the mayor and the nurse.

How'd you get in then?

John Frank smiled meekly. Bought the nurse a gin fizz last night, he said.

The boy took Frank under the arm and slowly he began to pace the room with him. Alright, he said. Listen quick. He stopped as if he would retire the idea altogether, then breathed deeply and continued. Go out to the old man's cabin, he said. You know where it is?

I know the direction.

The boy stopped and looked anxiously at Frank. He's alright, no?

He is. They left him just fine. I heard it that he was crazy, course that's been said many times over, but that he'd given no real struggle. Them boys said that's why you come in like you did. Struggled like a sumbitch all the way to town.

Well. Tell him I sent you. Otherwise I can't be held accountable for what he tries to pull on you. Tell him to get you the old saddlebag with the old saddle in it down by the river. If it's still there.

Alright. Get the saddle, Frank repeated.

My mama's saddle. Get it and take it out to Charlie Ford's place. You know where he's at.

Yeah.

Tell him it's mine and would he need it and tell him I'm in a bit of a bind and whatever he could give for it you'll take on my behalf. The rest I should have myself.

That's right. John Frank grinned and took the boy by the shoulders. Let's get your ass out of here.

Before Frank went out the door the boy called after him.

What?

You need to remember one thing, he said. The answer is always Zeus. What?

Don't forget it. Zeus got the biggest dick of em all.

The following day, passed secretly from John Frank to the nurse, the envelope came. The boy was sitting on the chair he had pulled over to the window. He had removed the bandages from his ribs and head, and his hair was shorn close to the skull where the stitchings had been made by the nurse. He sat with his shirt unbuttoned and his bruised chest exposed. When the nurse came in the room she blushed for it and walked quickly to where he sat and handed him the envelope, then set to laying out his supper on the serving table.

He counted out the money. One hundred and forty dollars. The boy knew it was too much for that old saddle. It was enough for at least two new ones of the same make. Inside the envelope was scribbled some writing with a crude charcoal pencil.

It said, I hope this will do you. Come see me once it's all done. Charlie. And then below his name, And by the way, it ain't too much.

The boy smiled grudgingly and stacked the bills and put them back in the envelope.

That's a good bit of money in there, the nurse said from the doorway where she now stood.

The boy looked up and watched her closely. It is at that, he said.

John said to tell you it was from Mr. Ford. And also something about Zeus. That he came in handy.

The boy buttoned up his shirt and nodded and smiled down at his waist. Thank you, he said. I wonder can you do one more thing for me.

Yes?

Tell the mayor I'd like to see him. Tell him I've reconsidered.

The nurse looked up and openly beamed at him, then forced her smile down. Yes sir, she said. I will. Right now.

When she had gone he pulled off one of his boots and turned down the heel of it from where he pinched out a wad of crumpled bills, which he then smoothed out in his lap and counted to make seventy dollars even. He placed ten of those in the envelope from Charlie Ford and returned the remaining sixty to the boot and pulled it back on his foot and sat and waited for them to come.

It was just nightfall when the nurse called on him and found him still sitting where he had been in the morning. He followed her down the hallway without shackles or chains of any kind. One of the Ralston brothers stood outside the mayor's office with his arms crossed at his chest. He did not look at the boy but merely pushed open the door and let him by.

He heard the mayor's boots before he saw his face. The mayor turned slowly in his chair and motioned to the guard for the door to be closed. He shifted his spectacles on his nose and smiled casually at the boy.

Please, he said in his tremorless voice. Sit down.

The boy sat.

You are looking well. The mayor regarded him with a genuine look. Quite well, he said.

I'm in need of my hat.

Your hat?

Yeah. My hat.

I do not have such a hat, I am afraid. Perhaps it was left behind. After the . . .

The mayor searched for the words.

After the scuffle. He smiled again and more crookedly at the boy. But if you have brought what is necessary, you can find it yourself. He made a flourish with his hands. Otherwise I can have someone bring it to you, he said. Here.

I have it, the boy said.

The mayor raised a single eyebrow and tugged on his beard. Do you, he said.

The boy produced the envelope from his pocket and placed it on the desk. He pushed it across to the mayor's hands. With his eyes unrooted from the boy's face the mayor gradually leaned forward and took up the envelope, then turned his chair away. When he turned back he was smiling robustly.

This is one hundred and fifty dollars. Fifty short of what has been asked of you.

It's all I got. If you want I can pay the rest later.

No, no. You see, you cannot work for me anymore. He made a pointing gesture at the desk. You cannot stay here anymore.

So I'll be gone. You want that so much, ain't it worth fifty dollars to you?

The mayor stood and walked across the room. He went by one of the dark wood shelves that was lit up brightly by the candelabra beside it and picked up one of the glass train engines. He turned it over in his hand and studied it deliberately. He closed his fingers around it and set it down again. It is agreed then, he said. You may leave at your leisure. You will gather up your things and go far away from here.

The boy nodded. He looked across the room at the mayor with his purple eye upon him. How much you figure for the girl, he said.

The mayor's brow creased in distaste and he walked to the back of the boy's chair and put his hands on it.

You have heard, then, about the girl.

The boy stayed silent. He looked straight ahead at the desk.

What exactly is the business you have with her?

It ain't any business.

Ah, the mayor said, touching the rims of his glasses, but it is. I believe that you are fond of her. I believe you would like very much to see her live. She is, after all, quite pretty for a negress.

Maybe it's that I don't want to see anyone die.

The mayor went to the drink cart which stood beneath the raised blinds and poured a thumbnail of whiskey and brought it to his lips.

Maybe, he said. But sometimes it is necessary. She is not an innocent, you see. None of them were. Including you. She was unlucky, yes. But I do not think of it entirely as death. You must learn to understand this. That it is an action. A necessary act in which something is given for the greater well-being.

The mayor sipped from beneath his heavy beard and adjusted his glasses again and set the tumbler down and folded his hands behind his back.

It is like trading a ripe apple for a rotting one, he said. When the freshly fallen apple is picked up and the old one is crushed beneath the heel, there is a new order. A new order is created by that. The old worm-ridden apple is forgotten, and the other is brought to the mouth where it revitalizes that which the old apple could not.

The boy's eyes quickened and he pushed back the chair violently.

It was her all along, he said, standing now and facing the mayor. I think it was always going to be her. All you're sayin is she'll be the one least missed. That she's chosen to show death. Not to show lost life, cause no one cares about her life. But death's enough to put fear in the heart. Death's all you need. It ain't life gone out, it's just the goddamn picture. It's the picture of death you want.

The mayor took up the whiskey glass again and rolled the rim around his lips.

I am not the great changer, he said calmly. I am not the one who bleeds life and death into the earth. A man is given one life and one life only. It is as substantial as a tree or bush or doe. It comes and is gone. A man lives and learns or does not learn and then is gone. Your life is not the blessed possession you would like to imagine. I am seeking order, he said more sharply. He set the tumbler down again. As perhaps you are, though you cannot see it. The girl's life does not change things in the vast order of the world, it only changes things here. It makes order here. That is all we can do. A small bit of order amidst the outstanding chaos. It is simply an example, you are right in that. It is simply what must be done in a world where everything that is done must be.

The mayor sat behind the desk again and crossed his legs. He held his hands for the boy to sit as well but he would not.

I know how you see things, the mayor went on. Once I saw them much in the same way. Perhaps to a lesser degree, but the same. I see how the land is inside you and how you imagine it goes with you in a way you understand. And you expect the same from the people who inhabit this land. All things one great presence sweeping through time on the merits of its own simplicity. As if time will not disturb it if you wish it not to. As if the changes around you were unwound from your own hand. And perhaps what exhausts you most and what you clearly do not understand is the fact that underneath, where you are, everything is strong and solid and peerless, yet on the surface, where the real world resides, everything is subject to flux. Everything is in turmoil.

The mayor removed his glasses and rubbed his eyes. He held the spectacles up to the candlelight, then put them on again and leaned across the desk.

Because of this you are like a desert of sadness, he said. No one comes to you to agree with your notions of right and wrong. You have only nature's laws. Absolute laws that are neither spoken nor attainable by words. Understand this. These are not the laws that apply here. These are the ones as children we may have hoped the world is obedient to, but they are never in case the true ones. In truth they are not of this world. They are God's illusions cast down for some greater purpose we cannot fathom, nor can we accomplish. I do not think this distinction is clear in your mind. And because of it you are like a desert of sadness. No one goes to the desert. No one goes to kneel and speak words of comfort. No one goes to mourn or pray for it. And do you know why this is? It is because the desert is no place, just as the workings by which you wish to see the world turn are in fact no workings at all. They are that which is imagined. They are dream, and no more.

The mayor tipped his head and looked at the boy over his spectacles. He seemed pleased by his words. The boy turned his eyes away. For a long while they remained silent. The mayor watched the boy who was leaning against the bookshelves.

It's all bullshit, the boy finally said. He straightened himself from the shelving. I ain't pretending to be like you and I ain't tryin to find your good side. I just want the truth. Great new town of the West ought to begin with that. My mother gone and now my father too, and never did I see the perfect law in that.

The boy paused and crossed the room and sat again. He leaned forward in the chair with his hands clenched upon the arms of it, his good eye red and sharp upon the mayor.

I know they called for it, he said.

Who and for what?

The people. Those Ralston boys. Someone above your common code. They called for her to hang and not by no random lot.

The mayor leaned away.

This is not about you, son.

Tell me it was random then. Tell me that at least.

The mayor took off his glasses again and set them on his desk and groomed down his beard with the back of his hand.

Tell me.

It was, the mayor started, but before he could finish the door swung open and from it came a voice.

Nothing in this world is random.

The mayor scrambled up his glasses from the desk. The boy turned in his chair. The figure at the door stepped out of the lit hallway and into the candle flames. It was the Englishman from the mountains.

My lawyer, the mayor said hastily.

Before he could go on, the Englishman motioned the guard into the room and spoke coolly to the boy. And you will be gone from here, he said. One way or another.

Then he turned from the door and the guard came forward. The boy made to stand when the mayor nodded solemnly to the guard, but just as he was rising the pistol butt once again came down to lay darkness upon the light in his eyes.

HE SAT WITH his elbows on the table while the old man worked up a pot of coffee. By the time he'd returned it was very late and bitterly cold with the wind slashing through the empty window frames and the last blow from the Ralston brother still ringing in his ear.

How'd you get back here?

Walked.

Someone came out here and said he was a friend of yours. Went rummaging through your things.

John.

Yeah. That was him. Sort of nervous little fella. Kept goin on about Zeus's dick.

The old man turned from the stove and brought forth the coffee and placed the mugs on the table. They banged you up pretty good, he said.

I know it.

You reckon they'll leave off you now?

No. Not if I stay. They expect me to be gone right soon.

But you won't be.

No. I won't.

They drank. The old man fumbled for a pack of cigarettes from his shirt pockets and took one out and handed the pack to the boy. These are yours anyway, he said.

Keep em if you want.

The old man shrugged and put the cigarettes away in his pocket. What's become of the girl? he said

She's to be hung. Like I thought it. Like I knew.

The old man lowered his head uncertainly and scratched his arms. What will you do?

I don't see but one choice. I'll get her loose before they . . .

The boy paused and nodded to himself.

I'll get her loose, he said.

How do you aim to do that?

The boy shook his head. I don't know, he said.

They sat and drank their coffee in the windy dark.

They didn't bother you too much, I hope, the boy said.

Naw. What good would it've been to em? Old buzzard like me made of nothin but booze and bones. Naw, they tried to scare me but I knowed their faces from a long time ago when they was young and they seen that and maybe took ashamed. Told me not to take you in no more is all.

But you did.

I did. Yep. No matter.

The old man turned away and nodded plainly and with some embarrassment. They watched the outside. The clouds were thick and sticky with rain and after a long time the boy stood and went to the back of the room and laid out his bedroll still twisted and turned inside out from the night of his arrest.

You'll sleep alright now. I done cleared out the tub.

The boy looked up at the old man, then over the rim of the tub. The old man was nodding slowly with his hands raised up. I quit it, he said. Day after they took you.

Why?

I don't rightly know. I figure I could have given forth a good fight if I wasn't so much made of liquid. Maybe drawn some blood from them fuckers. He crushed down the stub of his cigarette in the stone bowl on the table and grinned at the boy, gnawing on his gums as though to work a barb from the back of his mouth. Next time I'll be ready, he said.

Nineteen

THE CHILL OF the norther that came boring down from the mountains woke the boy and the old man equally and they rose together before dawn and sat again with a fresh pot of coffee. The old man sat shivering with his blanket clenched at his throat and the boy fixed up a bowl of eggs which they split between them along with a quarter loaf of bread. After a few minutes the boy pushed his plate away and rose and began to pace the cabin floor. The old man was hunched down and hefting forksful of eggs into his mouth.

Given me quite a hunger, he said, not drinkin and all. You goin to finish that?

The boy turned back a hand toward his untouched eggs. The old man pulled the plate across the table and worked the pepper mill over it.

Least you got a haircut out of it, he said.

He crooked his neck around to smile at the boy. The boy was staring off out the window. A blank portrait, even the dips and rises in the land flattened by the sad dispersion of light.

I'll get someone to fit some plate glass for the windows, the boy said.

I'd prefer only some good burnin wood.

And something to seal them with.

I'll be fine with some dry wood.

Look at you shiverin, the boy said. I'll get some glass.

He turned back and walked to the table and pushed back the blanket from the old man's chest and reached in his pocket and took out the pack of cigarettes. He ran a match down the table and pulled it lit.

When's it to be then? the old man asked quietly through the smoke.

Three days. Saturday.

The old man guffawed. Just in time for their sabbath, he said.

The boy walked the floor a while longer. When he finished the cigarette he thumbed it in the bowl. He found his hat in the back of the room and punched it out as even as he could and set it on his head.

I got to get on, he said.

They don't want you here no more, boy. Where you think you're goin?

The boy gazed across the room. The old man shook his head at the look and pulled the blanket back to his chin and worked his fork impatiently through the eggs.

Go on then, he said. I fed the horses while they had you down there. He looked up at the boy through his fierce gray eyes. I reckon I'll be prepared to do it again.

He dismounted his horse in front of Garrets and stroked the mare under the gaze of some early-rising passersby. He heard them whispering as he went up the porch steps, but he did not look up. There was little left he believed he had not heard and there was nothing he believed could worsen things and whatever remained of his name could be carried away on the wind and without consequence.

Jane was waiting for him at the door with her apron strings loose in her fingers and her arms held out for him.

Come on in here, she said.

She smiled wide and sad and took him around his caved shoulders, then held him back at arm's length. You look tired, she said.

Yes ma'am. I've heard it said and I believe it.

She led him to his booth in the back. No one else was in the cantina except the cook who looked out from the plate window momentarily then disappeared into the kitchen.

Jane brought him coffee and an ashtray. The boy thumbed loose the pack of cigarettes he'd taken from the old man and set them on the table.

Bring me whatever you got, he said. I believe I'm ready to eat.

I'll bring you a feast, she said.

The boy took up his cigarettes and shook one loose and turned to the window. There were blinds drawn over it and the boy looked them over and pulled them apart with his fingers and eyed through to the plaza. It was cold-looking and nearly empty with the norther winds picking up the dust in great cones. Even the Indian women were absent from the tree. Only the innkeeper was across the way, sweeping off his porch and blowing on his hands from time to time. Before too long the boy's breath drew up a fog on the glass and he let the blinds drop shut.

The waitress returned with a fried steak and red corn tamales and a bowl of beans cooked with mint leaves. When you've finished with that I've got a nice mincemeat pie for you, she said. Just like I promised.

The boy made a slight nod to her, but she lingered by the table with the apron strings twisted around her fingers and finally she sat down across from him in the booth. You alright? she said.

Alright as I can be, I reckon.

You heard about the hangin and all. It really will be.

Yes ma'am.

Makes me sick to my stomach.

Your mayor ain't the saint you thought he was.

No, she said. I guess he's not.

They sat in silence for a moment, the waitress still watching the boy uncomfortably. How's the steak?

He looked up at her from his plate. After a moment he said, It's good, Miss Jane.

She nodded absently. She kept watching him with her fingers still knotted in the apron strings. They hurt you pretty bad, did they?

They left me alive at least.

Do you know that girl? The one you were lookin after when you broke into the mayor's place?

I know her. Yes ma'am.

How?

The boy looked up from his plate again and studied her face, so hardened and drawn with lines yet innocent even to him. I just know her Miss Jane. You know what I mean?

She smiled at him and pushed back her yellow hair nervously. I'm sorry, she said.

Don't be.

Let me get you more coffee.

She slid from the booth and came back with the pot and poured it for him. How about that pie? she said

He lit a cigarette while she went back into the kitchen and turned it in his fingers. Miss Jane brought out the pie. He picked at it for a while, drinking his coffee in small swallows. He asked her for a glass of water and she brought it to him. When he finished the pie he motioned her back from the bar where she had been watching him from the corner of her eye.

How much do I owe you?

The waitress smiled dimly and placed a tentative hand on the back of his neck. This one's on the house, she said.

Let me pay you.

Trude. Darlin. You paid enough.

He looked up at her standing there above him and rubbed his hands together and rapped the table with his knuckles and rose.

Be careful now, she said. I don't want to wait so long between visits again. She smiled full at him. You've become my best customer.

She put a hand on his, then withdrew it and pressed both against her stomach.

By the way, the boy said, inclining his chin toward the window. What are them blinds about?

Miss Jane pulled her eyes off him and looked to the window and sighed and went and flipped her fingers through the wooden slats and looked out a moment at the writhing willow tree, then turned back to the boy.

Some people just don't like to watch the winter come, she said.

He spent the morning in an alley adjacent to the town hall, waiting for John Frank to come out. People had begun to appear in doorways, on the plaza, riding in cars. Children crossed sullenly behind the barbershop and toward the schoolhouse. The departure of the warm months seemed finally to appear in the people's dress. Black dusters rode the men's backs like old-time capes and long gray shawls were held bundled over the petticoats of the women who clutched at their breasts as if the cold would inflict them. The boy watched all of this from a wooden crate he sat upon with his hat low and his knees drawn to his chest.

All morning long he sat smoking and listening to the crisp winds turn the corners of the building and from time to time looking off to where he had left his horse deep in the alley. He watched a purse maker down the way rocking slowly in a chair on the porch of the general store with a blanket across her lap while she cut lengths of brass straps. In the distance he could see the railroad workers gathering in circles along the track line and could hear the drill bits driving into the ground and the railing of the foreman's whistle after which the men would shift sluggishly farther down the line where they raised their tamps and sledges into the cold sunlight.

A mime artist who came and stood under the willow tree held the boy's attention for a while. He was trying to gather an audience from those passing with wild theatrical acrobatics. His face was painted powder white and before him stood a beaten copper drum with a single bill leafing over the rim. A black tear was painted on his left cheek and he repeatedly feigned wiping it away when someone came near but there it stayed all morning until he finally picked up the drum with a few loose coins clattering in it and went away.

An hour later John Frank appeared at the door of the town hall and came down the porch steps. The boy gripped a small rock he had been turning in his hand and threw it toward the porch. It skidded and bounced by Frank's feet. John Frank stopped and looked around. The boy stood obscured by a wall and he thrust out his hand into the open air and waved it furiously. Frank came jogging into the alleyway where the boy had pressed his back against the wall.

What the hell, he huffed. You know you shouldn't be here.

I know it.

I see you're not plannin to leave, then. John Frank shook his head at the boy's silence. He put his hands on his hips and breathed down at his feet. When he'd gotten his breath he looked up at the boy. He regarded his worn and dusted clothing and the ragged look around his eyes, then sat himself on the crate. You look like shit, he said.

Yes, I believe we've covered that.

I don't have words that'll make you feel any better.

I wouldn't imagine you would.

Shit, John Frank said. His eyes darted down the alleyway and back onto the plaza. We can't stay here. Let's take a ride.

I thought you hated horses.

Just put me up and not say another word about it.

The boy went down the alley and got the mare and wrestled John Frank onto the back of the saddle. Don't forget to breathe, he said.

I know where we can go, Frank said. I go there sometimes when there's considering to be done. Go back that way.

He cocked a thumb over his shoulder and the boy put a boot in front of Frank's face and eased into the saddle with the Italian ducking under his leg. They rode out of town and down a long slope through seep willow and salt grass and into a dense patch of skunkbrush with the wind on them and the mare snorting as she footed her way through the high and ripping bramble.

John Frank clenched his hands around the boy's chest and gasped out directions as they went. The sun was all lost under wide ribbons of cloud and the landscape lay flat and unadorned. They downstepped again and came out of a stand of cottonwoods by an arroyo cutting and in the west a small pond of water perhaps once a lake that had dried beyond repair. By the side of that murky pond was a small red-brick barn with one wall completely razed to rubble. Here it is, John Frank called.

They let down by the water's edge. The boy walked Triften to an iron rail standing by the barn door. John Frank sat in the weeds and caught his breath.

Used to be the site of a ranch owned by a man named Foster, he said. First man to drink with me. You can imagine I liked him pretty good. He cut out of here some five years ago. Went to bookkeep for a livery stable in West Virginia. Said he was glad to go back East. Nobody claimed it since this little lake got sucked dry. No fish here no more neither. No water worth a damn but to wet your face with, and even then I believe it'd be a hazard. I just like it on account of it's quiet and I like the look of them junipers yonder.

229

The boy looked out and crossed his arms over his chest. After a few moments he sat down next to Frank.

Horse rider and nature lover in one day, he said. I never would've guessed it.

John Frank dropped his head between his knees and grinned.

Testament to the human spirit, he said.

They sat a long time. They sat crosslegged on the hardened firmament and picked at the weeds beside them. The clouds rimmed over the sky. They watched the heat of their breath rise and fade into the clay bowl of the lake and finally John Frank spoke with a slow heave. I guess you really do love her then, he said.

The boy did not move but kept looking straight ahead at the desolate water.

And I guess you plan to see it through, one way or the other.

One way or the other, the boy repeated quietly.

Beneath the sounds of the wind he told John Frank about the lawyer and the mountains. He told him what the lawyer had done and what he was now doing.

He dumped the baby in the river? Good lord. And all she done was steal a rake to fetch it with? Jesus and the twelve disciples.

You can see how it comes out, the boy said. No way he'll let her stay around with all he's got goin with the mayor.

Why the hell did he bring her here in the first place?

I don't know. I reckon to have something to abuse. Lots of nights travelin alone, he probably figured. I don't want to even imagine what he done to her. Couldn't even imagine it.

But the boy could imagine it and he squinted his eyes and rubbed his shaven head to ward off the vision.

So what is there to do about it now?

The boy glanced over the slope of his shoulder at Frank. I think you know, he said.

John Frank shook his head severely. Now you know that's impossible, he said. Mayor's got himself guarded good as the president, and he regrets lettin you walk already. I bet he knows we're here right now.

John Frank paused and glanced around, then spoke in a hushed tone.

Not to mention that piece-of-work newsman Trewitt been followin him around like a dog for the past month. Says he's goin to write a big story about the mayor and the town and send it off to his Washington boys. The Cultivation of the West, he's goin to call it. I heard him say it with my own ears. It won't work for you, bud. I mean, I suppose none of this makes a damn to you, but I'm tellin you, you got a better chance in outstrippin a train.

He looked pleadingly at the boy. The boy pursed his lips and held up his hands. Alright then, he said. I guess I'll have to outstrip it.

John Frank paused considerably. He gazed out at the trees across the rim of the lake.

One last thing I guess I ought to tell you then, he sighed. There's a chance you can still see her. She's to go to the old church to see the priest. He's comin down from San Suelo to hear her confessions and give her penance and all. She's to go there at noon on Friday. Nobody's really there no more since they started work on the new church and I imagine you could sneak yourself in before they come. That is if they don't find you out before then. You still got today and tomorrow to stay on the lam and I hope you'll at least honor that.

The boy stayed looking out at the junipers in the distance. The wind grew colder with each sweep across the plainland and they each huddled in their jackets and stuffed their hands into their pockets.

I wish I could do more, you know? Frank said. Bring the jail keys to you or tie up the mayor or some shit like that. But it ain't no picture show, Trude. I wouldn't even know where to begin. Wouldn't even know how to tie a good knot. Shit.

Don't think of it, the boy said. You done more for me than anyone I can recall.

They watched the arms of the trees shiver and roll upon themselves for a long time and at length the boy stood and put out his hand to John Frank and John Frank took it and the boy dragged him to his feet. Come on, he said. I'll ride you back.

What about the lawyer? Frank asked.

The boy pulled on his gloves and righted his hat. We'll meet yet, he said.

I don't think so. Way I understand it is even he's got himself guarded by the Ralstons now. And he ain't never been easy to find in the first place, has he?

No. But we'll meet yet.

You think he'll give down his milk about it all?

The boy almost laughed. No, he said. I don't.

So what do you aim to do?

The boy held his laced hands for John Frank to step into and hefted him into the saddle. I aim to make him soft where he'd been hard.

They rode the back country and came upon the outskirts of town, whereupon John Frank said he should walk the rest of the way and that he'd rather anyway. My ass is killin me, he said. The boy got down with him.

It was late now though no trace of sun or moon could be found, and all the day had seemed to pass as if it were the same hour which itself was untraceable. The wind was very cold and the mountains appeared to be pulsing in the distance and the world itself seemed gray and black and even the trees leaned heavy with age and decay.

The boy and the Italian stood before each other as if not knowing what it was they wanted to say or how to say it or if it would be worth saying at all. John Frank said again that he was damn sorry and the boy took him by the shoulders and they embraced for a moment in that cold and empty place. Perhaps they both knew that it might very well be the last time they saw each other for a long time and if not for a long time then forever.

The boy watched John Frank go down the road, making exaggerated bowlegged strides and looking back at the boy with a sad grin on his face. When he was all but out of sight the boy mounted his mare again and took up the reins and said, Best get on, and they did, riding the country that went deeper and colder than he could remember from all days before.

FIVE HOURS OF solitude by the old man's river found the boy wrapped in his bedroll and sitting on the banks of the water. The old man was inside sick and yellow since he put the bottle away. The boy could hear him hacking and once he heard a long desperate oath muttered through the cabin walls. Birds called out thinly, their songs falling brittle and bare from the sparse trees. He rubbed his shaven head and under the bedroll he held his ribs which had started to ache with the darkening weather.

The boy sat alone hour into hour as he had grown to do and he knew the ways of solitude and that in solitude it was fruitless to try to speed the passage of time or worry about its passing but rather that it was better to sit and watch. Sit and watch and let it go by and not think of what things were being lost in that time because things would always be lost and whether they were lost in solitude or in a great shudder of the masses it mattered very little.

In the distance where the mountains stood formidably against the steel sky he thought he could see snow falling. In the gaunt light that lilted from those mountains he thought of her alone in her cell, her soft head resting on the flimsy pillow and her dark eyes turned down. He tried to imagine his mother's face before him, some of her words of comfort carried through the winds of his mind, but he could not. She had become lost to him among all new and other days, and what still remained to be done.

By and by he stood up, flicking the butt of his cigarette into the brush and going back inside the cabin. The old man sat sprawled and wrecked at the table. The boy went by his side and slapped him sharply on the back.

How you holdin up, old man.

Fuckin killin me, boy.

The boy went to the sink basin and returned with a cup of water. Take this, he said.

The old man held the cup to his trembling jaw and drank at it. Tastes like mud, he said.

The boy sat in the opposite chair and polished his pistol and shucked the old shells from the rifle and reloaded it and cleaned the barrels with a piece of chicken wire while the old man talked himself to sleep. When he had finished with the guns he sat with his hands folded on the table. After a long time he fingered his neck and lifted up the silver chain and grasped the silver amulet. For a while he just looked at it. For a while longer he ran his fingers over his mother's name. Then he polished it as well as he could and lowered it very carefully into his back pocket. He took up his guns and refilled the cup of water and set it on the table where the old man was mindlessly working his arms with his fingers while he slept, and went out the door.

He packed the rifle in the saddlebag and pushed his pistol into his belt and patted the mule's head and climbed onto the mare. They rode high on the mesa with the blue light of the mountains pouring down across the horse's chest. When he hit Old 17 he pulled up the reins and walked the horse down the road, holding his hand to his brow to shield his eyes from the sudden break of sun.

By the time the boy had adjusted his eyes to the glare and saw them standing in the road, it was too late to turn around. The guns they held aimed at him were long and familiar and they each rose in succession from a card table that had been situated in the road ditch. There were four this time, the waxed mustaches like dark blades upon their mouths. They stepped away from the table and the buckets of beer and ice. One of them held his cards up to the boy as if to call his bluff.

He was thirty yards away when he tried to make a turnaround and remount his horse. When he was up in the saddle he shot a glance back and saw the Ralstons piling into a car parked by the card table. He came down from the mare and dropped the reins and turned back and started walking down the road toward them.

The driver saw him coming. He called to the others and they all stepped out of the car. They met the boy in the middle of the road. One stepped forward with a grin and shucked the boy's pistol from his belt and slid the rifle loose from the saddlebag with the mare stepping nervously away. We meet again, he said.

It was the leader who had taken him to the river.

What'd ya think? You'd just mosey on out here and we'd lay down the red carpet for ya? He laughed heartily and looked around at his brothers. Who's this kid think he is? Jesse fuckin James? He came forward and took the boy under the arm. Someone'd like to talk to you.

He led him to the car. The boy made no protest at all. Get in, the leader said. Tie up that horse, he called to another.

One of the men got in front with the leader and another slid in the back with the boy and held his own pistol to the boy's cheek.

Why you wastin your time like this, boy? You must be dumb as dirt to waste your time on a girl. And some kind of nigger girl, no doubt. Somebody must've filled your head with rocks. You got rocks in your head, boy? He shook the boy's head with his free hand. I think I hear em bangin around in there. You hear em boys?

The men chuckled coldly and watched the road. When they reached the gate the boy saw the Englishman standing in the front yard throwing a horseshoe at an iron post driven into the ground across the brown lawn. When the car came into the drive the lawyer looked up and saw the boy in the backseat. He started across the lawn. His walk was slightly plagued by a slump in his shoulder where the boy had cut him. He came to the car and the car stopped next to him and he opened the door. Please, he said. I've been expecting you.

The Englishman stepped back and let the boy out and leaned into the car and thanked the men and told them to stand by. They nodded with prideful faces and set their guns in their laps.

You got it, the leader said.

The Englishman led the boy across the lawn to where a pair of wicker rockers sat in the grass. Sit, he said.

The boy stayed standing, looking around at the horseshoe posts and the chairs and the car, unbelieving it was the same empty place he had so long visited.

Yes, the lawyer said, watching the boy's eyes, I have been a long time in waiting for this matter to clear up. And you have been very persistent indeed. But after Saturday all will be well. Now sit, he said, drawing from his vest a small revolver and pointing it at the boy's chest.

The boy sat. The Englishman leaned daintily into the other chair and leveled the pistol at him and began rocking. He rocked with a steady push from his foot and waved the pistol around thoughtlessly. I should have killed you in the mountains, he said. And I could have. Very easily. Perhaps all this would not have gone so far. He paused the rocker and settled the pistol on the boy again. But it has.

You son of a bitch, the boy said.

Oh, the Englishman said, easing back in the rocker. It is not wise to take such a tone. Didn't your father ever tell you that it's not wise to insult a man who is holding a gun to your face?

If he did I don't recall nor do I care.

My, my, the Englishman said. The youthful spirit.

The boy made to stand and hit him but the Englishman spun and locked the pistol down on the boy's eyes. The boy slumped back into the chair again. He put his hand over his face. Then he looked up at the man again.

Why? he said.

The Englishman pressed the boy with a stare. Necessity, he said. That is why. Necessity. The Englishman sat and leaned out of the chair and put the pistol into the boy's chest. If it wasn't my doing, it would have been someone else's. I could have killed her before as well, you must know. But I spared her. I thought perhaps she'd let it pass and I would locate some job for her and she could try and have a go at it for herself. Very generous of me, you must agree. But she did not let it pass. He paused and withdrew the pistol and began again to rock. She had to go and steal that rake. Had to go and try to discredit my name before I even got settled in. Now how is a man to make a good name for himself with such fanfare surrounding him? Quite impossible, I assure you. This, at the very least, your simple mind understands.

She stole a rake, the boy said with the same lack of animation that stared out at him from the Englishman's eyes.

A rake, a car, a lock of hair. What is the difference among those things? I think you should be able to see it. It is not the object, it is the intent. The Englishman went on rocking. I am an indispensable figure for the mayor, he said. He needs me. He needs my reasoning. He is sometimes swayed by sentiment. In a business such as ours there is no room for sentiment. You, for example.

He waved the gun at the boy again, as if in offer of some trivial council.

The mayor should not have let you go. He knows this now, but here you are. Prepared to kill me, I'm sure. No, he should not have let you go but as I said, sometimes he is swayed by sentiment. He likes you, I believe. To a certain degree at least. He thinks you are foolish but he does not condemn you for it. Perhaps because in many ways, as in this case, he is foolish too. But you see, there must be some amount of condemnation for those who are foolish, just as there must be for those who aspire beyond their place or those who don't seem to have any sense about them at all. People like this are reckless and certainly dangerous and they have no regard for the way things are set up around them.

The boy sat very still. The Englishman kept rocking steadily as if he meant to torture the boy with the monotony of it. Now and again he glanced over at the car where the Ralstons were hipped up against the open doors of the car and watching them blankly.

See them, he said. Those men are not smart. But those men know it and know their place. I'm sure you have been made to understand such a thing. They do not try to leap from their confines.

The Englishman paused and put up a finger in retraction.

Not confines, he said. Boundaries. They know their boundaries. That, in turn, makes them smart. Not smart in an intellectual way, for such a cause is lost on them. But smart in the ways of the world. You don't seem to share that with them. And no matter how smart you may be otherwise, on the whole you are very stupid.

Which makes you the smartest man in the world, I imagine.

In this world, perhaps. Yes. The world of here. The world of this town.

The boy put his hands over his face. When he let them down the Englishman was still rocking, his eyes studying the boy.

I'd give you my word we'd never come back here again.

Your word? The Englishman raised his eyebrows. And what word would that be? he said. How young you are indeed.

Then you could watch us leave, the boy said. Have us followed all the way to the Yukon if it pleased you.

The Englishman shook his head and smiled. You truly do not understand, he said. I have been crossed by Delilah. I have been crossed by you. Do you think I did not notice the scratches on the lock of my docket you so long delivered to me? Shall I throw flowers at your departure for that, bid you a fond farewell into the setting sun? That would not be smart of me. That would make me a very stupid man.

He leaned forward and studied the boy's face with a false tenderness.

However, I have decided to let you go. Call it sentiment. Or call it the fact that I think to watch Delilah hang would be a fine lesson for you. Something to realign your thinking. Something that will show you at last that in this matter there is no choice for you. That in this matter you are relegated by your boundaries. The Englishman took a long breath and stopped rocking. So, he said. It is decided. Of course we will hold your guns here for safekeeping. And we will watch closely for you on Saturday. He turned away to the mountains again and smiled at them. Yes, he said. A reckoning for all.

The Englishman got up from the rocker. He raised his collar against the winds and looked around the yard. I believe the cold will put off my horseshoe game, he said. Unless you'd like to stay and play awhile.

He smiled into the empty stare of the boy, then sighed and waved the pistol about and called for the Ralstons who came trotting out into the yard.

TWENTY

HOURS BEFORE THE girl was to meet the priest the boy showed his face in town once more. When the glass cutter stepped down from his truck the boy got off the porch step and put up a finger in greeting. He was an excessively thin man and he came tugging on a pair of oat sack pants that were held up loosely by a pair of red suspenders, his too-large boots clomping indelicately in the early morning stillness. He stopped short huffing and looked at the boy, then came booting up the steps.

Been here long?

The boy stubbed out his cigarette on the porch floor and stood and put his hands in his pockets. Not too long, he said.

The glass cutter shifted the mug of coffee in his hand and fumbled through his keys. Friday usually finds me slow to start, he said. What time is it?

Just six, the boy said.

No wonder you been waitin. Come on in, he said.

He pushed the door open with a long creak. They stepped into the cool shade of the store. The man walked up to the front and put his

keys and coffee on the counter near a polished silver till. He went back
up to the front door and tilted open the shudders, the light arriving in a
single weak shaft along the floor. Then he came back and stepped
behind the counter still wrestling with his pants and took up a pencil
and slid it behind his ear and leaned on the counter and looked bemus-
edly at the boy. There was no sign that he registered who the boy was.

So what did you need from me that you come so early?

I'm in need of some plate glass.

What size?

I'd estimate it at three by four.

Big window.

Yes sir. And I need two of em.

The man lifted a pair of wire-rim glasses from the undershelving
and settled them on his nose. Let me go see what I got in back, he said.
You want some coffee? I'm fixin to put a pot on back here.

I'd appreciate it, the boy said.

The glass cutter was gone for some time. When he came back he
held a mug of coffee in each hand and set both on the counter.

Here you go. I put some sugar in it. That alright?

That's how I take it. Thank you.

The glass cutter sipped and shook his head at the mug.

Myself I like a little milk in mine but it ain't easy to find a fresh
bottle these days. Seems they more concerned about other things. Man
who used to sell milk and cheese come in here the other day with this
catalog on coolers. Stepped right up here, nothin said about the milk
I'd asked him for, only this long-winded speech about the two-hundred
model. Four compartments in this cooler. Never fail to keep things
cold. I told him all I wanted was some milk. How you goin to keep it
cold? he said to me.

The glass cutter shook his head at the boy, but the boy was watching the sun rise out on the road.

Man's been bringin me milk for five years, asks me how I'm goin to
keep it cold. And he knows I own the very first cooler in this town.
Men used to come and sip beer on my porch every Saturday. I
reminded him of it but he said it don't work like this two-hundred
model. Don't keep near as cold or well. So to that I just stood there
poker-faced as I could and asked him, asked him, Earl, what you think
I've been doin all these years? Don't you know how much I enjoy it

warm and spoiled? Earl didn't much care for that, told me to forget it. Said I'd come aknockin for it right soon. Well, I promised him I'd never be caught callin on a farmer wearin a silly brown suit like he was that day. Looked like somethin one of his calves shot from its ass.

The glass cutter looked into the black of his coffee and laughed sleepily. Ain't seen Earl in a while, he said.

The boy nodded and tried to hide the impatience in his smile and thanked the man again for the coffee. How about them windows? he said.

Right. I put a good cut on em. They're ready. And I reckon you'll need some sealing compound.

Yes sir.

Alright. You got a truck out there somewheres?

No sir. Got my horse.

The glass cutter took the glasses from his nose and set them back on the undershelving. Well, he said. I can have em drove out later.

There's no road to where I'm bringin em.

The glass cutter sipped thoughtfully at his mug. How you reckon to carry em then?

Just strap em up good. Can you pack em with some boards and paper?

I reckon we could put a try to it.

The glass cutter lit a pipe he brought from beneath the counter and tugged on his pants and brought the glass out and two tins of sealant which he placed in a small paper bag. Let's see what we can do, he said.

They wrapped the glass together with some broken tackboard scraps and taped up the glass with heavy brown packaging paper and they each carried a piece outside on their hips. They stitched up the glass on the horse's rump, tying it under her flanks and around the saddle and up the buttocks. The mare reared up and the boy coaxed her down and told her to be still and finally they had it on tight enough.

The boy turned to the glass cutter and asked him how much he owed him and he paid fourteen dollars even and the man thanked him and told him to take care with the glass then went back inside drawing on his pipe, a finger hitched around the back of his suspender branches. The boy put the sealant in the saddlebag, climbed on his horse and began to walk her down the road.

As he was passing under the willow tree he heard a door slam in the near distance. A few seconds later Thomas Trewitt came hustling onto the thoroughfare. When the boy saw him he hopped down from his horse and went swiftly toward him with his hands poised into fists. Trewitt did not turn to run but instead he held up his own hands and waved them at the boy. Only when the boy had him by the collar did the newsman start backstepping and slapping at the boy's hands.

Cultivation of the West, the boy hissed.

Trewitt kept slapping at the boy's hands. His face was screwed up and then he took the boy equally by the collar. You wait a minute here, he said with a forced hush. I came to tell you I'm sorry.

Sorry? Sorry for what? That you were full of shit about tryin?

No. Look here. Trewitt's breath was hot and fractious on the boy's face. I have tried, he said. There's nothing that will persuade him. I'm sorry.

The boy let down his hands. After he caught his breath Trewitt let go too.

You're sorry, the boy said dryly. What about the lawyer? There's your big story. Why don't you tell the people about him?

You mean the rumor about him and the girl.

Not the rumor. The fact.

The newsman wrung his hands together and looked down. Hell, he said. There is nothing I can do about it now. He paused a moment, then looked up sharply. It's not my fault, he said. And no one could do anything about it, even if they did care. It would be too dangerous for me. He looked down again. But I can promise you it will not go unrecorded.

Oh, the boy said, turning back to his horse who stood nosing the cold ground. Of course not. Great new West will be told for all the world.

Trewitt put up a hand to the boy's back. All of it, he called. Not just that. Nothing will be lost. All things will be recorded. All things will be told.

The boy got up on his horse again and began to walk her down the road. Trewitt started into a jog beside the mare. He was holding up a hand as though he wished the boy would shake it but the boy only frowned down at him then started the horse into a trot. Trewitt tried a few more steps, then pulled up and stood huffing in the middle of the road. He watched the boy stepping the horse into the high grass at the edge of town. You will be recorded too, he called.

By the time he cleared out into the hamlet it was already ten o'clock. The old man was riding the mule alongside the river and humming to himself. When he saw the boy coming he turned and came up the slope.

What in the hell, he said.

It's your windows.

I told ya I just needed some wood.

I told you I'd get some windows. Help me bring em down.

They undid the cording and removed the glass from the horse's back and walked each window to the cabin and leaned the packages under the empty window frames. The boy handed the old man the paper bag. You'll need this, he said.

The old man snatched up the bag and flung it to the ground. I can't do this, he said.

Why not?

The old man fumbled with his gnarled hands. He held them up to the boy. Shaking and twitching and thin to nothing but knuckle and bone.

I've got old, boy. It's still amazin to me I can make coffee.

Well I ain't doin it. I got to get on.

I ain't either. Told ya I just needed some wood.

Will you just look it over? He cut em to fit right.

I just imagine I can't is all.

The boy turned away from the old man and looked up at the muddy sun and the torn shreds of cloud before it. Noon was approaching quickly. I got to get on, he said.

You just got back. Where you off to now? You know they're bound to catch you.

The boy lifted his hat and squinted. He seemed at a loss to describe it, his eyes out on the sun as if it too awaited his answer. Goin to see God, he said at last.

Then he was up on the mare again and going down the hills with the old man watching him the same way he had so many times before. He put his hands on his hips when the boy was out of sight, then turned and hobbled back into the windy dark of the cabin.

THE CHURCH STOOD half toppled just east of town where the old adobe structures of the first settlers there had once stood. Now the church was skeletal, the red clay walls nearly washed out of their flaking white paint and the cross erected at the wooden gate angling down into the dust.

The boy came riding in the soft cold light. He walked the horse behind the church to the friary. The churchyard was a vast field of cracked red earth. Here and there fissured headstones protruded, offering little more than rubble and weeds. He hobbled the horse and came into the yard and bent by one of the stones, his hands clenched on his knees. There was no name or if there was it had gone away by the elements. He went to another as nameless as the first, then stood and spat and wiped his brow under his hat.

When he entered the church he took down his hat. He could not remember the last time he had been to church but he remembered going with his father and his father lowering his hat from his head as if in apology and how he had watched him and done the same.

Inside the air was cool and splayed from the shattered windows and it leaned in across the walls and floor like rivulets of water. The boy bent down and took the dirk knife from his boot and stood stockstill in the doorway. Smells of jasmine and wine and rot lingered. The floor was littered with parched missals and the sunburned husks of palm leaves. When he walked up the nave he could feel the dry clay shift under his boots. Dust billowed up from his tread, then froze and hung suspended in the light.

In front of the altar rail rose two long steps of Italian marble and behind the altar a basket for the alms. The altar was a thick cut of beech and perhaps the only thing untouched by the years. Upon it stood two chalices of pewter and one of bronze, though the cup had been tarnished green at the base. The boy picked it up and turned it in his hand.

The blood of Christ. He thought of his father again. Remembering what he always said when he returned from town Sunday nights. Only thing that place is good for is the blood. Then he would go staggering up the stairs with a fifth of bourbon or bootleg gin and pass into the bedroom where he would make no light to see by.

The boy stepped down from the altar and walked around to the side. Some birds cooed, then spun from the vigas. They went in a flurry out an empty window. He watched them go in the milky light. Down one of the aisles on the far side of the church's body was an alcove built as a confessional and inside it a pair of small stools and a curtain between. He looked around. The birds that had gone warbled again in the distance. Calling perhaps to welcome his soul or to warn it, or perhaps calling for no reason at all unless their own antique nature. He stood listening, his hands nervous around the rim of his hat, then with a shuffle and tread of dust he went toward the confessional.

He walked in and placed his hat on one of the stools, drawing the curtain along its ring chain until it unfolded in front of him. He sat in the darkness. He sat motionless in the dark and cold, listening to the wind shrilling through the broken glass of the windows and he sat for a very long time.

He tried to think of her coming up the road. He imagined her walking in the door long and clean and sad and beautiful. Imagined her hair pulled up and tossed along her shoulders and her shoulders slung back along her smooth neck and only her downcast eyes betraying the majesty of her.

He wondered what he would say to her when she came. This time he wanted to say nothing but only hold her and take her in his arms and let her fold into him like a blanket wrapped around one who is lost in sleep and then to push her long black hair from his face and kiss her eyes until they once again opened to him with that clear dark light.

When he heard the wind kick up and sweep through the chapel he raised his head from where it had been resting on his knees. He parted the curtains enough for one eye to see through. He held his breath. Nothing moved. And then she came.

She was led by the mayor himself. He was dressed grandly and shielding the boy's vision of her, closing the doors behind them and clearing out some curious townspeople who had come to watch and telling them to go on home. Then he moved aside to let her pass.

The boy watched her stepping free of chains down the dirt floor of the nave. He could smell her hair. She wore a long white cotton dress with a dipped neck and a white lace shawl and brown sandals with

open toes too cold for the weather. Her toes were painted pale pink
and her fingers too. Her long hair black as a lake was brushed out fine
and brought up behind her head with a white bow that was knotted
sadly and falling down along her back. Her lips were dark and red and
trembling.

She held her hands folded in front of her stomach as she came.
When she looked up at the altar he could see the glaze of her eyes in
the broken slats of sunlight, something in her shadowed aspect that
made it so he could scarcely manage to look upon her.

The mayor followed behind her at a distance. When he pushed
back his coat and folded his hands behind his back the boy saw the twin
pistols in his turquoise-studded belt. He gripped the knife tighter. He
looked back at the girl. She knelt on the first step in front of the altar
and bowed her head. The boy could see the skin of her neck stretching
along her shoulders and down her back and he had to breathe and
think only of his breathing to keep himself from rushing out for her.

The birds that had flown off came parting the light and dust, fluttering and floating, then perching themselves high above in the apse,
but the girl did not move at the sound of them. After a few moments
the mayor came forward. He seemed he would put a hand upon her
shoulder. He held his hand up behind her but then stopped and looked
down at her and at his hand and then he turned and sat himself in
the front pew and crossed his legs. For at least an hour he moved his
fingers through his beard deliberately and studied her, the boy watching both of them from behind the curtain. In all that time the girl did
not move.

At last the mayor stood and looked back at the closed door and
looked at his watch and walked toward the girl. With the dust from his
boots smoking up the light between them he spoke to her back.

Miss. He cut himself off and coughed into his hand. I must go, he
said woodenly. Padre Jiminez should have been here by now. I have
business to attend to. I will have the men who drove us here come
inside and wait with you. Do not—

He stopped himself again and watched the girl who had not turned
to face him and he watched her very seriously and the boy thought
sadly also.

Please do not try and flee them, he went on. I know what tomorrow
brings, but if the Ralston men are given any reason to—

He stopped himself once more. He coughed. When you are finished speaking with the priest they will escort you out. If he comes. If not . . .

The mayor paused when the door opened. He turned around. The boy let the curtain fall and shifted to the other side and peered out. The mayor raised a hand and bowed excessively as the vicar came up the pews.

The old priest's white mane of hair was windblown and his cheeks pocked with dirt. One of his arms was slung up in a green rag. In his other hand he held a small leather satchel limply by his side. He raised his satchel and gave the mayor a weary smile.

Padre, the mayor said, walking rapidly up the nave with one brief look back at the girl. ¿Qué paso?

El charro choco. Eso fue un accidente.

The priest gave his shoulders a slight rise and shook his head wistfully, his peaked eyebrows giving him the appearance of being in constant deliberation. The mayor put a hand on the priest's back.

¿Que tu hicistes? ¿Quien te trae aquí?

Uno de los muchachos de la cuidad. Eso no fue su culpa.

¿Tu brazo, esta roto?

Si. Yo pienso.

Will you be alright?

Seguro.

Eschucha, yo tengo que irme.

Go my son, the priest said firmly.

¿Estas seguro?

Si. Vayate. Dejame aquí con la muchacha. Vaya con Dios.

Pero, please bring her out to the men waiting in the car when you are finished. And be quick. He gave a slight nod at the priest's satchel. And remember, he said. Be careful too.

The priest frowned at the satchel and nodded.

The mayor inspected him once more, then bowed his head. Vaya con Dios, Padre.

Then the mayor was gone out the door. This time he did not look back.

The priest stepped down the nave, the shuffling of his feet almost obscene in the silence of the ruined church. He came and put a hand on the girl's shoulder and she turned to where some light came upon her and stayed caught in the hollow of her throat. She looked up at the priest with such a look of grief the boy turned away. Then she rose and stood in front of him. The priest gave a heavy sigh, leaning and setting his bag down and putting his hands on the girl's shoulders again and taking her soft hands in the wrinkled bags of his own. I'm sorry for you, he said. For you I am very sorry.

He spoke with heavy Spanish inflections and the girl nodded slowly at his words, then left her head resting on her chest. The priest looked around the church and shook his head at the floor.

You must understand, child, he said facing the girl again. These are no God's ways. These are no the ways of God but the ways of man and they are very different. No worry, though. God will bring you home.

She nodded again, a single band of blue light now riding across her cheek. The priest looked into her glistening eyes and let her hands go and she left them by her side and he leaned and took up his satchel and placed it on the altar.

You are ready to give penance and take holy communion?

She shifted her feet and stood erect before the altar and stepped up to the altar rail and gripped it to steady herself. It was so quiet in the half-light that the boy could hear her dress shift along her arms when she nodded again.

What is your name, child? So I may give it to God to take you in.

She shifted her feet again. She shook her head, her lips tense and fluttering but unable or unwilling to speak.

My dear, the priest said even more gently, you must tell me your name. God must recognize you when you ask forgiveness and come to his glory.

One hand went up to her neck. It paused there, then fell again. She covered her face with both hands with the pink fingertips quivering above her eyes.

Delilah. Her name is Delilah.

Both the girl and the priest were startled by the voice and the priest nearly backed into the altar when the boy shook open the curtain and came walking toward them.

What are you do here? he called. How you get in here? You are no supposed to be here. He held up a bony finger toward the door. You go now. This is sacred exchange. I call the men.

The boy kept coming. As he neared the altar he swung the knife up from his hip. He heard a low gasp from the girl but still he kept coming. The priest saw the blade and turned to his satchel and popped the latch open with his working arm and thrust his hand inside it. When he turned around again the pistol he held rigidly was pointed at the boy's stomach and the raised knife halted above the boy's shoulder. The priest's look was inexplicably placid. He rode back the hammer and pushed the nose of the gun into the boy's stomach. The boy and the priest stared at each other, the pace of their breath equal and loud in the quiet.

Please. Though the words barely escaped her lips, the priest turned and regarded her. Please, she said again and louder. Let him stay.

The priest inspected the girl's face as she let her head back onto her chest. He turned and grimaced at the boy.

I want him to stay.

For why you want him to stay?

The boy set the knife down on the floor and took a step backward. The priest studied him anew, his clothes disheveled and his shorn hair standing on end and his eyes drained white and blinking. Then he picked up the boy's knife and looked at the girl again. Alright, he said. He pitched the knife toward the back of the church. He lowered the gun but did not put it down. Any wrong and I call for the men, he said. Do not think I can no use this either. Now come here, and you do not molest.

No sir.

The boy walked past the girl, touching the tips of her fingers which remained at her side with the palm of his hand but not looking at her yet.

You help me since my arm is gone broken, the priest said. Open this bag, please.

The boy opened the bag and the priest told him what to remove and the boy removed a pewter dish and a round sterling box and a white cloth which the priest told him to lay over his forearm. Then the priest stepped down and told the boy to move back. Keep going, he said. When he felt the boy's distance was far enough away he came down to the girl and placed the pistol in his pant waist and put his hand on her cold forehead and spoke quietly to her.

A breeze came down through the cracked roofing and caused a shiver in the girl's shoulders. The birds above ruffled their feathers. The priest spoke to her of God's everlasting forgiveness and he spoke of His goodness and peaceful home in the heavens and he told her that no sin could not be redeemed by faith and love and then he asked her to speak her sins.

She looked at neither of them and with a rising voice she told the priest about her lost baby and the rake she had stolen and how she should have done more to save her child and perhaps even her own mother and father and the priest's brow grew heavy and he dipped his head down, then up at the ceiling, and finally he took his hand from her forehead where beads of sweat had begun to form.

The priest took the gun from his waist again and motioned the boy back to the altar. He came holding the box and dish. The priest told him to set the dish on the altar, then he made the sign of the cross over it. He told the boy to open the box and place one of the wafers on the dish and the boy did so. He set the box back down while the priest mumbled prayer over the dish. The boy smiled weakly at her as the priest spoke to the ceiling but she did not smile back. When he finished the blessing he labored down to one knee, genuflected, then rose and turned to the boy.

Please, he said. When I finish speaking, place the bread upon her tongue.

The boy gave the priest a sharp look, then moved forward. He tilted back his head and rubbed the base of his neck, looking around the church as if none of what was occurring at that moment in his life was meant to be occurring at all.

Good father, look upon this girl Delilah with your all-seeing eyes and know that she is ready for you in your palace on high. The body of Christ.

The priest nodded at the boy with the pistol flinching in his hand to make its own surrogate command. The boy turned and took up the chalky wafer from the dish on the altar. The girl leaned forward. Ever so slightly she parted her lips. Before she leaned back again the boy whispered to her and his face was very sad and pale.

No god will save you now, he said. All you got left is me.

She looked at the boy and then at the priest to see if he had heard but he had not. Then she began to cry.

The priest motioned the boy to use the cloth on his arm and he dabbed the girl's eyes until they were dry again. Is that it? he said.

That is all we can do for her here. God will take her the rest of the way.

Can I talk to her a minute then, before she goes.

The priest lowered his eyebrows on the boy. Solo un momento, he said grudgingly.

The boy stepped down and took her by the arm. Her eyes turned and came upon him, wet and lost on his face. He led her toward the confessional. Before he shut the curtain around them the priest raised up the pistol and called to the boy. Solo un momento, he said again.

Inside it was all but dark with only a thin film of gray light on the crimson curtains. He took her in his arms.

She was frail, more frail than he had imagined, and she gripped the collar of his shirt and wrung it in her fingers and he felt in her a strength he had not imagined either. He put his nose into the black ribbons of her hair. She kissed his neck. Then he leaned back and studied her face. All things he remembered and all those he had never known but perhaps had seen in his dreams. She remained still and silent and he took a long time with it. Trying to place in his memory the touch of her skin.

He passed his hand over the thin eyelids and across the hollowed cheek and the raised cheekbone. He touched below her lip a moon-shaped scar lighter than her true color. He pushed his hand through her brushed hair and at last he ran the back of his hand along her neck, and when he finally withdrew from her his head was humming and the weight of his own body seemed suddenly much greater and he straightened his knees to better bear himself.

She had her lips against his chest when he finally spoke to her.

It's alright, he said as softly as he could. I'll come for you tomorrow. Trude.

I'll be there. Tomorrow mornin. Just make sure you're lookin. I'll be there.

He felt himself rocking her in his arms, and when the priest called loudly from the altar he stopped. She put her arms around his neck and let her head fall to his shoulder and he held it there.

Then he reached into his back pocket and took hold of her hand and turned her palm up with his thumb. Take this, he said. This is yours now. He pressed the amulet into the throat of her palm.

The silver chain pooled across her cupped fingers and the girl grasped the amulet and read the name and once more she began to cry.

The boy closed it in her hand. He tried to smile at her. Only time you're allowed to take it off is when we go swimmin, he said.

Trude, she said. Her face was still against his shoulder. I can't.

He took her under the chin and raised her head up. You can too, he said. He tried to smile again. Call it collateral, he said. Or call it my promise.

The girl leaned away and placed her fisted hands on her chest. Then she raised her head to his with her eyes still closed and kissed him on the mouth. Your promise, she said.

She let her arms down then, turning and opening the curtain and walking toward the altar with the boy reaching out his hand for her once more. She took it, then let it go. He stood watching her walk away from him with the priest coming down the steps of the altar to lead her out.

The priest held the pistol up with his working hand. You stay right there, he called to the boy. Then he nodded at the girl to walk before him and they passed up toward the door while the boy walked slowly to the altar again with his hat held in both hands against his stomach. Before they had gone by each other entirely, she looked across the pews and through the scattered light. Something appeared in her face that had not been there before, and he saw in her eyes then that she believed him.

Twenty-one

THE WIND CAME ripping through the valley and he lifted his head from the horse's mane to take its sting upon him. He wanted it with him, wanted to endure everything in her name. Wanted to invoke her presence for all living things who understood what pain was and wanted them to see it in his face only and in no other face besides.

By the time he downtrotted onto the thoroughfare his breath was all but gone and the horse under him heaving too. His face was blotched red by the wind as if he'd been pelted with buckshot. He sprang down from the mare and left her standing in the road and went up the steps and in the door.

He walked past the old woman at the counter with the burnt remnant of a cigarette dangling precariously from his lips. She watched warily as he strode about the store, his eyes here and there, lost among the rows of canned goods and kerosene and firewood. The proprietor came out from behind the counter and she stood against the front of it with her glasses held shakily to her nose. Aren't you the boy, she started.

The boy wheeled around on his heels as if he'd forgotten she was in there with him. The woman gripped the counter behind her. She looked at his face. She looked at his clenched hands. Can I help you find something? she said.

What?

You need me to help you find something? She was almost whispering now.

He looked around again. A hat, he said after a moment. I need a hat.

She motioned to the back of the store. In the back, she said. I'll show you.

He followed her absently to a small hat stand where hung four woven Resistols and two black Stetsons. Let me have one of em, he said. He was already turned away and walking to the front of the store.

Which one, exactly?

Any of em.

She took down one of the Stetsons and checked the size and estimated it to his head, then came back to the counter where he was standing with the bills from his boot heel leafed open in his hands.

Any shirts?

He did not look up from the money he was counting nor did he seem to expect an answer from her. The proprietor set the hat on the counter. Yes, she said.

Pants?

Yes, she said again. They're all in the back.

Ring one up of each.

Well, the old woman fumbled. You want to look at them?

His eyes came up from the money and shifted around her head, settling nowhere. No, he said. You pick em.

She shook her head and went away. When she came back she was holding a black muslin button-up and a pair of denim jeans the color of coal.

Will these do? I don't rightly know without measuring you but I think they're about your size.

Those are fine. He didn't even look up from his hands. And three packs of cigarettes, he said.

She took the cigarettes from under the counter and tallied up his purchases and sacked them in two large paper bags and pushed them toward the boy's lowered hands. Nineteen dollars, she said.

He paid and took the bags in his fist and looked evenly at her. You got any guns back there?

No, the old woman said and in her face was a look that said she wouldn't tell him even if she did.

Outside he stuffed the clothes into the saddlebag, removing a pack of cigarettes beforehand and rising onto his mount and stopping briefly to look upon the willow tree. The wind blew its long cascade of arms down into the dust and high again and he saw once more that the Indian women were absent. He watched the barren arms of the tree twirl and sweep down in the bursts of wind and he watched the sprinkle of their silky catkins being blown down the road, fine and tender and lost on the spinning world.

The hand upon his boot shook twice before the boy noticed it. The rancher came around and stood in front of the boy's horse and waved a hand up at him.

That ain't no place for sleepin, he said. He smiled unsurely up at the boy. You alright?

The boy looked down and saw Charlie Ford standing with his hand on Triften's nose. Yeah, he said. I'm alright. What are you doin here?

A man's got to be in society every now and then. I was fixin to get a steak and a cup of coffee. Why don't you come along.

Well. I ought not to.

Well.

But I'd like to talk a minute, if you can spare it for me.

I can spare a handful. What is it you need?

The boy looked about furtively then motioned to Charlie Ford and walked the horse into a nearby alleyway. The boy tore open the fresh pack of cigarettes and cupped his hand over a match and lit it and looked out at the road.

I wanted to thank you for all you done for me, he said.

Don't think of it.

It was too much, you know.

No, Charlie Ford said. He smiled a little. I don't know it at all.

Well, the boy said, it was. That's why this time I'd like to do some bartering, and I hope to do better for you. He paused and looked into Charlie Ford's eyes. You, he started. I guess you heard about what all's happened down here. Why I needed your help and all.

Charlie Ford stopped smiling and pushed his hands deep into the pockets of his ranch coat and peered out at the plaza. Whatever you need, he said. Tell me.

The boy looked down at the unsmoked cigarette in his hand and flung it onto the ground.

I'm assumin you take the part opposed to the mayor, Ford said. And that makes the place where I hang my sympathies automatic.

The boy took up the reins and thanked the rancher and told him he'd be by the ranch as soon as he checked on the old man. To this Charlie Ford said that he'd wait on him and not to worry himself about when he came. The boy lowered his head and said that he'd have to stop doing favors for him or else he'd feel obliged. Charlie Ford came and patted the boy's boot again and told him there wasn't anything wrong with feeling obliged every once in a while. He patted the boy one more time on the leg and before he walked off toward Garrets he said that feeling obliged let you know you still had friends and that there was something you still cared about, and that that was no small thing. The boy held up the reins and spoke a small but fervent agreement under his breath and raised a hand and flicked the reins and went dusting down the road and into the coming storm clouds.

The room was clamorous with smoky light and the damp odor of flesh. The old man was still sitting as the boy had left him in the morning, rocking back slightly in the chair and staring up at the ceiling with slickened gray eyes.

You need to get yourself out more is what you need.

The old man turned at the boy's voice, an awkward heaviness in his motion. I need a drink, he managed.

Drink that water.

I'm sickern shit.

The old man sighed and righted the chair to the table and hunched down and spread his arms across it. The boy came and sat across from him and took his feeble arms in his hands. The old man started up at the boy's touch.

What is it now? he asked.

The boy looked down at the table. That holster you got in the cupboard, he said. You got a pistol to fit it?

What happened to yours?

I reckon the story of it ain't no good. It's gone though.

I can guess it might be, yeah. Look around if you like. He stopped and took his arms away and set them on his belly and began to scratch them. I won't waste a breath on askin what for, he said.

The boy got up and began to look around and paused when he saw where the old man had fixed the glass into the window frames.

I'll be damned, he said.

He turned to the old man who held up his arms and feigned reproach.

Yeah, I done it. Nearly killed me, ya sumbitch.

Hellfire, the boy said.

After a while he found the pistol wedged behind the crate of crickets. He cleaned the barrel with a piece of chicken wire and greased the gate and found also a box of shells scattered in the corner. He upheld them in his fingers and inspected them and loaded the chamber with them, old and fragile as they were in their rusted casings. He put the pistol in his belt and went out and fed the horse and mule and watered them and secured a lead rope on the mule. He paused a long time at the mule and finally took the rope off him. He collected all his belongings in the side-saddle sacks and put them back on the mare. Then he walked around the mule again, stroking his head and whispering softly to him.

The old man had risen and stood watching by the door. The boy rubbed the mule's nose and stepped back reluctantly, then nodded to himself and came back to where the old man was standing.

I'm leavin the mule with you, he said.

I know it. You always do.

No. I'm leavin him with you. He's yours. I think he's grown a likin for you anyway. Take him down by the river when you get to feelin better. He managed a thin smile. Maybe take him to town one night, he said. Find yourself a woman.

The old man squinted back and forth between the boy and the mule.

You ain't comin back, he said plainly.

No, the boy said.

The old man looked small and indistinct in the sparsity of the low-ceilinged cabin.

Well, the old man said, gathering himself proudly, you've earned your welcome here. I don't rightly know how, but you have. Now just you make sure not to upset old Zeus. He won't put up with none of your bullshit like I have.

The boy came forward and put out his hand. The old man took it and held it tight as he could. The boy let go, then put his hand on the stringy head that was slick with sweat and in one sudden motion he leaned down and kissed him flatly on the wrinkled shell of his crown. He leaned away and thought the old man would say something more but he did not.

The boy pushed two packs of cigarettes into the old man's hip pocket. Those should keep you for a while, he said. Then he went out and got on his horse. The old man watched as the boy quartered the mare and jogged her down by the river with the wind blustering upon them and the river splashing over the dead grass on the banks.

You come back, he said.

THERE WAS ALREADY a fire going at Charlie Ford's house when the boy came knocking. Ford opened the door and shifted the cigarette he was holding into the other hand and shook hands with the boy. He stepped aside with his hand on the doorknob. Come set, he said.

He showed the boy through a spacious room of hardwood occupied by sparse oak furniture and brass lamps. They went silently across the cold floors and into a long hallway where the walls remained bare and in the back of the ranch house he led the boy through another door and into a final room where the fire was burning.

Above a wide brown leather couch was a large framed portrait of the rancher's wife. She was sitting on a rocker in the middle of a wheat field with her feet wrapped back around the chair legs in the manner of a contented child. In one hand she held daisies and in the other a bowl filled with shavings of an unknown flower, all purple and white and orange and caught in the portrait spilling to the ground.

The boy stood studying the portrait with his hat in his hands. Charlie Ford stood behind him with his own hands folded behind his back and watched between the boy and his painted wife. Finally he motioned the boy to sit on the couch.

What's in the bowl, the boy said, sitting himself down and setting his hat beside him.

Charlie Ford roused his eyes from the portrait and let down his hands from his back. Saffron, he said. She loved the smell of it. Used to

257

cut it up and sprinkle it on the floor around our bed. Said it was what she smelled when she thought of me. Ain't that a funny thing to say? Lord, she was a funny thing.

Ford unbuttoned his breast pocket and withdrew a pack of cigarettes and handed one to the boy. Then he sat in one of the oak chairs that stood without symmetry around the room and hefted himself near the couch with his hands gripping the back of the chair. He leaned back and looked up at the portrait and shook his head, then smiled broadly at the boy.

So, he said. You were talkin about a barter if I'm not mistaken. What can I do?

Well. The boy swept a hand back and forth over the bristle of his hair. I was wondering if I could trade you for a horse, he said.

What's the matter with Triften?

The boy shook a finger. No, he said. Nothin's wrong with her.

Charlie Ford's eyes centered on the boy's and he opened his mouth slightly and tilted back his head. Oh, he said. Well. You mean the girl you was talkin about. Delilah, ain't it? He studied the boy's face and smoked and tapped his cigarette in an ashtray on the low butcher-block table that stood between them. He nodded to himself before the boy could answer.

I wish they'd just let her be, the boy said.

Well, Ford said, leaning up off the chair back, the mayor down there thinks that law without teeth ain't no law at all. Now myself, I tend to be of the thinkin that law without brains is even worse. He sucked at his bottom lip with disgust. But I can't imagine what you're plannin to do to get her out of it now, he said.

The boy rubbed his head again and stubbed out his cigarette in the ashtray. He was looking past the rancher and into the flames from the fireplace behind him. He gritted his teeth. Hellfire upon this place, he said. He exhaled long and slow into his cupped hands. Just ride in is the best way I've been able to figure, he said. Just ride into the plaza and fire off the guns if such a thing is called for to get her free.

He stopped and his face fell suddenly slack at his own words and his eyes glassed over on the flames.

You ever tore off a piece before, son?

Sir?

Shot a gun. You ever done it? What I mean by that is have you ever used it?

The boy's hands went down from his head and began to fiddle with the hat beside him. Shot at birds and barrels, he said. And I shot a sick bovine once.

Charlie Ford shook his head. Shooting a man's a different thing entire, he said.

The boy looked off quickly to the side of the room. I know it, he said. But I don't care what happens to me no more.

Charlie Ford glanced once more and keenly at the portrait on the wall.

When I lost Ann Marie I thought I was done myself, he said in a tone much quieter and slower than he'd used with the boy before. Thought about it even. One shot under the chin. It's a simple thing, really. But after a while passed I knew how wrong that thinkin was. And dark. Ain't nothin good ever comes from dark thoughts. Now that may be a simple sayin from a simple man but it's true. You look out at this land uninterrupted as many days and years as I have, and these things'll get sifted out of you.

He put a hand across the table. He did not seem to want the boy to take it, but only meant to solicit him to listen.

But I see where you're at, Trude. It's the girl and the girl only and nothin beyond it. It ain't nothin to be ashamed of neither. Most men think there's weakness in turnin their hearts to women, but that ain't true. There's strength in it. And that's what I found out, and even it was there when I lost her.

Charlie Ford blew a long stream of smoke across the table in order to undo the boy from the pattern of his hands.

I ain't fool enough to think it ain't hard, and I ain't crude enough to try and lessen whatever it is that's between you two. And I know how it can seem to come from nowhere. That's almost the beauty in it. You and me know the same things in many ways, the lives we live. The life you was born to. The steadiness of work on the ranch, the same every day. The change in the chores that comes only in the change of the seasons. The comfort in that. This here ain't a business, though. A woman in you is as much a thing correctable as it is foreseeable. And it ain't always a thing you can put your hands to for to mold how you want it. I imagine I was already in pieces over Ann Marie before we even met. I know how that can happen. Now that's somethin fine and special and terrible to lose but you got to understand that things will keep goin even when it's down to just one of you left. Don't get me wrong, not a day goes by I don't miss that girl.

Charlie Ford shook his head very slowly. The firelight poured up behind him. His thick burly figure seemed suddenly diminished by the slackness of his shoulders.

She may not be around for me to talk to or touch, but the strength of her is in me still. And for that I know I've got no choice but to go on, even now. Because I imagine she has memories of me too, how she sees me. Strong, she'd say, full of energy. Maybe proud. What would she think of me if I myself disappear? What would she think if she saw me put a bullet in my head, which is what you're sayin more or less. What would Delilah think if she saw you walk into certain death?

He shook his head again, even slower this time.

No son, he said. You got to keep goin on. There ain't no sense in givin yourself up too. There ain't no strength in that.

The boy's hands came away from his hat and he squeezed them together a moment and looked at them. Then his eyes quickened and he looked up at Charlie Ford.

I know it, he said. But I've got to at least try for her. If you'd had the chance, you'd have done the same thing for your wife. He looked hard across the table. You'd do the same thing.

Charlie Ford leaned his elbows onto his knees and peered up at the portrait above the boy for a long time. Alright, he said.

And that was all that was said for a long while. They listened to the fire crackle. Charlie Ford continued looking at the portrait. The boy watched his face deepen upon it. It looked like he meant to summon a word or two from the flat canvas of her face.

You got to be careful, Charlie Ford said at last. You understand me? Be careful who sees you until tomorrow mornin and what they see you doin. And what with. What a man carries can tell you exactly what he's done the last few days.

And what do I look like I've been doin? the boy said.

Charlie Ford raised his eyebrows. Gettin ready, he said.

They sat silent for a moment longer with the shadows of the flames writhing on the walls.

What kind of horse? Ford said.

The boy leaned forward and took out a cigarette and lit it and dashed the match into the ashtray.

Doesn't matter, he said. Whatever you got to spare.

Charlie Ford rubbed his jaw.

Well, he said. I reckon I could put you up with one of the Morgs. I've got a good little saddle horse, he can rack even, but I think he'd be too young for mountain ridin. And I don't think a quarter horse would do much good unless he'd been worked in em, which mine haven't. I reckon the Morgan's the best bet. He's a little unmindful but takes well to the reins. Not so big like he should be, but big enough for her.

I aim to give you everything I got, the boy said. I bought some new clothes and a hat so I'm squared away with that. I got some forty dollars yet and all my other clothes you can have, except my coat and gloves. And you can have one of my saddlebags and a hackamore and bridle reins. Two bits I don't have any use for. Got a gad piece probably not worth a damn but it's yours. And a knife I don't reckon I'll need.

The boy rubbed his head, his eyes shifting back and forth from the fire to the table. Well, he said. I reckon I ought to keep that.

Charlie Ford raised a hand. Now hold on son. I don't need nothin from you. I'm prepared to give you the horse.

No sir. I'll just keep the knife. And my bedroll. But the rest is yours. I don't want nothin.

The boy's face narrowed. Damn it, Charlie, he said. I want you to have it.

It was the first time the boy had used his name and it was then that the rancher saw what the boy meant by it. He closed his eyes. Alright, he said. But I want you to keep the money and I want you to listen to what I have to say about this now. I want you to listen to me right now.

Alright then.

The boy fell back onto the couch and put his hat in his lap and set his hands over the crown. Charlie Ford got up from his chair and went to the fire and threw another log on the flames.

I want you to know first of all that I appreciate what you're tryin to do. No matter what I've said. It ain't often that such an effort'll be made for anything or in any direction. Goodness don't got much to do with the world no more. I'm proud of you, boy. I guess that's all I mean to say. He turned from the fire and nodded. Then with the metal stoking stake raised in his hand he pointed toward the back of the house. That bein said, I want you to take my truck with you tonight.

The boy's eyes shot up from his hat. He was already shaking his head. Charlie Ford turned the stake toward the boy and raised his free hand to ease him back again. Now hold on, he said.

I don't know how to drive.

I know it. I'll teach it to you. It won't take but ten minutes. Now listen.

The rancher made expansive gestures with the stake and his shadow leapt behind him like a bear rearing among the pale painted walls. He explained to the boy how they wouldn't expect him in a truck and how it would be faster and easier to get away with. He told him that though he hadn't driven since his wife died in her own truck, he kept his in good shape and more than likely he'd be able to outrun anything that gave chase. He said if he made it out clear he could drive back to the ranch and pick up the horses and be gone into the mountains with not a scent of his breath left by the time they picked up his tracks. Lastly he resaid that they wouldn't expect him to come that way and the surprise of it alone would work in his favor.

The boy tried helplessly to refuse the logic of Charlie Ford's plan but could not. Charlie Ford set the stake against the fireplace and both men drew up the collars of their coats tight upon their necks and plodded out into the thick grass where the truck was parked aslant from four unused stalls at the rear of the property.

The truck was rusted at the tire wells but the rest was clean and russet-colored, though covered by a thin film of dust. The seats squelched when they got up in it. The boy sat in the passenger seat and shifted his knees from the dash and pushed back his hat.

Now don't look like that. It's ain't a tough thing. Look down here at the pedals. You got the clutch and the gas and the brake. Steerin's easy. Just turn when you want to turn and keep the wheel steady when you want to go straight.

Charlie Ford rummaged through his coat and brought forth a key tied to a leather thong and put it in the ignition.

Give down on the clutch to start it. When it catches, ease up on the clutch and throw the gearshift up here. This is first gear. Got four altogether. Put down on the gas the same time you let go of the clutch.

When you're wantin to shift into the next gear to go faster, do the same. Start with the clutch, move the gearshift, and step on the gas.

Charlie Ford nodded at the boy and drove the truck out onto the high grass and into the gravel wash of his drive. The blousy evening light glittered before the headlights when he pulled them on. He stopped the truck after a while, going through the instructions again and recounting a number of situations he might find himself in and what to do if they indeed occurred.

The boy listened listlessly and regarded the numbers on the gauges with an apprehensive eye, all the while remembering back to the nights of riding in his father's truck, how he would bury his head deep in the upholstery of the backseat while his father swerved down the black country roads. And how every once in a while he would crane his neck up and gaze upon the speedometer for which he did not know the purpose of the ascending needle but took it to show the rise of blood in his father's face and the endlessly increasing and immense silence of his mother who sat rigid in the front seat.

It seems too much, he said.

Charlie Ford gave a sigh. You know it ain't too much, he said. Most people your age been drivin a number of years and I don't believe half of em as smart as you. Now get over here.

Ford got out and crossed the headlights where his face took an obscene and warped illumination. When he got to the passenger side the boy slid himself behind the wheel and ran his fingers over the dash. He looked down at the heavy square pedals. Charlie Ford hopped into the passenger seat and turned off the truck and motioned for the boy to start it again.

It was two hours counting before Charlie Ford was convinced the boy could drive. He took him back and forth down the gravel path, letting him crank it and drive out on the open road and swing into reverse and bring the truck around again.

When the boy finally got down from the truck he crouched in the grass and looked to where his horse stood grazing, holding for a long moment the dark swatch of the mare's mane in the quiver of his eye.

Charlie Ford led the boy over to the barn where he served up coffee. He asked the boy where he would stay the night and the boy told him he planned to stay at the inn on the plaza to be close and ready.

Best make yourself quiet as a cat, was all Ford said. Then for a while he asked the boy questions about what he should do on a road like this or that until finally the boy said he couldn't talk about it anymore and that he'd take the truck that night and leave his horse and wasn't that enough to satisfy him.

I could come with you, Charlie Ford said.

The boy shook his head at his coffee.

I figured you'd say that. Thank you, but I reckon it ought to be just me.

Charlie Ford managed a smile. And I figured you'd say that, he said.

They drank coffee with the darkness now full in the valley, and after a while the boy got up and brought down his saddlebags from his horse and piled all the things he had promised the rancher onto the barn floor. He looked down at the pile and almost began to take it up again, but at last he turned and spat and shook his head and said, It's all yours.

Charlie Ford looked uncertainly over the ragged heap of leather and metal and cloth, but he thanked the boy kindly and told him he best be getting down the road.

In the cool night air he walked the boy out to the truck again with only the sound of their boots in the grass. When the boy climbed in and got the motor cranked Charlie Ford leaned into the open window and told him again how he had to be strong no matter what happened. Lastly he told the boy that he admired him for what he was doing and that he was right, he would have done the same for his wife, and that if he had had a son of his own, he'd of hoped he would come out just like him.

To this the boy lowered his head and frowned at his lap, saying if he had had a father half as fine as him, but then stopped and nodded at his feet, saying finally that he would see him in the afternoon and to have the horses ready.

Twenty-two

IN THE WAN light of the quarter moon the boy motored the truck to the back of the inn and parked it askew to the proprietor's barn. He shut off the engine and the lights and came down with his hat in one hand and his rucksack with the new clothes in the other. A fine mist had risen up from the damp earth to slide silently across the grass, and it settled around the boy's ankles as he walked to the barn.

The proprietor's horse was tending to her stall in near darkness, shuffling her hindquarters through the soiled hay beneath her. When the boy came forward she looked up. He set down his rucksack and took her lean jaw in his hand. Even without the light he could see the sick hunger in her eyes. Her unclipped feet were sodden with manure. He stroked her and went across the cold dirt of the barn floor and brought back a tin bowl of water from the spigot and set it before her.

He sat against the stall gate and listened to the countryside and smoked. He sat for nearly an hour and he seldom moved. Listening and smoking and remembering those sounds and smells that he once knew every day. The quiet insistence of the night and the wilderness was somehow comforting, with the raw smell of the horses and hay and worn-down leather rising above it all. After he rose and fondled the horse's head, he flicked away the stub of his cigarette and went walking to the inn.

The innkeeper came rubbing his eyes from the door behind the counter after the third ring of the bell. He squinted at the boy and twisted the ends of his glasses behind his ears and sighed.

Time at last to come of age? he said. Find yourself whichever one you like. Go on up there. Them girls are always eager for a virgin. Always titterin on about you anyways. Not that I could rightly see why. Lookin at you don't seem to do nobody no favors. He smirked at the boy and opened the shabby ledger and thumbed through the loose sheets of paper. I can't read this, he said. I'll just go on and call Janis down here. First poke in the weeds don't make no difference but for a hole.

I ain't interested in no Janis, the boy said. I ain't here for none of that. I need a room.

The proprietor looked up from his ledger.

Ah, he said after a moment. He squinted at the boy cunningly. Ain't you in some trouble with the mayor? Something about tomorrow's show, ain't it?

Tomorrow's what?

The hangin, boy. The goddamn show.

The boy only looked down at his hands. Right, he said. The show.

Far as I've heard you should be gone from here, the innkeeper said cheerfully. The fact you're still hangin around is probably worth a good piece to the mayor I'm sure.

The boy stared at the man awhile. Then he leaned down to the floor and produced a twenty-dollar bill from his boot heel and set it on the counter. The innkeeper smiled at the money and picked it up and pushed it into his shirt pocket. I'd say that's about right, he said. He smiled again. Nothin personal, he said. You understand.

The boy sidled up to the counter and rested his fists upon it. You understand you got a horse out back there?

The innkeeper stayed studying the tablet for a room. Yeah, he said absently, I know it.

I was just wonderin if you remembered. Cause it seems it might be the other way around.

The innkeeper raised his head from the ledger and handed him a key. Room's on the front right, he said. Upstairs.

The boy tossed a plug of bills onto the counter. And that's for the room, he said. Maybe you ought to think about usin some of it on that horse instead of on women that ain't your wife.

The proprietor slammed his palms down on the counter. Damnation, he said. I can't even believe this. You tryin to tell me in one sentence you know more about horses and women than I do? You little son of a bitch.

I ain't talkin about women or horses. I don't know what to tell you about them. What I'm talkin about is quittin, that's all.

The innkeeper glared at the boy a moment longer, then slammed the ledger shut and ripped down the glasses from his face and slung them on the counter and walked off for the door.

Well thank God for that, he said.

It was the same room he had been given when he first arrived in town. He closed the door behind him and turned the knob on the lamp. The room swelled with a soft yellow glow. The bedcovers were drawn tight and the tablets and pencils on the side desk were even to the thumb. He placed his rucksack on the footstool at the base of the bed and sat down and pulled off his boots. Then he dragged the chair to the window and looked down on the plaza.

His eyes immediately fell on what he had not seen before, the skeletal structure of the hanging platform. There were no lights around the plaza that evening but he could see it in the moon glow. He watched it for a long time, the hard firm beams of it, the long and rigid shadows it cast upon the earth.

Some time later, long into the night, his eyes opened to the sound of someone walking beneath the window. He righted himself in the chair he had slumped over in and saw the shape of a boot behind the hanging posts. He saw it alone and then stepping with its twin to eclipse the moonlight on the road, then he saw them turn and walk and slowly turn again. When the boots stopped and turned a third time, in profile against the pale blue light, he recognized the beard of the mayor.

The mayor looked up at the wooden beams, then higher up into the sky, then at his feet. He walked again and stopped and turned and did the same pace over again. He pulled at his beard and took down his glasses from his face and wiped them on his shirtsleeve. The boy leaned forward and scrambled for his boots and pulled them on but before he rose again the mayor was walking swiftly away. The boy pressed his face to the window and looked out in quiet desperation to where the mayor's shadow soon vanished and the moon fell behind the clouds and darkness settled once again to shape in a darker hue the gallows below.

He rose before dawn and walked down the cold floor of the hallway toward the bathroom with the faint moaning of whores already beginning or still finishing from the night before. He closed the door, a mournful click, and filled the tub with hot water. He stripped and stepped into the tub and shaved and washed himself and stepped once more from the water and out of the dark steamed room with a towel clinging to his sunken hips.

He dressed in his newly purchased clothes and scrubbed the mud from his boots and sat on the edge of the bed and pulled them on. He combed back his hair with his hands and situated the new hat on his head, moving it this way and that until it sat straight. He rubbed his face and turned his hat around once more and buttoned his shirt to the middle of his chest and folded the sleeve cuffs over his forearms. Then he stood and crossed the room and regarded himself in the gilded mirror.

He could have been a young man calling on his sweetheart. Or a soldier returned from war and on his way to a dinner where his family had gathered to receive his arrival. Or just a regular boy his age, dressed for the first day of his job at an office in town where they would pay for his schooling and room and board until he found a wife and a place for them to live. He pulled the brim of his hat lower still and he knew that he could have been a number of things but he knew also that he was none of them and that he never would be.

He turned away from the mirror and went to the window and looked out. No one was walking the street. There was no visible sun nor moon and the town lay in a light so flat it seemed no light at all. He withdrew the knife from his rucksack and slid it in the small scabbard he'd tied to his leg just under the cuff of his boot. Then he took out the old man's pistol. He held it in his hands and stared at it a long time.

When he came to Old 17 he veered the truck into a low ditch and cut off the engine. The cottonwoods along the bank of the road and out toward the Englishman's house were thin and unknitted by winter's coming but packed densely together, densely enough to cover his approach.

He walked swiftly along the stream, a quarter mile away from the road. The sun made its first clean rise in the east, dashing red coins of light upon the trickling water he stepped through. He stumbled along the rocks and swathed through the brush with a low swishing sound when he emerged from the stream.

After about a half an hour he stopped and listened. Voices rose from the distant road. He could tell they were at their card games already, shouting and drinking and calling for queens and diamonds.

When he cleared out from the cottonwoods almost an hour later, he could see the back of the Englishman's house cloistered by the light of the cold sun. He looked up and estimated it was nearly seven o'clock, five hours before the girl would be led from the prison house to the willow tree.

He walked along some flattened logs and down into the soft earth and shuttled through an open field toward a copse of box elders rising dark and feathered behind the house. There he found a wide trunk of a tree that had been cut down and he glanced around for any sign of the Ralstons and finally sat. He undid his shirt pocket and rustled out a cigarette with his chilled and shaking fingers and lit it and began his watch.

Not long after, he saw some of the guards emerge at the edges of the front yard. Then they turned and disappeared again. There were two of them from what he could make out and he smoked and watched them as the sun mounted a sky now loaded with a heavy basket of cloud. They would come into his view, then turn and fall toward the house again in slow repetition. He tugged his jacket around his neck and blew steady streams of smoke at his feet. He knew the Englishman would come out sometime. He waited. His gun was tucked to his side and after a while he took it from his belt and ran his fingers over the steel barrel, pointing it and bringing it down and flipping it on the ground by his side. He lit another cigarette and inspected the yard.

Along the northern edge of the property stood a jagged row of acacia which appeared at some point to have been subject to a firestorm. The thin trunks of the trees corded one another and their blackened limbs lay sunken and tangled. They stretched out all the way past the water well behind the house and as he waited he listened to the wind tearing through the old branches.

An hour of waiting soon became two and then three. The two men in the front of the house kept up their pacing all morning long, pausing only to exchange a few words or pass cigarettes. They had long-barreled rifles slung over their shoulders and they held the stocks in the cups of their hands.

The sun rose higher yet, splitting the clouds and bringing not heat but simply a bright glare that shed everything around him of its shadow. The house stood cold and bare in the white wash of light. The guards winced and pulled their hats low. Nothing moved save those men and the failing limbs of the acacia which whined and clattered in the periodic gales of wind and the boy knew he could not wait any longer.

Just as he began to rise from the tree trunk he heard a door open in the front of the house. He leaned forward into a squat. The Englishman was down in the yard. The Ralstons fell back out of view. He could hear muffled voices and a sharp command upon which the guards reappeared together at the edge of the yard. They sat against a fence pole facing out at the road and went to smoking and shaking their heads.

The Englishman's hands were held loosely behind his back as he strolled toward the back of the house. He wore a dark blue suit with the waistcoat slung over his shoulders. Before he saw if the Englishman was wearing a weapon himself, the boy was up and crossing through the field and into the trees.

He stepped over the husks of bark and twigs, gliding swiftly with his knife raised out of his boot and his pistol resituated in his belt. Halfway to the house he looked up. The guards were still sitting with their backs to him, watching the road. The Englishman was lowering the bucket into the well, standing with one hand in his pocket while the other moved the wheel crank. The boy pressed on. When he was parallel with the Englishman he lightened his steps. At last he stood silent and listened for the guards. There was nothing save the grind of the wheel crank and the creak of the bucket. He waited in hopes that the Englishman would lower his head to watch after the bucket, and a moment later he did.

As the boy came forward a strong wind made the Englishman look up, but before he could turn or speak the boy had his hand clenched over his mouth and the knife poised at his throat. For a moment the Englishman struggled, but when the blade of the knife exacted itself against his powdered skin he withdrew.

The boy spoke only once, saying, Walk out there.

They went slowly at first along the trees and then with the boy's elbow against the Englishman's back they upstepped toward the box elders. The boy looked back and saw the two Ralston brothers facing each other, one holding a lit match and the other cupping his hands around it. They did not see the two figures walking out through the blazing field nor did they look up again until the boy had him well inside the grove.

He lowered the Englishman to the tree stump. The Englishman's hands trembled by his sides but his face appeared unmoved. The boy told him he would kill him right there if he tried to call out. He asked the Englishman if he understood and the Englishman tilted his head and smiled under the boy's hand. The boy took the blade from his neck and took away his hand from his face and came around and stood facing him. He drew the pistol from his belt and tapped it against the Englishman's head.

Here we are again, the Englishman said calmly. Wasting our time on a little black whore.

The boy brought down the chamber of the gun against the side of his face. The Englishman fell back against the trunk and smiled, exposing his bloodstained teeth. Blood also ran from the Englishman's ear, but he only eased himself back on the stump and watched the boy. This will not save her, he said blandly. Or you. What do you think? Do you think you are a revolutionary? Such men no longer exist. Did you truly think that?

No, the boy said. I don't. And this ain't no revolt.

Ah. The Englishman smiled obliquely and shook his head. Then what, young monument of justice, is it?

It's a reckoning.

The Englishman went mute. He was looking into the eyes of the boy now, no longer eyes but shells of eyes.

The boy raised the pistol. The Englishman saw it come up from the boy's waist to his own face. He watched the boy but he was no longer smiling.

The reports from the pistol clipped twice then vanished into the wide empty country. The wind spun up, plunging out of the trees and across the field. The body of the Englishman jerked back with the force of the bullets, then went limp to the ground. The boy leaned down and put a hand upon him and tore off the golden chevron from the dead man's waistcoat.

Then he was going across the field with the nubs of old wheat stalks brushing his knees. Down from the mountains the terraced light raced across the valley. He did not look across the field to see if the Ralstons saw him but went headlong toward the stream with his breath rattling out of his chest. He fumbled with the pin as he went and clamped it across the front of his jacket. He listened to his feet splashing through the water and he held his hat down against the wind.

When he reached the truck nothing had altered except for a new armada of clouds that had once again stolen the light from the sky. He leaned on the hood to catch his wind and looked down the road. He saw dust swirling and the flat red line at which the road slipped from sight. He climbed up in the cab and cranked the engine. The truck sputtered under his heavy foot and his body bounced up and down as he spun the truck out of the ditch and onto the road. Then he shoved the gearshift higher and sped off toward the town.

When the sun came clean he craned his neck out the window and looked up. He knew he had cut it close but there was time yet. It was not much past eleven from all he could tell. He moved the truck into fourth gear, clinging to the wheel as if it alone were the force behind his driving. He fumbled once, knocking the gearshift down to third, and the truck sputtered and died.

When he had the truck moving again he saw the thoroughfare coming into sight. He could make out the assembly already gathered around the tree. People were crowded all the way around the perimeter of the plaza, standing on porch steps, crouched in the road. There were no children to be seen but a few who clung to their fathers' legs and pressed their faces into their pants. He could not see the scaffolding for the tree branches but he saw the mayor standing by and he saw his hand raised decisively and he saw his hand drop.

He slammed hard on the gas pedal. As he came to the plaza rim the boy was met by a maze of cars and trucks parked on the road and the road's edge and in the grass. They offered no clear path through, as though some malevolent metal garrison had been set against him. He swerved the wheel of the truck and braked and wove his way through, clipping bumpers and doors and bumping the pistol off the seat. When he was nearly through the frozen traffic the truck hit the front wheel of a remaining car and jerked back and died again.

It wheezed when he turned the key and he cranked the engine again and more viciously, whatever curses from his lips lost in the engine's surge. When it caught he put the gear forward and drove into the open road. As he came abreast of the willow tree he slowed the truck and leaned across the seat and squinted against the light, reaching blindly to the floor for his gun. Some of the people turned at the sound of his truck but their eyes quickly returned to the tree.

He rode on to the left and steered the truck around. He could see the crowd clearly now. All seemed subject to the same torpid motion. The faces lolling in the cloudlight. The eyes going to slits, then opening wide. Hands of women going to their mouths. The men lowering their hats from their heads. He came around. He saw the mayor standing with a knife at his side. His face seemed drained of any thought at all.

The boy pressed down on the brake and pitched open the door and spilled his body over the hood. When he regained his balance and looked up he saw the wooden platform. There were no shoes on her feet and the first thing he saw was that the child-pink paint upon her toes matched that of her fingers. Then he saw the silver amulet glistening faintly from the caved pool of her throat.

One of her feet kicked briefly. He was yet thirty yards from her. Her color had already blanched and was going paler yet. Nothing could transport him to her side fast enough, and yet there she was.

With one swift motion he leveled the pistol in his hands and cocked back the trigger. Three of the Ralstons came down from the steps of Garrets's porch floor and began walking toward him.

The gun crackled and jogged back in his cupped hands. The men who were coming for him ducked, then began to rush forward but stopped when they saw where the bullet had gone.

The tiny motions of Delilah's body stopped all at once as if summoned into stillness by a command unheard by all but her. The mayor started from the scattered shadows of the tree to find the boy crouching by the truck and holding his head, his hat dashed to the ground and rocking on the pavement in the wind.

All the hushed crowd turned and watched him now. After a while the boy rose again to his feet. The mayor stepped to the front of the gallows where the body of the girl now hung folded in her blood-stained dress with the noose around her neck guiding her eyes to the sky. He put a hand up to the Ralstons and they stepped back. The boy came slowly forward. The crowd so silent only the swish of his trousers and the skidding of his boots could be heard. He held his head low until he came face-to-face with the mayor, then raised both his head and the pistol in unison.

The mayor looked down and gripped his beard. Some of the women in the forefront gasped and the Ralstons came forward again. The mayor held up his hand firmly. Stay there, he said.

The boy looked around. He saw Miss Jane, her eyes covered by her hands. He saw the railroad men still sooted in their work clothes and he recognized the face of the storyteller he had sat with on the mesa wall. He saw Thomas Trewitt standing by with a camera and flashbulb limp in his hands. He saw the old woman from the general store. She was weeping. He looked around for John Frank but did not see him anywhere. Perhaps he had known that the boy would not want him to come, that he would not be able to save her.

He turned back to the mayor. No words occurred from either of them until the mayor spoke to a man dressed in formal black attire on the platform beside them. Cut her down, he said.

The boy raised the pistol to the mayor again. No, he said. You cut her down. He shook his head at the gun in his hand. If you think you're fit to hang her, you're fit to cut her down.

The mayor hesitated, looking up at the body from the platform. Then he looked upon the boy. The boy did not seem to be where he stood. The mayor could have simply ungripped the pistol from his hand but he did not. He stepped up to the scaffolding with his knife and cut the girl down.

He caught her over his left shoulder and dropped the knife and took her slight body in his arms. He shuttled her down his chest, then laid her down on the wooden pallet that had been prepared for her and removed the noose. Someone handed him a blanket and he covered her body, for the first time looking full at her, the face of a child.

He came down and stood before the boy. People began to lean in again but he stayed them with his palm. He seemed he would speak again. He put a hand on his beard.

I imagine there is one more life you would like to take, he said.

The boy's eyes came away from the pallet.

A desert of sadness, he said to his feet. He looked up at the mayor. That's what you called me. And maybe you're right. You, though. He looked at his feet again. You're just a desert.

With that he lowered the pistol away from the mayor's chest. No, he said. There's nothin left here I want.

He stood briefly as before, then unclipped the golden chevron from his jacket and dropped it at the mayor's feet and went up to collect the body. The mayor stared down at the pin for a long time but would not pick it up. Then he stepped away, raising a hand once more to keep off the Ralstons. Before the boy had gone by, the mayor crossed in front of him and put up a hand to the boy's chest. They stood for a few seconds looking at one another.

I don't want no apology, the boy said before the mayor could speak. He pushed past the mayor's raised hand. Whatever you're offerin, I don't want it. And if you aim to kill me too, you just go on and do it now.

He held her around the shoulders and under the knees and once he began walking through the crowd he did not look back. When he pulled the truck door open he turned with her body sagging down in his arms. The mayor watched with his eyes slightly upraised from his canted head but he did not move nor did he make any further motion to the Ralstons. When the boy had placed the girl's body in the passenger seat of the truck he closed the door and walked around and climbed in and was gone.

He held her close as he had waited so long to do, going up the road toward the north. From the fallen strap of her dress the crumpled photograph fell by his feet and he bent and picked it up and pushed it into his shirt pocket. Then he held her against his neck. The road was empty. The sun stayed beneath the clouds, the truck humming through the wind and tearing up the colorless earth beneath them.

THE OLD MAN was standing at the door when he saw the boy on the far side of the river. Small black-red globes of dirt flung from the shovel the boy had found in his yard. The old man came down from the cabin. He started off toward the river but instead he sat down and watched on. The silver amulet was tight around the boy's neck and it shimmered in the dying sun. The old man watched him dig long into the evening, the boy's body grading deeper into the earth until only his head was above the ground and then only the head of the shovel. After some time the boy climbed out of the pit and stood looking into it.

The grave he dug for Delilah was nearly nine feet deep. He took off his hat and wiped the sweat from his brow and spat to his side. He had not looked at her body since he carried it out here and he would not look at it again.

He wanted only to bury her now. To bury her deep. Deeper into the world than those places where he walked. Deeper than his mother. Deeper than the place he had buried himself that day.

When the boy was finally finished filling the grave the old man looked across the river at his body silhouetted against the cold sky. The boy leaned and rocked and leaned again, until at last he placed his hat upon his head and began to walk through the quivering trees.

Charlie Ford was off cutting brush along the pasture fences when the truck formed out of the darkness. He saw the way the boy was holding his head and he set down his ax.

He helped him down from the truck and put his arm over his shoulder and led him toward the house. The boy stopped them there, weakly gripping the rancher's forearm.

Just take me to my horse, he said.

Charlie Ford stood on the hay floor and watched as the boy set the horse for riding. He placed the pad delicately on the mare's back and soothed her with his hands across her chest. He set the saddle on and shifted it and centered the pad and took down the cinches with the wind turning through the stable fence and the light of the moon spreading about his feet.

When he was finished he sat by her feet. Charlie Ford came forward to give the horse her hackamore. He looked down at the boy. He was holding his hat in his lap and turning it with a terrible deliberateness.

After a long time the boy raised his head. I shot her before she was dead, he said. Before they killed her. She was dying. She was about to die. He raised his eyebrows at Charlie Ford, then looked down again. I couldn't bear the notion of her dyin at their hands.

You did the best you could, Charlie Ford said.

But I should have been there sooner. I should have known they might do it early on account of me. I had all the time. I could have. I had all the time.

He fumbled for more explanation, but he could not go on.

No you didn't, Charlie Ford said. You done all you could. He paused. I want you to stay on here a while.

The boy looked square at him. Charlie Ford nodded at the look in his eyes.

What do you aim to do now, then?

Get clear of this country. That's one thing for sure.

I'm sorry.

Yeah. I know it. The boy lowered his head again and ground his fist in the dirt. I know you are, he said.

Where will you go?

I don't know. To Colorado, I reckon. To the north country. Seems like up there's the kind of wilderness I belong to. So that's where I aim to go, but I don't know. I aimed at it once before and look where I am.

Charlie Ford set down the bridle reins and took the boy by the lapels of his jacket and straightened the collar. Well, he said. You promise me you'll go easy when you go.

I'd like that, Charlie. I'd like to go easy but I don't got any promise I could put to it.

Charlie Ford acquiesced with a hand raised to his hat and a tug of the brim. He went up to the boy's mare and stroked her nose. You take care of Trude now, you hear?

The boy got up on the mare with the rancher holding the reins again. When he was set in the saddle Charlie Ford asked him once more if he'd like to stay but the boy only lowered his head and Charlie Ford handed up the reins and the boy took them and touched the horse with his boot and the mare raised her nose then kicked her feet against the darkened earth.

V

TWENTY-THREE

HE RODE WITH the black twisting trees and nothing besides. He rode all night and all morning, stopping only when Triften needed water. He rode the plateland that was sucked down into the horizon with a dull constancy, and he thought little of where he was going as he went. As he had with his father before he rode swiftly, laying up in hillside groves to watch for a pursuit, but no one came.

In the early evening of the following day he upstepped the horse from an arroyo and came upon a small Indian pueblo in a basin of barbed pine trees. The road he hit at the pueblo edge was hardly a road and more a path worn by feet. The sky was clear and the evening sun struck yellow on both adobe and tree. He came down from the mare and took down his hat and held it against his pale chest. He looked off to where people were gathered in what seemed formal assembly. He led his horse up the road.

They were of the Zuni tribe and all were brightly dressed and standing upon a fine carpet of pine needles and white flowers. On a small wooden step the chief stood before them. The boy stopped along the rim of the gathering and tied his horse to a nearby tree. The chief was making flowing gestures with his arms and he was very old and weather-worn and slow in his movements. Directly in front of him stood a young man and woman and they were the only ones among the gathered who were plainly dressed.

He knew at once it was a wedding ceremony. He turned to go but a hand caught him by the arm and turned him back. It was a woman with a young face and hair that was pure white and long to the back of her knees and unbound by any cord or garment. He saw the scrutiny in her eyes and he stood still, saying nothing. The woman's face was intense upon him and he shifted under her gaze. Then she looked at his horse and at the boy once more and her face softened. No white men, she said.

He made to take hold of the mare's reins but she only squeezed his arm tighter.

No white men except for today. Today you stay, she said. For a ceremony of love everyone who come here they stay.

He looked off behind her hair at the gathering. The sun lay copper on the slim face of the bride. He shook his head but the woman would not let go of his arm. She guided him firmly toward the assembly as the witnesses all bent to sit at the chief's command. They stepped among the crossings of legs where some eyes turned curiously at him, and at last she pulled him seated by his jacket sleeve.

The language of the chief was unknown to the boy but there was a gentleness to it that held his attention. He presided over the congregation with his dark pitted eyes and all watched his face keenly save the lovers whose gaze stayed fixed on each other.

When the ceremony was over all stood and began to walk toward the makeshift gazebo that had been erected in a small circle of pines. The woman with the long hair led the boy along by the arm. No one looked his way nor would the boy have noticed if they did.

There was a tarpaulin of cloth thin as silk strung up over four old cattle posts that had been squared and pounded into the ground. Under it was a long table of dark wood. Around the table in the open air stood several small tables and smaller chairs where the others sat with their knees high to eat. The woman with the white hair pointed the boy to set himself at one of the tables on the periphery. He leaned down and took hold of one of the chair backs and lowered himself into it.

Within a few moments young girls arrived from across the road bearing great platters of posole and red corn tamales and loaves of skinned corn paste and wooden bowls of hominy and blue corn dumpling soup. One girl carried a large box filled with cut leaves of tobacco and corn husks to roll them in. Another balanced three jugs of water in her arms.

When the boy and the woman were served the woman leaned toward him and told him to eat for it was a feast and that it was a holy one that not even he, a white man, could deny.

They ate. It grew dark quickly. The same girls who had served the food crossed the road again and came back carrying long poles with rags soaked in kerosene at the tips. They planted them around the gazebo, the tallest among them igniting the rags with an old silver lighter. The space around them incandesced in a remarkable green among the trees, and after the woman had seen the boy eat a sufficient amount of food she rose and told him she would return shortly.

He turned in the chair to watch her. People drifted in and out of the canopy presenting gifts to the father of the groom, who would study them and bow his head gratefully, then pass them to the father of the bride, who would then hand them to his daughter. The woman with the white hair offered up a large turquoise stone that did not seem to have been fashioned for ornament, but for what purpose the boy did not know.

When the woman returned and sat again the boy spoke for the first time, asking her what her gift was and what it could be used for. The woman swept her white hair back from her shoulder and shook her head and said that it was not these things that mattered, but only how much the gift meant to the giver. How cherished was the thing being given away.

She watched the boy smoke in the flutter of light. Each time she caught his eye he looked down. The early noises of celebration one by one subsided with the approach of nightfall. Those who still remained at their tables leaned against the low backs of their chairs and passed the box of tobacco and watched the night unfold. After a while the woman asked the boy for a name.

Trude, he said. Trude Mason.

The woman pushed her hair aside again and smiled mournfully. I did not mean yours, she said.

Whose then?

The girl's. Tell me the girl's name.

He looked away at the trees. She moved her chair closer to him. When she touched his hair with her fingers he flinched and recoiled from her hand. He kept his eyes on the trees and the woman watched his face and shook her head. So young, she said.

That was all she said for a while. She watched the moon slide in and out of the trees and her face against it lit up blue. When she turned to him again he looked away and she spoke to him slowly and with a great quietness.

She told the boy that love appears to people as the sky. That there is a landscape in the world of love that one may travel through. Free to pick and choose, she said. To discover hidden places. She said that with grief this was not so. She said that grief was like a tree. Like the trees he now looked upon. It could not be moved or shaken loose. Nor could it be uprooted and carried away. It planted itself in the heart like a dagger clot in stone.

She paused only briefly and then said with some sadness that love and grief indeed took a very long time to join together rightly in one's heart. That they were complicated forces, the sky and the tree. But she said that no matter how complicated they became, that when the heart found a place to hold them together as one, they could be lived with.

When he rose from his chair the woman did not try to stop him. He walked to the marriage table under the canopy. All that remained at the table were the gifts that had been given to the new couple and a drape of muslin covering them. He stared down at the table. The last green slivers of light bent and faltered on the dying kerosene rags. He unbuttoned his shirt slowly and slowly drew the silver amulet from his throat, lifting it over his head and placing it upon the cloth. He touched it once more, turning its small brightness in his fingers, then withdrew his hand. When he turned the woman was standing before him.

What is that? she asked him.

The boy glanced down at his hands which he held open on his stomach. It was Delilah's, he said. It was my wife's.

He turned to go. She walked with him to his horse. When he was up in his mount he bent down and took his hat down and thanked the woman for her kindness.

Before he kicked the horse on and disappeared down the road the woman put a hand on the mare and with the other she grasped the boy's stirruped boot, telling him that no matter how sorrowful a love was, what was important was that love still remained in his heart. We are not long for this world, she said. And that however fine and true any story of love may be, what was more important was that love remained in his heart, for in the heart is where it would always continue to begin.

TWO WEEKS LATER the boy was riding the mountains again. He had loosed the shoes from Triften's feet and bought a new saddlebag and filled it with tins of beans and hard bread and a gallon jug of water.

He passed through Cibola County where he talked to many men about the country to the north and about ranchers they knew who might be looking to take him on. He studied maps laid out crudely by traders and foragers and he carved himself a path up through McKinley County riding by the edge of the Tularosas and toward Apache Mountain in San Juan County which would lead him across the border and into towns named Durango and Silverton and Ouray in the state of Colorado.

He stopped for a few hours on certain days, taking odd jobs that required bodies who could move things around. In some towns he slept in hotels and listened for the sounds of the wild beneath the telephone exchanges from other rooms and the thrumming of trucks on the faraway roads. Far from sight and sound were the highways of distant cities he never knew or believed he would, but at times lying on cot or grass he envisioned them and what they might mean in the long space of things.

In the days since he had left the town he had scarcely slept, but his exhaustion went past his body. In his eyes was some past so darkly original, built by a world extinguishing and in some places already extinguished and from which even its own witnesses, of which he was one, could no longer be called forth for study.

Yet when he rode during the day his thoughts sometimes cleared and he rode with her and her riding was all the beauty and light and wind that lay trapped in tree and field and the water that went running south, always running south, down the mountains and into the nameless crystal ocean that he kept in his pocket, where she would soak her hair and swim and emerge from the water and walk to where he stood on the bank waiting for her.

At the end of the first month of winter he rode into a valley where he came upon a wooden signpost stuck crookedly in the earth. Scrawled upon it with indigo an arrow pointed northwest toward a frozen creekbed. It read, Juanita's Herbal Remedies. For Sale. Thank You.

It was growing late and cold. His chest and forearms had grown thick again with the heavy labors he took on, and he passed one broad hand across the rubble of his face. The terrain on which he rode was now replete with thornbrush and gravel washes and the moon was dimming under the clouds.

In a strangely geometric half circle of ponderosa pines the boy came upon a tremendous campfire around which several bodies reclined. Behind them were raised broad tents with fur pelts and beads hanging over the stake posts like the trappers of old. They were lanternlit from the inside and the boy could see hands moving within them.

He came down from his horse twenty yards from the camp and walked to the fire. When he was nearly on top of them a woman looked up, her eyes like green moons in the firelight. She stood slowly but smoothly, an odd elegance to her movement which betrayed her shabby dress. She came toward the boy with her hands upraised.

Come on over, she said easily. You look mighty tired.

Her hair was wound up by a bright orange scarf and her smile seemed involuntary. Some of the others who sat around the fire, men and women both, looked up and smiled at the boy with similar smiles. He studied them all for a moment, then went around the fire and sat with the woman.

She gave the names of all the people who sat at the fire and he gave his own, and all leaned forward still smiling and taking his hard callused hand in the soft warmth of their own.

I'm Rosemary, not least of all, the woman said when the introductions were through. She put a hand on the boy's leg. Are you hungry?

No, the boy said, though he was very much so, I reckon I'm alright.

For a while they asked him questions. Who he was. Where he was going. Why he was going there. He answered them briefly, their faces warm and red and intent on his words and the slow way in which he put them forth.

When the questions waned Rosemary produced a pipe from the folds of her skirt and offered it to the boy but he waved it away. I don't guess I need that, he said.

The keepers of the campfire smiled among themselves. They smoked and sat and kept the fire going long into the night. The boy talked a little more but mostly he sat listening, until at last the laughter subsided and the fire drew down and they one by one laid back their heads.

When all was quiet the boy pulled off his hat and leaned back against the log he had been sitting on. He folded his hands over his stomach and closed his eyes, and that night he dreamed once more his dream of childhood. Yet in his dream he stood on a road, and in this dream the very same bear he had hunted in the mountains lumbered toward him out of the distant forest. Only when the bear was inches from the boy's chest did it stop. They stood in the road looking at each other. Then all at once the boy walked to the bear's side and put his hand upon its neck.

The white field they walked through was a blinding white. It covered everything. Only the snow and the approaching forest and both sun and moon all but gone and all the sky fading around them. The pines rose in a majestic white only slightly discernible from the rest of the world. The boy held fast to the bear's neck. They went and went, deeper into the white trees, deeper into the snow. The white sun and trees and the white earth drawing back, receding into deeper whites and thicker trees, the bear silent and leading the boy into the scorching white of the world where he now slept, would always sleep.

In the morning he woke to the smell of coffee and chicory and the heat of a new fire. He sat up and tugged on his boots. Everyone was gone from the fire's circle save the woman Rosemary who came by and handed him a ceramic mug. He leaned forward from the log he had slept on and coughed into his hand and rubbed his head and sipped the coffee. It tasted sweet and he was very thirsty and drank it quickly. The woman smiled down at him and after a moment she sat beside him.

She asked him if he had a cigarette and he said he did. He took two from the battered pack in his breast pocket and lit them both and handed one to Rosemary.

She took it and thanked him and both looked out at the land. The sunlight was reddening behind the snowcapped mountains and it sparkled on the thin white dusting that had fallen to settle around them during the night.

They smoked. After some time Rosemary got up and returned with a plate of potatoes seasoned with pepper and blackened by wood smoke. She handed it to him and sat again.

Will you have much farther to go? she asked.

A week. Maybe two.

You can stay here as long as you want.

Well, he said, picking at the potatoes, thank you. But I best get on.

He put down the plate and pulled out his new billfold and leafed through the bills. The woman stopped him with her hand.

Other things are sold here, she said, the least of which is food. You won't make it without your money. Not on that horse. Keep it.

I'll make it, he said. He held the money out to her. I've got plenty.

She took her hand from his and put it on his raw face. I hope you always do, she said.

He rode out that morning in an unseasonal heat, passing through low rolling hills with the green stems of grass still glistening through the mist of snow. The mare's feet kicked up the white powder like moondust and the boy slackened his jacket collar from his neck and yaed her into the rising sun. Later in the morning he reached a down-slope at the edge of the field he had been traveling in. He whoaed the horse and came down.

He sat on a rock that was kept bare of snow by the sprawling aspen it rested under. A creek ran along the base of the coming Tularosa Mountains and he gazed across it to where a pack of wolves slick with snow nosed the ground, lingered by the water, then ran away.

He considered what a man in Cibola County had told him about the country up there while they had sat eating at a roadside diner. He had told him that much of it was still wild beyond what he could prob-ably imagine and that it was a place even the government had not yet attempted to rule. He said up there was where whoever put the world together went shithouse crazy. He said he'd find plenty of ranch work up there. That it was all that Colorado was good for. That and mining. He said also that he had gone to work in the town of Grand Junction a few years back but the winters had been too much for him. He told the boy one day he'd sat up from his tick and thought upon it, and that he'd left that very day. He said that a man's got to follow what's in his mind. That if ever there was a tough question put to him, a man should count on his mind to put things right.

To that the boy had smiled and nodded. He lifted the mug of coffee he had been drinking and told the man that he wished it was that way but in truth it was not.

For a long time the boy tilted his head up at the sky and smoked and looked out at the land. He turned and watched Triften foot the earth, still trying to reclaim her knowledge of that terrain. Then he turned back and leaned on his elbows. He took off his hat. His hair was growing long again and he put a hand through it to let the rare winter heat bear down upon his face. He rubbed his eyes and gazed back at the creek, putting his eye to one strand of water. He followed it until its path crashed and blended with a greater rope, watching it all tumble past and glinting in the sheaves of light, the only thing fit to mark it.

Soon he would be in that Colorado country the man had spoken of. And soon the sun would rise up from behind the mountains to stay with him the length of the day.

Acknowledgments

FOR THEIR FAITH and friendship, thanks to Bob Reiss, Tom Bissell, Sloan Harris, Jennifer Barth, Dennis Sampson, Eric Vrooman, Mike O'Sullivan, Mimi Dow, and Robert Cording. For the company of their song, thanks to Lucinda and Merle. A special thanks to my traveling partner Thad Weitz for his sharp eye and unreasonable sense of humor, and to Cassie Gainer for all the time and light she has given to me.

Finally and above all thanks to my parents Robert and Cathy, my brother Brian Gatewood, my sister Germaine Gatewood, and all my Gatewood family; Cristina McGinniss; Johnny, Al, and all the Germains, especially, and always, Nancy Germain.

LaVergne, TN USA
10 April 2011
223598LV00002B/57/A